Long Journey
to the
South River

Leif Lundquist

COMRECO AB
Källvik, 185 91 Vaxholm, Sweden
Ph. +46-8-541 754 05
E-mail: postkontoret@comreco.se

ISBN-978-91-974941-1-3
September 2009

Edition 1.2, December, 2009

Leif Lundquist started writing fiction ten years ago after a long career in high-tech business and a life of traveling. He has lived in Holland and England, two nations who together with Sweden colonized North America along the Atlantic coast. In the 1960s he lived in the USA, in New Jersey, which was once part Dutch and part Swedish. He now lives in his native Sweden, but spends winters in Tucson, Arizona. He's a member of the Swedish Colonial Society (www.colonialswedes.org) and the editor of the Swedish website "Nya Sverige i Nordamerika" (www.colonialswedes.se), dedicated to the history of New Sweden. He has written essays and stories and a book "Vinteröken" [Winter Desert] about Southern Arizona.

With deep gratitude to all who contributed

The writing of this book was in itself a long journey, and many people helped me along the way. The people from the Swedish Colonial Society in the US showed great hospitality and generosity: Kim-Eric Williams, Peter Craig, Herbert Rambo, Mary McCoy, Earl & Sylvia Seppala, Max Dooley, and Edie Rohrman coached us in the history of New Sweden and guided us around the area on the Delaware. Captain Lauren Morgens on the modern Kalmar Nyckel demonstrated with warmth and aplomb the skills needed to sail a 17th century ship. Hans Duned from Kalmar, Sweden (twin city of Wilmington, Delaware) made the introductions. Along the way I picked up invaluable local color, not to mention loads of wonderful details from the past. Thank you all!

In Germany we followed the 17th century trails of the Swedes, to all the places in the book. People we didn't know helped us everywhere. Thanks to the Wolgast Museum curator who showed us around, the people in Lützen who made the 360-odd years since Gustavus Adolphus died seem like blink of an eye, and the anonymous man in Magdeburg who helped us find our way across town when we were totally lost.

Thanks to my wife Margot who, with infinite patience, has not only traveled with me to all these places and endured my chatter about the story, but who has also been of great help with editing the text. Finally, I thank our son Johan, who designed the cover.

Vaxholm, Sweden, in April 2009.

Leif Lundquist

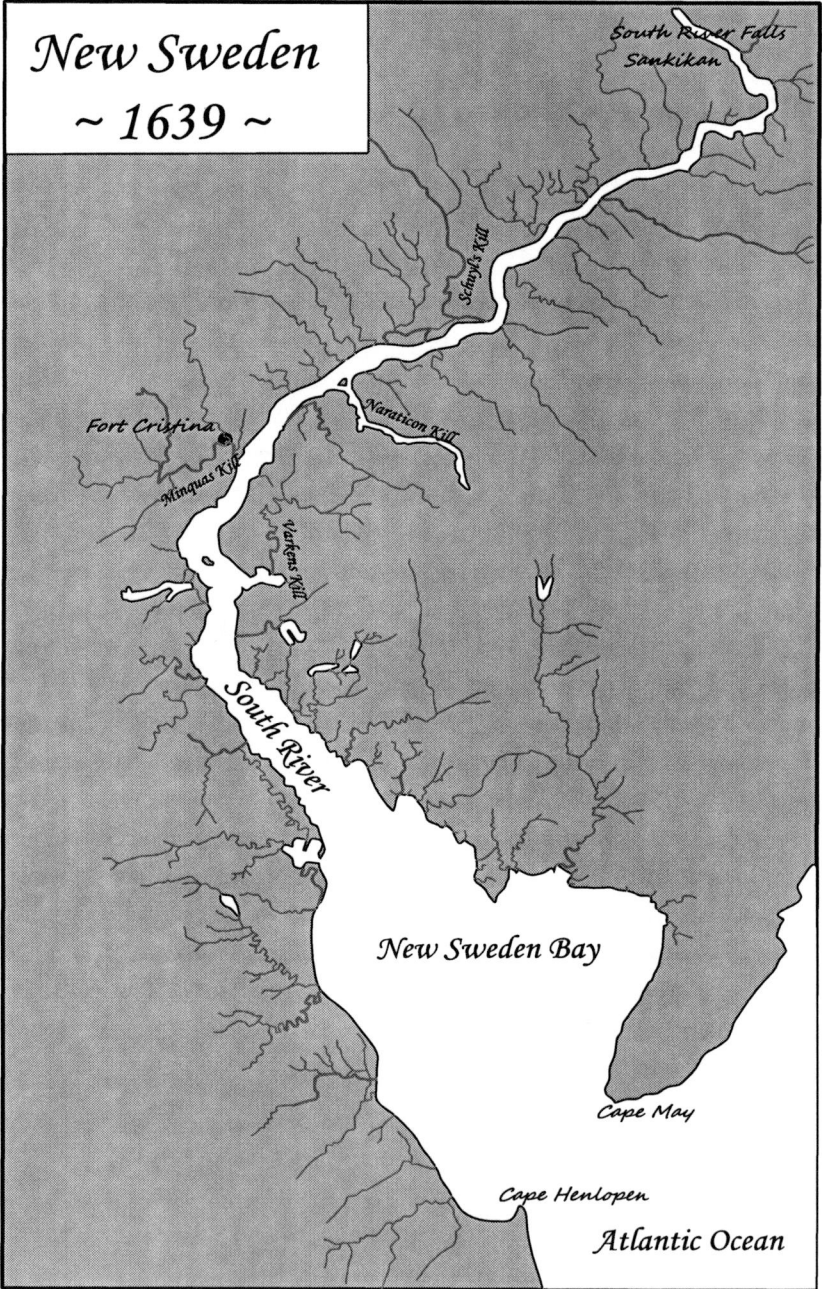

New Sweden
~ 1639 ~

South River Falls
Sankikan

Schuyl's Kill

Fort Cristina

Minquas Kil

Naraticon Kill

Varkens Kill

South River

New Sweden Bay

Cape May

Cape Henlopen

Atlantic Ocean

Europe ~ 1632

Contents

Prologue

The people who came to the South River settlement were forever changed. Ben, Liisa, Caitrin, Esa, and the others were no longer Europeans; they were part of a new world. My story is fiction, but it could well have happened — and some of it did!

Three hundred and thirty years after the fact, I first visited the site where Swedish soldiers, convicts, indentured workers, and a handful of free men had first landed in 1638. The park on the Christina River in Wilmington, Delaware was a small, quiet oasis; the focal point was, and still is, Carl Milles's Calmare Nyckel monument, which had recently been dedicated. It's a site lovingly kept by Swedish descendants, fighting against the incursion of industry and the fogs of time.

Why did the Swedish colonists come? Over the years, I asked myself this question and as I learned more and more about New Sweden I began to see the risky commercial enterprise as a part of national ambitions, or more likely of the ambitions of the powerful rulers and rich merchants. Today we would call it a start-up venture, the difference being of course that in the 17th century commerce, military and political power went hand-in-hand. Sweden, Holland, and England were mighty powers in Europe, and like the other two, Sweden wanted to fill its coffers by trading the riches of the new world. This was long before the United States of America, long before the Revolution. The Western world's focus was on Europe and the relationships between the European countries – who were constantly at war. The New Sweden venture was like a leaf at the end of a branch on a huge tree, the Swedish nation, rooted on all the shores of the Baltic. When storms gathered, there was a great risk that the leaf would fall off and sink to the bottom of the sea.

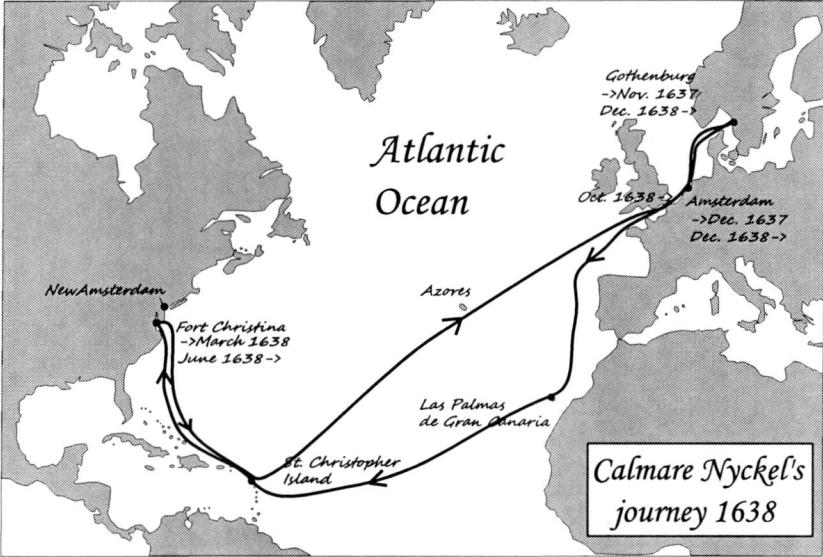

Gothenburg
->Nov. 1637
Dec. 1638->

Atlantic
Ocean

Oct. 1638->   Amsterdam
->Dec. 1637
Dec. 1638->

NewAmsterdam

Azores

Fort Christina
->March 1638
June 1638->

Las Palmas
de Gran Canaria

St. Christopher
Island

Calmare Nyckel's
journey 1638

1. The North Sea

The ship heeled again, the humming of the rigging increased to a high-pitched whine, and the passengers fumbled in the darkness for any handhold they could find to help them stay in their bunks. The heeling didn't stop, and a woman cried out, "Dear God, help me! We're capsizing!"

The North Sea storm had been tossing Calmare Nyckel around for hours, and in the black of the night, the world in the passenger hold of the pinnace was rolling and heaving with each wave. Water gushed across the deck above and leaked down into the hold, where it sloshed over the already wet floor before slowly seeping down through gratings into the bilge of the ship. The hull creaked as the planks moved against each other pulling at the nails holding them together. Below the waterline, hidden from view, little cracks had formed between the planks and little holes around the rusty nails, and the relentless pressure of the sea was creating rivulets that added more water in the bilge, making the ship sluggish and plowing her bow deeper in the water.

The ship continued to heel and they heard a large bang that sounded like a cannon shot. A man's voice, "We've hit a rock! I must get out!" There was another bang. Calmare Nyckel stopped heeling and slowly began righting herself. Something had snapped or been cut on deck, relieving some of the pressure on the sails. But the pitching and rolling continued; the storm was not over yet.

Lieutenant Ben Fogel, employee of the company that owned Calmare Nyckel, was in his bunk trying to sleep; soon it would be morning, and like most of the others he hadn't been able to sleep much during the storm. During a lull in the noise, he heard a lot of activity up on deck – sailors running around, sails flapping, and orders being shouted. His bunk rose and lifted him, he hung suspended for a moment then dropped as the ship plunged down the back of a wave. The woman cried out again, "We'll die here! We'll never get to New Sweden!"

He called to her in the darkness, "Don't be alarmed! It's only a storm! It won't last!"

But he was alarmed, not because of the storm, but because he sensed that Calmare Nyckel was slowing down, and he could hear water sloshing below him. "She must be shipping water!" he thought. Carefully he stepped out of his bunk, put his clothes and shoes on, and made his way aft to the ladder that led to the deck. He had to feel his way in the darkness, hanging on to a line strung along the side of the hold. He made his way up the ladder, and counting the time between gushes of water leaking through, he opened the hatch and climbed out halfway between two waves. He pushed the hatch shut and secured the latch, but just as he was done a rogue wave came across the deck. Ben lost his footing and slid down the deck toward the lee side, pushed by the water running over the side. He hit the gunwale and the water pulled him toward an opening, but his hand found a shroud, and he held on for dear life while the water disappeared over the side. Before the next wave came, he scrambled to a more secure place higher up on the windward side under the bridge.

The noise from the waves crashing, the rigging humming, lines banging against wooden spars and masts and snapping in the wind, was deafening. He slipped, but somebody grabbed his coat and pulled him back up, where he found a line to hold on to. A head next to his screamed into his ears, "Fogel, what are you doing on deck?" It was Mr. Jongehans, one of the ship's officers.

"I wanted to see for myself what's going on. The passengers are terrified."

"Well, they don't need to be. It's too early in the season for a really bad storm, and we can weather this."

"Are we shipping water?"

The wind drowned his voice, and Jongehans put his face close to Ben's ear and yelled, "What?"

"She moves like a heavy battleship, not a fast pinnace! Are we shipping water?"

They were both hanging on to a line strung along the side so as not to lose their balance when the ship rolled. Jongehans looked at him for a moment before answering.

"Yes, we are. The captain has ordered us to man the pumps, and I'm on my way to inspect the lower regions and the hull." Jongehans grabbed the line with both hands as Calmare Nyckel heeled over and sank down into a trough at the same time. Behind them the two steersmen pushed the whipstaff down, moving the tiller and the rudder to compensate for the ships' yawing.

Jongehans went on, "Would you like to come with me?"

"Yes!"

Jongehans opened a door that took them into the steersman's cabin under the poop deck, where two sailors were taking turns with the whipstaff. From side to side at the top of the forward wall there was a slit in the wall, a narrow opening through which they could see the deck, even though the main mast and the rigging restricted their view. The men at the whipstaff were wearing raincoats to protect them from the showers that the winds and the waves sent in through the window.

Jongehans opened a side door to a narrow space with a ladder going down. They climbed down below deck and walked to the pump room behind the main mast; the tossing of the ship made it difficult to move around, the ceiling was low, and they had to walk hunched down. Jongehans carried an oil lamp, and their shadows floated on the walls as they shifted positions when the ship moved. Ahead of them another lamp cast a weak glow over the pumps and the men working them. Two sailors were pushing the seesaw handles of one of the ship's pumps up and down, while two others rested, bracing themselves against the walls.

Jongehans asked, "How are things going?"

One of the sailors at the wall replied, "I think we can hold the water back, Sir, but it's hard work, and we can only take short turns."

"How high is the water?" Jongehans asked.

"It's still below the floor in the lower cargo hold."

Calmare Nyckel suddenly pitched forward; the pumping stopped while the men at the pump just held on to the handles in order not to fall. Then the room became level again for a moment, long enough for the men to start pumping again. And so it went, the ship was never still, the pump room pitched and rolled constantly, and the pumpers braced themselves between the floor and the pump handles, now and then losing purchase when their feet slipped.

Jongehans and Ben climbed down to the lowest cargo hold. Jongehans held his lamp close to the inside of the hull and said, "Look at this!" He pointed to the planks; water was running down the side. Jongehans put his hand over one of the bolts that held two planks together. He put his hand to his mouth and tasted the water. "Seawater, and I can feel it coming through." He handed the oil lamp to Ben. "Hold this!" he said. He took out a knife and scraped around the bolt. The rusty head came off in his hand. "Damn!" he said, "If they're all like this, the whole hull could break up."

They continued along the hull, holding their heads down, squeezing through narrow spaces between bulkheads and the hull. The ship kept up its dance to the stormy music played by wind and waves. Up, down – lean to port, lean to starboard – pitch forward and rise again. The heavy cargo next to them creaked, pushed against the restraining bulkheads, and pulled at lines and nets that held it down; if anything broke and the cargo started to shift, Calmare Nyckel's dance might become a drunkard's wobble that could end in her falling down and not getting up again.

Not all the bolts were bad, but they found more rusty bolts; in several places the bolts had given way, and small cracks had opened between the planks; the constant movement of the water, the waves working to widen the cracks little by little. The hull was wet from sea water trickling down the inside slowly, slowly filling the bilge. They made their way back up to the pumps; the sailors looked expectantly at Jongehans, who said, "You're right! We're holding our own, but we'll need to keep the pumps going. I'll send down more hands." He turned to Ben, "I'll go tell the Captain. Why don't you go back to the passengers and calm them down. By morning I think this storm will be gone, and we'll take another look when we have daylight."

Jongehans was partly right and by morning the winds had calmed down some; the sound in the rigging was back to a comforting low hum, and there were patches of blue sky appearing above them. But the storm had roused the sea, and huge grey swells, their frazzled white tops curling and breaking, lifted the pinnace just to drop her down into troughs where the water towered around the ship. The passengers were allowed on deck again, but the rolling and heaving of the ship made many of them seasick, and Ben was joined on deck by several passengers whose faces were turning various bilious shades of green. They were on their way to the New World, where they would become settlers, but now many of them only wanted to die.

It was September 1639 when Calmare Nyckel weighed anchor, left Gothenburg on the west coast of Sweden, and headed out on the Skagerrak. From there she went west to the North Sea, where she would turn south through the English Channel, and go past the Iberian Peninsula and along the African coast to the Canary Islands. Then she would let the trade winds blow her over to the Caribbean Islands. After a couple of trading stops making deliveries, looking for return cargo, taking on water and provisions she would set her sails for the final leg through the West Indies up along the North American coast to the mouth of the South River at what would much later be known as the Delaware Bay. Calmare Nyckel had made its first journey to the South River settlement in 1638, and she was returning to New Sweden with more settlers. In 1639 sailing ships did not travel fast; her second voyage across the Atlantic to New Sweden was going to take at least four months. It was a good plan, but the storm would change all of that.

Next to Ben stood a man in a black frock, with a black hat on his head. From under the brim of the hat, light brown hair hung limply down over his collar. His dark beard was trimmed and framed his pale, seasick face. He was a bit unsteady on the rolling deck and held on to a line.

The man turned to Ben and said, "The storm was frightening. This is my first time at sea, do you think it'll get worse?"

Ben replied, "I hope not, but it'll soon be winter and perhaps there will be some more storms on the Atlantic. I've never been that far, but I've heard sailors talk about storms on the way to America. But don't worry, you should get used to the ship's movements after a few days."

"We are all in God's hands, and I've prayed for a safe passage."

"You must be of the church?"

As the ship sank down into another trough between two waves, the man took a deep breath and replied. "I'm Reorus Torkillus, pastor in the Lutheran church. I've been called to service in New Sweden; the Queen wants our countrymen to hear the gospel in their own tongue."

He continued, "How about you, are you a sailor?"

"I've been a sailor, a soldier, and an innkeeper. I would have liked to stay an innkeeper, but now by the Queen's order I'll be a settler. It's a long story."

"I'd like to hear it, if you don't mind telling it."

"I don't mind, and we will have a lot of time to tell stories before we get to America."

The conversation ended there. Calmare Nyckel rolled sharply to port and the Reverend Torkillus temporarily suspended his relations with the heavens and paid homage to Ran, the storm goddess while hanging over the railing.

Ben noticed that Calmare Nyckel had changed course during the night and was heading southeast toward the Dutch coast. The passengers were talking about the commotion last night, making guesses about what had happened, when Mr. Jongehans came down from the bridge. He addressed them briefly, then turned around and left.

"What did he say?" asked a woman. "I don't understand Dutch."

"He said that the ship is leaking, and that we have to go to Holland and get the hull repaired," Ben answered.

"We're sinking!" shrieked the woman.

"Dear God, save us!" cried another.

"No, no, don't worry," said Ben, "it's a slow leak and they are pumping out the water. Mr. Jongehans said that we will be in Medemblik in a couple of days, if the weather holds."

Pastor Torkillus suggested that they all kneel and pray for the ship, its crew and passengers, and its safe voyage to Holland. He led them in prayer and, just for good measure, in singing a hymn as well. His strong voice sang out over the deck, the familiar incantations seemed to calm most people and they gradually dispersed. Some went below and others sat in groups talking. Pastor Torkillus turned to Ben and asked, "Was that all he said?"

"Well, he also said that he may need volunteers to man the pumps in a couple of days or if the weather gets worse."

"Let's hope we reach Medemblik soon."

The next morning, the wind had decreased but turned to southeasterly. Calmare Nyckel had to turn and tack against the wind. Mr. Jongehans came down to the passenger quarters and sought out Ben.

"Fogel, I need your help. Could you find some strong men to relieve my men at the pumps? The captain wants to assign more of our crew to working the sails."

Ben talked to the other passengers and found a group of young farm boys who, eager for any kind of activity, said they would help. He asked Pastor Torkillus to look for more volunteers, and then the young men followed Mr. Jongehans to the pumps. They climbed down below deck and walked to the pumps behind the main mast; the tossing of the ship made it difficult to move around. The oil lamp cast a weak glow over the pumps and the men working them. Their faces were streaming with sweat, and their eyes were blank with fatigue.

One of the pumpers had a large bruise on his cheek, and there was blood on his shirt collar. "I lost my grip and hit my head against the bulkhead," he said.

It took two men to work one pump, and the flickering light of the lamp fell on the other. Dark stains of blood glistened along the edge of his hands on the pump handles. A third man was sitting, bracing himself against the bulkhead, holding his open hands in front of him; the palms of his hands and his fingered were colored an angry red where open sores had replaced the skin.

The volunteers relieved the sailors, who were sent up on deck by Mr. Jongehans. It took a while for the new group to get the pumps going evenly and to keep a steady rhythm. They had to brace themselves against the tossing and turning of the ship, and at the same time pump and pump. One of the boys, Anders, threw up immediately, and next to him his friend Nils looked ashen. It was hard work and they worked in pairs taking half-hour turns, the seasick boys going up on deck between turns.

Mr. Jongehans came back and told them, "I've been back down to the bilge and looked around. She's not leaking badly, but there is a steady trickle of water coming in around old nails and between the hull planks. We'll need to keep both pumps going until we get to Medemblik."

This meant that they needed twice as many men at the pumps at all times. Pastor Torkillus found some more passengers that could help, Mr. Jongehans reassigned a couple of the sailors, and it seemed for now as if they had enough people to man the pumps.

In the beginning the men felt strong and kept up a banter, but as they got wearier the chatter became less and then it stopped altogether. The only sounds you could hear were the men breathing, the pump going up and down, the pounding of the waves, the hissing wind, and the humming from the rigging. Life in the pump room became an endless stream of alternating fatigue and oblivion – nothing mattered beyond the next stroke or the next rest period.

The wind was against them, but slowly Calmare Nyckel made headway toward the Marsdiep, the entrance to the Zuidersee and safe harbors.

2. Innkeepers

Ben's real name was Benjamin Hyeronimous Magnusson. His father, Magnus, had been a sailor who had found his Dutch bride, Anneke, at a harbor tavern in Volendam. Magnus was a tall blond man of Viking stock with a booming laugh and an openness that won him many friends. His clear blue eyes and gentle hands endeared him to the girls. Anneke looked nothing like a Viking bride; her Huguenot grandparents had moved from France to Holland to escape the persecution of the Catholics. She was small, with black curly hair and brown, almost black eyes. But her eyes could sparkle and when Magnus came into the inn where she worked, they would glitter like the phosphorescence that follows a ship in the night.

Back when Magnus was thirteen years old, King Karl IX had decided to build a new city that would allow ships to go directly from Sweden to the North Sea without paying a toll to the Danes. It was built at the mouth of the river Gotha, which poured into the sea from the land of Goths. The King named the city Gothenburg, and he invited Dutch traders to come and settle. Sweden exported copper, iron, tar, and wood through the Gothenburg port, and Magnus's parents had a small inn there to serve traders, travelers, and ships' crews. The settlement grew, but Denmark's King Kristian IV was not very happy about either the competition with Danish merchants or the loss of tolls.

Like many young men living on the coast, Magnus had gone to sea. He was nineteen, and in 1611 he was sailing on the Dutch ship Noorderlicht between Sweden and Holland. When his ship was about to return to Gothenburg, he had received word that Danish troops had attacked the settlement and burned most of it to the ground. His parents had barely been able to get away, but they were safe and had moved back inland. He signed off Noorderlicht in Volendam and was looking for a ship that would take him home. It was difficult with the Danish blockade, and besides there was the matter of Anneke; he was growing more and more fond of her.

Letters took a long time and delivery was not always reliable, but over the years they would get news from home now and then. They had heard that Gothenburg was being rebuilt, trade was picking up, the Dutch traders were coming back and Magnus's parents had started a new inn, but it would take six more years before he could return home with his bride and their first child, Benjamin.

Times were still difficult, and soon after coming back to Sweden, Magnus had gone back to sea. Anneke and Benjamin had moved in with his parents and become working members of the innkeeping family. Magnus had continued his mariner's life, coming home once or twice every year, and two more times leaving Anneke to bear him a child. Then one year when Ben was ten, Magnus didn't come home at all. His ship had been lost on the North Sea, the wet grave of many sailors.

Magnus' father and mother had grown old very fast after his death, and Anneke soon took over the inn. She renamed it Molen, remembering the windmills along the Zuidersee. In the Gothenburg harbor it was known simply as "The Dutch Inn". They all lived in the rooms behind the inn, and Ben, his brother Maximilian and his sister Alexandra grew up among visitors from all over the world. They would sit among the sailors, who told stories and talked longingly about their own children, whom they hardly ever saw.

Ben had the build of his Viking father blended with the Huguenot looks of his mother. He had a dark complexion and curly brown hair – but his eyes were pale blue. He was quick to smile and got along well with everybody. His brother Max was a carbon copy of his father; Anneke often found herself looking at Max and thinking of Magnus. Alex took after her mother. She also had quite a temper and when she got angry, her eyes would frost over and her mouth would become a thin, straight line across her face.

As Anneke's children got older, they would come home from school and help out at the inn each afternoon. This was the time when the sailors came to eat and get away from their ships. As the evening wore on, things got livelier; the ale and schnapps flowed, the local floozies arrived to charm the pants off the sailors, and now and then a fight broke out.

Anneke presided over all of this, and when things looked as if they would get out of hand, she would send in one of her seven-foot barmen to settle things down. By that time, however, the children would be safely tucked away in their beds. At least most of the time – sometimes they would sneak over to the inn and secretly watch and listen.

The sailors would tell stories about their travels, about faraway places and people, but also about the perils – the ships that got lost and ran up on rocks, bad storms when men would be washed overboard, and pirates that would do unspeakable things to the crew of any ship they conquered. The stories would get better as the storyteller downed one tankard of ale after another; there were three-ale stories, five-ale stories, and even those that would last until the storyteller nodded off.

Tom, an old English sailor, worked on a ship that plied the North Sea from Newcastle to Gothenburg. He had a golden chain around his neck, he was missing the bottom half of one ear; the other had a ring in it. Two fingers were missing from his left hand and half of the index finger on the right. Tom would sit at the inn with what was left of his hands around the ale mug and tell stories. Now and then he would pause, take a sip of ale, wipe his mouth and, after a bit of prompting, go on.

Ben's favorite was a five-ale story about Tom's adventures sailing with Francis Drake around the world. Tom told them about ransacking Spanish ships going back from South America to Spain laden with silver, finding their way through the archipelago at the bottom of South America, pillaging Spanish cities in Chile and Peru, finding California, continuing across the Pacific to the Spice Islands to load up with cloves, and then finally setting sail back toward England. It took three years and Drake lost over half his crew, which was not unexpected in those days.

"Francis Drake was a pirate, but he was the Queen's pirate," the old sailor would say, reaching for his third ale.

By the fourth ale, Drake was back in England. There he had delivered treasures and spices to the Queen, who in return had knighted him Sir Francis Drake. That put an added responsibility on Drake, and with the Queen's blessings he was now off burning and looting more Spanish possessions.

Tom had signed on Walter Raleigh's ship, which in 1585 went to the New World across the Atlantic to form a new state, Virginia, and to bring back tobacco to the Old World. He told the children about beautiful beaches, high mountains, and huge forests along the Atlantic coast, but also about the natives.

"There are lots of Indians of different tribes living everywhere. They speak many different languages, and they don't understand the ways of the Europeans. That's a problem already, and it's not going to go away," the old sailor said and finished his fifth ale.

Sweden was at war in Europe, and Gothenburg was an important hub for the supply lines to the army in Germany. There were yards where ships were built and overhauled, and the harbor itself was very busy. Soldiers, provisions, and arms would be loaded on ships that would travel in convoys to Prussia, to return with maimed soldiers and war booty. The crews of the ships would come to the Molen, bringing news and stories from the battlefields of Europe. The fires of war were spreading and the stories of slaughter and mayhem just got worse.

Ben wasn't sure exactly when he became an innkeeper, but by the time he was sixteen his mother would often leave him to run the inn while she went back to the house. Ben's grandfather had died the year before, and his grandmother was bedridden and failing. Ben had started helping out with the inn years before. He would come home from school and his mother would give him a broom and ask him to sweep the floor before dinner, and then assign him to picking up and washing dishes. He didn't like the work, but there wasn't much he could do about it; his mother needed the help.

One slow afternoon in June, the door of the inn opened and a sailor came in and sat down. He was dressed in navy clothes, and his gait marked him as someone who had just come off a ship. He took off his jacket; his weather-beaten face and arms were tanned a deep brown. Ben recognized the man, whom he seen several times at the inn, and he walked over.

"Good afternoon, Harald, it's been a long time since I saw you!"

"Hello, Ben! Yes it has, I've been away for six months."

Harald Arneson was boatswain on the naval ship Gothia. He asked Ben for a tankard of ale, and when Ben brought it over, Harald said, "Sit down and join me, it's been such a long time since I had a sane moment."

Ben got a glass of his own and sat down. Each took a swig. It was quiet for a long time, and then Ben asked, "We hear a lot about the war, what's it like?"

"Well, we just picked up over two hundred wounded men from Rostock. They were packed in like sardines everywhere we could find room for them. Many never made it; they died of their wounds, and we started burying them at sea the first day out. But that was only the beginning."

He paused, took another swig of ale and continued, "After a couple of days the flux started spreading, first among the wounded, then it spread to the healthier men, and then to some of the crew. By the time we arrived in Gothenburg, half the people on the ship were ill. It was a real shithouse!"

"Where are the soldiers now?"

"Those who could walk or find conveyance are on their way home, and the sick are in field hospitals outside the city. When the living had left the ship, there were still many left; they're resting in the cemeteries now."

"Are you going out again right away?"

"Yes, soon, but Gothia needs an overhaul and will be in port for a month. I'll stay around for two weeks, but then I'm shipping out on the merchant ship Svala for a run to Holland and Scotland."

Harald looked at Ben for a moment and said, "I remember your father – he was a sailor, wasn't he?"

"Yes."

"How old are you?"

"Sixteen."

"Would you like to come along on Svala? I need another hand on deck. The captain is a good man, and Svala is a good little ship."

Ben had no illusions about the life of a sailor, he had seen too many broken-down men coming off the ships, and he had already seen many leave and never come back. But at sixteen he felt immortal, and the prospect of a sea voyage was alluring. He told Harald that he would need to talk to his mother.

When Anneke heard about the idea, she flatly refused. "Your father was lost at sea, and now I'll lose you too! And what about the Molen? Who will help me here?"

"Max is old enough to help you. He has already begun to work at the inn now and then. And I won't be gone forever."

It took a week before she reluctantly gave in. Harald was taking his meals regularly at the Molen, and he talked to Anneke. "Let him go, he will be fine, it's an easy run. It's summer and the weather will be good. And it will also keep him from being conscripted into the army and sent to fight the papists."

The soldiers in the Swedish army fighting in Europe came from every-where; only about a quarter or perhaps a third came from Sweden and Finland. Even so, with such a small population the drain of young men was great. As the war continued, traveling army recruiters were asking for more and more conscripted soldiers. By royal decree, any boy over fifteen years of age was eligible for service. A village would be asked to supply and pay for one or more soldiers. Many villages lost so many young men that the women who remained behind had to step in and take over much of the day-to-day work.

So in the summer of 1630, when the Swedish King Gustavus Adolphus landed in Peenemünde in Pomerania and started marching south with twenty six thousand men, Ben was on the ship Svala sailing west from Gothenburg around The Skaw, the northernmost point on Danish Jutland. She continued across Skagerrak, and south over the North Sea to the mouth of the Zuiderzee, where she made her first port in Enkhuizen, in North Holland.

Harald's promise of an easy run came true. The winds were moderate, the northern summer nights were short, and it never got really dark. Ben was the youngest on board, and got saddled with all the menial chores. He had to clean the fo'c'sle, wash up after meals and swab decks, but he also had to pull his weight on the lines when sails were set or lowered. Being the youngest also meant going aloft often, not always because it was needed; the older seamen were not above sending him up on a fool's errand. That is, until one day when he was sent up to the main top one day to tighten "the imaginary line".

Svala was pitching and rolling in the swells of the North Sea, and it didn't take Ben long to realize that he was getting seasick. Still, aware of his duties, he kept on climbing up the mast as it swayed violently back and forth. All of a sudden his stomach revolted and he spewed forth his latest meal straight out in the air. A shower of salt herring and sour ale poured down on his elders, who were imprudently standing downwind. From then on, Ben still had to do the menial chores, but he was no longer sent aloft needlessly.

Enkhuizen, with over twenty thousand inhabitants, was the third largest city in North Holland; only Amsterdam and Haarlem were larger. Its location on the western coast of the Zuiderzee made it a perfect deep water port for the large Dutch merchant fleet that traveled all over the known world. It was one of the homes of VOC, Vereenigde Oostindische Compagnie, the United East India Company.

It was midday when they approached Enkhuizen, moving slowly in a light wind. They first saw the masts of the many ships already at anchor, then the ships. There was an armada of tenders under sails and oars that carried the cargoes to and from the docks. As they got closer Ben could see the wall with seven pointed bastions that protected the city. A pilot came aboard and guided Svala to her anchorage, and soon she was at rest, all her sails furled.

The VOC agent came aboard, and the captain negotiated the sale of his cargo of tar and iron, as well as the purchase of the return load of salt and spices. The captain and the agent knew each other from past dealings, and besides, the cargo came from a Dutch merchant in Gothenburg who would also take the salt and spices when Svala returned.

The deal was concluded quickly and sealed with a glass of Dutch genever, followed for the sake of fairness by a glass of Swedish aquavit. The agent also took Svala's mail and left a bag of mail for her to take. The unloading of the cargo was to begin the next morning, and the captain gave half the crew some eagerly-awaited shore leave for the evening. "I need some of you to be on port watch all the time, and this way I know that at least half of you will be sober."

The ship's skiff took Ben and Harald dockside. As they approached, the din of the city got louder and louder. There were many taverns along the dock, and the streets were crowded with sailors, beggars, prostitutes, hawkers, and vendors of all kinds. Horse-drawn wagons carried ships' cargoes between tenders and warehouses; there were delivery wagons, cabs, and fine carriages. Dogs were fighting over scraps of food. There were no fine shops; to find those you would have to get away from the harbor. But there were many men in fine clothes and many trade offices. Signs on the shops told of silk, spices, tobacco, tea, porcelain, furniture and more, all part of the East India trade.

Ben and Harald walked along the harbor street. It reeked of horse manure, fish, garbage, and salt water, but Ben felt invigorated by the teeming life ashore. He listened to the people haggling or just talking; he heard Dutch, German, English, French, and a few languages that he didn't recognize. The rattling of a chimney sweep's chains and the bell of a knife sharpener going from door to door mixed with the clanging of a smith's hammer and the hawkers' shouts.

"Fresh cod, I've got fresh cod!"

"Mister, do you want to have a good time!"

"Pictures! I can draw your portrait in twenty minutes!"

"Rhinoceros horn from Africa! Mister, you'll impress the ladies!"

"Candy, sweet candy from India!"

"Come see the hunchback and the fattest woman on earth!"

"Fresh greens straight from the country!"

"Want me to shine your boots, mister?

"North Sea herring!"

A vendor held a herring in front of his face, but Ben had had his fill of herring aboard ship, and declined. Harald, who was getting hungry, bought one, held it high by the tail and in the proper Dutch way sucked the meat off the bones like a calf sucking on a cow's teat. They continued to a little square, wandering among stalls where crumbs from the rich East India trade were hawked. They walked past a spice seller and their noses picked up whiffs of nutmeg and cinnamon in the air. Suddenly Ben felt something on his back and he heard the tinkling of coins. A busker's monkey had jumped onto his shoulder and was holding out a little copper cup looking for more coins. Next to them a man with a wooden leg was cranking a hurdy-gurdy, a young boy with bells on his arms and legs was dancing to the droning music.

They stopped and watched for a while. Harald dropped a coin in the monkey's cup, and said, "That herring made me thirsty, it's time for some ale."

They found a tavern called Het Papegaai, and stepped through a low door into a smoke-filled room where they sat down and asked the barmaid to bring them some ale, bread, and fish soup. The food and drink came and they tucked in. It didn't take long until a couple of local women started circling like sharks around their fish bowls. Ben didn't put up any resistance, but when he was beginning to enjoy being pawed by a hustling blond with deep wrinkles around her eyes, tobacco-stained teeth, and magnificent breasts that were held up by a tight bodice, Harald moved in and explained kindly to the woman that unless she let go of her young catch, he would personally kick her ample behind out the door.

She assessed his size and the probability that she could muster up enough supporters to challenge him, but decided there was easier prey elsewhere and said to Ben, "Good night, sweet boy! Come back some other time when your Cerberus has drowned."

16

From Enkhuizen Svala set sail for Edinburgh, where she would take on board a contingent of Scottish mercenaries whom they would bring back to Gothenburg. There the Scots were transferred to Gothia, whose overhaul had been completed. Gothia was heading for Pomerania, where the mercenaries would join Gustavus Adolphus's army, but Ben's first sea voyage was over, and he signed off the ship and returned home.

The fires of war in Europe consumed more and more men, the King was stepping up his demand for fresh soldiers, and recruiters in Sweden were getting more insistent. When Ben was eighteen, the day came when he had to go stand in front of the neighborhood conscription committee.

The recruiting captain had decided that this was the year when he would begin to give his new recruits their own unique family names. This was an army tradition in the making. The Swedish Army wanted to get away from common patronymic last names, where they would have thousands of young men whose last names were simply their father's first names with "son" tagged on, creating a confusing abundance of Larssons, Svenssons, and Erikssons. The renaming practice would last over a hundred years, filling the country with generations of very special soldier names. Ben's captain was going down a list of birds' names, but just as he got to Ben he had reached the end. He was thinking of starting all over again, just adding a number, but then he asked Ben about his full name. "Benjamin Hyeronimous Magnusson" answered Ben.

"I've too many sons of Magnus. Where does your mother come from?"

"Volendam, south of Edam in North Holland."

"Spreekt je Nederlands?"

"Ja, mijnheer."

"Well then, we'd better give you a proper European family name – I'm out of bird names, but we will call you Fogel, just bird."

Anneke had always spoken Dutch to her children, first out of necessity, and then out of habit. Ben spoke fluent Dutch and with all the foreign visitors at the inn, he could also manage English and German. The captain was very pleased to get a soldier who could speak so many languages, and assigned him to a company that was going to Germany to join Gustavus Adolphus's army fighting against what the King called "the Papal deluge approaching our shores".

It was 1632 and the war between Protestants and Catholics had been going on for fourteen years. Sweden was at the peak of its imperial power, ruling most of the nations around the Baltic, with the exceptions of Denmark and the Habsburg enclaves; its navy controlled the seas and Gustavus Adolphus had over one hundred thirty thousand soldiers of different nationalities fighting for him in Europe. The Dutch were rich and powerful as well, and they had joined the Protestant alliance in the war against Catholic Spain and the Habsburg empire. The alliance was strong, but the Habsburg General Albrecht von Wallenstein was making plans to draw the Swedish king into battle at Lützen.

3. Going to War

Anneke packed a pouch of food and drink for Ben, who had to report to his regiment. The recruiting captain had given him two days to settle things at home, and pick up anything he needed. Before Ben went home to say goodbye, he was given a new grey uniform with the wide-brimmed hat of a musketeer. It used to be the practice that every neighborhood was to provide their recruits with the necessary gear and a backpack for carrying anything the soldier wasn't wearing, but six years ago the King had decreed that the soldiers should use standardized clothing and ordered centralized production of uniforms. Weapons were now also mass-produced at Swedish foundries and steel mills.

Ben walked up the hill from the Molen, then turned around and waved to his mother, his brother, his sister, and his grandmother, who were all standing at the door. It was early morning, the harbor was still quiet, and the water lay calm and glittering in the warm sunshine. He stood there waving to his family, and for a moment it seemed to Ben that the world held its breath. Then he turned his back on his childhood, and walked off to go to war.

A training camp where the recruits would learn the basics of soldiering had been set up on a field outside the town. Ben arrived at the camp midday and was told to report to Sergeant-Major Petersson. The sergeant-major looked at the notes made by the recruiting captain and said, "We are setting up a new company that will be leaving for Germany in three weeks. Fogel will be assigned to assist the company commander's staff with interpretation and translations, but first you need basic army training. Go and report to Mr. Rask in the next room!"

Ben walked in search of Rask, who assigned him to a tent and then told him that his training would start the next morning. An orderly took him over to the tent, and showed him a pile of blankets and mattress covers. Outside there was a pile of straw, and the orderly said, "Fill your mattress cover with this! It will probably be the most comfortable bed you'll have for a long time."

Ben put his mattress on the ground in the tent, arranged his coat to be a pillow and stowed his gear on the ground behind the bed. He was the first one to arrive, but when he was finished with his preparations the other recruits started to dribble in one by one. The first one was a boy who looked to be no more than fourteen years old. His clothes were worn and had been patched many times; he was very thin, his hair was matted and his face grimy with road dust. He sat down on the ground and looked at Ben. "I have been walking for four days to get here, and I haven't had anything to eat for the last two days."

Ben fished out an apple from his backpack and gave it to the boy.

"What's your name?" Ben asked.

"Henrik Svensson, but they changed that to Henrik Skata."

"A magpie! Welcome, my name is Fogel."

Soon more recruits arrived. It must have been the season of birds at the recruiting sessions. First a thrush, a finch, and a raven arrived: Anders Trast, Per Fink and Johan Korp. Then there was a relapse to the old names when Sven Nilsson and Nils Svensson arrived. The last one in was a short boy with a thin face. When they asked him what his name was, he mumbled, "Hans Vessla."

"A weasel in the birdhouse, how will that work?" Ben said shaking his head.

At eighteen Ben was the oldest recruit; the others were between fourteen and sixteen. None of them had ever been away from home before, but like most young men everywhere they put on courageous faces. Sven and Anders came from the same village, and they had been the last men there to be drafted. Now there were only women, small children and a few old men left to tend the village farms.

They spent the next three weeks practicing. They were each issued a grey jacket, blue trousers with long grey gaiters, and a wide-brimmed musketeer's hat. Each was armed with a sword, a musket, a bandolier for ammunition, and a musket fork for support while firing. They practiced loading the gun quickly, shooting, reloading, and shooting again. They were shown how to thrust and slash with their swords. Swords were meant for hand-to-hand combat, but they could also be useful to bring down a horse. Mr. Rask told them, "If you get that close to an enemy rider, aim for the horse. You can bring it down with a slash at the legs, cutting the tendons. Then you can take the rider when he falls to the ground."

Ben shuddered at the cruelty implied in the instructions, but kept a straight face. He was a military man now, and his childhood morals would have to change, at least in warfare.

Three weeks of training was not enough time in which to learn very much, but the King had ordered the mobilization of more and more army battalions, and he wanted them right away. Rask knew that time was short, and he ran the boys ragged. Each night they fell exhausted into their beds and it seemed as if reveille was sounded two seconds after their heads hit the pillows. Sunday, after the morning church service, the obligatory cleaning of clothes, weapon maintenance and the subsequent inspection, was their only time off.

On their first day, Rask warned them about running away. He told them about recruits who had broken down and run away, only to be caught and put in the dungeons at Fort Elfsborg. But in spite of the warnings, Trast was missing one Monday morning. It took Rask's men another week to find him, but when they did, they first brought him back to camp for the other recruits to see. He sat behind bars in a prison wagon, his clothes torn, his face dirty, and his hair matted. He had a broken arm and there was blood on his shirt. The camp commander sternly assembled all the recruits, had them stand at attention and addressed them.

"The King has ordered that every able-bodied Swedish man should serve his country in the war against the papists. The Pope and his Catholic emperor are at this moment planning to invade our shores. This is a time when we must stand fast behind our King and his noble generals and admirals to meet the threat of this unholy alliance."

He pointed to Trast in the prison wagon and continued. "This man has broken the trust of the King, and he must be punished. However, he is very young, and will be given a chance to redeem himself. He will go to prison, but he will also get the chance later to make amends and join the King's army in Germany directly from prison." He dismissed the recruits and the wagon with the prisoner left for the fort.

When the next ship for Germany was ready for departure, Trast would be given a choice of going directly to Germany, albeit in shackles, or staying in prison. After a few weeks in the wet, cold, dark cells at the fort with little to eat and drink, most of the young escapees chose to go.

"But if you think you can run away in Germany, think again!" Rask told his recruits. "There the punishment for desertion is death."

Ben's company was commanded by Baron Rupert von Lans. Captain von Lans was twenty-five years old and was already a battle-scarred army veteran. Since his older brother would inherit the family landholdings, his family had used its influence and secured him an army commission with the staff of Field Marshal Gustav Horn, one of Gustavus Adolphus's commanders. Von Lans had been with Horn at the battle of Breitenfeld a year ago, when the Swedish army soundly defeated the imperial army under General Johann Tilly.

At Breitenfeld von Lans had demonstrated a talent for organizing the soldiers and getting them ready for battle. The Swedish tactic was to move ahead aggressively, alternating artillery and musket fire with forward movements to engage Tilly's soldiers. Von Lans had trained his company well; he kept a cool head and held his men under tight control. When Gustavus Adolphus decided to turn the right flank to counter Tilly's move to go around the Swedes, von Lans led his men in setting up the new lines with artillery, cavalry and infantry of pikemen and musketeers. Horn then gave orders to attack, and waves of alternating cavalry and infantry pressed back Tilly's army.

The Swedes had been practicing platoon fire, a powerful new musketeer technique that they now put into practice. Three lines of musketeers fired at the same time; light artillery fire was added and between the explosive firings the pikemen would attack and drive back the Catholic cavalry against their own infantry. After hours of Protestant attacks the middle of the Tilly line broke and the Catholic cavalry retreated in total confusion, abandoning the infantry.

The Catholic infantry didn't give up, but kept on fighting. Horn ordered his cavalry forward and the mayhem continued with hand-to-hand combat. The Catholic army slowly started to collapse under the pressure, but on the hills behind them, their artillery kept on bombarding the oncoming Swedes. Horn ordered von Lans and his men to follow him in an attack on the gun emplacements. Von Lans went around the infantry battleground and came up on the gunners from behind. The Swedes fell on the Habsburg soldiers from the back and captured much of their artillery, which they then turned on Tilly's army.

It was a bloody, lengthy battle. When it was finally over the imperial Habsburg army had lost more than half of its soldiers, and the total death toll would rise to over twenty thousand – most of them killed the first day. This first evening the battlefield was covered with thousands of bodies; many wounded soldiers who couldn't get away were killed by roving bands of peasants scavenging the field of carnage. Surgeons had set up field hospitals and were hard at work cutting, sawing, and sewing. Some of the wounded would survive, but many would die later of infections. Four thousand horses lay rotting, and the air was laden with the stench and the moaning of the wounded as the smoke slowly drifted away. During the battle, the Protestant supply wagons had retreated and then been ransacked, and there was little food for the tired, hungry soldiers, who gathered around campfires in the middle of the battlefield. The dust from the battle settled and night came.

The victory at Breitenfeld whetted Gustavus Adolphus's appetite for more conquests. The Midnight Lion decided to move south toward Bavaria. He needed more troops, and his commanders sent several young officers back to Sweden to draft new recruits and set up new companies and bring them to Germany. Baron von Lans was ordered by Horn to go to the western part of Sweden.

Three weeks after Ben had joined the army, von Lans led the new musketeer company down to the docks, where they boarded ships bound for Germany. The summer was almost over and the trees were beginning to change colors. But the days were still warm and the late summer breezes carried them out on the Kattegat, where they turned south. A few days into the trip, Captain von Lans was in the officers' mess, and he sent for Ben.

When Ben came into the mess, von Lans was sitting at the table. His long dark hair was tied back in a neat ponytail, his face was clean-shaven, and his shirt was open at the collar. His coat hung on the chair next to him, and in front of him he had a pile of documents. He was writing and Ben waited patiently for him to say something. Finally von Lans looked up.

"Fogel, you will be part of my staff. We are going to have Dutch and German contingents, and I'll need you to be an interpreter and a courier. Do you know how to ride a horse?"

Ben, who had grown up by the sea and never been on a horse, answered, "Not very well, Sir."

"Well, you'll have to learn after we land in Stralsund." He continued, "You will be part of the King's Guard and my Sergeant; go see Rask about a new uniform."

Dismissed, Ben went in search of Rask, whom he found down in one of the ship's store rooms. "Captain von Lans told me to see you about a new blue uniform. I'm joining the King's Guard."

"I know," said Rask, "come with me and we'll find one."

They walked over to a pile of clothes in the back and Rask started rifling through the pile. "Here is one," he said, "oh, no, you don't want that." The jacket had a rip right across the sleeve, and there was a brown spot where it had been cut. The next one had a hole on the chest, and Ben realized that all the uniforms had been used and taken off their previous owners before they had been buried.

"Don't worry," said Rask, "they have all been cleaned. Here is one that has hardly been used." He took out a jacket with no visible scars and handed it to Ben.

There wasn't much for the soldiers to do aboard the ships. Von Lans and the other officers had their own quarters, and the soldiers didn't see much of them. Rask and his men had them assemble on deck in the morning for inspection and a session of weapon training, but most of the time they just waited.

The late summer breezes pushed the convoy slowly through Öresund. The ships flew Swedish flags, stayed fairly close together and posted gun crews on watch – they had Denmark on both sides. Out of the narrow strait they continued south, heading for Swedish-held territory. A little over a week out of Gothenburg the ships turned south into Strelasund in Pomerania, where they would anchor in the harbor of Stralsund, center of the Swedish occupation of the southern shores of the Baltic Sea. They were not alone; this was a busy shipping lane with troop and supply ships coming and going. Ben was standing on deck as the southwesterly breeze pushed them along toward their anchorage. Ben's ship had furled most of it sails and was moving slowly. Coming toward them, going north out on the Baltic Sea with all her square sails set for speed was a three-masted pinnace flying the blue and yellow Swedish three-tailed naval flag. As she passed them, Ben could read the name Calmare Nyckel on the stern.

4. Pomerania

The harbor was crowded and they had to lie at anchor in a road-stead north of the town for two days before they could get a place at the docks. Gustavus Adolphus now commanded an army of one hundred fifty thousand men, and Stralsund was a busy port. Supplies, troops, horses, weapons, ammunition and everything else that the war machine craved came on ships across the Baltic. On the return trips the ships carried sick and maimed men that were unfit for further fighting as well as war booty, some of it for the King, some for the generals, some for the Protestant church, and some for private traders.

Mainland Sweden's southernmost seaport in the Baltic was Calmar and there was a constant stream of ships between Calmar and Stralsund. The business of war was brisk, and supply lines, as always, crucial. Four years ago, the same year that Gustavus Adolphus's pride the royal ship Wasa sank on her maiden voyage, the "Imperial Generalissimus" Wallenstein tried to cut the Protestant supply lines by a siege of Stralsund. Scottish and Swedish soldiers held the town and fought off the attack, putting the Pomeranian port securely in Swedish hands.

Ben's ship was towed into port and made fast alongside the dock. Unloading began immediately, and the solders were ordered to fall in on land. Ben had been ordered by Captain von Lans to go with the troops to their camp outside Stralsund and join the Guard stationed there. Now Rask took command and no sooner had they gotten off the ship and put their heavy gear on supply wagons than they were moving. They marched along the town wall and away from Stralsund. It was mid-September, a warm day in early autumn, and the leaves were still summer-green. Behind the troops the supply wagons lumbered. Some of them carried women and children; the army had a large following of families. The wagons also held a motley crew of mistresses, cooks, maids, whores, fortune-tellers, peddlers, and just about anybody, man or woman, that had any relationship to the soldiers or simply saw an opportunity in the vast congregation of men with lots of idle time and short prospects.

The road was well-traveled and had deep ruts from the wheels of carriages, wagons, and horse-drawn guns as well as carts pulled and pushed by sweaty men, women, and children. It was muddy and the mud was mixed with equal parts horse manure and piss. The cacophony from the road assaulted them; people shouted, wagons clattered, wheels squeaked, dogs barked, oxen bellowed in protest and from little fires along the roadside prostitutes called out their invitations. Soldiers on crutches worked their way slow step by slow step back towards Stralsund and the looming safety of the ship that would take them home. From bouncing wagons the boys could hear the cries and moans of the sick and wounded. Beggars shoved their amputated limbs and festering sores toward them; some just sat at the side of the road with empty cups and blank faces.

The suddenness of the sights and sounds, the smell and the loud noise unnerved the boys and the troops instinctively pulled together, finding comfort in a steady pace of walking. Young Skata had sought out Ben and was marching next to him. Vessla had joined them. He asked, "Do you know where we're going?"

Ben replied, "The Captain told me we have a camp about fifteen miles from Stralsund. We should get there today."

Skata asked, "Is this still Sweden?"

"No, it is Pomerania, but our King rules the land. His army fought off the Emperor's army that was trying to take Stralsund. Now it is ours."

"How do you know all of this?"

"We have a lot of soldiers and sailors coming to the inn in Gothenburg. They are always telling us stories from the war."

The road crossed a field into a forest of tall, green fir trees. The weather turned and the wind picked up, blowing lightly at first, but slowly picking up strength. The wind came from behind them, and the soldiers pulled up their coat collars. It got darker as they got farther into the forest and the sun disappeared behind a cloud. There was a smattering of hooves behind them. Two horses came galloping down the road. The riders in grey coats and hats were bent forward, urging the horses on. Each horse was carrying two big saddlebags that were tied down to keep them from flapping. The horses frothed at the mouth and were lathered with sweat.

As the riders passed, wet splashes rained over the marching soldiers. Vessla said, "They must be couriers. I wonder what's in the bags?"

Before anybody could answer, they heard more horses. A large troop of cavalry men came from behind. Each rider held the hackamore of an extra packhorse carrying bundles of supplies, personal gear, and weapons. The riders were dressed in long black coats with hoods that covered up their faces. Ben caught a glimpse of a pale, grinning face and large black eyes under the hood. The riders were cantering side by side in pairs, and with the extra packhorses they forced the foot soldiers over. The marching troop became a confused mass of individuals trying to get out of the horses' and each others' way. One horse spooked and started going sideways and soon it was bucking and kicking. A kick landed on the packhorse, which pulled back at the hackamore so hard that the rider had to let it go. The riders behind the kicking horse tried to pull back, and the foot soldiers scattered off the road.

More black coats on horses came from behind and got pushed into the mêlée, more horses started kicking, one reared up on his hind legs and danced around looking for an escape. Hooves were flying, soldiers shouting and the horses snorted and rolled their eyes in panic. Then it all quieted down as fast as it started, and the black cavalry disappeared down the road. But one soldier was left on the road, lying face down in the mud. Two men went over to him and rolled him over. It was Vessla; his face was dirty, his clothes torn and he was moaning. Ben kneeled by him and asked, "What happened to you?"

Vessla looked at him and his mouth moved as he tried to say something. It came out as a frothy whisper through the blood seeping out of his mouth, "A horse… kicked ….. me. I was trying to get away. It kicked me, and I fell."

Somewhere in the forest away from the road a woman started wailing. It was a high-pitched sound, rising and falling.

"Where did it kick you?"

Vessla pointed to the side of his chest and whispered, "It hurts."

"Can you sit up?"

The boy tried to raise himself up on his elbows, but the pain was too much, his face turned pale, and he fell back with his head in Ben's lap. Ben held him, but his eyes rolled back and his face got even whiter. He cried out with pain, then slumped down and Ben felt a chill go through him. He shouted, "Hans, Hans!" but Vessla didn't respond.

A man came over, saying, "I'm a surgeon, let me look at him." He bent over and gently lifted Vessla from Ben's cramp-like grip and laid him down on the ground. The surgeon put his head on the boy's chest, listened and then looked up. "I'm sorry," he said, "but he's dead."

Ben stammered numbly, "But, but, I just talked to him." He felt as if everything around him was disappearing, as if doors were slamming shut between him and the rest of the world. He saw the surgeon's mouth move, but he heard only the wail coming from the forest. Then it too faded away.

It seemed like an eternity, but the doors slowly opened again, and he heard the surgeon's voice. "There's nothing you can do, have a drink of water. You there, help this man get on his feet."

Ben felt hands grabbing his arms and helping him in his struggle to get up. Somebody put a bottle of water to his mouth, but he shook off his helpers. "I'm alright" he said, even though it wasn't at all true. The shock of his first encounter with death, and the suddenness of it, felt like weights hanging from his shoulders.

Rask had come over to see what was going on. He saw the young soldiers standing around aimlessly, looking shocked, and he quickly ordered them to fall in again. They put Vessla's body in a supply wagon, and the march toward war was resumed. They walked for most of the day, and by late afternoon they came to the Martinshof camp.

5. Camp Martinshof

As soon as the troop ship anchored at the roadstead outside Stralsund, a tender came to pick up the officers onboard. On shore a courier gave Captain von Lans an envelope with the seal of the Swedish Governor of Prussia. He opened it and found a summons to come to Würzburg for a meeting. He was to leave immediately with an escort from the King's Guards. It would be a long trip as Würzburg was over three hundred miles further south. Von Lans gave instructions for the new recruits to his deputy, Lieutenant Storm, who had accompanied the courier.

"Here is a list of forty men that I want for the King's Guard. Go to Camp Martinshof and prepare for their arrival and training. Rask will lead the march from Stralsund, but he will hand these forty over to your command when they arrive at the camp. The first thing they will need to learn is how to ride. Here is letter with a requisition for horses, instructors and stable boys that you should present with my compliments to the Martinshof commander Kapitän Freiherr von Lutz."

He continued, "We are bringing uniforms on the ship. They will go in the supply wagons with Rask and the new recruits. I made some appointments onboard the troop ship, and these men have already been issued uniforms onboard, but please make sure all our new men get the new yellow uniforms of the King's Guard. I should be back in a couple of weeks. Any questions?"

"What about weapons, Sir?"

"Let them keep their swords for now, but they will need to replace their infantry muskets with the short cavalry model," replied Von Lans and added, "Please look after a new Sergeant named Ben Fogel. He speaks

Dutch fluently as well as some other languages, and that will be very useful for us. But he needs to learn how to be a cavalryman."

Von Lans bid adieu to Storm, got a couple of light saddlebags that his aide had packed and headed south with his escorts. They would ride all day, changing horses along the way, but it would take them over a week to get to Würzburg and the meeting with Axel Oxenstierna.

Next to the King, Oxenstierna was the most powerful man in Sweden, and some would say he had more power than the King. When Gustavus Adolphus became king at age seventeen, Oxenstierna, who was twenty-eight, became the Chancellor of the Realm, the highest ranking advisor to the King. Oxenstierna's family was a longstanding member of the nobility, and he had already made a name for himself with Karl IXth, Gustavus Adolphus's father. When Karl died, Oxenstierna negotiated an agreement with the new king that strengthened not only his power and influence, but that of all of the nobility.

The King was the most powerful person in the country, but he ruled the country together with the Parliament of the Four Estates, which repre-sented the people, at least some of them. The four estates were Nobility, Clergy, Burghers or townsmen, and Yeomen or freehold farmers. Tenant farmers, farmhands, servants, women, and other miscellaneous riff-raff of the times had no direct representation. But even the estates them-selves were not four equals; the most influential was, not surprisingly, the nobility. There were only a few thousand noblemen in the whole country, but they were rich and they owned substantial property. They also had a great many privileges – some of their land was exempt from taxes, and some were tax collectors with the right to keep some of the proceeds for themselves.

There had always been a tug of war between the King and the nobility about the power to rule and tax. Both would use the other estates in parliament to leverage their influence, and the tides of power would flow back and forth. But the influence of local noblemen over their neighbors and serfs was very strong, and no king could rule without the support of the First Estate.

Oxenstierna came from a rich and already influential family with a lineage dating back in to the middle ages beyond the thirteenth century, and he was a master in the game of politics. His agreement with Gustavus Adolphus strengthened the influence of the nobility. The King agreed not to start a war or make peace without the counsel of parliament. Tax collectors were put directly under the County Governors, all of whom were noblemen. Other privileges given to the nobility included a monopoly on civil servant appointments.

Gustavus Adolphus, grandchild of Gustav Vasa, was the foremost member of the ruling class, and he was happy to oblige his fellow noblemen. He would continue the practice of issuing royal grants for country estates as a reward for services to the Crown. The grants didn't come without catches; the price was unequivocal loyalty and those who fell out of favor would find their grants revoked and their property handed over to a new favorite. At best they would be out of favor, perhaps going into exile, at worst they were beheaded. Like in all royal courts there was the usual intrigue, backbiting, fawning and struggle for power and the King's attention. Oxenstierna was a not only a master at this game, he was also an excellent administrator and he had the King's trust. Six years ago in 1626, he had been appointed Governor of all the Swedish holdings in Prussia. He was the man calling von Lans, and when Oxenstierna called, the only possible response for a Swedish officer was to get on his horse and ride quickly to answer the Chancellor's call.

It was dusk when the new recruits marched into Camp Martinshof. On each side of the road there were little encampments with tents, fires, and people preparing their evening meals. Ben was surprised to see women and children around the encampments. A soldier was sitting against a tree, his thin horse hobbled and nibbling on a small pile of hay. A musket was leaning against a tent pole. The tent itself was just a large piece of cloth on two poles with more cloth covering the ends. A woman was cooking some soup over the fire, and a baby was wrapped up in a blanket on the ground next to the fire.

The ground was hard and worn down by the use by the many tens of thousands of soldiers, wagons, and horses that the army had brought through. Ben looked up on a hill and saw the ruin of a farm that had been burned. The trees around it had green leaves, so it must have been some time ago.

They marched along the perimeter of the camp, along a row of larger tents with bunks for the soldiers. They walked down a row of mess tents; food and drink could be bought at shops set up along the side. The evening was still young, but especially the bars seemed to do a brisk business; lots of young soldiers stood around with large mugs of ale that had been brought to them by a cadre of barmaids winding their way among them with foaming tankards. The road was crowded, but the crowd made way for the new recruits. Voices called out to them:

"Stand aside! Greenhorns on the road!"

"Look, new cannon fodder!"

"Come and have a last drink with us!"

"Hey girls, don't forget to write home before you leave from here; there is no mail service from where you're going!"

They left the bars, the inns and the laughing voices behind them and turned the corner. Ahead was a large wooden building with tall palings around it. There were two large gates in the palings with soldiers guarding the entrance. The gates were open to let a horse-drawn wagon through, and on the wagon, three men were shackled to the bars of the high railing. As the troops marched by the gate, they could see what looked like a scaffolding, with ropes hanging from the top beam. They heard a loud thump, and Ben saw a sack dangling from the end of the rope. He shivered when he realized that they were passing a military prison and that the executioners were rehearsing a hanging. He remembered the warnings by the camp commander in Sweden that in Germany the punishment for desertion was death.

Past the prison, they came to a large open area, where troops were finishing their training for the day. At the far end there were cannons set up in formations. On the left side there were paddocks; soldiers and stable boys were taking saddles and bridles off the horses and giving them feed and water. A few riders were still on the field heading for the paddocks. On the right side there were fires with men gathered around them getting ready to bivouac for the night. A group was playing football; they had set up goal posts about fifty yards apart and a small crowd was cheering them on. Somebody missed a kick and the ball landed at Sven Nilsson's feet. He picked it up; the ball was made of soft pigskin stitched together around the animal's bladder.

Nilsson held the ball in his big hands and said, "I have one of these at home. We used to play a lot, but then the boys were sent away one by one to the army. I left the ball with my sister; soon her boys are old enough to play." He dropped the ball at his feet and kicked it back into the game.

They marched through a grove and arrived at an open field where Rask finally called a halt and addressed them, "This will be your camp for a while. Tonight you will sleep in the open; we'll set up only what is immediately necessary. Get some rest while I look around!"

32

He soon came back and ordered the supply wagons to set up at the edge of the grove. The troops were divided into smaller contingents and they settled down in the field. The horses were unhitched and brought down to drink at a stream that ran through the middle of the field. Kapitän von Lutz ran a well-organized camp, and firewood had been brought in and stacked in piles at the edge of the field. Soon fires were burning and the field kitchen was up and running. The boys lined up for a bowl of stew with ale and bread, walked back to the fire and sat down to eat.

Darkness fell and it got quieter around the fires. Ben pulled a blanket over himself, closed his eyes and fell fast asleep. The clouds had disappeared and the sky was bright with stars. Orion was rising, the fire in his belt glowing; he held his shield high, and his mace was ready to strike. But somewhere in the dark sky a scorpion was waiting.

Reveille was sounded just before dawn; after an hour of breakfast and morning chores, the bugler sounded assembly. When all were present and accounted for, Rask introduced Pastor Numinus, who would lead the morning prayers. The pastor stepped in front of the troops; he was a short man with a ruddy, round face and tobacco-stained teeth. His clothes were black; he wore a long coat, a vest that didn't quite fit around his ample belly, knee breeches and riding boots. Curls of black hair rolled out from under the round hat.

Pastor Numinus came from Finland and he spoke the lilting dialect of Finland Swedish. His voice rang out, "Our Father, please welcome these young men to thy holy cause of protecting the true faith of Christianity as you have told it to Martin Luther. Let them be brave in defending the world against the Devil's work by the unholy Catholic League and their heretic Habsburg Emperor. Bless our soldiers and let them be victorious in following our noble king and the yellow crosses of our blue flags in this holy fight against the papists and let us all repel the invasion of our lands. Forgive the sins of those that fall in this battle, and open your doors to them, that they will become holy martyrs for you. Father, be with us! Amen."

The service finished with a hymn and the recitation of the Lord's Prayer, after which Rask gave them the orders for the day. Tents were to be raised, latrines dug, water collection organized, firewood gathered, mess tents and a field kitchen put in places, all the routine chores of an army. Rask had been given von Lans's list of the men wanted for the King's Guard, and before dismissing the troops he told these men to stay behind.

Ben found himself in the company of his tent mates from Sweden: Per Fink, Johan Korp, Sven Nilsson, and Nils Svensson. Von Lans had requested forty men and Rask lined them up in a four-by-ten formation on the field, putting himself in front of the troops. Lieutenant Storm had been waiting on the side since the beginning of the prayers; he now stepped up in front of Rask who called out, "Attention!" and addressed Storm. "Lieutenant, forty men for the King's Guard reporting."

"Thank you Mr. Rask, I'll take over."

Rask saluted, turned, and marched away. Storm waited until he was out of the way and then ordered, "At ease, men!"

Lieutenant Johan Mats Storm was twenty-two years old and came from Vasa in Finland. His father and grandfather had also been soldiers, and Johan Mats had joined the army when he was sixteen. He now stood in front of the new recruits, dressed in an officer's red coat and cape, white leggings below red breeches tied under the knees. He wore a wide-brimmed black hat with a large white feather on top, and around his neck he had a slung a white scarf. His sword was sheathed, the sheath hanging at his side in a belt across his chest and shoulder. His long, wavy blond hair hung loose down to his shoulders, his face was clean-shaven but for a moustache, and he had several scars across his cheeks.

His clear blue eyes looked them over one by one, and then he said, "Good morning, my name is Lieutenant Storm, deputy for Captain von Lans. The captain has picked you to join his unit in the King's Guard. It is an honor to be in the Guard, but you will need more training. You will stay here at the new camp, you'll get new uniforms and muskets, and you'll practice riding until you know how to handle a horse in battle. We have three weeks until Captain von Lans is back from his mission. By then you will either have learned, or gone back to the infantry." When he said "infantry" his lips pursed and his brow wrinkled slightly, as if he had stepped on something unpleasant.

He went on with some practical details and then dismissed them until next morning to set up their tents, find uniforms and get ready for their new life in the cavalry. They spent the next three weeks learning how to handle horses and to ride. Most of the boys came from farms where they had horses, but for Ben and a few others, it was all new. But at the end of the three weeks, only one boy was deemed hopeless and sent back to the infantry. One had broken an arm falling off, one had gotten kicked on the shin, and one's foot had been stepped on by a horse; he was limping on crutches around the camp. The rest of them, Ben included, were still intact, and the initial excruciating pain in their buttocks and thighs was mostly gone. They kept their swords but their foot soldier muskets had been replaced by a shorter model better suited for firing from a horse, and they had learned how to steer a horse with one hand free to hold the sword. Some of them could steer the horse using only their legs and body weight, leaving both hands free for firing the musket. Replacements for the injured and the hopeless had been brought in and they were busy trying to catch up.

But it was all unreal and seemed like a game. They slashed with their swords at sacks full of hay, they fired blanks, and when they or the horses got tired, they rested. At night they sat around the fires or went to the camp drinking holes; there was a lot of talking, laughing and stealing away into the shadows with the barmaids. They almost forgot that they were going to war.

6. The Chancellor's Orders

Von Lans and his escort approached Würzburg on a cloudy but un-seasonally warm afternoon. Their last horses were tired and they let them walk slowly along the winding road leading toward the walled medieval city on the right bank of the river Main. Vineyards covered the hills on both sides of the road; many of them were neglected and overgrown, some were burned and trampled. But some had survived the worst ravages of war, and old men, women, and children, were busy working along the rows of vines. They were cleaning up and pruning the vines after the summer harvest. Some yards were late and their grapes were still being harvested and loaded on handcarts or in large baskets. The carts were wheeled and the baskets carried to wagons waiting at the edge of the vineyards. The wagons were drawn by oxen and a few sad-looking horses, leftovers, the last of the pick, scrawny with their ribs sticking out, old, lame, and poorly fed; every good horse for miles around Würzburg had been appropriated by the conquering armies that succeeded each other in ruling the area.

Gustavus Adolphus had conquered Würzburg the year before and von Lans knew that its citizens had to pay tributes to the Swedish king. Oxenstierna commanded a large army stationed around the town, and a lot of the harvest would go to paying and feeding the soldiers camped in the countryside. As they were getting closer to the city, they saw more and more soldiers; outside the city wall a large area was covered with tents, men, horses, wagons, and all the accompanying human flotsam and jetsam. Guards were posted around the camps and along the roads, and they had to go through several checkpoints. They entered the city through one of the gates in the city wall and continued along the city streets. Several houses had been burnt or ransacked; there were beggars reaching for handouts, many people had come from the countryside seeking refuge within the city walls. They came to the river and another checkpoint at the bridge that had carried people across the Main since Roman times. From time to time the bridge had been destroyed by flood or by marauding armies; it had just been rebuilt after the last battle. The bridge was guarded by Scottish soldiers serving the Protestant cause as mercenaries in Gustavus Adolphus's army.

To the southwest the land rose into high hills; a road wound its way up the hillsides through the vineyards to the top where they could see the Marienberg fortress. It had been captured by the Swedes last year; it was a bloody battle that started when the King knocked on the city gate using a petard that blew the gate off. The eight thousand citizens of Würzburg faced twenty thousand soldiers that stood outside the gate. Citizens began fleeing the city, some of them seeking refuge in the Marienberg fortress, but the next day Würzburg surrendered, saving the city from being ransacked and burned to the ground.

An offer to surrender was sent to the Governor of Marienberg but it was rejected out of hand; the Governor thought it was a preposterous idea to even consider that the mighty fortress that covered the top of the hill, with its high, thick walls and deep fosses between the walls and the steep hillsides should not be able to withstand any attack. There were about one thousand Catholic soldiers defending the fortress, and Marienberg's booming cannons kept firing at the advancing armies. Gustavus Adolphus ordered an attack. Scottish and Swedish soldiers crossed the river, clawed their way up the hillside and after three days of assault overcame the fortress defenders.

The battle ended in a pandemonium of pillage and massacre, when the conquering soldiers started to plunder the fort. The cries for mercy slowly died out as the vanquishers executed Marienberg's defenders, soldiers, and priests one by one. Valuable arms, provisions, and Catholic treasures fell into the hands of the Swedes.

Marienberg was now Oxenstierna's headquarters in Würzburg. The cannons remained on the emplacements surrounding the fortress but now they were manned by Swedes, and a there was a guard of Swedish soldiers posted all around. Von Lans's contingent crossed the Main bridge and followed the road along the river and up the hill to Marienberg. They showed their credentials to the guards at the fortress drawbridge and entered. Inside they were met by the officer-of-the-day, who saluted von

Lans. "Welcome to Marienberg, Captain! I am Lieutenant Alfred Moren. My men will show your men where to stable the horses and where their quarters are. I'll take you to the officer's lodgings."

Von Lans returned the salute and introduced himself, "Captain Rupert von Lans." He got off his horse with a voluptuous sigh, "Arghh, I don't think I'll ever be able to sit down or stretch my legs again."

His escort took the horses to be stabled, and to find their quarters. Lieutenant Moren accompanied von Lans to his room. The officer's quarters were one flight up in the eastern wing of the fortress, and through his small window he could see the river below and the city on the opposite side. A bastioned wall bending from north to south protected the city toward the east; on the western side there was only the one bridge across the Main. Army camps were spread out on the open land outside the city wall.

He sent word with Moren to the Chancellor that he had arrived and asked when he should present himself. Oxenstierna, not a man to lose any time, invited him for dinner that evening. Von Lans had a bath, and lay down for a rest after the long ride. At eight in the evening, an aide woke him up; he dressed and set out by foot to the chancellor's apartment. He knocked on the door and Oxenstierna's footman opened.

"Baron von Lans to see Count Oxenstierna."

"Good evening Sir, the Chancellor is expecting you. Let me take your coat and please follow me."

The footman walked down a corridor, opened a door, and held it open for von Lans. It was a small dining room with a table set for three. A fire was burning, and there were three armchairs and a couple of small side tables set around the fireplace. The footman pointed to the armchairs and said, "Please sit down, I'll tell the Chancellor you're here," and left the room. Von Lans sat down and waited; he looked into the fire and thought about why he might have been called. As a young boy with his father in Parliament in Stockholm, he had seen Oxenstierna but had never before spoken to him.

A quarter of an hour went by, then the door opened and the Chancellor entered the room. Von Lans was not surprised to see that behind him came Field Marshal Gustav Horn, his commander. Horn had married Oxenstierna's daughter, Kristina Axelsdotter, four years ago and they had had two children. Kristina had come to Germany to join her husband the year before, but soon after she arrived she died in an outbreak of the plague. Her death was a blow to both Horn and his father-in-law, and while neither of them would admit it, they seemed to find comfort with each other. Horn was the man who had sent von Lans to Sweden on a recruiting mission, and it was he who had especially ordered von Lans to find new recruits for the King's Guard. Von Lans rose to greet them.

Oxenstierna was now forty-five years old, and his dark hair and long black beard were beginning to show a few grey streaks. He was dressed for comfort, baggy black trousers, a white shirt open at the collar, a brown sweater, and slippers made from sheepskin. He walked in with the confident, easy stride of a man who knew his rightful place as a leader, much like a wolf at the head of a pack. His clear eyes looked straight at von Lans, and his smile was warm as he shook von Lans's hand and said,

"Welcome Baron, I'm glad to see you here. The Field Marshal has spoken a great deal about you."

He stepped aside as Horn shook hands with von Lans. The footman poured three glasses of wine, which he served on a silver tray engraved with the image of an ox's horned forehead, the Oxenstierna coat of arms. He offered the first glass to the chancellor who sloshed the wine around his glass, inhaled the aroma through his mighty nose, and nodded to the footman, who then served the others. Oxenstierna raised his glass and looked at Horn and von Lans and said "Skål, gentlemen!" The two officers put their heels together, straightened their backs, raised their glasses and answered "Skål, Herr Chancellor." Each took a sip from his glass, then they bowed their heads slightly over their still-raised glasses and the ancient ceremonial greeting distilled into male formality was complete.

They exchanged a few pleasantries about traveling and, in the manner of all travelers, lamented about spending long hours in the saddle. Finishing the wine, they sat down to dinner, Oxenstierna at the end of the table, with Horn on his right and von Lans across the table from his commander. It was a simple dinner of vegetable soup, bread, a small roast of wild boar with turnips. The footman served red Würzburger wine and water from nearby mountains.

Oxenstierna took command of the conversation, asking von Lans about his travel to Sweden and the difficulties in finding new recruits for the army. Von Lans replied, "The recruits are getting younger and younger. The villagers grumble about losing their men; they claim they don't have enough men to work the farms, and they cannot raise enough money to pay for their uniforms and weapons."

"Do you think this is true, or is it just the same old complaints about taxes?"

"I think there is some truth in it, there is a shortage of available young men," von Lans replied.

Oxenstierna paused for a moment as he chewed on the boar roast. He swallowed and said, "We need men in both places, here to fight and at home to work hard so they can pay the taxes to help the King pay for the war. War is a business and you need money coming in to pay for all the expenses – people, weapons, ammunition, food, clothes, transport, horses, and everything else an army needs."

The footman cleared the table and brought them some cheese, bread, grapes and a sweet white wine. Oxenstierna continued to talk about the war. He was surprisingly forthcoming about the problems of the state and the difficulties in keeping an army supplied and ready for action. His manner was formal but open, he would engage both Horn and von Lans in debate. He and Horn often disagreed, but von Lans noticed that Horn knew when to hold back and defer to his father-in-law. Horn was the paramount officer who liked to take action and face the enemy, and he and von Lans reminisced about the battle at Breitenfeld, when the Swedes trounced General Tilly's army.

"It was close, but when we managed to turn the troops against Tilly's flanking movement and fight him off, the tide turned in our favor" said Horn and looked at von Lans, "Your attack on his artillery was brilliant. That settled it."

Oxenstierna was the consummate strategist statesman who wanted to conserve his assets, minimize his costs, and maximize his profits. He said, "Breitenfeld was a brilliant success for us, and it had to be done. The King is very pleased. But going into battle is a very risky business."

They finished the meal and moved over to the armchairs around the fire. The footman brought plum brandy, poured it into three glasses and quietly left the room. Oxenstierna continued, "Winning our cause with as few losses as possible should be our goal. If we can move the enemy without battle, if we can conquer territory without a fight, if we can get supplies and finance our expenses without troop losses; that would be perfect. The venture of war is to scare the opposition to provide what you want with as few expenses and as low a risk as possible."

"We need large sums of money and lots of supplies to keep our army going. Only some of that can come from home, most has to come from the occupied area. So it has always been in wars and so it will always be. An army is a beast of prey, it eats and when the prey is gone it has to move on. A battle ravages an area, and quickly exhausts the tributes the army can command from the local population."

He paused, sipped his brandy, and Horn said, "That is all very well, but the enemy will not sit still while we conquer more and more of Germany. General von Pappenheim is on the move again and Wallenstein is now massing his Habsburg troops around Lützen."

Oxenstierna replied, "Yes, and we will have to fight again soon. But think of how we took Würzburg last year. Our troops surrounded the city, and at the threat of being burned and plundered, the citizens agreed to a tribute of eighty thousand rixdollars in return for our protection. Our venture cost was very low and the risk very small. This year München paid out three hundred thousand rixdollars. It is true that we compete with the Catholic League for tributes and that the supply is limited, but we made a net profit on the Würzburg and München operations, whereas Breitenfeld incurred a loss that we have to recover."

He held his hand out and swept it in front of him as if showing the room, and said, "Governor Keller, who commanded this fortress, was not as accommodating as the citizens of Würzburg. He decided to fight, but after three days of our attacks, he lost. Unfortunately, things then got out of hand; our soldiers wanted revenge for the Catholic destruction of Magdeburg in the spring."

He turned to von Lans and continued, "Baron, I have talked about these practical and administrative aspects of the war to give you a bit of background for the mission that General Horn and I have in mind for you. I hope I have made you understand how important these matters are to the success of the King's undertaking and Sweden's plans for the Baltic area. Now, we want you to take charge of collecting tributes and taxes in Germany as well as the distribution of monies to the Protestant armies here in Germany. Some money, gold, and captured war goods belonging to the Crown or its servants need to be transported back to Sweden."

Both Oxenstierna and Horn looked intently at von Lans, who hesitated a moment. But there was only one way forward and he replied, "Chancellor, I'll be happy to take on this mission. It will be a challenge and there will be surprises, but I am sure we can overcome most obstacles with a bit of planning ahead."

Horn smiled at the younger man and said, "Von Lans, we understand surprises. What we are looking for is a man who can work well under pressure and meet surprises with flexibility and imagination. Now, what do you think you'll need?"

"General, I'll need many things, but most of all I'll need a contingent of good men and officers. Liutenenant Storm is training the new recruits from Gothenburg right now. I would like them, but they have never been in battle and they need seasoning and the experience that comes with time. If I could have a contingent of experienced men from my old company that would help a great deal."

Horn interjected, "I anticipated your request for experienced cavalrymen, and I've ordered two young second lieutenants who served under you earlier to pick out three dozen men and come here. They should arrive from Trier within a couple of days."

"Thank you, General."

"Anything else?"

"Horses and wagons to carry money chests, gold barrels, and other goods."

Oxenstierna, who was a good listener, said, "Very good, prepare a list of men and material that you need and present it to me tomorrow. I'll sign the order and you can get to work. I assume you will need to go back to Camp Martinshof and collect the other men and gear. You will liaise with my paymaster Commander Filip Martius, whom I have borrowed from the Navy."

Horn continued, "To mark the importance of your appointment, you will be promoted to Colonel in the King's Guard. You may want to promote some of your officers and men to give them the necessary authority. Please include any such requests in your list. I'll be your commanding officer, but you will take your mission orders from the Chancellor."

"General, I'm honored by the opportunity."

Von Lans knew that none of this could have happened without Gustavus Adolphus's knowledge and consent, but this was left unsaid. He had many questions, but he needed to collect his thoughts and prepare his list of requests. It was getting late, and with the main issue of the evening out of the way, all three sank back into their chairs like slowly deflating balloons. It got very quiet for a few minutes, then Oxenstierna yawned, stood up, tossed back the last of his brandy and said, "Gentlemen, I think we're finished for tonight. Colonel, I'll expect your requests tomorrow afternoon. I'll say good night now to both of you. Gustav, I'll see you in the morning." He hesitated a moment and added, "We'll need a name for the new company, and considering the color of their uniforms, why don't we call it the Flaxen Guard?" He walked to the door, opened it and left the room.

Horn turned to von Lans and said, "You did well tonight, but don't underestimate the difficulties of the job. We've had several problems, both with the collection itself and with the transportation. Highwaymen have attacked several transports that have been too vulnerable and poorly guarded. Some of the roads go through country ravished by famine and disease. You will have to avoid areas and towns where the plague is rife."

Von Lans nodded and replied, "I understand. We'll need to keep our transport operations clandestine and unobtrusive as far as we can."

"Yes, and when it comes to collections, you'll need to be firm and sometimes you may have to be very firm. The Chancellor has been known to order the burning of hostile villages to make examples for others. And don't expect anybody to be grateful even though we may have reduced their suffering; for the population it is mostly a matter of avoiding a greater evil for a lesser one. For us it is vital to collect tributes, without them our armies will starve."

They sat back in their chairs at the fire and continued talking for a little while about many of the practical matters of the mission. Then Horn walked von Lans to the front door, where von Lans bid him good night and walked back to his quarters. His head was churning with all the impressions from the evening, and it took him a while in bed to calm down. Eventually the need for rest took over and he fell asleep.

7. The First Mission

The Chancellor was leaving Würzburg for Frankfurt, but before he left he signed von Lans's orders and an accreditation letter with the Chancellor's seal on it. Oxenstierna also prepared an encrypted letter to the King confirming the appointment as well as separate coded letters to the top generals introducing von Lans and his mission. It would take several weeks for the letters to reach their destinations, but it would take von Lans longer before he could get back to Stralsund.

Von Lans met several times with Commander Martius; he turned out to be quiet, unimposing man with a razor-sharp mind. He first took von Lans across the courtyard to the corner of the fortress, where they stopped at a door guarded by soldiers. Martius unlocked the door and they entered a dusky room; the only light came from two small barred windows. The guard brought a lit torch and put in a holder on the wall and then stepped back outside. Von Lans looked around and saw chests, flags and standards rolled up on poles, paintings, piles of books, ceremonial swords, pistols with handles made of polished hardwood with inlays of silver and pearl, decorated armors, and much more. Martius said, "Look around, Colonel, this is part of the treasures from Marienberg." He opened a chest; it was full of gold and silver coins and jewelry. He opened another that held chalices and crosses inlaid with precious stones that must have come from the Marienberg bishop's treasures. The third held books, Martius took out a large leather-covered book with with golden ornaments on and said, "This handwritten Old Testament is about five hundred years old." He took up another, opened it to show a map and continued, "This book of maps was printed in Mainz about two hundred years ago. It is one of the earliest printed books and perhaps it comes from the Gutenberg printers."

Martius put the books back, closed the chests of war booty and said, "The Chancellor wants you to take some of this to Wolgast for shipping to Sweden. You can't take everything, but we've sorted out some rare books and other things and packed them in chests for you. But now let's go back and I'll tell you the rest." They left the booty room and von Lans gave the torch to the guard while Martius locked the door, and they walked back across the courtyard. Back in his office Martius pulled out large sheets of paper with columns of numbers, from which he produced a list of targets for collecting tributes. He wanted von Lans to pay a visit to two villages in Sachsen, but said, "First you need to take a small chest of money to Kapitän von Lutz, the commander of Camp Martinshof, then the goods from here to Wolgast. There we'd like you pick up forty thousand rixdollars and take it to His Majesty's paymaster, Mr. Cyril Heidelmann in Erfurt in Sachsen. Then you should go to Wilfenheim and Kaltdorf near Erfurt; they are both behind in their payments." He gave von Lans the details for each place, and continued, "Bring back the tributes to Marienberg; after that the Chancellor will probably need you and your men for an important transport to Sweden." Little did he know how his plans were to be disrupted and yet how prophetic his comment was.

Field Marshal Horn had gone back from Würzburg to the Alsace border with Spanish Netherlands, where he would continue his battles with the Catholic League. Three days after von Lans had first met with Oxenstierna and Horn, the troops from Trier arrived. They set up camp below Marienberg, and the same afternoon the two young officers Horn had put in charge rode up the hill to report to von Lans. They were shown to the officers' drawing room, where von Lans was working at a desk in a corner. Second Lieutenant Peder Falkenberg and Second Lieutenant Cassius von Birger, their hats off, bowed to von Lans who smiled when he recognized the two officers. They had been his standard-bearers at Breitenfeld, each leading a cavalry platoon in battle. He said, "Gentlemen, it is good to see you again. How was your trip?"

Falkenberg answered, "Captain, it is nice to see you too, Sir. The trip was uneventful, and we came as quickly as we could. We are bringing thirty-six men and half a dozen packhorses, and the men have set up camp on the bank of the river. Our orders from General Horn were to bring all our gear as well as weapons, and not to leave anything behind."

Von Lans nodded and looked around the room, where other officers where talking, reading, and playing cards. "It is a nice afternoon, why don't we take a walk around Marienberg. There are several overlooks where we can sit and talk. I'll get the steward to bring us basket with a bottle of Würzburger wine, water, and some bread and cheese." He called the steward over and made his request, and then led the way out into the courtyard and through the gate. They walked along the fosse on a path that wound around the fortress. The sun was low in the west and as they came around the corner on the sunny side of Marienberg, they could see how their long shadows crept toward the fortress wall.

While they walked, von Lans described the mission to the two men. They walked all around the fortress and came back to the drawbridge; there was a table with couple of benches facing the river. The steward had set the table for them and left the basket with wine and food. They sat down and served themselves; below them the Main flowed slowly under the stone bridge and the afternoon sun lit up the roofs of the old Roman city and the hills behind the city walls. At the military camps evening fires were being lit, and the smoke rose straight up in the still air. When von Lans was finished with his description, he cut a piece of cheese, put in on a slice of bread, ate it slowly, and finally said, "I want each of you to command a Flaxen Guard platoon." He stretched his legs out, leaned back, put his boots up on the bench, held out his glass to von Birger for more wine, and continued, "This is not a battle mission, even though we must be fully prepared for fights. Our mission is to bring in the war tribute with a minimum of conflicts; we'll use force when necessary, but only then and to make a point. We'll go around areas where we may encounter the Papists, rather than fight them. This means we will become experts at finding our way. We'll use trusted local guides and scouting missions to see what's ahead."

He went on, "We'll need to have transport wagons for some of the goods as well as our own gear. That will slow us down and make it harder to find clandestine and safe routes, but there is no choice. When we can, we'll set up camp with other Protestant units, but there will still be guard duty for the men."

Falkenberg asked, "Captain, right now the men are tired and could do with a bit of rest. Is there anything you want us to do before we leave?"

"You will need to find two wagons, foursomes I think, but I'll discuss this with Commander Martius. I'll come down and see the men tomorrow, and we can go through what we need. For now, give your men some time to rest during the next couple of days, as we have a long ride ahead of us."

Darkness was approaching, and Falkenberg and von Birger needed to get back to camp before it got too dark. The three men walked back into the courtyard, and the younger men got their horses and mounted them. They saluted von Lans, turned their horses around and rode out through the gate heading down the hill.

Four weeks later, the Würzburg troops arrived at Camp Martinshof where they delivered the money chests to Kapitän von Lutz. Their first mission accomplished, Von Lans quickly rounded up Storm and the new recruits and in mid-October, 1632, the Flaxen Guards set out at dawn from Camp Martinshof. Colonel von Lans and Captain Storm led the troops assisted by two Pomeranian guides, the two officers' orderlies right behind them. Then came Lieutenants Falkenberg and von Birger, followed by the cavalry and grooms leading the spare horses. Sergeants Ben Fogel and Rolf Byske from Stockholm had the tail positions. In the middle of the cavalry they had three covered wagons, one with the war booty from Würzburg, the others lightly loaded with their own gear and supplies. Each wagon was drawn by a team of four horses. The driver controlled the horses, not from a seat on the wagon, but from his saddle on one of the rear horses; which one he used depended on the driver's habits. Right-handed drivers liked to ride on the left side and vice versa; that way the driver had his best hand toward the other three horses, which made it easier to hold the reins of the team with one hand.

Their first destination, Wolgast, was about thirty miles from Camp Martinshof on the eastern coast of Pomerania. Wolgast itself was protected from the sea by the Usedom island where Gustavus Adolphus had first landed at Peenemünde two years ago. Wolgast was securely in the hands of the Swedes. Enemy ships couldn't get near its harbor, and it was a good port for the Swedish supply lines. The Flaxen Guard arrived late and settled in for the night at the military camp outside the city.

They woke up in the middle of a grey cloud; during the night a Baltic fog had drifted in over the coastal area. The thick fog blanketed all of Wolgast, and it was very quiet. After tending to their horses and having their breakfast, von Lans called them to assembly. He stood in front of the troops, and said, "Today we will ride to the harbor outside Wolgast where HMS Snabben is waiting at the roadstead. We'll deliver the goods from Würzburg and then collect chests containing some very important goods that we will transport from here to a destination I will reveal when we leave Wolgast. From now on, I want every man to be on high alert all the time. These chests are our responsibility, and every man must have his weapons loaded and ready at all times."

He ordered them into their saddles, the wagons fell in line and the train of men, horses, and wagons moved out. They soon arrived at the small harbor, where a tender from HMS Snabben was tied alongside the wharf with navy guards posted all around. The wagons pulled up to the dock, and Captain Storm ordered von Birger and his platoon to stay in the saddle and stand guard. Von Birger posted the men in two half circles around the wagons to guard the loading. Falkenberg's platoon dismounted, some tended the horses, the coachmen held their four-somes, and the rest of the men were assigned to loading duties. Von Lans went aboard the Snabben tender which took him out to the ship, where he presented his orders from the Chancellor to the ship's commander, Commodore Helmerin. About an hour later the loading could start.

The forty thousand rixdollars that the Flaxen Guard was to bring to the King's paymaster were packed in twenty chests and it took several runs with the Snabben tender. Each chest weighed close to two hundred pounds, and it took four men to carry it and lift it onto a wagon. The wagons had special stowage space, big enough to hold the chests, under a false floor. When all the chests had been loaded, they secured their loads with straps and put back the false floor. On top they loaded their own supply of weapons, ammunition, blankets, clothes, food and tents and then closed the covers; they were ready to go. Von Lans turned to Storm and said, "I want one platoon up front and the other following the wagons. I'll take the lead and you cover the rear for now." The captain ordered Falkenberg and von Birger to position their platoons; they all got back in their saddles and took their places. In front of each wagon the driver sat on his horse, a second driver rode behind with the spare horses. When the men and wagons were all in place, Von Lans turned and saluted Snabben's commander, who had come along for the final run of the tender, and said, "Goodbye Commodore!"

Helmerin returned the salute and replied, "Godspeed Colonel, I hope your journey will be safe."

Von Lans lifted his hand and pointed forward. He nudged his horse and the Flaxen Guard started their two-hundred-fifty-mile march from

Wolgast back the way they came, through the duchies of Pomerania, Brandenburg and Saxony to the city of Erfurt.

8. Wasteland

Ben was riding next to his platoon leader, Lieutenant Falkenberg; they had been on the road for seven days. The flat Pomeranian landscape around them was bleak and marked by war, many burned-down houses, overgrown abandoned fields, pockmarks of water-filled holes from explosions and cannon fire, long-dead animals picked to the bones, dead trees, half trees where the tops had been blown off, burned trees, trees with hanging ropes still dangling from the bottom branches, and here and there graves, some recently made, many unmarked, some with hastily made crosses. But now and then, by some miracle, a tree had survived the human battles, a green beacon in a field of destruction.

They were following an old trading road, but there was little traffic. The armies had left, the ravaged earth could no longer feed the farmers and there was no one left to plunder. They made slow progress, the speed determined by the wagons. The Colonel never moved before scouts came back and reported what was ahead. When he deemed the road safe, he ordered the wagons onward to the next rendezvous with the scouts. Ben had been on several scouting missions, and he enjoyed the break from the monotonous riding. It was a challenge to venture into the unknown and to come back on time, so that the wagons were not held up unnecessarily.

From the front they heard the call, "Send out a new scouting party!" Falkenberg turned to Ben and said, "I believe it is our turn, take Korp and Nilsson! It is two miles to the next rendezvous; Byske's patrol should be on their way back from there. Continue about another two miles and then come back and report." Ben signaled his old tent mates from Gothenburg to follow him, and they urged their horses into a slow canter, saluting the Colonel when they passed him at the head of the troops.

Ben had found that he loved to ride, and since they spent many long hours every day in the saddle, liking it was helpful. Sure, there were bad days when his body ached everywhere, when it was raining all day and the road turned into a strip of mud, or when he got a particularly ornery horse, but generally he felt comfortable in the saddle. This morning the road was hard, not too many ruts and holes, and they could keep up the slow canter. There were a few travelers walking along the road and it seemed very peaceful. After mile or so they saw the dust of approaching riders; it was Byske and his men. They stopped and Byske said, "The road is clear for about another mile; I left a marker there. But from the hill where we turned, we could see something going on further down the road. There were several people gathered in the middle of the road. I'll report back, but you'd better check it out. Leave my marker there if the coast is clear."

Byske and his men disappeared behind them, and Ben's patrol moved on. The land appeared flat from a distance, but up close it undulated with rises and dips among which the old road slithered back and forth, up and down across the wasted landscape like a flattened snake. They picked up Byske's marker at the top of a hillock; ahead of them they could see about a half a mile down the road. There was some movement on the road and Ben thought, "It must be the gathering that Byske mentioned." He slowed his horse to a walk and said, "Let's be careful, here the land is open, but right behind the people there is a woods. That's a perfect place for an ambush."

They each put their reins in one hand, the other ready to draw the sword, and moved carefully up the road toward the woods. As they got closer they saw that the gathering was only an old woman and two children. They were prying something out of an overturned wagon and then they disappeared behind it. Ben turned to Korp and Nilsson and said, "Stay back and keep a watch on the woods, I'll see what they're doing." He rode up to the overturned wagon and looked over the edge.

An old wrinkled face with a toothless mouth stared up at him; her dirty, tattered clothes hung like wilted spider webs over her thin body, a few strands of white hair stuck out from under her head cover, which was made of some kind of fur and decorated with black crow's feathers that hung down the sides of her head like limp wings. Two boys of about nine or ten with eyes sunken by hunger into black holes hid behind her. On the ground lay the dead horse that had been pulling their wagon until its heart caved in of exhaustion and starvation. The woman had a knife in her hand and she was trying to cut pieces of meat off the horse's shrunken body. A mangy three-legged dog was pulling at the entrails through a hole in the horse's stomach.

The woman took a look at Ben, muttered something incomprehensible and went back to her hacking. The boys just stared at Ben; the dog didn't take any notice of him. Looking at them, Ben asked, "What happened?" The woman ignored him, she just kept on cutting the horse and muttering to herself. Ben looked at the boys, but they hid their faces behind the old woman. He rode around the wagon looking for clues, when out of the corner of his eyes he saw some movement between the road and the woods. He quickly turned the horse around and rode back to the other two. "Did you see that?" he said.

"Yes!" Korp answered. "Somebody is out there."

"Let's go look!" Ben said, and the three of them spread out and rode quickly toward the woods. When they came closer, Nilsson spied somebody trying to get ahead of them into the cover of the trees. "There!" he shouted and pointed, and all three converged on the runner, who was not very fast and had no chance of outrunning the horses. The two men on the flanks cut in between the woods and the runner, and soon the three of them surrounded their prey. They stared down at a girl, she looked to be about thirteen, but she was so emaciated and her face so pale and drawn that it was impossible to tell her real age. She was breathing hard and trembling with fear at the sight of the three soldiers, with their swords drawn, sitting high on snorting horses trampling back and forth, closing her in.

Ben looked around, but he couldn't see any more people. He looked at the girl and said, "Don't be afraid, we won't hurt you." She kept her eyes down, but managed a little nod. Ben continued, "We saw the old lady and the two boys with the dead horse. Were you with them?" She nodded again without looking up.

"Are there any more of you?" Ben asked. She shook her head, so he went on, "Is that your horse and wagon?" Another nod.

He raised his voice, "Look at me, who drove the horse if there are only the four of you?" Her head rose slightly, and she cast a quick glance at him and whispered something.

"What?"

Her voice a little louder, "I d-d-did, ….. Sir."

"What happened?"

By now she had calmed down a bit and she looked up, although not straight at him, and replied, "We lived in Magdeburg and our house was burned by Catholic soldiers." Now the words gushed out of her mouth like a flood. "All the men were killed, we hid outside in the country, but there was nothing to eat, we've been scrounging for food everywhere, the horse was old, he just laid down and died on the road, we have a little wheelbarrow for the horse meat; my grandmother is going loony, she talks to herself and she takes the food from the boys, we're hungry all the time, we eat grass and leaves...."

Ben tried to interrupt her, "Wait, wait!" She clamped her mouth shut and lowered her head again.

"Have you seen anybody else here?" Ben asked. She shook her head vigorously.

"All right!" he said, "Come back to the wagon with us, take what you can and then go into the woods and hide far away from the road. You can't be here when our troops are coming through. We need to clear the road, come quickly." He turned to Korp and Nilsson and said, "Check out the road through the woods and look for tracks leading into the woods, but be careful."

Ben rode back to the wagon, the girl following him. She got the boys to help her load the wheelbarrow with a few bundles from the wagon and a little of the stringy horse meat. She tried to get her grandmother to get up, but the old woman wouldn't budge from the horse; she was trying to chew a bit of raw meat with her toothless gums. Ben looked at them, and took out a loaf of bread from his saddle bag, gave it to the girl and said, "Use this as bait!" She broke off a piece, took one bite, gave some to the boys, put the rest in a bag, then she showed the bread to the old woman and said, "Oma, come with us, I have some bread for you." The old woman's eyes lit up with a sly shine, she muttered something, then slowly got up and tottered after the girl and the wheelbarrow pushed by the two boys. Ben called to the girl, "Don't forget to hide!" The four wretches with their meager pack disappeared toward the woods. Ben knew they were only trying to survive a religious power struggle of which they had little part, a struggle that only brought them suffering and death, a struggle they didn't want, a struggle where the best thing they could do was to try to avoid any army that would only ravage what little they had left.

Korp and Nilsson came back and reported that they had been to where the woods ended and beyond. "After the woods the road continues in more open land," Korp reported, "We haven't seen any tracks or signs of anybody in the woods."

Ben replied, "Fine, now let's get the wagon and the horse off the road before the rest of the Flaxen Guard arrives." They unhitched the dead horse from the wagon, righted it, and hitched the wagon to one of their own horses instead; they moved the wagon up to the edge of the road and well in among the trees. Ben thought to himself, "Maybe the wretches can use the wagon for shelter." They tied a rope around the dead horse, and connected it to a second rope wrapped around the saddle horns of Korp's and Nilsson's horses. The two riders urged their horses off the road and into the terrain, pulling the dead horse away from the road.

With the road cleared, Ben put down Byske's marker and they continued. They made a few detours into the woods, but didn't find anything unusual. Once out of the woods they went back to a canter and sped down the road ahead. Back on the other side of the woods, the rumble of the approaching Flaxen Guards could be heard. Byske had reported to the Colonel, who ordered a tightening of the formation and cautioned everybody to be extra alert. A scout came back with Byske's marker; the Colonel called up Falkenberg and von Birger and said, "The patrol ahead haven't found anything suspicious, but just to be sure, let's speed things up a bit until we're through the woods."

The train of riders and wagons picked up speed and the dust rose as it rumbled past the dead horse. The three-legged dog was back pulling at the entrails from the horse's stomach. On top of the carcass sat four big black crows; they looked for a moment at the passing riders, but soon lost interest and went back to picking at the horse. The eyes were gone, and they were working on the lips and nose. More carrion eaters would join them later, and in a couple of weeks, only the skeleton would be left.

9. Werben

The Flaxen Guard continued southwest toward Werben, a Swedish stronghold on the river Elbe. Von Lans was a hard taskmaster who wanted the guard to keep a low profile but move swiftly. He was very aware that the fortunes of war could easily change, and scouts were ordered to pick up any news from travelers and villagers. The best sources were the Swedish couriers and friendly troops, but sometimes they would not see any allies for days. Rumors were rampant and contradictory, and it took a long time for news to travel by horseback or foot. The fog of war spread far from the battlefields, and they could never be sure that what they heard was really true.

And yet they had to move on. Scouts reconnoitered ahead and came back to report, and the troops and wagons kept on moving. Von Lans and Captain Storm took turns at the head of the caravan, the other covering the rear. The wagons set the pace, a slow but steady one. The fall weather was still warm, but the travel days were long and the breaks always seemed too short to allow them a chance to really rest. First the horses had to be attended to and guards posted, and not until then could the men stretch out on the ground and eat their meager rations. Only at night did they get a warm meal, a soup made from dried vegetables with slices of pork. The experienced soldier always carried his own stash of bread and whatever else he could buy, commandeer, or steal along the way. Von Lans had ruled out carrying any alcohol on the wagons, but many soldiers carried their own little flasks of aquavit to relieve the monotony of the evenings.

As they got closer to Werben, the flotsam and jetsam from the war washing up on the road increased. They passed refugees with no homes to go back to, invalid soldiers trying to make it home, beggars displaying their broken limbs, lethargic children, many of whom had scars from wounds and diseases, and women selling the only thing they had left, their own bodies, for a pittance. Occasionally they saw somebody who had succumbed to disease and starvation, the body slumped over at the side of the road, the remains quickly being picked over for anything worth taking. They heard the bells of the charnel wagons that would pick up unclaimed corpses and take them to nearby mass graves.

They reached the eastern shore of the Elbe River across from Werben on the other side. The Swedes had set up a large camp on the plains on the western shore between the walls of the town and the river. The army had taken control of nearby ferries as well as set up their own between the eastern shore of the Elbe and the camp. There were long lines at the crossings, but von Lans's letter from Oxenstierna secured them passages on the next ferries.

Ben was standing at the railing of the ferry. The river was swift and to hold the ferry from drifting down the river, a long line had been tied from the ferry to anchor poles upstream, allowing the ferry to swing back and forth across the river like a pendulum. Ben thought of home; in the corner of the Molen his mother had an old clock. He could see her going to the clock every morning, adjusting the hands and restarting the pendulum.

It was an afternoon at the end of October when they finally reached the Werben camp; they had been moving for many days, only stopping at night. The men and the horses were weary, everybody needed rest, and they also needed to restore their diminishing supply of provisions.

Von Lans presented his credentials from Chancellor Oxenstierna to the camp commander, Major Ian McCully from Edinburgh, whose Scottish mercenary troupes served Gustavus Adolphus in Werben. The major offered his help and said that the next morning they could replenish their supplies from the camp stores. "Stay as long as you need," he said hospitably.

Von Lans replied, "Thank you, we'll need to move on, but tomorrow we'll stay here."

"Fine, and please come to dinner with me tomorrow night. Bring any of your officers that are free."

The next evening von Lans put Falkenberg and von Birger in charge of the guard while he and Storm went to Major McCully's dining tent. There they were introduced to his wife, Sarah, a tall young woman with a blond head of hair that spoke of Nordic ancestry. McCully introduced her to the Swedes and said, "My wife has been staying with me for a while. It is a long way to travel from Edinburgh, but we enjoy our short times together. Right now Werben is quiet, but I get reports of outbreaks of plague south of here, so Mrs. McCully will return to Scotland presently."

Von Lans bowed to Mrs. McCully and said, "How delightful to meet a lady! Perhaps we can all forget the business of war for a few hours." He continued, "Madam, you remind me of the fair women at home. Did you husband fetch you from across the North Sea?"

Mrs. McCully laughed, "Thank you Colonel, but I think that I found him. My father was in the army, and Ian was in his regiment. And I assure you that I am Scottish from way back, although there is probably some Viking blood in my ancestry."

They sat down to dinner, and for a few hours they could almost forgot the war; they talked about their lives before the army claimed them, their homes, family, and friends. Toasts were exchanged, and they drank to their respective kings. They told jokes, the Scots about the English and the Swedes about the Danes. Then, toward the end of the meal, Mrs. McCully confided that her husband had a nice singing voice.

They sang – McCully began with a song about the highlands and the lochs of Scotland. Then his wife joined him in a lamenting ballad about a maiden whose true love died at sea and when she found out, she went to the shore and walked out into the water to join him in death. When they were finished there were tears in Storm's eyes and he said, "I know that one, but in our song he is lost in the forest on a dark winter night, and she drowns in an icy river." He proceeded to sing, and his strong baritone rang out with the singsong of Swedish born in Finland. When his last note faded away, they all sat quiet for a minute, trying to hold on to the magic of the music.

Dinner over, Mrs. McCully bid them goodnight and left the men to talk. The camp commander had some news about the Catholic troop movements. The Habsburg General Pappenheim was moving toward Halle, south of Magdeburg, and the Flaxen Guard would be wise to take a route around both cities. "I'll ask one of my officers who has just come from Erfurt to advise you and your scouts on the best route to take," Major McCully said.

They broke camp the next morning and set their course south. The land began to rise as they came closer to the Harz Mountains. The weather was changing, clouds were forming and the temperature dropping. Soon it would be November. Erfurt was about a hundred miles away by the shortest route, but to avoid any confrontation with Pappenheim's troops, von Lans decided to stay west of the Elbe, move south toward Magdeburg, and then go west of Halle to Eisleben and directly to Erfurt. It was a slower but safer route.

Magdeburg was still in ruins from the Catholic army's massacre a year ago. The Flaxen Guard passed west of the burnt-out city – the terror of the Black Death was strong. Gustavus Adolphus was also blamed for not having defended Magdeburg against Tilly's army, and von Lans didn't want any confrontations with the homeless squatters around what was left of the city.

They came to Eisleben and camped on a hillside overlooking the town. As the day turned into dusk, the hillocks of copper mine tailings formed a ragged contour against the sky. The wind had died down, and soon they could see fires and torches in the valley around Eisleben. Over to the west they could see more of the Hartz Mountains and tomorrow they would follow the foothills south toward Erfurt. Lieutenant Falkenberg was in charge of guard duty and had ordered Ben to post men around the camp. Ben had just finished a check on the guards, and he was sitting at the campfire with the other soldiers when a horse and rider approached. Nilsson and Svensson stood guard at the approach road, and Nilsson aimed his gun at the rider and called out, "Halt! Who goes there?"

The figure, wearing a long black cloak and the feathered hat of a Swedish officer, brought the horse to a stop and answered, "I'm Pastor Numinus of the Swedish Army. May I join you?"

Ben, who had heard the exchange, came running and said to the rider, "Wait there!" He said to the guards, "Nilsson, get the Lieutenant! I'll hold your weapon."

He took over Nilsson's rifle pointing at the visitor, and Nilsson ran off to get Falkenberg. Ben said, "Pastor Numinus, would you please take off your hat so I can see your face."

The rider did as he was asked and Ben recognized the ruddy, round face and tobacco-stained teeth from the sermon at Camp Martinshof. When Falkenberg arrived, he told him so, but Falkenberg, who hadn't met the Pastor, asked him to dismount and surrender his weapons before he would let him into the camp.

Numinus got off his horse, turned over his sword and a pistol to Falkenberg, and walked into the camp, where he tied up his horse with the others. He took his saddlebag, pulled the collar of his cloak tight, and walked over to join the soldiers at the campfire saying, "It's a cold evening, I just need to warm up a bit and get something to eat before I get back into Eisleben." He opened the saddlebag and took out some bread, a piece of ham, and a flask of wine, then sat down close to the fire. He wrapped his cloak around him, brought out his knife and cut a piece of ham, put it on a slice of bread and took a bite. He washed down the food with a swig from the flask.

When Ben came off duty, he went to the fire to heat up some soup. The Pastor was still there, and Ben heard him say, "I came to Eisleben because this is where Martin Luther was born. Every Protestant should make a pilgrimage to Eisleben."

He looked at the young men around the fire and continued, "Do you boys know about Martin Luther?"

It was very quiet, but then Korp guessed, "He was a Protestant general."

"Not quite, does anyone else know?"

"He was a carpenter who made doors," said Fink hesitantly.

Byske laughed and broke in, "No, no, he was a monk!"

"Yes, but he was more than that – he is the reason we are all fighting the Catholics. Martin Luther was an Augustine monk in Erfurt. He became a priest in Wittenberg but broke with the Catholic faith."

Pastor Numinus took another swig of wine, belched, and continued, "He thought the Catholic Church had become a seller of indulgences – charging for God's forgiveness – and had lost the meaning of the true Gospel. And here we are, over a hundred years after Luther nailed his Ninety-five Theses about the Pope, penance and the indulgence extortions to the door of his Wittenberg church; the two sides are still fighting. It's been a long war and it isn't over yet."

With that the Pastor sank to the ground, the flask dropped out of his hand, and he soon began to snore. Ben picked up his cloak and covered him. Soon he turned in himself. If the weather held, they were only a couple of days from Erfurt.

10.   Chance Encounter

The next morning the clouds were hanging over the hills to the west, and as they got under way a light drizzle began. Scouts were sent out and came back with reports that the road ahead seemed clear. They didn't expect any enemy troops to be this far west, and von Lans thought they could relax a little. The day went by without any incidents, they camped for the night and the following morning they slogged on again.

About midday Ben was out front with Korp and Nilsson when they saw a group of riders coming from the south. Nilsson stayed back, prepared to ride back with a warning while Ben and Korp rode ahead. The soldiers came closer and Ben saw that they were wearing Swedish uniforms. About ten men, several of them high officers, came first, and a Colonel approached the two Flaxen Guards calling out, "Who are you?"

"Sir, I'm Sergeant Fogel, this is Soldier Korp, and we are with a Swedish company commanded by Colonel von Lans," Ben replied.

The Colonel turned back and said something to a man in the middle of the group. Ben couldn't quite see him, but as the man came forward, he saw that he was wearing a general's uniform; he was short and rotund, but a good rider, sitting well on a sleek brown horse. Korp whispered to Ben, "It's the King, it's the King!"

The man in the general's uniform stopped by Ben, took a water bottle that was handed to him, and drank out of it. His gaze directly on Ben, he said, "Sergeant, you must be part of the Flaxen Guard!"

Ben had only seen pictures of the King and didn't know what to say at first. Von Lans had given clear instructions not to reveal their identity. Gustavus Adolphus saw his hesitation, smiled and said, "Don't worry Sergeant, you needn't conceal the identity of your unit – I'm not going to attack my own Guards. But we would like to meet your commander, so would you please ride back with us?"

Ben, straightening himself in his saddle, finally found his tongue, "Yes, Your Highness, but may I send my man to announce to Colonel von Lans that you are coming? He may otherwise be suspicious seeing us coming back with a group of armed men."

"Very well, but let one of my officers go with him." The King turned to his officers and asked, "Does anyone here know von Lans? Colonel Friedrich, weren't you with Horn at Breitenfeld?"

"Yes Sir, I was, and I know von Lans."

"Then off you go!"

Ben took Colonel Friedrich over to Nilsson, who had been watching at a distance for signs of any possible danger. The Colonel went ahead with Nilsson, while Ben and Korp escorted the King and his contingency back toward the Flaxen Guards.

Gustavus Adolphus seemed in an excellent mood, and he asked Ben about his family. Ben told the story of his Swedish sailor father, his Dutch mother, and the Molen. The King listened and said, "My wife is German and I know that it can be hard for a woman to marry a foreigner and have to learn a new language and new customs. At least your mother and father loved each other, even if they only had a short time together – and look at you – you have the benefit of knowing several languages. We need more people like you."

They saw the Flaxen Guards stopped at the side of the road just ahead of them. The King turned to Ben and said, "Thank you, Sergeant, and Godspeed." Ben took off his hat, replying, "May God bless Your Majesty," and urged his horse to the side with Korp to let Gustavus Adolphus lead the way to the meeting with the Flaxen Guards.

Von Lans had ordered a short break; it was time for a watch change, putting new soldiers on active duty and letting the others relax. The horses also needed water and rest; the draft horses were switched for fresh ones. They had stopped off the road on a rise where they could see ahead. Storm and von Lans were standing off to the side, their horses being attended to by their grooms. Soldiers were busy unhitching the draft horses, others were waiting with the relief horses; yet others were sitting on the grass, their horses' heads in buckets of water or stretching to nibble the yellow grass.

Storm looked down the road ahead, and saw two figures on horse-back coming toward them. They were too far away to be seen clearly, but he thought he recognized Soldier Nilsson, but not the second rider, although his uniform looked familiar. He turned to von Lans and said, "There is someone coming back with Nilsson; I can't see Fogel and Korp."

Von Lans got out his spyglass and looked at the riders. He said, "I know that man, he is a Swedish officer, and last time I saw him was at Breitenfeld. What is he doing here?" He called out, "Groomsman, bring me my horse! Falkenberg, get two men and come with me! Storm, you take over here. Make sure the guards are where they should be and on the alert, the rest of you finish what you're doing and look sharp!"

The quiet time was over, the orders flew, and the horses snorted when the men saddled them up. The posted guards straightened up, the jackets, coats, and hats that had been taken off were quickly pulled back on, and weapons were held close at hand. The Flaxen Guard was still changing the watch, but the sense of ease was gone and there was a tension in the air. After all, underneath the loads of army supplies they were carrying twenty chests of rixdollars, through a countryside where a person could get killed for refusing to hand over his torn overcoat.

Von Lans and his men approached the two riders, their horses at a slow canter. The two men halted and waited for the group to come closer. Colonel Friedrich held up a hand in a greeting, smiled, and said, "Rupert, it's been a long time!"

"Heinz, it's been almost a year. I didn't expect to see you here." He returned the greeting and continued, "I thought you worked for Horn, is he here?"

"Yes, I did work for the Field Marshal. No, he's not here. I'm now with another of our officers."

Von Lans looked at Nilsson, then turned back to the Colonel, "You must have met our men, but where are the others?"

"Don't worry, they're on their way back to you. Our group met them up the road and my commander would like to meet you. He sent me ahead with Nilsson to make an introduction."

Von Lans beckoned to Friedrich to come away from the men, and then he said quietly, "Heinz, my mission is a bit delicate; I'm not sure I can let a group of armed men, even if they are Swedish, come too close. Who is your commander?"

Friedrich, who had enjoyed keeping von Lans on tenterhooks, smiled and replied, "Relax, he's your commander as well, in fact he's our Commander-in-Chief."

Von Lans's face was blank, "Yes?" Then it dawned on him, "The King is here?"

"He is on his way from Erfurt to Leipzig to join his army. We met your men and the King decided he wanted to see the Flaxen Guards. It will be a brief visit, we don't have much time to spare."

"Then let's go back and make ourselves ready!"

Von Lans turned his horse around, told the others to follow, and they cantered back to the Guards. Storm, in the meantime had made sure the draft horses had been changed, and the men and their horses were ready.

Von Lans and the others arrived in a cloud of dust; they came to a quick halt and he immediately ordered, "Everybody on their horses and at their posts, we're having an important visitor!"

They had just enough time to collect their gear and mount their horses before Gustavus Adolphus and his men rode up to them. Nilsson had told a few who the visitor was, but most men were in the dark. Von Lans, his horse still breathing hard with puffs of steam coming from its nostrils and mist rising from around the rider, sat at the head of the Guard. He took off his hat with a sweeping gesture and greeted the King, "Welcome, Your Highness, I'm Colonel Rupert von Lans, and we are your Highness's Flaxen Guards."

Gustavus Adolphus acknowledged the greeting and replied, "Thank you, Colonel, we're very happy to see you. The Chancellor has told me he expects great things from you." He looked over the men, the horses, the wagons, turned to the troops, and said, "Soldiers, you're doing a very important job for our country, and I am sure the job is being done well. This is a chance meeting, and we can't stay, but our thoughts are with you.

He turned to von Lans, "Colonel, can you ride with me for a little while? Bring your escort for the return, but it won't be long."

The King turned his horses and he and his entourage started north toward Leipzig. Von Lans rode next to the King who stopped after a while, and took out a sealed letter from his saddlebag. On the outside he had written "Maria Eleonora."

"Colonel, I would like you to take this personally to the Queen. She is in Erfurt, where I left her a few days ago."

"I will do that, Sir. Would you like me to give her any message?"

"Just tell her that my heart belongs to her."

The royal visit was over so fast; many men still had no idea who the man on the brown horse was, and Svensson asked von Birger, "Lieutenant, who was that?"

"That was the Midnight Lion, Gustavus Adolphus, King of Sweden."

"Really, that was the King? What is he doing here?"

"I don't know, but it must have something to do with Pappenheim moving his army toward Halle."

The Guards were marching again, the November sky covered with low clouds, and ground fog hanging in the lower valleys. In the afternoon it started to rain and the already rutted road turned into a river of mud. The horses struggled with the wagons, heaving through mud holes and over rocks. One wagon went too far to the side and the wheels sank into a ditch. They hitched up more horses to pull it out, men put their backs into pushing the spokes of the wheels, and with a squelching sound the mud let go. The rain increased and that night they spent huddled miserably in their tents trying to dry their clothes.

11.   Erfurt

Two days later the Flaxen guard approached Erfurt, a city long held by the Protestant alliance. They came over a hill and ahead of them they could see the city inside its protective walls. The river Gera ran along the western side and over the river three hills rose; on the top of the highest one they saw scaffoldings and the partly finished construction of a large fortress. They entered the city and went straight to Oxenstierna's paymaster, Mr. Cyril Heidelmann, whose offices were inside the thick walls of an old monastery. Guards were posted at the gate; when they saw the armed men and their wagons approach the monastery, a flurry of activities started. Extra guards came running out the gate, and a heavy iron grate closed behind them. Von Lans presented his credentials to the Sergeant at Arms, and a few minutes later the gates opened again and they could bring their wagons into the courtyard, where Heidelmann met them. At the corner of the yard there was a stone house that looked like a large bunker with no windows. Heidelmann greeted von Lans, pointed at the stone house and said, "This is our treasury, please bring the chests over here."

While the men unloaded the chests of rixdollars and carried them into the treasury, Heidelmann and von Lans talked. Heidelmann swept his arm around and pointed at the buildings around the courtyard.

"This used to be a Catholic monastery – Augustinian monks settled here when they first came to Erfurt in the thirteenth century. It's also where Martin Luther first became a monk over a century ago."

Von Lans replied, "It doesn't look like a monastery."

"Well, it isn't anymore. After the Reformation the Catholics left, and it is now used by the city government. You have seen the building that's going up on the hill across the river. That will be our new Petersberg fortress, and I'm using this place until we can move in up there."

Von Lans looked at the wagons, where the load of chests was getting smaller.

"I'm glad these are safely in your hands. Do you have any messages with further orders for me?"

Heidelmann had recently seen Chancellor Oxenstierna and he said, "Your orders are still to go to Wilfenheim and Kaltdorf to collect their tributes, but after that you should report back here."

Von Lans replied, "We need a few days to replenish our supplies and to let the horses and men rest a little."

"Very well, today is the fifth of November, can you leave on the tenth?"

Von Lans nodded and said, "Yes, that will fine, but what about the plague? We've been warned there are several villages that have been struck."

"There are small outbreaks here and there; I'll give you the latest reports before you leave, but be careful. We don't want you to bring the Black Death to Erfurt. I'd rather you cancelled these missions if you have any indications of an outbreak."

They watched as the last few chests were being unloaded. Von Lans turned to Heidelmann and said, "I have another errand, I have to personally deliver a letter to the Queen from her husband. She doesn't know me and I need an introduction; could you help me?"

"Certainly! As a matter of fact, I need to see her this afternoon. I'll take you myself. Get yourself and your men organized, and meet me here at three."

"Thank you."

The last chest was safely in the treasury, and the Flaxen Guard mounted their horses to set up camp in the fields outside the city. Von Lans sent for Ben, who arrived still in his dusty clothes and boots covered by mud. Von Lans said, "Fogel, clean up your horse, brush the road dust off your uniform, and polish your boots! We're going to see a lady in Erfurt, and I may need you to interpret. Meet me outside the old monastery gate at three, but don't tell anyone where we're going."

He dismissed Ben, who went to find Korp and Nilsson and said, "Give me a hand grooming my horse; the Colonel wants me to go with him, and I have to look presentable. I'll need to wash and change clothes."

While the men took care of his horse, Ben washed. The water was ice-cold and he was shivering, so he quickly dried himself, put on his only clean shirt, and brushed off his only pair of breeches. He washed the mud off his boots and brought out a chunk of saddle soap to polish them. Finally he put his sword back on and went to mount his horse. He turned to the men and asked, "How do I look?"

Nilsson, unaware of Ben's mission, answered with an approving chuckle, "Like a gentleman on his way to a finer whorehouse!"

He was waiting when von Lans and Heidelmann escorted by one of his guards rode through the old monastery gate. Von Lans beckoned to Ben to fall in behind them, and explained to Heidelmann, "Sergeant Fogel here speaks several languages, and he also met the King on the way here."

Heidelmann nodded to Ben, "Sergeant!"

Heidelmann led the way through the narrow streets until they came to a wider street opening up into a square. He turned to von Lans and said, "This is the Anger, an old dyer's market and a center for rich Erfurt merchants – the lady lives here."

The commerce in the market was in full swing with vendors taking up two thirds of the square – the rest had been cordoned off by soldiers. When they approached the only entrance to the cordoned-off area, the guards at the gate saluted Heidelmann, and opened the turnpike to let them through. They stopped at number eleven, where two valets took their horses and their swords. Heidelmann led the way up the stairs to the front door with von Lans and Ben following closely behind. The front door opened and a servant greeted them in German, "Welcome, Mr. Heidelmann, you're expected." He took their coats and continued, "Her Highness is in the drawing room. Shall I announce you?"

"Thank you Mr. Von Pentz, but would you please first show Colonel von Lans and his Sergeant a place to wait. I would like to introduce the Colonel to the Queen. He has a message for her."

"Very well, Sir. Gentlemen, please come with me."

Mr. Adam Von Pentz, Chamberlain of the private household of Queen Maria Eleonora of Sweden, opened a door to a small sitting room and showed them in. Before he closed the door he said, "I'll ask the maid to light a fire and to bring you some fruit and something to drink."

There were chairs and a sofa in the sitting room, but the two men stood at the window of the sitting room looking out at the Anger; it was getting darker and torches were being lit and placed around the square and the stalls to fend away the dark. Von Lans said, "Fogel, I brought you along not just because of your language skills, but also because you met and spoke to the King. The Queen may want to ask you about that."

Just then the door was opened. Mr. Von Pentz held it, and Maria Eleonora walked into the room followed by Heidelmann. The Queen was the daughter of the Prince of Brandenburg, and she had married the King twelve years earlier after lengthy negotiations led by Oxenstierna. She was a small woman with a pale but shapely face and wavy light brown hair providing a wide frame for her eyes and high forehead. She wore a long dress that swept the floor, and she had a shawl draped over her shoulders and around her neck. Ben thought she was a beautiful woman, but there was an air of nervousness around her. When she spoke her voice had a high pitch and it almost trembled.

She nodded a greeting and addressed von Lans, "I understand you have a message for me."

"Yes, Your Highness, the King gave me this letter for you." He brought out the letter and handed it to her.

She took one glance at her name on the letter, and said, "I'll read this later, but first you must tell me about the meeting."

"Well, Sergeant Fogel was the first one to see the royal party. The Sergeant was on a scouting mission ahead of my troops, when the King arrived with his party."

The Queen turned to Ben, "Tell me everything about it."

Ben told her about the meeting, the King's questions about his own family and his answers. When he finished with the King's comments about the difficulties of marrying into another language and another culture, a look of melancholy came over her face. When he was finished, Maria Eleonora was quiet a moment, then she looked straight at Ben and said, "Sergeant, your mother and I may have a lot in common. Thank you for telling me all of this."

She turned to von Lans, "Colonel, please come with me into the drawing room, I'd like to read the letter and talk to you. Mr. Heidelmann, you may join us." She smiled a quick smile at Ben, then turned and led the way out.

Alone in the sitting room, Ben sat down in one of the chairs and let out a sigh. It had been a long journey, and now that the tension was gone, tiredness got the upper hand. He closed his eyes just for a moment, but they stayed closed and soon he was sound asleep. He dreamt that he was back at the Molen; the inn was empty and quiet, he was sitting by the window looking out at the harbor. He could hear the noise of people outside. Somebody came in through the back door and said something. It sounded like Alex, but he couldn't quite make it out. The voice spoke again, but he still couldn't hear.

He woke up halfway, still drowsy from the sleep. The voice spoke again, *"Mochst wos zum eissen?"* Startled, he opened his eyes; it wasn't Alex, but a stranger, a girl standing at the table where she had put a bowl of fruit and a pitcher of wine. Ben, still not really awake, replied, *"Bedankt, Alex."* She looked at him and switched into Dutch, "Mr. von Pentz sent me up to ask you if you were hungry." She had started a fire, and she went over to put another log on the grate, then turned and looked at Ben, "Who is Alex?"

Ben stood up and stretched, "Sorry, I wasn't sure where I was. I thought you were my sister." He looked around and asked, "Did I sleep for long? Are the others still here?"

"I've been here about half an hour trying to get this fire going. Yes, your Colonel is still with the Queen."

Ben went to the table and took an apple. He was hungry and he wolfed down the apple quickly. The girl was still fussing with the fire; the wood was damp and it wouldn't start properly. Ben went over, got the bellows hanging on the wall and started blowing on the kindling that was burning under the damp logs.

"What is your name?" he said.

"Emilia – Emilia Hout." She stood up, and held up her hands that had black soot on them. There was some soot on her sleeve, and when she wiped her brow with her arm the tip of her nose became black as well.

Irritated, she wailed, "Look at this, it always happens when I try to light this dratted fire."

Ben looked at her and couldn't help smiling. He saw now that she was about fifteen, a few years older than Alex. She had blond hair combed back and held in a severe knot, a white cap, and a long dress with a white apron. Ben thought she was pretty even with the sooty face; her green eyes were lively, even if under her furrowed brow, they now looked like they were made of steel.

The fire was looking better, and Ben said, "Emilia Hout, I think you need to wash your face. I'll watch the fire."

"Oh, it looks like it'll burn now."

She put a screen in front of the fire, and continued, "Come with me to the kitchen, we'll find something better than an apple for you." He looked hesitant and she added, "I'll tell Mr. von Pentz where you are, he just brought dinner for three into the drawing room. I think your Colonel is staying a while."

Emilia brought him downstairs to the kitchen; it was warmer there than upstairs, with a fire burning in a large cooking stove. Ben took off his hat and coat and sat down at a large battered oak table. The stove and the copper flue above it took up the better part of one wall. The outside wall had windows that looked into a small vegetable garden surrounded by a hedge. Under the windows there was a counter, and the wall between the windows and the counter was taken up by knives, choppers, spatulas, copper ladles, wooden spoons and other cooking implements.

Emilia asked the cook, who was cutting some meat at the counter, "Can you spare some of your good pea soup and some bread, Mrs. Hahn? Mr. von Pentz asked me to give our guest something to eat." She turned to Ben, "What is your name?"

"Sergeant Ben Fogel."

He nodded to the cook and added, "Good evening, Mrs. Hahn."

"Good evening Mr. Fogel, your soup's on its way."

Emilia disappeared to wash her face, and Mrs. Hahn served him a bowl of thick green pea soup, ladling up large pieces of the fat sausage it contained. She put a loaf of brown bread and a knife next to him. Ben cut a piece of bread, dipped it in the soup, put it in his mouth, savored the taste and said, "Oh, this is good!"

Mrs. Hahn smiled and replied, "Thank you, I hope so. The King likes this, he wants to serve it to the army, but I told him, "Where will you get all the peas?"

Emilia came back and sat down. Ben looked at her and once again he was reminded of his little sister. He told her about his family, and Emilia replied that, like him, she had also a Dutch mother, but a German father who served with Gustavus Adolphus. She didn't know where her father was, but she thought he was somewhere not too far away. Her mother had a stand in the Anger market, where Mr. von Pentz and Mrs. Hahn bought a lot of their food. Emilia had been helping her mother at the stand for many years, and when Mrs. Hahn needed some extra help in the kitchen, she had asked Emilia's mother if the girl could come in to help. With the Queen in residence, there was a lot of work to be done, and by now Emilia was part of the domestic help.

A bell rang, and Emilia went to answer Mr. von Pentz's call. She came back and told Ben that he was wanted. Colonel von Lans had asked that he should get the horses ready; the audience with the Queen was over and they were leaving. Ben rose, put on his coat and hat, thanked Mrs. Hahn for the meal, turned to Emilia and said, *"Tot ziens, meisje!"* He went out the back door and around the house to the stable where they had left their horses.

When he had left, Emilia said to Mrs. Hahn, "I'm not a little girl, I'm fifteen – and I'll see him again, I just know it!"

12.   The King is Dead

O n the fields northeast of the little town called Lützen two armies were getting ready to do battle. On the northwestern side of the Leipzig road, the Habsburg Field Marshal Albrecht von Wallenstein had assembled ten thousand foot soldiers and seven thousand cavalrymen. On his right flank, among the windmills on a hill, Wallenstein had placed his heavy artillery. Pappenheim was several hours away, but on his way to assist Wallenstein with another two thousand cavalrymen. On the southeastern side of the road Gustavus Adolphus was getting ready to advance with thirteen thousand foot soldiers and six thousand cavalrymen. The small town of Lützen was burning, the smoke mixed with the November fog, and the visibility was already poor. As the battle started and the smoke from the guns spread over the battlegrounds, it would get even worse.

It was the sixth of November, 1632; the battle went on all day, and at the end seven thousand men, about half from each side, were dead, and thousands more wounded. There wasn't a second day of battle; Wallenstein retreated during the night and the Swedes were too exhausted to pursue him. There was no clear winner, as both sides had suffered great losses and their commands were severely damaged. Field Marshal Gottfried Heinrich von Pappenheim was mortally wounded, and worst of all for the Swedes, the Midnight Lion, Gustavus Adolphus, lay dead on the battlefield.

In Erfurt the Flaxen Guard rested. After they had spent a day setting up camp and tending to housekeeping duties, Storm paid them their salaries and gave them two days of leave. After the long journey the soldiers were rather tired of each others' company and they spread out. Some went directly to Erfurt's many taverns to get drunk and to find a lady of their choice; at their meager salary that usually meant standing in line outside a small cubbyhole down by the river, waiting their turns, before being served five minutes of pretended rapture. Some went to church and prayed that they would get out of the war alive and some stayed around the camp to write letters to the people back home, those who couldn't write getting help from those who could.

The two days of leave passed quickly. Soon it was time get back to duty and get ready to depart. On November ninth they finished their preparations, and the next morning they were going to leave. It was getting dark, with a slight drizzle in the air when von Lans and Storm walked around the camp inspecting the preparations. When they had finished their round they were standing by the horses at the entrance to the camp and Storm said, "Well, it looks like we're ready to go. What time do you want to start?"

"Let's be ready to leave at first light."

Von Lans continued, "It is quiet here. Why don't you put our Sergeants in charge, find von Birger and Falkenberg, and bring them to my tent. I have a couple of bottles of wine that we need to finish before we leave."

Later the four Flaxen Guard officers were sitting in von Lans's tent. In the middle was a small wood stove that labored to keep the November cold out. His orderly had set the small camp table with bottles of wine, sausages, and bread. Storm raised his glass to propose a toast, "Here's to the successful mission completed!" They drank and von Lans added, "To the King, I hope he is victorious!"

"To the King!"

They heard the noise of someone approaching outside, and voice saying, "May I come in, Sir?" It was Ben and he was carrying an envelope that he handed to von Lans saying, "This came from Mr. Heidelmann, the messenger says it's urgent!"

"Thank you, Sergeant!"

He opened the envelope and read the message. It was short note scribbled in haste. He looked puzzled and read it out loud to the other officers.

"Come quickly to the treasury, something that may delay your departure has come up. Heidelmann."

"I have no idea what this is about," von Lans said, "but I'd better go see him. Falkenberg, you'd better come with me."

The two men had their horses saddled, and accompanied by two soldiers with torches they rode into Erfurt to the old monastery. They were shown into Heidelmann's quarters, where the royal paymaster met them. He looked distraught and strode back and forth while he spoke, "A courier bag just came through on its way to Chancellor Oxenstierna. It's already on its way from here with a new courier on a fresh horse, but the bag also contained a message for us." Heidelmann wanted to continue, but he choked and couldn't talk for a moment. The two men sensed that they shouldn't interrupt; they stood quietly while Heidelmann collected himself. After a while he continued, "There has been big battle near Lützen. We had almost twenty thousand men and the Catholics about the same. Many thousands have been killed in one day, but worst of all …." His voice broke again but they heard him say, "They say the King is dead."

Heidelmann sat down, got up, and sat down again. He looked up at von Lans and said, "The dispatch had been sent in such a hurry, there are no details. I can't be really sure that it's true until I know more, and I can't tell the Queen until I know for sure. Colonel, I need somebody I can trust, I need your help to find out what has happened." His elbows on the table, his face pale, he put his head in his hands and moaned, "This means the end of everything – what am I going to tell the Queen – such a disaster."

Von Lans sat down opposite him, took his wrists and gently pulled Heidelmann's hands away from his face. "This is terrible news if it's true," he said, "and of course, I'll help you. But we need to think clearly."

Heidelmann looked at him, "Yes, I know, but it's such a shock."

They sat silently; each man thinking about what this news meant to them. Heidelmann had worked as the King's paymaster for many years, and he had come to like the man behind the official façade. Falkenberg thought of the man they met briefly quite by chance just a little over a week ago. Von Lans thought about the conversations he had just had with the Queen about her husband.

The color was coming back to Heidelmann's face, and he composed himself. He said, "Colonel, can you go to Lützen and see for yourself? Send back reports whenever you can, but come back immediately when you're certain – then I can tell the Queen."

Von Lans replied, "I'll go to Lützen with a few men. Lieutenant Falkenberg here will go with me. He may return early with a first report. We'll leave at daylight."

They discussed the details for a while. Heidelmann was recovering from his despair and seemed happier when he could get on with the bureaucratic process of preparing written orders and letters of introduction for von Lans. They also had the rest of the Flaxen Guard to consider, but decided that the tribute mission would go ahead. Heidelmann didn't think it involved any difficulties and thought that Storm and von Birger should be able to handle the collection with a reduced contingent. They should be back by the time von Lans returned from Lützen.

When they were done, Heidelmann said, "I'll send a dispatch to the Chancellor. Now the whole burden of leadership will fall on his shoulders."

Von Lans and his men left the monastery and returned to their camp, where Von Lans sent for Storm to brief him, and Falkenberg went looking for Ben. He found him sitting at the campfire. "Fogel," Falkenberg said, "our plans have been changed. I'll need you and two of your best riders to go with the Colonel and me on a special mission tomorrow."

"I'd like to take Fink and Korp, they're both excellent riders."

"Very good! Get your best horses and bring a set of spare horses as well. Bring your weapons but only minimal gear, as we have a hundred-mile ride ahead of us. Be ready to leave at dawn."

13.   The Battlefield

The Erfurt dawn always comes late in November and the next morning it came even later because the already weak morning sunlight of the season was locked out by low clouds meeting the ground fog that had grown overnight like a fuzzy fungus. Dawn came reluctantly, but gradually the bubbles of light surrounding the torches and fires that had been lit for the night expanded into a grey mass of low, misty light. The five men, von Lans, Falkenberg, Fogel, Fink, and Korp, set out at first light, but it was slow going. They had a long ride ahead of them, and they couldn't run the horses too hard. The poor visibility made it even worse, and they had to slow them to a walk.

It didn't get much better as the day wore on, and by mid-afternoon they were not even halfway. After another couple of hours of riding, they stopped at a Swedish camp to bivouac for the night. The camp that normally held over a thousand soldiers and their followers was quiet. There were women and children waiting for husbands and fathers, and a small guard force to look after the camp and take care of the spare horses left behind when the main contingency went off to fight. The people in the camp didn't know much about what had happened. They had heard from the odd traveler that there had been a terrible battle, but had no news about the outcome.

Next morning Ben was awakened before dawn by the sound of wagon wheels creaking, horses snorting, and people talking, all of it accompanied by a hum of strange noises. He emerged from sleep to see a train of wagons entering the camp, and behind them an endless line of riders and foot soldiers. He stood up and walked toward the procession and the hum separated into sounds of moaning and crying. It was the wounded and dead returning from the battle; those who couldn't walk or ride were

76

sitting on the wagons next to stacks of dead bodies. Most horses had two riders, a cavalry man and a wounded soldier clinging to his back; some were pulling travois with wounded soldiers. There were foot soldiers walking, some unhurt but tired, some needed the help of others, and some hobbling by themselves with the help of makeshift crutches.

The pace was very slow and the cries of the wounded rang out as the wagons and the travois bumped over the ruts in the road. Ben couldn't see the end of the procession; they just kept on coming. The women and children were gathering along the side of the road looking for their kin. Now and then a woman would see her husband, a child would see its father and run toward the procession. A soldier with a bloody bandage around his head dropped wearily to the ground at the side of the road. Another with a bandage across his blinded eyes was led off by his weeping wife.

And there were more and more. The cries of the waiting kin blended with those of the wounded. A woman collapsed by the wagon next to her dead husband. Horses shivering from exhaustion were released into the paddocks, where some of them just laid down and refused to get up.

They were all awake now, looking at the stream of the tired and wounded men flowing relentlessly into the camp. Von Lans spotted a young officer riding along the procession. He walked over and hailed him.

"Captain, where are you coming from?"

The officer stopped and replied, "Directly from the battlefield at Lützen. I've been collecting what is left of our company and I'm bringing them back here."

"How many men have you lost?"

"Over a third died in the battle, and another third is in poor shape."

The young man had been wounded in his right arm and he was holding the reins with the left. His horse moved, startled by a wagon, and the captain winced. He continued, "But we beat the papists, they ran off during the night, and all of their heavy artillery is now ours."

"Captain, I've been asked to find out what happened to the King. Can you give me any news?"

"It's very confusing. I was at the left flank and the King was over on the right. I've heard that he was wounded and some say he is dead. The battle is over, but the battlefield is covered with dead and wounded. The healthy men are trying to move the wounded to the field hospitals and charnel wagons are picking up the dead. It'll be a long time before it's all done."

"Thank you, Captain, I'll have to go there to see for myself."

They saddled their horses, left the camp, and rode up along the muddy road and the murmuring stream of soldiers flowing back from the battlefield. As they got closer to Lützen the stream turned into a thick jam of men, horses, and wagons jostling for space. Fights broke out now and then when weariness made tempers flare. Along the side of the road a charnel wagon had broken down. The pale and sometimes mutilated feet of the dead stuck out from under a cover, and a group of men was trying to raise the wagon to free the broken wheel. Wounded soldiers who had run out of strength sat dazed by the road, seeing nothing but their own misery; some who had given up lay slumped on the ground.

Slowly they made headway and after a couple of hours they could see smoke rising up ahead. During the battle Lützen had been put to the torch, and fires were still smoldering. The villagers had been trying to save what they could. They didn't have much, and there were pathetic heaps of their scanty belongings next to the smoking ruins.

Von Lans led the way through the village and out toward the battlefield. On a hill near the village, they could see flags flying. Von Lans raised his arm to order a halt. He turned around, pointed up the hill and said, "See those flags up there?"

Ben looked up the hill; the slope had been torn down by attacking soldiers and the hillside had turned into muck. Bushes and trees had been ripped out of the ground by explosions, trampled by horses and pummeled by soldiers' feet. At the top of the dirty gray hill a cluster of flags and standards fluttered ¬— some were torn and others had holes in them. Ben recognized the Swedish flag, but he didn't know the others.

Von Lans continued, "Those are all Protestant banners; the big one next to the Swedish flag belongs to General Bernhard, Duke of Sachsen-Weimar, a loyal ally to the cause."

He looked around the countryside and said, "Let's go! There must be a command post up there, and we can get a better look over the battlefield."

They made their way slowly up the hillside, skirting the worst area of craters and fallen trees. Most of the dead soldiers had been removed, but there were many horse carcasses left on the ground. The sickly smell of death filled the air.

At the top of the hill was a row of wooden windmills and a miller's cottage. Several windmills had been hit by cannon fire; the largest one, at the end of the row, had one wing missing. With only three left, the mill looked like a great headless bird opening its wings to the sides. The bird had drooping feathers hanging from the wings; the big feathers were swaying back and forth in the light wind. They came closer and the feathers turned into men, their hands tied behind their backs and nooses around their necks.

"Catholic informants," said von Lans, "I imagine it's our side's revenge for losses in taking the hill."

In front of the windmills was a battery of cannons pointing down the hill. Protestant troops were busy hooking the big guns to horses that would reposition them to secure the hill against any attempt by the Catholics to retake it and the artillery. Other troops were posted around the top, but nobody stopped their approach. Von Lans halted and asked one of the soldiers, "Where is your commander?"

The soldier pointed to the miller's cottage surrounded by troops, "Over there, Sir!"

The cottage seemed to have survived the battle with little damage. Outside Bernhard's standards were flying; they had been under fire during the battle, but now stood there as marks of victory. They rode up to the guards at the door where von Lans ordered a halt. The two officers dismounted and handed their reins to Korp and Fink. Von Lans asked one of the guards, "Is General Bernhard here?"

"Sir, who may I say is asking?"

"Colonel Rupert von Lans from the Royal Flaxen Guard. I'd like to see the General on an urgent matter!"

"Please wait here while I ask."

The guard went inside in search of his commanding officer, who could relay the request to the General. After a little while the guard returned together with a young Lieutenant, who saluted von Lans and said, "The General asks if you are the von Lans he knew from Breitenfeld?"

"I am."

"Then please follow me!"

Von Lans nodded and turned around, "Falkenberg, come with me; Fogel, you and the rest wait outside. See if you can find some water and feed for the horses!"

He turned back and he and Falkenberg followed the guard officer into the cottage. They stooped low to get through the low doorway into a small entryway. The guard asked them to leave their weapons there, and led them through another low door into the cottage. There was only one room; in one corner there was a fireplace used both for heating and cooking. In the opposite corner a bed was covered by a pile of overcoats and hats. On a kitchen counter next to the fireplace there were platters with remnants of dried ham, cheese and brown bread, and jugs of water. Red embers were glowing softly in the fireplace, and it was quite warm in the cottage.

The Duke of Sachsen-Weimar was in the middle of a group of his officers gathered around a table covered by maps. To prevent the maps from curling up they had weighted down the edges with their swords and pistols. It was a grey November afternoon, and the two small windows didn't provide much light. There were oil lamps and candles placed around the room and on the table, casting flickering shadows of the men on the cottage walls.

When von Lans entered the cottage, Bernhard was talking and pointing to the map, "We need more men to the north to secure the perimeter. And send out scouts, Wallenstein may decide to fight again!" He looked up, "Does anyone know if Pappenheim is really dead or just wounded?"

 Bernhard was only three years older than von Lans, but he was a veteran soldier. His long dark hair was tied back behind his head, and his thick moustache drooped down the sides of his mouth. His face had several scars from cuts received in earlier battles, and he would soon have another; his left hand was wrapped in a bandage. He looked up and saw von Lans and Falkenberg enter the tent and said to his officers, "Gentlemen, please continue. I need to have a word with our visitors." He stepped away from the table, turned to von Lans, held out his hand and said, *"Herr Baron von Lans, willkommen!"*

Ben and the two soldiers went in search of water for the horses. The guards had told them to look for a makeshift paddock at the edge of the hill, where they would find both water and feed brought in by General Bernhard's cavalry. They rode over to the paddock; it was filled with tired horses attended to by a group of cavalrymen. Many horses had cuts and bruises from the battle, and some were limping badly. Ben approached one of the men at the paddock and asked if they could get some water and feed for their horses.

"Help yourselves, there is water in those troughs and bales of hay by the gate," the man replied.

"Thank you!"

They dismounted and led the horses into the paddock. While the horses drank and fed, they talked to the cavalrymen. Ben asked about the battle.

A man with a bandage around his left arm slowly rocked his head back and forth and said, "It was a very long and awful day, and we tried to charge up the hill twice. We had lots of cavalry and foot soldiers, but the heavy artillery at the top pounded us and we had to fall back each time. The hillside was full of our wounded and dead. The gunfire and the screaming and moaning of the wounded were terrible....." He shook his head slowly, his eyes filled with tears, and his voice broke.

They waited while he regained his composure and continued, "When the Duke ordered a third attack, we all thought it was madness, but we went ahead anyway. It was as if there was nothing more to lose, just charge, charge, charge. It was madness, but somehow we finally made it and took the hill. The first ones up went crazy and cut down the Papist soldiers that were still there. By the time it was dark, the hill was ours, and the remaining enemy had retreated."

Ben said, "We've heard that the King is dead. What happened?"

Another man leaning on a crutch fashioned from tree branches, answered, "We don't know for sure, but we heard that he got shot during the morning. They've told us the Duke is now commanding the army, but everything is so confusing." He pointed to the east and said, "Look at this, the countryside is destroyed as far as you can see."

Ben went over to the edge of the hill and looked out over the plains where the battle had been fought. Almost forty thousand men, horses, and wagons had trampled the earth into a muddy swamp as far as he could see. The normally busy road from Lützen to Leipzig had disappeared into the muck. There were encampments of soldiers spread out along the edges of the worst areas of destruction. Smoke rose from fires where the soldiers were burning anything that would provide them with a little bit of warmth. Flocks of hobbled horses stumbled around bales of scavenged hay and drank at craters filled with muddy water. It was almost a week after the battle, but charnel wagons were still collecting the dead, or what was left of them. He could see a few tents set up, which must be field hospitals. Outside them were litters with men waiting their turns, and Ben shuddered. He knew that treatment in a field hospital was as close to a death sentence as a wounded soldier could come.

81

There was a break in the clouds and a spot of sunlight moved across the battlefield. It lit up the field hospital, moved slowly across the wounded soldiers, caught a man raising his gun to the head of a horse lying on the ground kicking its legs spasmodically. He saw a puff of smoke from the gun and the horse lay still. The beam of light moved on toward the edge of the hill and a crater with an exploded cannon at the bottom, found two men, one leading his sightless companion down the hill away from the carnage on the hillside; it went up the broken hillside where it stopped for a moment. The clouds rearranged themselves and the sunbeam swept toward Lützen. There it stopped, shining on the ruins of burnt-out houses, still smoldering, the smoke rising straight up. Then slowly the light faded as the hole in the clouds got smaller and smaller until it finally disappeared.

Ben's eyes followed the beam of light. He heard a hum from the battlefield, but he was too far away to distinguish any sounds. But the vivid highlights of the battlefield were searing the inside of his head. When the light disappeared, he heard Korp saying, "It seems so unreal from here, like a painting."

Ben replied, "Yes, I feel like we're not a part of it, we're only visitors."

14.   The Parsonage

"Time to go! Let's get the horses saddled up! The Colonel will meet us at the cottage!"

Ben turned around – Falkenberg had walked from the cottage to convey von Lans's orders that they were ready to move out. They saddled all the horses, and rode over to the miller's cottage. Von Lans was standing outside the door talking to one of Bernhard's aides. Ben heard him say, "We'll go there so I can tell the Queen that I've seen the King's body. Then we'll head straight back to Erfurt tomorrow. I'll see to it that the Duke's message gets to the Chancellor. Thank you for all your help."

He shook the officer's hand, turned around and walked over to Korp, who was holding his horse. Korp handed him the reins – von Lans put his foot into the stirrup, swung his other leg over the horse and settled into the saddle ready for the ride. He turned his horse toward the men, looked at them quietly for a little while and then said, "The King died a few days ago; he was shot several times during a cavalry battle. The situation is still very confusing, but General Bernhard has taken command for the moment, and he told me what happened. We're going to see the body ourselves, and I want all of you as witnesses, so that in case something happens to one of us, the others can go back to Erfurt and tell Mr. Heidelmann – who must tell the Queen."

He continued, "The body has been taken to the village of Meuchen not very far from here. We'll go there directly. Everybody ready?" Nobody said anything – they just nodded. Von Lans waited a moment, then shortened his reins, turned his horse around, and kicked its sides lightly. The horse started walking and the four others fell in behind him. They rode down the hill away from the windmills, through the charred town of Lützen. There had been gardens at the edge of town along the road to Meuchen, but they had been trampled by troops, and many of the trees were shot to pieces. A bloody torn shirt dangled from a broken branch. There wasn't much left of the road. Most of it had been turned into mud during the battle, and they made their way slowly. They crossed Flossgraben, a canal, where some of the worst encounters had taken place. Broken wagons, corpses of horses and soldiers floated in the water, many of them entangled in gruesome jams of flotsam. The sickly stench of death was in the air.

Gradually the destruction around them lessened. The road was still muddy and you could see that soldiers had marched across the surrounding fields, but there were fewer signs of battle. Instead there were makeshift camps around the supply wagons, people gathered around fires, women cooking their evening meals, a few children playing – it almost looked like the end of a normal, quiet day in the life of an army. The day was nearly over, it was getting darker, and the battlefield disappeared into the blessed anonymity of the November night.

They came to Meuchen, a small village consisting of a church and a few dozen houses spread out at the junction of the road to Weissenfels. The narrow road became a cobblestone street between two rows of low thatched-roof houses set closely together. Traffic had been diverted around the village. The flood of cavalrymen, infantry soldiers, wagons of all kinds, hurried messengers pushing through on sweaty, snorting horses, coming and going, had split into two streams on either side of the village, to join again at the other end of the village. Before the battle, the village had been commandeered by the Swedish army and the main street going through the village was blocked by Swedish soldiers; they had lit fires by the road and von Lans recognized the King's Guard huddled around one of the fires.

They made their way slowly through the throng to the guard post. A young lieutenant came up to them and von Lans handed him the letter of introduction from Heidelmann and said, "My name is Colonel von Lans of the Flaxen Guards. Is Colonel Friedrich here? I need to see him urgently, and I'd like to bring my men with me."

The Lieutenant took the letter and read it carefully. He handed it back and motioned to the guards to open the gate, then put his hand to the rim of his hat in a salute and said, "Follow the street to the church.

You will find the Colonel in the parsonage. It's the largest house in the village, and it's next to the church. There will be more guards there."

They rode down the street. It was now dark, but torches had been lit along the street; the shadows they cast undulated back and forth against the sides of the houses. Once each house had had a narrow garden toward the street, but like the gardens in Lützen they had been trampled by the passing armies. The din of the bifurcated stream of traffic, squeezing the village in its tight embrace, was muffled by the houses, and an eerie silence took over. The only loud noise was the clattering of the hooves of their horses on the cobblestones. Few people were out, mostly soldiers posted at the doors, but they passed one house where two villagers were sitting silently on the front steps.

There were more torches as they approached the church. The church and the adjacent cemetery were fenced in by a low stone wall, and there was a small gate in it between the parsonage and the church. Another wall went around the parsonage, completing the enclosure of God's holdings in Meuchen at the large main gate facing the village street. There were guards posted at the main gate and along the outside wall as far as they could see by the flickering light of the torches. Inside the gate, the light from the torches on the steps fell on an open wagon parked at the parsonage front door. The shaft at the front was resting on the ground. On the wagon they could see a plain wooden coffin, and next to the wagon a soldier was holding a folded bundle of cloth that looked like a Swedish flag.

At the gate Von Lans repeated his request to see Colonel Friedrich, and they were asked to wait. They dismounted and led the horses to an old stone water trough at the side of the gate. Von Lans said, "Let's have something to eat ourselves while we wait." They were traveling light and didn't have much in the way of provisions, but after the long ride, the stale bread and hard cheese tasted fine.

They had waited for about an hour, when the parsonage door opened and Colonel Friedrich walked down the stairs and through the gate. Ben hardly recognized him as the cheerful, spirited officer they had met only a little over a week ago. He looked tired and drawn, he was limping, and his clothes had rips in them. He walked up to them and addressed von Lans, "Rupert, it's a good to see you so soon again, but I wish the circumstances could have been better."

"I've heard, I visited General Bernhard today, and he told me what has happened. Were you with the King during the battle?"

"Yes, but there was little I could do. It was a mêlée, and when Gustavus was shot, I was in the middle of a fight myself. He was hit in the arm and then several times in the body and finally in the head. His bodyguard tried to shield him, but he was killed as well."

Until then, they had all referred to the King as if he was still alive, but now von Lans unconsciously changed his manner of speaking and said, "Is the King's body still here?"

"Yes, we are making preparations for a transport to Weissenfels. The body will be accompanied by the Guard, and they will move fast. We're still not sure everything is secure here, despite our victory in battle."

"Heinz, I'm on a mission to see for myself that the King is dead and report back to Mr. Heidelmann, who will tell the Queen. I'd like to bring my men with me as witnesses, in case something happens to me on our way back."

"I thought as much, when I heard that you were here. Leave your horses with the guards – they'll take care of them – and come with me."

Friedrich led the way through the gate, up the front steps, and into the parsonage. It was hardly any warmer in there than outside, and they kept their outdoor clothes on. They followed Friedrich into a large room. In a corner was a fireplace, but there was no fire going. Instead the windows were opened, letting in the cold November air. Friedrich turned to them and said, "We're trying to preserve the body as well as we can until we can find an embalmer. That's why we keep it cold in here and light as few candles as possible. We're also about to move the body to the church, where it is colder."

Ben's eyes were slowly getting used to the dimness in the parsonage. He looked around the room, where most of the light came from six cande-labras placed around the edges of a large table in the middle of the room. The oil lamps on the walls were not lit, and there were more unlit candles on side tables along the wall. A desk and a chair were placed under the window at one end of the room. He could see bookcases along the oppo-site wall; on top of them were pictures of several stern men in black, presumably a string of Meuchen parsons. He saw chairs that had been pushed away from the table into corners and along the walls. There were several people standing, sitting, and milling around, some of whom Ben recognized from their earlier encounter with the King. He had expected it to be very quiet, but it wasn't. There was a murmur of voices, small parties of officers were standing around talking, somebody was laughing, there was a card game going on in one corner, and you could hear the sound of coins clinking.

He walked into the room behind von Lans and Falkenberg, and they all took off their hats. On the table lay the body of The Midnight Lion, Gustavus Adolphus, King of Sweden. Around him several people were busy: a field surgeon was examining his wounds, a tailor was trying to repair the King's clothes, somebody was trying to clean the dried blood from his coat, another was busy combing his beard. The surgeon's instruments were on a tray next to him, and on the floor there were bowls of bloody rags. At the end of the table a man dressed in black stood with his head bowed, his hands clasped in prayer – his words cut through the noise and Ben recognized the lilting voice of Pastor Numinus. The light from the candelabras made the table and the people around it look like a stage in the middle of the room, the center of everybody's attention being the royal body. Ben thought of the man he'd met on the way to Erfurt, a man still very much alive, who had asked about his family and talked about his wife's difficulties in adjusting to Sweden.

Von Lans greeted several of the officers around the table, while his men kept in the background. He spoke to the surgeon. "I'll tell the Queen that he died in battle leading his troops, but I'd also like to tell her that he didn't suffer." The surgeon looked up from his examination and replied, "He's been shot several times, and there are many stab wounds as well, but he was killed by a single bullet through the head. I can't tell you if he really suffered before that, but it must have happened very fast."

Von Lans turned to Friedrich and asked, "Heinz, is there anything I can take back to the Queen, something personal that she will recognize as belonging to the King?"

Friedrich looked at the surgeon questioningly, "Any amulet or a ring?" The surgeon thought for a moment, then opened the King's shirt. Around his neck was a thin silver chain with a locket. He took it off and handed it to von Lans, who opened the locket. Inside was a miniature portrait of Maria Eleonora, and a small lock of hair. Before he closed the locket he showed it and its contents to his men. He put the locket and the chain in his breast pocket, turned to Friedrich and the surgeon and said, "Thank you. I'll deliver this to Her Majesty as speedily as I can."

Von Lans stepped back from the table, put his hat on, and asked his men to do the same. The room stirred with royal attendants, officers, and hangers-on; in the middle of the murmuring crowd, the five men faced the table, stood at attention and raised their hands in a salute to the Midnight Lion, then turned and made their way out of the room. In the corner, somebody threw a silver rixdollar onto the card table. It rolled off the edge and fell, clanging as it hit the stone floor in front of the cold fireplace.

Friedrich arranged accommodations for the night and meals for everybody. The officers stayed with other officers and Ben and the others found beds in tents put up for the guards. Ben was bone-tired, but found it hard to go to sleep. When he finally fell asleep he dreamt about being in the middle of a battle. Everything was silent but he saw the King fighting off attackers, then falling off his horse and disappearing among wounded soldiers. He saw guns firing without a sound, horses rolling their eyes in terror as they fell, and on the hills on the horizon windmills with bodies dangling from their slowly turning wings. A rider, with a gray hood hiding the rider's face, came charging at him, a sword held high ready to slice at him. When the rider came closer the hood blew off and he saw the grinning face of his attacker. It was the old woman from the road, and she was riding on her dead horse. He dodged the attack, but his horse stumbled, and he slowly slid off his horse toward the bloodstained water of a canal. Somebody called out his name. It was Hans Vessla standing in the canal. Ben couldn't understand it – Vessla had died on the road on their first day in Germany. As he fell toward the red water, he heard Vessla cry out, "Sergeant, help me!"

He opened his eyes and sat up abruptly, shivering. Korp stood next to his bed and he was saying, "Sergeant, you're dreaming! Wake up, it's morning and it's soon time to go."

It took them three days to get back to Erfurt. On the first day out of Meuchen, Falkenberg's horse went lame. They had tried to change horses in Meuchen, but the only ones available looked even worse than their own. So they pushed on, trying not to drive the tired horses too hard, but in the afternoon Falkenberg's horse started to limp. They rested, but there was no change. The horse was reluctant to put weight on his right front leg. An hour ago, they had passed the Swedish camp where they had stayed before, and there was little to do but to go back and look for a replacement. At the camp, von Lans had to use all his authority and power of persuasion to find a replacement for the lame horse. In the end he succeeded, but by that time it was too late to go on, and they might as well let the other horses rest as well.

Finally, in the late afternoon of the third day, they walked in through the gates of Erfurt leading their tired horses.

15. The House on the Anger

They went straight to their old camp. Captain Storm and the rest of the Flaxen Guard had already come back from their mission and were waiting for them at the camp. The five men were tired after the long ride, and they were very happy when Storm ordered a couple of soldiers to help them unsaddle, feed, and water their horses. Von Lans, warm from the ride, unbuttoned his coat, took off his hat and wiped his brow with a dusty kerchief. He flung his saddlebags over his shoulder and said to Ben, "Fogel, you and the other two, take your time and rest tonight. But stay around tomorrow, I may need you." Then he turned to von Birger. "Lieutenant, would you please send a man to Mr. Heidelmann with a message that I'll be there in an hour. Then join us in my tent."

With Storm and Falkenberg in tow he walked toward his tent. Ben, Korp, and Fink sat down by the campfire with the rest of the soldiers. Nils Svensson brought them bowls of hot soup made from sauerkraut and carrots with slices of sausages. He said, "We got this in Kaltdorf." Ben swallowed a mouthful of soup and replied, "After three days in the saddle, eating nothing but old bread and ham that was getting worse by the hour, this tastes heavenly!" He took a few more mouthfuls. Byske, sitting across the fire from Ben, asked, "Tell us! Is it true? Is the King dead?"

"Yes, he is, we all saw his body."

Ben went on to tell them what they had seen and done, and that there was no doubt. The man they had met on their way to Erfurt was no longer; a battle had been won, but there was to be a shift in the fortunes of war.

Falkenberg went to change his dusty clothes and join the other officers. While von Lans washed up and changed clothes, his aide set a table

90

for them. Somewhere he had managed to pilfer a white linen tablecloth and napkins as well as tableware. But the soup was the same as for the soldiers, even if it was served in bowls made of fine china and eaten with silver spoons. They ate quickly and von Lans told the officers about their journey and about the King's death. He said, "The King will be taken to Weissenfels, where they'll prepare the body for the return to Sweden. But first the Queen must be informed, and she and Chancellor Oxenstierna must consent to the arrangements."

Their hasty dinner over, von Lans ordered up a couple of horses and he and Falkenberg rode to the old monastery to report to Mr. Cyril Heidelmann, the late King's paymaster and the Queen's confidante.

The following morning von Lans sent for Ben to escort him and Heidelmann to see the Queen. They arrived at the house on the Anger, and the chamberlain, Mr. von Pentz, led them into the drawing room. He looked anxious and worried, and he turned to Heidelmann. "Is it true then? His Majesty is dead?"

"Yes, I'm afraid he is."

"Her Majesty doesn't know. We have heard so many rumors, but I haven't had the courage to tell her yet. We hoped the rumors wouldn't be true."

He wrung his hands in despair. "But now there is no other way. Will you tell her?"

Heidelmann nodded. "Yes, but would you please have one of her ladies in attendance when we do it?"

"Yes, I'll do that. Please wait here while I make the arrangements. The Duchess Eleonore is here."

Von Pentz opened the door and left the room. Von Lans looked at Heidelmann and said, "She really doesn't know anything yet?"

"No."

Ben stood at the window behind von Lans and Heidelmann who sat down in two armchairs next to small table. On the opposite side of the table were more chairs and a couch, and on the table was a vase with yellow and orange asters that must have come from the greenhouse behind the house. Ben looked out through the window at the Anger; the market was open; people were walking along the stalls picking things up and putting them down; vendors and customers were bargaining; it was business as usual. The three men waited in silence.

The door opened, von Pentz held it open and Maria Eleonora entered the room escorted by the Duchess Eleonore Dorothea von Anhalt-Dessau, the wife of Duke Wilhelm of Sachsen-Weimar, an ally of Gustavus Adolphus and Governor of Erfurt. The Duchess was only a few years younger than the Queen; they were both born into the German aristocracy, and politics, family, and marriage had linked their destinies together in Erfurt.

Behind them came Mrs. Hahn and Emilia with two tea trays. The two men stood up, the Queen greeted them and sat down on the couch, the Duchess in a chair next to her. She introduced von Lans and Heidelmann to the Duchess and invited them to sit down. The room got quiet while von Pentz helped Mrs. Hahn to set the table with tea cups, plates, two pots of tea, milk, sugar, and plates of cakes. Mrs. Hahn and Emilia, with a quick smile at Ben, then left, while von Pentz served the tea. Maria Eleonora fidgeted nervously with a handkerchief. Nobody said anything, until von Pentz was finished, when he said, "Your Highness, I'll be downstairs if you need anything else." Maria Eleonora nodded and von Pentz turned and left the room.

Maria Eleonora looked at von Lans. "Colonel, I understand you have been to Lützen. What news can you bring me?"

Von Lans hesitated, unsure of his voice, he looked at the Queen and took a deep breath. "Your Highness, there is no good way to tell you this…."

He saw the Queen's face turn pale, and heard her breath catch. He went on. "My men and I have been to Lützen and back. There has been a big battle, in which the King took command and charged ahead of his troops. But now I must tell you that he was killed during the battle. He fought bravely….."

He stopped, interrupted by a crash of broken china and a piercing cry that sliced through the room, closing out all other sounds. Maria Eleonora had stood up and her face was like an open wound that she tried to cover with her bare hands. She was shaking all over, and out of her mouth came a wail – rising, sinking, and rising again. The Duchess came to her side to try to hold her; the men stood up not quite knowing what to do. The Duchess held the shivering Maria Eleonora in her arms, looked at Ben and shouted, "Go get Mrs. Hahn and the girl, I need their help. Quickly!"

Ben ran out of the room toward the kitchen. Turning a corner he collided with von Pentz, who was running toward the drawing room. Ben cried out, "It's the Queen!" and continued running. He burst into the kitchen. "Mrs. Hahn, Emilia! Come quickly, the Queen is ill! The Duchess needs your help!"

The two women got up and followed him back to the drawing room. On the way he explained. "The King died in battle, and Colonel von Lans had to tell her, but before he could finish, she broke down screaming and shaking." They came back into the drawing room. Maria Eleonora was lying on the couch, her feet on a pillow, head resting in the Duchess's lap. One hand clasped Eleonore Dorothea's hand, the other was balled into a fist over her mouth. The scream had turned into a low moaning sound, but she was still shivering. Mrs. Hahn went into an adjoining room and came back with a down cover that she put over Maria Eleonora, gently tucking it around her. Emilia brought a glass of water.

Heidelmann said, "Perhaps it is best if we let the ladies attend to the Queen. Von Lans, we can all wait elsewhere." He looked at von Pentz and continued, "You'd better find Her Majesty's doctor, and ask him to come immediately." He started for the door; von Lans and Ben followed.

"No!"

The whisper came from the couch.

"Don't go, I want to know! Colonel, wait!"

Heidelmann stopped. Von Lans almost bumped in to him before he came to a halt as well. Ben hadn't begun to move and stayed where he was. Heidelmann went back to the couch, crouched down and said quietly, "You Highness, we can come back later, when you've had a chance to rest from the shock."

"No, I must know!"

Maria Eleonora's voice was stronger, the shivering had stopped, and she took a small sip of the water offered by Emilia.

So with the Queen on the couch, the Duchess of Sachsen-Weimar holding her hand, the cook Mrs. Hahn getting another pillow, Emilia helping her to sip from the water glass, and Mr. Cyril Heidelmann, the King's paymaster and Sergeant Ben Fogel of the Royal Flaxen Guard standing behind him, von Lans told her the story of her husband's death. Before he began, he brought out the locket and put it in her hand. He spoke gently, slowly telling her everything about their travel and what they had learned. Maria Eleonora listened quietly, tears streaming down her cheeks, her hand clasping the locket to her chest.

When von Lans was nearly finished, the door opened and von Pentz came in followed by a man carrying a small satchel. He was Dr. Trepp, the Queen's physician in ordinary. Von Lans finished and stepped aside to let the doctor through. Von Pentz spoke: "I've told the doctor what has happened."

Dr. Trepp sat down by the distraught Queen; tears were making lines in the powder on her face, but she had calmed down and was breathing normally again. The doctor looked at the gathering around the couch and said, "I'd like to have some privacy with Her Majesty. Perhaps the Duchess would like to stay, but could the rest of you please leave. Mrs. Hahn, please bring some more hot tea!"

Heidelmann and von Lans with Ben following behind went to the nearby sitting room. Emilia went with Mrs. Hahn to make more tea, and von Pentz disappeared as well. Heidelmann sat down by the fire in the sitting room, unbuttoned his coat and tie and sighed, "Thank God that's over. I hope the doctor can give the poor woman something to calm her down so she can rest."

Von Lans replied, "Yes, it wasn't easy. I watched her face and the despair welling up in her eyes, and I really had to force myself to tell her." He was quiet for a while, then added, "What now?"

There was a knock on the door; it opened and Emilia came in with the tea tray. When she put it on the table, Heidelmann said, "Thank you, but we may need something stronger to go with this. Is there any of Mrs. Hahn's good plum brandy?"

"I'll look, Sir."

Ben came forward. "I can come with you and get it!" He looked at von Lans. "That's if it's alright with you, Sir?"

"Fine, you go along."

When Emilia and Ben came into the kitchen, Emilia started looking around for the brandy. She opened several cupboard doors, but couldn't find it. She got more and more frustrated, and finally she banged a door shut, and started crying. She put her face against the wall and sobbed. Ben walked up to her, put his hand on her shoulder and said, "There, there!" She turned around, put her arms around him and clung to him, her head on his shoulder. Ben, taken by surprise by her sudden show of emotions, stood still for a second, then put his arms around her shoulders and held her.

They stood there in their embrace. Slowly Emilia calmed down and her sobbing stopped, and finally she let go of him. She whispered, "I feel so sorry for her, but I'm glad you're here."

He held his hand against her cheek and smiled at her. "Me too."

Emilia dried her cheeks and went to the right cupboard to get the plum brandy. She handed it and a couple of glasses to Ben and said, "You must bring this up now – I'm fine." He took the brandy and left reluctantly.

Outside the sitting room he met Dr. Trepp coming from the Queen. Ben put down the brandy and opened the door to let the doctor enter first. Von Pentz was standing inside talking to Heidelmann and von Lans. When Dr. Trepp came through the door, Heidelmann looked up and asked, "Doctor, how is she?"

"I've given her some laudanum, and she was taken back in her bedroom to rest. The Duchess is with her, and von Pentz has sent word to the Duke."

"Is there anything we can do?"

"Not right now. I expect she'll sleep a lot today."

"Thank you, Doctor," – he looked at von Pentz – "and you too, Mr. von Pentz. Please keep me posted if anything happens."

"I will."

Von Pentz nodded, and Heidelmann looked at von Lans. "There isn't much more we can do here for now."

"No, let's go back."

Von Lans looked at Ben. "Fogel, you keep in close touch with Mr. von Pentz, and keep me informed about what is happening. Use your men as messengers, and have at least one posted here at all times, beginning tonight. I'll inform your Lieutenant."

"Yes, Sir!"

"Mr. von Pentz, send for me anytime you need to!" von Lans concluded.

"Thank you, Colonel, I will!"

Back at the camp, von Lans briefed his officers, and when Ben went to see Lieutenant Falkenberg, he had already decided to assign Korp, Fink, Nilsson and Svensson to him. Falkenberg said, "Fogel, I think there will be more turmoil and more orders to come. You'll have to keep your ear to the ground, and listen carefully to what goes on."

"Yes, Sir!"

Ben brought his four men together and told them about the visit to the Anger house and what their orders were to be. He sent Korp and Nilsson to take the first watch at the house and gave them instructions to report to Mr. von Pentz. From now on Ben and his men alternated between the Anger house and camp; two men were always at the house. Von Pentz gave them the use of a small room near the kitchen, and they could keep their horses with the guards outside.

The whole house was in mourning, clothes were changed to black, and all the curtains were draped with black mourning crape. The guards at the gate wore black bands around their hats, and all around Erfurt officers and soldiers put on black armbands. The Duchess spent a lot of time at the house attending the Queen, and Duke Wilhelm was a frequent visitor. They and others brought their own servants, and there was a constant stream of coachmen, maids, and messengers downstairs. With all the comings and goings, von Pentz was very happy when Ben volunteered his men to give a hand with the increased workload. It wasn't entirely altruistic on Ben's part, for it also provided him with excellent information about everything that went on. Ben was amazed to learn how little privacy the Queen had from her servants.

Maria Eleonora kept mostly to her rooms. Now and then, day or night, she would sweep through the house like a black shadow. She left the running of the household to von Pentz. One morning she called for him. When he arrived she handed him a letter. "Please read this, I want you to arrange for a courier to go to Weissenfels."

Von Pentz put on his reading glasses and read the letter. Maria Eleonora waited, her hands fiddling with the locket on the chain around her neck; it was the locket von Lans had brought back from Meuchen. He hesitated, cleared his throat. "Your Highness, do you really want this?"

"Yes, I do. Please find a reliable courier and send him to Weissenfels. Here is my seal." She handed him her signet ring.

"Yes, Ma'am, if you wish." He folded the letter carefully, went to her desk, and took out the sealing wax, warmed it over a candle, dripped warm wax onto the letter, and pressed the signet ring into the soft wax.

He put the letter into an envelope, and handed it back to Maria Eleonora, who wrote the address on the outside.

Ben reported daily to von Lans about what they heard and saw in the house. Both von Lans and Heidelmann came to call, but the Queen was in such a state that she wouldn't see them. One afternoon they arrived when Duke Wilhelm was there, and he invited them into the sitting room. They talked about the Queen's condition, and the Duke said, "Sometimes she is very quiet for long periods, then she gets very agitated. My wife tells me she has long crying spells. She also misses her daughter, Princess Christina, and wants to bring her here."

"But she is only six, and it is not safe here." Heidelmann replied.

"We tell the Queen that, and she agrees, but then she comes back with the same request."

"I wonder what the Chancellor would think? He is the Princess's guardian now."

"Well, we'll soon find out, he's coming here in a few days."

"Oxenstierna? That's good, we need him – now more than ever."

Two days later a carriage escorted by a large contingency of guards arrived. Ben heard it coming and went to look across the hedge at the side of the house. Von Pentz was at the gate greeting the two men who stepped out of the carriage.

"Chancellor Oxenstierna, we're very glad to see you – and you, Mr. Martius!"

He quickly ordered servants to carry luggage and help the coachmen, then led the two visitors to the door and into the house.

Ben walked back to the kitchen where Emilia and Mrs. Hahn were busy preparing dinner. "The Chancellor just arrived." He looked at Nilsson who was sitting at the table. "Don't go anywhere, you'll need to ride to the camp with a message soon."

They waited in the kitchen. It didn't take long before they heard von Pentz' steps on the stairs. He came to the kitchen and gave orders to set up a meal for the visitors in the upstairs dining room. He turned to Ben. "Sergeant, the Chancellor would like to see Duke Wilhelm – I'll take care of that – but he also wants Colonel von Lans and Mr. Heidelmann to join him. Can you arrange that?"

"Yes, but does he want them right away?"

"As soon as possible, he said."

"Very well. What about the Queen, will she be there as well?"

"I don't know, but I doubt it. She had a bad night and the doctor has given her some laudanum."

Ben turned to Nilsson. "You ride to the camp! Talk to Lieutenant Falkenberg first, he'll tell the Colonel and Mr. Heidelmann. If you can't find the Lieutenant, you'll have to find them yourself. Tell them that Chancellor Oxenstierna has arrived, and that the Chancellor is asking them to join him here urgently."

Nilsson left to saddle his horse and ride to the camp.

Upstairs in the dining room, Oxenstierna and Martius were eating. They had changed clothes, washed the travel dust off their faces, and Oxenstierna had taken a nap. Now they were eating quietly, the only noises heard were the crackling of the fire and sounds of chewing. They had traveled together for several days and had run out of subjects. Oxenstierna also felt the weight of the moment. He had been very close to the young king, and he felt a great loss.

There was a knock on the door and von Pentz came into the room. "Chancellor, the Duke is on his way, Mr. Heidelmann and Colonel von Lans have just arrived."

"Will the Duke be long?"

"A quarter of an hour, he said."

"Show them all in when the Duke has arrived."

"Very well, Sir."

Von Pentz left, and the two men finished their meals. Oxenstierna broke the silence. "Well, what do you think? Shall we get von Lans for the job?"

"I think so. He's done well with his assignments so far, and the Queen seems to trust him. His most delicate responsibility will be to deal with the Queen, but not let her divert him from the main task."

"Hmmh!"

There was another knock on the door, and von Pentz brought Duke Wilhelm of Sachsen-Weimar followed by Mr. Heidelmann and von Lans into the room. Oxenstierna greeted them, they shook hands with Martius, and all of them sat down around Maria Eleonora's dining room table. Von Pentz served some wine and water and left. Oxenstierna said, "Tell me everything you know about what has happened."

Heidelmann started, "We first heard that the armies were gathering at Lützen, then came the odd report that the King had been killed, so I sent von Lans up to see for himself." He stopped and looked at von Lans, who told about their journey to the battlefield, his meeting with Duke Wilhelm's brother Bernhard, the body on the table at the parsonage in Meuchen, and their return to Erfurt. Heidelmann continued with the account of how they told the Queen and her ensuing collapse.

Oxenstierna asked, "How is she now?"

Duke Wilhelm replied. "My wife has been with her since then, and the Queen is still very distraught. Her mood goes up and down, but she is slowly, slowly getting better. She seems to have found some solace and strength from arranging everything in the house in royal mourning. The Queen ....."

The dining room door opened suddenly, and in through the door came Maria Eleonora. Behind her von Lans could see the Duchess of Sachsen-Weimar looking quite distraught herself. Both women wore black; the Queen had a black veil draped over her head; her face was pale white and the pupils of her eyes had narrowed to the size of tiny black pearls. The men rose, Martius so fast that he spilled his wine all over his lap. The Queen had a black wooden box in her hands. A piece of mourning crape had been tied around it, making a bow on top. Her voice was surprisingly strong.

"Axel, I just heard that you were here. Why didn't you let me know right away?"

"Your Highness, you were asleep, and we didn't want to wake you." Oxenstierna pulled out his chair, "Please sit down with us, we're talking about these terrible events."

"I want to see Christina, she doesn't know her father is dead. I want to go to my husband."

"I know, we'll need to make plans for all of this."

Maria Eleonora still standing, turned and looked directly at von Lans, "Colonel, you told me that the King had told you 'Just tell her that my heart belongs to her.' "

"Yes, he did."

Maria Eleonora held out the black box and said. "Well, now it really does."

Von Lans looked puzzled, "Your Highness?"

Her voice quivered, "I have his heart here, and it will stay with me as long as I live."

It was dead quiet in the room. After what von Lans felt to be an eternity, the Duchess moved up to Maria Eleonora, put her arm around her shoulder, and said, "Your Highness, isn't it better if we let the men talk and make plans? The Chancellor can report to you in the morning."

Oxenstierna continued, "I think that's a good idea, we can talk this through, and tomorrow you and I can decide what we must do." Maria Eleonora nodded, and clutching the black box under one arm, her other arm supported by the Duchess, she walked out of the room.

16.   New Orders

The five men sat down again and Oxenstierna looked at von Lans. "What was that all about?" Von Lans told him about the chance meeting with Gustavus Adolphus, and how he had delivered the King's letter and his message to the Queen. When he was finished, he shook his head in disbelief. "Do you really think she has the King's heart in that box?"

"Well, stranger things have happened. But she couldn't have gotten it without help. Talk to von Pentz later, he must know. But now let me hear the rest of what Duke Wilhelm has to tell."

The Duke didn't have much more to add, but he concluded by saying, "The Queen's desolation is real, she grieves the loss of her husband, and she wants everybody to grieve with her. It will take a long time before this is all over."

Oxenstierna thought for a moment. "There is much more to this than just the Queen's personal grief. We have a whole nation to consider as well as the war and our allies. The Crown Princess is just a child, and we'll have to protect the succession."

He looked around the table, pausing for a moment at each face, looking straight at them. "The Queen needs to grieve, and we must let her. Let the nation grieve as well. Let's bring the King home with all due ceremonies, with pomp and circumstance. We can do it slowly, and everywhere along the route we'll give the people a chance to pay their respects to the Midnight Lion on his final journey."

His eyes stopped at von Lans. "Colonel, I want you to escort the Queen and follow the King's body home. You'll have to hand over the Flaxen Guard to your Captain, but take the men you need for the escort, and we'll find more for the Guard." He turned to Wilhelm. "My dear

Duke, I hope we can count on your and your wife's help in arranging things for the Queen."

"Chancellor, you can count on us." Wilhelm turned to von Lans. "Colonel, let's talk later!"

Von Lans had expected new orders, but not this. Oxenstierna looked at him. "Colonel, you look concerned!"

"No, no Sir, just surprised." He searched for words. "That'll be fine, but why me?"

"The Queen seems to trust you…. I trust you."

"Very well, Sir, it will be an honor. I'll need a few days to get organized, but I don't think the Queen is ready to travel just yet anyway."

"I agree with you."

Oxenstierna took a drink from his wineglass. "Let's keep all of this to ourselves until I've spoken to the Queen. I'll see her tomorrow, and I don't think she'll have any objections. It'll also give her something to think about and something to do." He stood up. "Unless you hear otherwise, let's meet back here tomorrow night." The meeting was over.

Ben was sitting in the kitchen with von Pentz, when von Lans came down the stairs and through the door. They both stood up, but von Lans waved at them to remain seated. He looked a bit perplexed as he took off his coat, unbuttoned his shirt collar, and sat down. "What a day – I need a schnapps!" Von Pentz got up, brought a bottle and a glass and poured the cold colorless schnapps to the brim of the glass. Von Lans lifted the glass and downed half of the contents in one gulp.

"Aaahh!" He put the glass down and said. "Mr. von Pentz, Her Majesty came rushing into the dining room surprising us all. She had a black wooden box in her hands, and she declared that it contained the King's heart. – Tell me this isn't true, and what in the world is going on!"

Von Pentz looked embarrassed. "She swore me to secrecy, but if she has told you, I don't see why I can't tell you now." He put the bottle on the table and sat down.

"Her Majesty called me to her room a day or so after she had received the bad news from you. She showed me a letter she had written to Colonel Heinz Friedrich – I think you know him – where she asks him – no, tells him – that she wants the have the King's heart. She wants the surgeon to remove it and send it to her. I pleaded with her, but she was very adamant and wouldn't hear of any objections. So I sent one of my most trusted men to Weissenfels with the letter. He came back yesterday with the black box."

"Wooh – that is a strange tale! What is she going to do with it?"

"I don't know. She keeps the box in her room. Perhaps she feels that she needs something from a husband that was always away, and now has left her forever?"

"Well, don't say anything to anybody else – that goes for you too, Fogel! The Chancellor will talk to her, and they will make plans for the King's funeral. It has to be in Sweden, of course, and we will know soon what they decide. In the meantime, not a word to anyone!"

He drank the rest of the schnapps, put down the glass and said. "Fogel, keep your men on watch here at the house, and don't change anything! I'll be back here tomorrow." He rose from the table, tucked in his shirt, buttoned his shirt collar, and put his coat back on. "I'm heading back to the camp, but first I need to have a word with Duke Wilhelm." He picked up his hat, walked through the door, and started up the stairs.

Early the next morning there was a knock on Ben's door. It was still dark and Ben was sound asleep and made no move to get up. But then somebody shook him and said, "Mr. Fogel – Mr. Fogel! Wake up!" Ben opened his eyes and through the darkness and the fog of remaining sleep he looked up and saw the chamberlain's face lit up by a candle in his hand. Von Pentz must just have gotten out of bed, he was unshaven and not fully dressed. He was wearing trousers held up by black suspenders and a shirt without a collar.

"The Chancellor wants to see Colonel von Lans this afternoon. Could you please send one of your men with the message?"

"I'll go myself."

"Thank you. Tell the Colonel that the Chancellor will be leaving tomorrow." Von Pentz left the candle on the table and went out into the kitchen, where Emilia was already busy preparing a breakfast tray for upstairs.

The November morning was still dark when Ben emerged from the room; it would be about three more weeks until the days would slowly get longer. Emilia had put a plate on the table with some bread and cheese. He sat down and she brought him a cup of warm milk. Ben reached out and put his hand on her arm. "How are you?"

She stopped next to him. "Oh, I'm fine, but it's all so confusing." Her hand went to his head and she absentmindedly began to twirl a strand of his hair. His hand went from her arm to her waist and around the back of her. He pulled her closer, and she put both arms around his head against her chest.

There were approaching steps in the corridor and she quickly let go, and when Mrs. Hahn entered the kitchen, Emilia was at the counter chopping vegetables and Ben was drinking his warm milk.

Ben left for the camp as soon as it got light. He found von Lans in his tent talking to Captain Storm. He saw Ben. "Come in Fogel, any news from the Anger house?"

Ben saluted. "God morning, Sir. I have a message from Mr. von Pentz. The Chancellor will be leaving tomorrow, and he would like to see you this afternoon."

"Thank you Sergeant, tell Mr. von Pentz that I'll be there. And – Fogel – go see Lieutenant Falkenberg, before you go back. He'll have some orders for you."

"Yes, Sir!"

Ben walked over to the Lieutenant's tent. Falkenberg was sorting papers from a box into his saddlebag. Ben took off his hat at the door, and said, "The Colonel wanted me to see you, Sir."

Falkenberg looked up, put a pile of papers down on the ground next to several others, and burst out, "Look at this mess, I'm supposed to be soldier, not a paper pusher! This army is getting too complicated with all the requisitions, lists, orders and all with copies. How many men do they think we have who can write?" He shuffled through several piles on the floor and finally extracted several pieces of paper, which he handed to Ben. "Colonel von Lans is taking half of the Flaxen Guard, including me, you, and your troop to provide escort for the Queen. The Colonel is in charge, and we must find wagons and supplies for about forty men. Here is a preliminary list. Talk to the Queen's chamberlain and see if he can help us find these things."

He looked with disgust at the piles on the floor. "We must be prepared to leave within the week. I need to sort out this mess, and get the men ready, but I'll come to the Anger house tomorrow. You might as well bring all your men there and help in any way you can."

Von Lans arrived at the Anger house early afternoon, and was shown into the drawing room where Duke Wilhelm was already waiting. A few minutes later Oxenstierna and Martius joined them and they all sat down in the armchairs by the fire. Oxenstierna wasted no time on small talk.

"Gentlemen, I've had a long conversation with the Queen, and she agrees with my plan. She will leave as quickly as possible to follow Gustavus's coffin all the way back to Sweden. It's a long journey, and with the winter coming, it'll take some time to complete. I have received reports that the coffin will go from Weissenfels, to Wittenberg, Brandenburg and on to Spandau, where they will wait for the Queen to arrive." He paused for a moment. "Now to the matter of Her Majesty's escort."

Oxenstierna looked at Wilhelm who replied. "The Colonel and I met last night. He can tell you about the military plans, but for the Queen's personal support, my wife will accompany her at least to Spandau. Where do the Queen and the coffin go from there?"

"To Wolgast, where we will wait for a suitable transport to Sweden."

"Well, in Spandau the Queen will be back with her Brandenburg family, but if necessary, the Duchess can accompany the Queen to Wolgast as well. Perhaps we can consider these arrangements later."

"Yes, Erfurt needs the Duchess as well, but this takes care of our immediate concerns. Thank your wife for me."

"I will."

Oxenstierna turned to von Lans. "Colonel?"

Von Lans replied. "I will take half of my men with me, including Lieutenant Falkenberg. The Flaxen Guard needs to be restored to its original numbers, but Captain Storm can take over the command. I'd like to suggest that you also promote him to Major, to mark the importance of the mission."

"We'll do that – Martius, you're taking notes, I hope."

Martius, who had note papers on a board in his lap, was scribbling fast and just nodded. Oxenstierna asked, "When can you leave? The Queen is very anxious to get going."

Von Lans replied. "We propose to take a smaller party, – the Queen, the Duchess, two maids and light luggage – and leave in a just a few days. The Duke is arranging for changes of horses along the way, allowing us to move faster. Lieutenant Falkenberg will leave another few days later with the rest of the Queen's party and the main supply wagons. They should get to Spandau maybe two weeks after the Queen."

He added, "With the two parties we'll need some more men, but Duke Wilhelm has kindly offered to lend me the extra soldiers."

"Excellent! Anything else I need to know?"

Both men shook their heads.

"Very well, and thank you both. I'll go and tell Her Majesty. Why don't you stay here with Martius, and help him to prepare the paperwork for me to sign before I leave."

Oxenstierna stood up followed by the others. He shook hands with von Lans and said, "Godspeed Colonel – take good care of our Queen." He turned and left the room.

Despite its gloomy trappings of grief, the Anger house was a hive of activity. Oxenstierna and Martius left the next day, but before they left Martius briefed von Pentz and Heidelmann about the plans. Von Pentz needed to arrange the moving of the royal household. Heidelmann would stay in Erfurt, but he had to make all the payments and provide travelling funds. Ben, with Falkenberg's list in his hand, was very busy shopping with Mrs. Hahn. His men carried the supplies back to the Anger house where the piles grew in the storage room. He hardly saw Emilia, who was helping with the packing, but he knew that she would be going to Wolgast with the royal household.

The Queen and her advance party left, escorted by von Lans and a small contingency of guards, and the rest of the party followed a few days later. Falkenberg led the march out of Erfurt, followed by half his soldiers, four carriages with household servants, six wagons of luggage and supplies, coachmen, groomsmen, and spare horses in a long column. Falkenberg had given Ben the task of covering the rear, and assigned him the rest of the soldiers. It took more than an hour just to get the caravan going, but finally the last wagon left the Anger house. The soldiers followed, and as the last to leave, Ben looked back at the empty space in front of the house. The window shutters were closed; the black mourning crape at the front door had been torn by the porters; the remaining pieces were wet from the rain and stuck to the door like dirty bandages. A contingency of guards remained behind to clear out the guard posts, but soon that would be finished, and they would go back to the army camps outside Erfurt.

It was cold, raining, and snowing off and on, the roads were muddy and the deep ruts filled with water. In the mornings, the puddles were frozen and the ice crackled as it broke under the feet of the leading horses. They had to wrap their legs with cloth rags to protect them from the sharp edges of the broken ice. They made slow progress; you could have walked just as fast. The carriages bounced up and down, inside them it was stuffy and the small windows foggy. Several of the passengers were sickened by the motion, and they had to make frequent stops. Some tried to walk for a while, but the roads were not made for fine shoes. The carriages had seats for the coachmen, but every wagon coachman had to ride on one of his draft horses. Only the carriage passengers were protected against wind and rain. When it rained or snowed all the others had to hover inside their great coats, collars pulled up and buttoned, and hats pulled down.

They followed the same route as the Queen's advance party, stopping along the way. The soldiers would set up camp, posting guards around it, and the Queen's household would find rooms at inns, parsonages, and the houses of local gentry. It was a slow process, but gradually the caravan moved north. The December evenings were long and cold and the soldiers made fires for cooking and keeping warm. When all the evening chores were done, the off-duty soldiers sat around the fires and talked. When there was an inn nearby, they went there.

Ben saw Emilia almost every evening when he was not on guard duty. He would join her, Mrs. Hahn and the others at the inn or they would come by the camp. They'd sit and talk about everything under the sun ¬— what else was there to do? He felt very comfortable with Emilia and she, obviously, with him. But she was young and he treated her a bit as though she was his younger sister, a fact that was infuriating her, particularly since he didn't notice that he was doing it.

One late evening Mrs. Hahn comforted her. "Be patient, child, you have a lot of time ahead of you."

Emilia's face didn't show any patience whatsoever. "Oh, but with this wretched war, who knows how long we'll live?"

It took them almost two weeks to get to Spandau, at the junction of the Havel and Spree rivers. Just north of the river junction the Havel widens into a lake and at the southern end, surrounded by water, was the old Spandau citadel, a square fort with four arrow-shaped bastions at each corner. Two years ago the Swedes had taken the fort and made it into a Swedish army stronghold, and one of Gustavus Adolphus's many headquarters. About a day's ride to the east along the Spree were the twin cities of Berlin and Cölln.

Ben was riding with Falkenberg at the head of the caravan, when they first saw Spandau. It was a cold, clear, windy day. The air was crisp, but the low December sun didn't provide much warmth against the icy wind. Ahead of them was a small village surrounded by a wall that went all the way to the water's edge. The road went to a gate in the southern wall but it also continued east along the wall toward the Havel. Vendors had set up their stalls against the wall; they wore winter coats and hats or scarves wrapped around their head against the cold. At the river there were boats loading and unloading, and porters carrying loads on their backs and horse-drawn wagons were hauling goods to and from the boats.

Falkenberg said, "The last dispatch we received said that the King's cortege had reached Spandau. That was several days ago, let's see if they are still here."

They were approaching the river and the bridge leading to a strip of land on the southern side of the citadel. They could see more and more of the fort. Ben pointed to the citadel. "Look Sir, the flag! They must be here." Behind the corner bastion at the top of a round watchtower, the yellow and blue flag complete with the royal insignia was flying at half-staff.

Falkenberg halted the column to talk to the Sergeant in charge of the guards posted at the bridge. "Good afternoon, Sergeant, we're coming with the Queen's household. Is Her Majesty here?"

The Sergeant saluted and replied, "You must be Lieutenant Falkenberg?"

"I am."

"You're expected. Follow me, please! I'll take you through the next guard post into the fort."

A couple of saddled horses were tied to the railing of the bridge. The Sergeant untied one, sat up and signaled to Falkenberg to start up the caravan behind him. They crossed the bridge and continued along the canal next to the fort until they came to another bridge that crossed the canal. There were more guards at the canal bridge, but the Sergeant spoke to them, and they turned to cross the canal. On the other side there was a gate in the curtain wall that went between the corner bastions. It opened and the long caravan with Maria Eleonora's household clattered through into the Spandau citadel.

17.   Spandau Citadel

Inside the citadel was a large courtyard, several buildings tucked against the walls, and, in the southwest corner, the round tower they had seen from the road. There were more soldiers inside wearing several different uniforms and Ben asked the guard Sergeant, "Who are all these troops?"

"Many are Swedish already posted here, but there is also a company of Duke Wilhelm's soldiers. They arrived with the King's cortege, and I hear they'll accompany the coffin to Wolgast and the ship for Sweden."

Falkenberg asked, "So the King's body is here?"

"Yes, his coffin is over in that hall over there!" The Sergeant pointed to a brick building near the tower by the western wall. Pikemen in long black coats had been posted around the building, their pikes reversed with the points on the ground, and each man had a black band of mourning crape around his hat. At the door of the building, there were several flags and standards held by more soldiers. In among the Swedish flags, Ben recognized the Sachsen-Weimar colors from the windmill hill above Lützen, and the Brandenburg coat of arms from the Anger house.

The Sergeant directed them to an open area, where they could park their wagons, the passengers could alight from their carriages, and the soldiers dismount. He showed them where they could put their horses, and the barracks where the soldiers could lodge. Von Pentz, Mrs. Hahn and the others were taken to rooms near the Queen. Finally he said to Falkenberg, "I think that's all for now, we're a bit crowded, but I hope you can manage."

"We'll be fine, but where can I find Colonel von Lans?"

"His lodging is in the officer's quarters not too far from yours. I'll find him and tell him you have arrived."

"Thank you, Sergeant."

By the time they had taken care of the horses and unloaded what they wanted from the wagons, it was almost dark. The Queen's servants disappeared to their quarters. The soldiers were tired after two weeks on the road. They had a meal at the barracks mess hall, and then most of them went to find a bunk where they could lay down. Falkenberg had ordered them to stay at the citadel until he knew what plans von Lans had for them.

Falkenberg was in the officer's mess; he had finished the meal and was sitting with a group of young Weimar officers who were part of the royal escort. Lieutenant Schumacher introduced himself, "I'm the second son of a brewer, so I had to join the army. My older brother will take over the brewery." He smiled and continued, "I don't know which is best, but at least I didn't have to become a monk like my younger brother."

Falkenberg asked, "Tell me about the funeral cortege."

"Well, it's a slow, slow march, and we seem to improvise as we go. The undertakers in Weissenfels had to embalm and dress the body, and they couldn't find a suitable coffin. It rained all the way to Wittenberg. We didn't have a proper hearse and the coffin leaked, so the first thing we had to do there was to open it up, dry out the coffin and change the King's clothes."

Schumacher shook his head and continued, "Luckily we had sent word ahead and when we arrived the undertakers were ready for us. They worked all night, and by the next morning the citizens of Wittenberg could got to see a properly attired King resting on a golden bed."

"Did you make more stops?"

"Everywhere we went, people came out to see the cortege. Several times we stopped overnight in a village and put the coffin in their church with an honor guard around it. The news spread fast and when it was time for the village pastor to hold the evening service, the church would be packed. Afterwards they would all file past the coffin. They would bring little gifts, dried flowers, homemade little crosses, and light candles near the altar."

"No wonder it takes such a long time."

"Yes!" Schumacher looked around to make sure nobody else was listening; he leaned over toward Falkenberg, and lowered his voice. "Sometimes I feel like we are part of a big carnival. – Step right up! – Come and see the Midnight Lion at rest!"

He leaned back in his chair again. "I suppose it serves a purpose. Kings always leave this earth with pomp and circumstance."

Falkenberg looked at him, raised his glass and said, "Here's to Gustavus Adolphus, his trip has been long and adventurous, but it's not over yet. Now the Queen is joining the cortege with her household and a contingency of Flaxen Guards. It may not be a joyous carnival, but it's entertainment no less, and the caravan is getting longer."

He stood up, his glass held high, "To the King."

They all stood up, "To the King."

Behind Falkenberg, a voice echoed, "Very well, gentlemen – to the King!" Falkenberg turned around and saw von Lans coming toward them. He raised his glass with them as he, somewhat unsteady on his feet, approached the group. Schumacher got another chair, and von Lans sat down next to Falkenberg. As he did so Falkenberg caught a whiff of flowery perfume, and he also noticed that the shirt of the normally meticulous Colonel was missing a button.

Von Lans waved at them to sit down, and called a waiter to fill their glasses, but then he became all business. He asked Falkenberg about their trip and the condition of the household party, and after listening to Falkenberg's account, he said, "Everybody needs a few days for house-keeping and rest, but then we'll all move to Wolgast together."

Von Lans took a sip from his wine glass and continued. "I've agreed with Duke Wilhelm that we'll share the duties with his troops and the King's own guard. We'll alternate guards around the coffin, alternate the order in the cortege, and we'll show all the colors – Swedish, Brandenburg, Weimar, Scottish etc. – along the way." He looked at Schumacher and then at Falkenberg. "You two will have to work out the logistics."

The two Lieutenants replied almost at the same time. "Yes, Sir! Yes, Sir!"

Falkenberg asked, "How is the Queen, Sir?"

"Under the circumstances, quite well. The travel was difficult, but she hasn't complained at all." He put his hand on his shirt where the button was missing and continued, "The Duchess Eleonore has been a great help, she is a very resourceful woman…" His voice lowered as if he was speaking to himself, "…and she's also very beautiful."

18.   Prenzlau

They didn't get much time to rest. Two days later the cortege was getting ready to leave Spandau in the morning. Ben was awakened before sunrise, it was time to pack their last things, put the draft horses before the wagons, and saddle up their own. It was dark and cold and the only light in the citadel courtyard came from torches placed all around. There was a line of torches flanking the honor guard when they carried out the royal coffin and put it in a covered black hearse drawn by four black horses with waving black feather plumes on their heads. The carriages for the Queen's attendants and her household servants were brought out, and one by one they filled with passengers. The coachmen lined up the carriages and wagons and held the draft horses ready; the cavalrymen mounted up and they were ready to go.

The Queen's carriage was brought out, stairs were put in front of the coach door and von Lans went to fetch the Queen in her quarters. The door opened, von Lans stepped out, and he held the door to let four ladies dressed in black mourning clothes through. It was the Queen and the Duchess followed by their travel attendants. The Queen was carrying a black box wrapped with black crape under one arm and holding on to Duchess with the other. The Duchess had a silvery scarf around her neck; it sparkled in the light from the torches. They walked slowly down the wet steps. One of the attendants took the door while Von Lans went around the ladies and opened the door to the coach; he offered his hand to the Queen. As she stepped on the stairs to the coach, she slipped. The Queen didn't fall, but she had to let go of the black box to catch herself, and the box with the King's heart in it dropped with a loud clap on the cobblestones.

It had been very quiet during the Queen's walk to the coach. The only sound was the whooshing from the horses' steamy breaths. The noise of the box' falling on the cobblestones reverberated in the quietude inside the courtyard. A horse behind the Queen's coach neighed, startled, then a few other horses joined in, and hooves danced on the cobbles. But it was quickly over. Von Lans bent down and picked up the box, wiped off some dirt, and handed it to the Queen through the door. The Duchess and two attendants stepped into the coach and the footman closed the door and stowed the stairs.

Schumacher's cavalry men were going to lead the caravan out of Spandau with the Lieutenant himself taking the point position. Falkenberg's job was getting everybody into the cortege in the right order. Ben and his troop had been assigned to direct all the carriages and troops to their places and to take their places at the rear.

The pale autumn dawn was breaking when Shumacher raised his hand and pointed forward toward the Spandau gate. His men followed him out through the gate, across the bridge to the strip of land, and turned right to the next bridge leading across the Havel to the town. After Shumacher's cavalry came von Lans and Colonel Heinz Friedrich riding side by side ahead of the royal hearse and the Queen's coach. They were followed by more cavalry, a cannon drawn by two horses, the Queen's household carriages, supply wagons, more soldiers, spare horses, another cannon, a wagon of cannonballs, more cavalry, and ammunition wagons. Along the procession waved flags, regimental standards and pennants of all colors.

All of Spandau had known that Gustavus Adolphus' body was at the citadel and when Schumacher some time before they left had sent out an advance contingency of soldiers to clear the way through town, the news flew fast that the royal funeral cortege was leaving Spandau. Now the street was lined with curious citizens. When Schumacher led the slow procession through the city a quiet hush fell over the crowd, and when the hearse and the Queen's carriage passed, the women curtsied and the men took off their hats and bowed.

It was a long caravan; when Schumacher rode through Spandau, Ben was still in the courtyard of the citadel directing participants to their places in the cortege. Gradually the courtyard emptied, and finally he ordered his men to the end of the line. He looked around the courtyard – it was empty but for a few caretakers – and then, as the last man in the

113

procession, he rode out through the citadel gate. It was daylight, a few rays of sunshine came from the eastern horizon, but cloudy overhead, and he thought to himself, "It's getting colder. It feels like there's snow in the air."

For the next few days the weather held, and they made good progress. They came to Prenzlau, where they planned to rest for a couple of days. On the shortest day of the year, at winter solstice, Gustavus Adolphus's coffin was on display in St. Mary's Church, while the troops alternated between guard duty, resting, and repairs. Ben's horse had lost a shoe; he wasn't the only one with horse problems and there was a long line at the farrier's down by the lake. It was getting colder by the day, and he was waiting his turn, trying to keep warm by the smith's coal fire. He looked down the street and saw Emilia walking along toward him with a basket on her arm. He called her name, she looked up and saw him; a smile came over her face.

She was dressed in a warm coat with a shawl wrapped around her head and shoulders. On her hands were woolen mittens. Her cheeks were rosy and her breath made little white puffs in the cold. She came up to the fire, put down the basket and took off her mittens. "You look cold," she said, "feel these!" She put her hands on his cheeks. They were warm against his cold skin. He put his hands over hers and said, "That feels good, why are you so warm?"

"I've walked from our lodgings to several markets looking for flour, butter, egg, milk, maybe some turnips. There is so little and it's not very good. Look!" She showed him the basket, and there were only a few eggs, and three turnips in it.

"Let me go with you, this will take some time anyway."

Ben agreed with the farrier that he would be back in a couple of hours He put his horse in one of the stalls, and picked up Emilia's basket.

"Let's go!"

They walked along the water and up the hill through a gate in the city wall, making a loop through the center of town toward the tallest building in Prenzlau, the tower of the St. Mary's Church. The day before, Ben had been on guard duty at the King's coffin, and he knew that around the church there were several farmers' markets. A thin layer of ice covered the Unterückersea, and there were many boats tied up in the harbor. Business was slow, but a few small fishing boats had braved the winter seas and were selling their catch at the docks.

114

Emilia bought fish from one vendor, haggling about the price until the fisherman finally gave in with a shrug of his shoulders, "Well, since it's almost Christmas." He wrapped the fresh fish in a piece of cloth and handed the package to Ben to put in the basket. They moved on.

Along the street from the harbor to the Church they found more vendors, and they stopped for more haggling. They talked and laughed a lot as they walked along the busy street. They came to a woman who was selling jewelry, and Emilia looked at the necklaces with drops of yellow amber. She picked one up and held the amber up to the light. Inside was a tiny moth that had been entombed when it took a wrong turn one night millions of years ago and got stuck in the resin leaking from an ancient tree. "Look how pretty it is!" she said.

"Yes – would you like it?"

Her face lit up, but she shook her head. "No, you shouldn't. It's too expensive."

"Let's see."

Now it was Ben's turn to bargain. He turned to the vendor. "How much."

"Two rixdollars!"

"My Dutch mother told me never to pay the asking price. I'll give you half a dollar."

The vendor, a big woman wrapped in a sheep skin coat, rolled her eyes to the skies, and shook her head. "No, no, that's impossible. I'm an old woman trying to feed her family." Ben turned and started to move away, when the woman called out.

"One and a half dollars!"

Ben stopped and turned back to her, then slowly put his hand in his pocket and took out two rixdollars. He turned his pocket inside out, shook it, looked at the woman, and showed her the two dollars he had in his hand. "My mother also taught me never to spend everything I have. This is all I've got. I'll give you one!"

The woman looked at Emilia and said, "It's for her, isn't it?"

"Yes."

"Well then, since it's almost Christmas. But you promise me to be good to her." The woman smiled a big toothless smile and handed over the necklace.

Ben paid her and said to Emilia. "Let's see if it fits." She took off her shawl, and opened her coat, and he placed the necklace around her neck.

She smiled at him, came closer, raised herself on her toes and gave him a slow kiss.

Behind her the vendor woman said, "Young lady, you be good to him too!"

They walked off and Emilia fingered her necklace and said. "Thank you! I'd like to meet your mother sometime. She taught you well."

"Better than you think." Ben put his hand in another pocket and took out two rixdollars. "She also taught me never to keep all my money in one pocket."

Emilia giggled and hooked her arm through his. "Let's go up to the church!"

They heard yelling and soldiers shouting orders as they came closer to St. Mary's Church. The church was at the side of the square. There were guards posted all around it, and a throng of people outside the front door. As Ben and Emilia entered the square, the guards were pushing the crowd aside to make way for a group of soldiers coming through the door. In the middle they dragged two young men, hands tied at their backs, blood streaming down their bearded faces. One man was screaming hoarsely, "Long live Pope Urban and the only true creed. Praised be the Lord!" The other continued, "Free us from Luther's heretics!"

The soldiers had their swords out. One raised his and slashed it down toward the shoulder of one of the men. The man screamed in agony when the sword made a deep gash at the top of his arm and blood gushed out. Another soldier shoved the second man, who fell on the ground, and the wounded man stumbled and fell on top of him. Soldiers in the back stumbled as well and more swords came out. It was a mêlée and Ben and Emilia could only see the backs of soldiers thrusting and slashing into the middle. People around started to scream and try to run away, but those on the outside were still pushing to get in.

Then, just as abruptly as it started, it was over. The crowd backed off, it got quiet, and the soldiers stood up and sheathed their swords. But on the ground, the two Catholic intruders lay dead next to one soldier who was bleeding badly from a chest wound. He had been stabbed by one of his own. Ben recognized the soldier; he was one of the Sachsen-Weimar guards. The wounded soldier was helped up by other soldiers, who took him back into the church. The others picked up the bodies of the two young men by the arms, dragged them off to the side of the church, and put them on a wagon. The crowd was very quiet, but then a voice from the back called out, "Death to the Papists, may they rot in hell!" More voices chimed in, "Death to the Papists! Let's hang them!" The crowd started to push toward the wagon with the two bodies.

The soldiers couldn't hold them back, and the angry mob pushed them aside and surrounded the wagon. Hands reached into the wagon and dragged out the two bodies. The mob kicked them and tore at their clothes. Soon they were naked, and the clothes were tossed around as trophies. At the side of the church, workmen had erected a scaffolding to repair the wall. There were ropes and pulleys to bring material up and down the scaffolding. The two naked bodies were dragged over to the scaffolding, ropes were tied around their ankles, and eager hands started to pull at the other ends. Soon two bloody and dirty corpses were hanging upside down, their dangling arms searching in vain for the ground, two scarecrows on the wall of St. Mary's Church in Prenzlau. The anger of the mob spent, the people stood below staring at the consummation of religious zealotry. The shouts and screams turned into a quiet murmur, and the crowd began to disperse.

Ben and Emilia were standing at the edge of the square away from the church. Emilia had grabbed Ben's hand and was holding it in a tight grip, her knuckles going white. Now Ben put his hand on hers and said, "Best not to stay here, you should go back to your lodgings. I'll walk with you, we'll need to warn the Queen's guards, but then I must go back and report to my Lieutenant."

They hurried back toward Emilia's lodgings; she was staying close to the Queen's residence. Ben quickly found the duty officer and told him what had happened. The officer responded, "Tell your Lieutenant that we'll double up on the guard here, and that I have enough men for now. He can send his men to assist the troops at the church."

"Yes, Sir."

"Colonel von Lans is here, I'll tell him right away. You'd better hurry back to camp." The duty officer went to find his reinforcement guards, and Ben looked at Emilia. "You should be safe from now. I'll be off!"

She gave him a quick hug, "Yes, I'll be fine. Go!"

Ben ran back to his camp, and looked for Falkenberg. He found him in his tent, and when the Lieutenant heard his report he said. "Get all our men, and go to the church! Have them fully armed and bring your horses as well. This could get out of hand, unless we show some strength right away. I'll go to the Queen's residence and find the Colonel. Then I'll come to the church."

Ben went to get the men. Some were asleep, some were eating a meal, others were just sitting around the fires and talking. The normally quiet camp exploded with activity as the men ran around getting dressed, getting their weapons, finding their horses, putting bridles and saddles on. Ben was still without his horse, and when he came upon Fink saddling his own, he told him. "My horse is still at the farrier's! Go get it! I'll take yours for now."

"Yes, Sir. I'll catch up with you at the church, shall I?

"Do that, but hurry!"

Fink quickly finished tightening the cinch, and ran off toward the harbor clutching his sword and gun under his arms. The others mounted up, and when everybody was ready, Ben ordered a quick ride toward the church square. He added, "Be prepared to take out your swords, but leave them sheathed for now."

They swept through the narrow streets, hooves clopping on the cobblestones. When they entered the church square, things appeared to have calmed down. There were gatherings of townspeople around the square, but the Sachsen-Weimar guards had formed a ring around the church. Near the church door Lieutenant Schumacher was talking to his officers. "No more visitors inside and make sure we have full control all around the church."

Ben rode up to Schumacher. "Lieutenant, how can we help?"

"Glad you're here! I want to secure the whole square. Could you and your men move the townspeople off the square and guard the entry points?"

"Yes Sir, we'll do that."

Ben ordered his troops to spread out sideways, forming a wedge, and they rode toward the edge of the square. On their horses they stood high above the crowd, and when he asked the people to move off the square, the compact line of cavalry behind him didn't invite argument. It was also beginning to snow, and the chill of the snow seemed to cool the mob down. There were murmurings, but then the crowd began to disperse into the narrow streets and alleys that led away from the square, and slowly the square emptied of townspeople. Ben put guards at each entry point but kept half a dozen men to form a roving patrol that moved around the square ready to assist the guards in case of trouble. A few curiosity seekers remained behind the guards, peering between them at the square full of soldiers. The snow fall was getting heavier, the large wet flakes sticking to the cold bodies still hanging from the scaffolding.

Fink arrived with Ben's horse, its shiny new shoes throwing little sparks against the cobblestones. They exchanged horses and Ben ordered Fink to join the roving patrol.

"Sergeant!"

One of the entry guards was calling him, and when Ben looked his way, the guard motioned to him to come over. Next to the guard von Lans followed by Falkenberg were entering the square on their horses, and Ben kicked the sides of his horse and went to meet them. Von Lans had come as quickly as he could. His horse had white lines of lather across its withers and down the sides around the saddle. It was breathing hard and chewing on the bit as von Lans was trying to calm it down. Slowly his horse settled down, and von Lans asked, "Fogel, what's happened?"

Ben told them the whole story from the time he and Emilia had come to see the church, about the young men, the crowd's anger, getting help for Schumacher's troops. He finished by saying, "Things seem to have quieted down, but I don't know if there are more angry Catholics biding their time."

While he was talking, Lieutenant Schumacher had joined them. He saluted von Lans, "Colonel."

Von Lans returned the salute, "Lieutenant, what started the whole thing?"

"The two stood in line, just like the others, to see the coffin and look at the King through the window in the coffin. When it was their turn, they took out some bottles from under their shirts and splattered the contents – it looked like blood – all over the coffin. They shouted, 'The blood of Christ shall drown the heretics!' When my men attempted to grab them, they brought out knives, but they didn't have a chance against all the guards, who quickly disarmed them and brought them outside."

"Is everything secure now?"

"Yes, we've cleared the church of visitors and searched it. We found spots of blood in a corner under a pew. They must have hidden the knives and the bottles inside the church several days ago. This was no spontaneous attack."

"Well, I wish they were still alive to tell us who they were."

The snowing had increased. By now they could hardly see across the square, and the soldiers were lighting torches and fires for the oncoming night. The ground was getting white, and little piles of snow were forming on the soles of the feet of the dead young and around the ropes holding them high in the air. Von Lans rode over to the scaffolding, and the others followed. He looked at the bodies and said to Schumacher, "Cut them down and find an undertaker. But put the bodies under guard somewhere secure. I want to find out who they were."

Schumacher gave his men the orders. Von Lans waited until he was finished, and then led them in a ride around the square, inspecting all the guard posts. He had a few comments here and there, but seemed generally satisfied that the entries were secure. They rode back to the church and stopped at the front door. Von Lans turned and ordered, "Sergeant Fogel, stay here with your patrol and guards. Lieutenants, please come with me. I want to have a look inside." Falkenberg and Schumacher also dismounted, and the three horses were left with one of the guards. Falkenberg looked at Ben, "Make sure the men are on guard for anything that can happen! I'll be back very soon." The three officers disappeared through the door of St. Mary's Church.

19.   Snow Falling

Inside the church it was hot. There were soldiers posted around Gustavus Adolphus's coffin, at the doors and around the church and candles were lit everywhere. The three officers inspected the guards and von Lans acknowledged the men coming to attention as they walked by. He stopped by the wounded soldier, a young boy, who was lying on one of the pew under blanket. The surgeon had just finished cleaning up his chest wound and wrapping a bandage around him. The boy's face was ashen and he was coughing into a red-stained towel. Von Lans asked the surgeon. "How is he?"

"Well Sir, I've stopped the bleeding on the outside, but I don't know how much damage there is on the inside."

Von Lans put his hand on the soldier's arm and said. "You're a brave man, how old are you?"

"Fourteen, Sir," the boy whispered, then coughed and spat more blood into the towel.

"I'll tell the Queen about your bravery. Now I'll let the surgeon take care of you."

They walked through the church and into the vestry. There were two soldiers guarding the room, but Schumacher asked them to leave and closed the door behind them. Von Lans was taking his hat and coat off. The two others did the same, and they all sat down on a couple of benches along the wall. Von Lans sighed, "What a mess." He sat quiet for a while and then continued. "Colonel Friedrich is with the Queen and he has enough men to guard her for now. But we don't have enough men for increased guard duty around the clock."

He looked at Schumacher, "Lieutenant, we have to consider the Duchess Eleonore as well. She was going to leave us before Wolgast, but that means you and your men would have to go with her, and we can't split our forces until we know what this attack is all about."

"I agree," Schumacher replied, "but what does the Duchess think?"

"She doesn't know much about this yet, but she was prepared to stay with the Queen all the way to Wolgast."

"Fine, my troops can certainly stay with you until we get there."

"Excellent, in Wolgast we have more Swedish troops and the security of the castle." Von Lans paused, stood up, pulled at his vest and sat down again. He continued, "We don't have enough men here in Prenzlau for around-the-clock guard of the church and the Queen's residence."

Falkenberg broke in, "Sir, until we know who or what is behind the attack, we'll be like sitting ducks here."

"I know, but we can't be seen as running away either. The plan was to spend Christmas here and then move on. Christmas is only three days away, and everybody could do with a rest as well."

"That's still a long time to keep our guards on full alert."

Von Lans nodded, thought for a while, stood up again, fidgeted with his vest, sat down, but then a look of resolution came over his face. "Let's do this," he said, "let's use the weather as an excuse for moving out. We want to get to Wolgast before the winter is really upon us. That way we can consolidate our forces and keep everybody together to protect the cortege and the Queen."

"What about the Queen, will she agree?" asked Schumacher.

"I'll take care of that – with the help of the Duchess. I'll go straight back and talk to the Duchess, and also to Colonel Friedrich. Von Lans looked at Falkenberg, "Do you want to stay here with your troops?"

"Yes Sir, I'd better do that."

"Fine, but let me have Fogel. I'll send him back to you with my orders."

"Very good, Sir."

Schumacher had one more question. "What about the attackers, Sir? Whom do you want to look into what's behind the attack?"

"Why don't we ask the Duke of Brandenburg to handle the matter? Can you send a courier to the Duke with a message?"

"I can do better than that. There is a contingency of his troops stationed here. I'll talk with their commander."

They put their coats back on and left the vestry. As they came out into the church, they saw the surgeon getting up and wiping his hands on a blood-stained cloth. His assistant unfolded a white sheet, shook it out into the air above the boy soldier, and gently let it fall over his body. He pulled it over the boy's face, and straightened it out. Von Lans looked at the surgeon, who shook his head with the look of a man who had seen too many dead boy soldiers.

Outside Falkenberg took over the command of his troops from Ben, and told him to go with von Lans. The Colonel was in no mood for talk, and they rode back to the Queen's residence in silence. The stable boys took their horses, and they entered the house by a side door leading to the downstairs. From the kitchen there were stairs leading to the upstairs hall. Von Lans started up the stairs, hesitated, then stopped and turned around. He looked at Ben, "Fogel, I'll be upstairs with Colonel Friederich. There will be some changes of our travel plans, but we need to make plans. Stay here, but be ready to go back to Lieutenant Falkenberg with my new orders."

"Yes, Sir, but what do I tell the household staff?"

"You can tell them what happened, but don't tell them anything about changing our plans. Tell them not to worry, there were only two crazy men, and they were caught."

"Very well, Sir!"

Von Lans turned back and started up the stairs. Ben stood at the bottom and began unbuckling his sword. He put the sword to the side, took off his coat, and sat down on the bottom step to pull off his boots. He heard the door at the top of the stairs open and a voice. "Rupert, I was so worried about you? You ran off in such a hurry, and then we heard the soldiers outside. What's happening….." The door closed and all he could hear were the muffled voices of von Lans and the Duchess Eleonore.

The cortege moved out the next day. The weather was still grey but no more snow had fallen during the night, and they made good headway. In the middle of the afternoon, they were about six miles from their next lodging, an estate owned by a distant cousin of the Duke of Brandenburg. A harbinger had been sent ahead to announce their arrival. Ben was at the head of the cortege with Falkenberg. The road had been going through open country for most of the day, but now they entered a pine forest. The land was flat, a few hillocks here and there. The ground around the pines was covered by heather interspersed by marshes where the pines thinned out just to close ranks on the other side. It was getting darker; Ben looked at the sky and said, "Lieutenant, I think we may see some snow."

"Yes, we only have a few hours left to go, but I think we'd better not slow down."

A few minutes later the first flakes fell, large white blobs of snow, only a few at first, but then more and soon they could hardly see anything ahead, only a white wall of snow. Falkenberg ordered a halt and sent Korp back along the cortege with orders to tighten up the caravan and not allow any stragglers. While they waited for his return, Ben pulled up his coat collar and tied a scarf around his hat. There was a strange sound like a moan from somewhere in the forest ahead. Falkenberg signed for silence. The sound came again, this time more like a high pitched howl, then it repeated and Ben thought out loud, "It's a wolf – no, it's a pack of wolves."

Falkenberg nodded, "Yes, I think you're right."

Korp appeared like a ghost out of the snow, back from the rear of the caravan. He rode up to the front and said," Lieutenant, the cortege has pulled together, everybody is ready to continue. The Colonel wants me to tell you that he'll stay by the Queen's carriage, but he asks that we move on."

"Thank you, Korp!" Falkenberg shouted toward the cortege hidden in billowing curtains of snow behind him. "Let's move out – but keep the line together!"

Falkenberg raised his arm and pointed forward and they set out again. The snow was beginning to accumulate on the ground, but they could still see the road ahead cutting a swath between the pines. The wolves continued their singing, but they seemed to be off the road. The snow didn't let up, and the going got more and more difficult. The riders could get through, but the carriages and the wagons were slowing down. The riders kept their heads down as far as possible to keep the snow away from their faces. The horses were shaking their heads back and forth for the same reason. The only ones protected were inside the carriages, but they couldn't see anything outside, and many of them were sickened by the motion and stale air.

A wolf howled nearby, there was a loud crack behind Ben and he heard a lot of commotion. Falkenberg raised his hand for the cortege to halt. "Fogel, go back and see what happened!" Ben turned his horse around, and started back along the road, along tired riders sitting bent over, their coat collars pulled up, snow on their hats and shoulders, and their horses steaming from melting snowflakes. He saw a group of people

124

around a carriage that was leaning over precariously. One wheel had come loose and the side door was hanging open; it was the Queen's carriage. He came closer and saw von Lans helping the Queen out through the door. She was pale, but appeared unhurt, and when she was safely away from the carriage, her maid put a blanket around her shoulders. Over on the side of the road, a soldier was clearing away snow from a log, where she could sit down. Another had cleared the ground and was starting a fire; von Lans had given the orders as soon as he saw the ladies were safe.

Maria Eleonora sat down, soon the Duchess joined her, but it wasn't over yet. The carriage was listing and pulling at the shaft between the draft horses; the horses' eyes were wide open and filled with fear. Several coachmen had been trying to keep them quiet, but now, when the passengers were out of danger, they began to unhitch the horses. The horses were hard to handle. Ben dismounted and went to help the coachmen, while von Lans got a team of soldiers to lift up the side of the carriage and put logs under the wheel axel.

They had a spare wheel, and once the horses were unhitched and the carriage righted, it didn't take the coachmen long to change the wheel. The snowfall began to let up and by the time the work was finished, it had thankfully stopped altogether. The soldiers and members of the Queen's household were milling around the fire heating water and soup to ward off the cold. The Queen herself and the Duchess were sitting with the rest of them, on the log in the middle of the group, soldiers' blankets over their shoulders, drinking hot tea served in army cups and eating dry biscuits. On the road in front of the broken carriage was the hearse with Gustavus Adolphus's body, and the flames of the fire shone through the glass onto the royal coffin through the little window casting light on the King's sleeping face. It had stopped snowing, but the ground and the trees were covered; the whiteness of the snow reflected the light from the fire among the trees. Now and then they'd hear a wolf howling, but the muffle of the snow made it sound like it was far away.

Von Lans came over to the Queen. "Your majesty, the carriage is repaired, and the horses hitched up. We can go on now."

"Thank you, Baron!" She stood up, gave the blanket to one of the soldiers, looked around and continued, "We thank you all for your help and company. Sitting here with you in the middle of the forest has been very comforting."

20. Christmas Travels

They continued down the road. It was getting dark but with torches and the reflections from the white snow the road was easy to see as it tunneled through the pines. Ben was again at the head of the caravan with Falkenberg. The pace was slow but steady and things seemed to go quite well. But then they heard a scream from the back, followed by another, and then another. Falkenberg halted the caravan again and said to Ben. "I think that's the Queen. You'd better go back and see what it is this time."

Ben turned and cantered toward the rear; soon he heard Maria Eleonora's wailing voice. "My heart, my heart, I must find my heart." He stopped by von Lans who was talking to the opened door of Maria Eleonora's carriage.

"Your Highness, we'll find it! I'll send a troop back immediately." The wail slowly subsided and turned into deep sobs, "I must have my heart back!"

Von Lans turned around and saw Ben. "Fogel, Her Majesty has lost something. Come with me." He rode over to the side and turned his horse away from the caravan. Ben followed and wheeled his horse around to face von Lans.

"Fogel, remember the story von Pentz told us in the kitchen in Erfurt? Her Majesty has been carrying that black box in the carriage. It must have fallen out during the accident."

"Do you want me to go back and look for it?"

"Yes, but I don't want the story to spread, if we can avoid it. Get four of your most trustworthy men and go find it. Don't just look, find it! We can't take the King home without his heart."

Von Lans went back to the royal carriage, and Ben turned around and rode back to get his men. He explained to Falkenberg, "The Queen has lost a box back there, and the Colonel wants me to go back and look for it. He wants me to take four men just in case we run into the wolf pack."

"Take the ones you need. We're not very far from the estate, and you can catch up with us there."

"It may take all night."

"That's fine, just be careful! Anklam is up ahead, we cross the river there, and then we go directly to Wolgast."

He took out a map from his pocket and gave it to Ben, "I don't have any extra guide to leave with you, but take this map."

Falkenberg looked at Ben, "Do you think you can find your way?"

Ben looked at the map and replied, "I think so, but I can always ask in Anklam."

"Good luck, I'll expect to see you in Wolgast."

"Thank you, Sir!"

Ben took Korp, Fink, Nilsson, and Svensson with him and rode back to the place of the accident, while the rest of the cortege continued. Ben told his men that they were looking for a black wooden box with black mourning crape tied around it. It was getting dark by now and they had to light torches to be able to see. They looked all around the place where the carriage wheel had fallen off, but they couldn't find anything. There had been no more snow, and the tracks in the snow came from the cortege, and all the people that had walked all over the place. But then Nilsson walked over to the edge of the trampled snow. There were some different tracks and he called to Ben. "Sergeant, over here!"

Ben walked over and Nilsson showed him some fresh tracks in the snow leading into the woods. "Look at these, the wolves must have been here."

"Yes!" Ben pointed to the ground. "But what is this?" There was a wide line in the snow along the wolf tracks. "It looks as if somebody has taken a wooden stick and pulled it along. Let's look!"

Ben and Nilsson took the torches and walked along the wolf tracks into the forest, while the other two brought the horses. Nilsson was the first to see it. "Look, a black veil!"

"No, I think I know what this is!" Ben picked up the torn black mourning crape from the snow. He held up his torch and saw wolf tracks all over the ground. In the middle there were dark stains, and when he looked closer it seemed to be fresh blood. He lifted up the torch again and there was a glint of light off to the side. There was the box, the reflection came from the silver lock. Nilsson walked over to the box, picked it up and brought it back to Ben.

"Is this it?" he asked.

"Yes, I'm sure, let me see."

Nilsson handed it over, but Ben didn't like what he saw. The box was empty.

They searched the area, but all they they found were more tracks and signs that the wolves had been fighting over some scraps of meat. They couldn't tell what it was, but Ben was getting a sinking feeling in his stomach. Finally he said, "There is nothing more here, let's follow the wolf tracks for a while more."

The tracks continued in a straight line, but then veered off on top of a different set of tracks. Korp pronounced them to be from a small sounder of boars. Soon they noticed blood on the tracks. The wolves must have reached their prey. But then the tracks divided. It looked like the sounder had divided and one single boar gotten away, while the wolves pursued the rest. Ben called a halt, "Let's stop this, we won't find anything."

Korp, who had followed the single boar track, turned to them and called out. "This one is hurt!" He turned around, took one step – and disappeared out of sight. At the same time a large, dark shape came charging out of a thicket. The wounded boar charged right past where Korp had been standing and then it also disappeared out of sight. Ben took out his sword and ran to help Korp. When he came to the knoll where Korp had been standing, he stopped. Below him lay Korp thrashing about in a flurry of snow, and next to him lay the boar. There was blood around his mouth and tusks, but he didn't move.

Ben with his sword ready moved toward the boar. It didn't seem to be breathing, there was a trace of blood along its tracks, but he wasn't taking any chances. Out of the snow flurry Korp came up like a whale for air, spouted snow and shook himself to get rid of the snow in his hair and on his clothes. Ben motioned to him to stay still, pointing at the boar. Korp froze and Ben moved closer, his sword held straight out in front of him.

The boar didn't move, and finally Ben was convinced the boar was indeed dead, and he put his weapons back. He turned to Korp. "You're one lucky soldier! This one weighs twice as much as you, and he just missed you. And look at those tusks!"

"I took one step off to the side and there was no ground. I fell into that pit."

It was a young male, and Ben remembered that they hadn't eaten for a long time. He was hungry, it was dark and they couldn't get back before the morning. "Let's make camp here and make a fire; we'll have a feast of wild boar tonight."

Svenson offered to cut up the boar. "I've slaughtered many pigs at the farm. I'll just need some help to hang it from a tree." Nilsson helped him while Korp took care of the horses. They were jittery, spooked by the boar's attack, but calmed down when Korp took out their feed bags. They were in a small clearing, and Fink and Ben flattened the snow. They cut down fir branches and covered the ground in a ring. Inside the ring Ben started a fire using several dead pine branches. Soon the fire was going, providing some welcome heat. Off to the side Korp was cleaning the boar, giving the innards to Nilsson to carry away from their camp. "Just in case the wolves decide to come back," he said.

Ben replied, "They are probably far away with their stomachs full of another boar from the sounder. They wouldn't have let this one get away unless they were hot on the tail of another, something a bit smaller than this one." Ben pointed at the blood-stained tusks. "There is also a wounded wolf out there, so the pack may lie low for a while."

"I hope you're right."

"So do I, but just in case, we'll keep the fire going and take watches during the night. I'll take the first one."

Korp was finished with the inside of the boar. He pulled out his hands and said. "This looks almost like it comes from a human. Who wants the boar's heart?"

Ben looked at the dark chunk of meat in Korp's hands, once the centerpiece of a living boar. "I'll take that!"

Korp was a good butcher and soon they had boar steaks roasting on the fire. It tasted good to eat fresh meat after many months of army fare. Ben took the heart and put it on a stick next to the fire. "It first needs to dry slowly. Boar's heart is a Dutch delicacy that my mother used to cook!" He turned the stick around several times to make sure all sides got evenly heated. One by one the others turned in, while Ben stood the first fire watch. It was getting colder and he gathered more wood to keep the fire going. Apart from the crackle of the burning wood, it was quiet all around them. It was the day before Christmas.

Ben woke up Nilsson who was to take the next watch. When Nilsson came to the fire, he noticed the stick with the heart was gone. "How did it taste?" he asked.

"I don't know! I went to get wood, and when I came back, the stick had fallen onto the fire and the whole thing burned."

"Well, I can't say it seemed very appetizing."

Nilsson went off to gather more wood while Ben laid down on the branches next to the fire and pulled his blanket over himself. Safely in his saddle bag was the Queen's black box with the mourning crape neatly tied around it. He slept like a baby.

21.   Wolgast Winter

Wagons, riders, foot travelers, and gaggles of domestic animals shared the icy road into Wolgast. The ruts and holes were filled with water mixed with broken ice, and the horses walked gingerly to avoid the worst of it. They passed scores of wounded soldiers heading for the ships that would take them home to Sweden. Some couldn't walk and sat or lay covered by worn blankets on wagons that bounced up and down. The screech of wheels mixed with the moaning of men in pain. The afternoon sun was low and lit up the flat landscape ahead of them. The effluvium of struggling animals and humankind hung over the road, but as they got closer to the coast the nor'easter brought a fresh smell of salt and seaweed. It reminded Ben of his days at home and at sea, but all of that seemed so far away and long ago.

Ben led his men down the hill along the town wall to the Peene channel that divided the mainland from Usedom, the island where Gustavus Adolphus had first landed a little over two years ago, thus marking Sweden's entry into the war. He knew they were about a day behind the funeral cortege. Along the road they had heard tales of the cortege passing through a day or two ahead of them.

"There'd been coaches, wagons, cavalry, and in the middle of the long caravan was the royal hearse and the Queen's coach."

It was cold, their horses were tired, and Fink's had lost a shoe. Ben ordered them to dismount and they walked slowly down the slippery cobblestone street toward the water. They crossed the bridge to Castle Island, on the western side of the Peene channel, where the Queen had her residence in the Wolgast castle. There were Flaxen Guard sentries at the gate and Byske greeted Ben, "Fogel, glad you're back! The Colonel wants to see you as soon as you arrive."

"Thank you, I'll go directly. Where is he?"

"In his quarters, I'll send a man with you."

They took their horses to the stable, and Ben opened his saddlebag to bring out the Queen's box. He turned to his men and said, "Take care of the horses, and then find your quarters. You've earned a rest."

He looked at his horse, "Oh, and bring my gear with you. I'll find you later." He turned to Byske's man, "Let's go find the Colonel."

Von Lans' quarters were high in the main building of the castle. The soldier brought Ben upstairs and left him as he knocked on the door.

"Enter!"

Ben opened the door and stepped inside. The large room was furnished with two groups with sofas, armchairs, and little tables scattered around. There were two windows, framed by heavy blue curtains, through which he could see the Peene channel and Usedom toward the east. There was an oak desk at one of the windows, covered with piles of documents. On the right was a door leading to another room; von Lans was coming through the door and behind him Ben saw a wide bed with a golden canopy against the wall. There was a black ladies' cloak and a silvery scarf on the bed.

Von Lans closed the door behind him. Ben saluted and von Lans returned the greeting and said, "Fogel, I'm glad to see you're back with us. How did it go?"

"Fine, Sir." He hesitated, "I think."

"Tell me!"

Ben told him everything that had happened, about the wolf pack and the boar that nearly killed Korp. He didn't leave anything out, and when he was finished he handed the Queen's box to von Lans and said, "Here it is, Sir."

Von Lans took the box and sat down at the desk. He offered Ben a chair on the other side of the desk. "Sit down, Sergeant, you must be tired, and I need some time to think." He opened the lid of the box but didn't say anything, he just stared at the contents with a look of deep concentration on his face. Finally he closed the lid, and said, "Fogel, I think you've saved the Queen a lot of grief." He stood up and looked at Ben who rose from his chair.

"Sergeant, all of this stays between you and me. I'll bring the box back to Her Majesty and explain to her that you found it near where it had fallen out of the coach." He continued, "The Queen will be very grateful to you, and I expect she'll want to thank you."

"Thank you, Sir, I understand."

"Very good! Now, you'd better report to Lieutenant Falkenberg and get settled in. The winter is upon us and I think we may be here for a while."

Ben saluted, turned around and went out through the door. Behind him a slow smile spread across von Lans' face. He rose and went back into the other room, muttering, "Miracles can still happen!"

They settled into a busy routine guarding Gustavus Adolphus's coffin and manning posts in and around the castle. The travel was over for now and some members of the cortege had to return home or move on to new duties. The first one to leave was Duchess Eleonore, escorted by Lieutenant Schumacher and his contingency of Sachsen-Weimar troops. Next Colonel Friedrich left to join Field Marshal Gustav Horn in Alsace.

Von Lans was now the ranking officer in charge of all the troops at the castle. He had the confidence of the Queen and he still reported directly to Oxenstierna. He quickly consolidated his position, and rapidly incorporated the small contingency of solders already at the castle. He negotiated with Kapitän von Lutz at Camp Martinshof for more troops. By the end of January the Flaxen Guard had doubled in size, and von Lans felt comfortable about having enough men to meet any emergency.

January went by very fast. Falkenberg assigned Ben to take charge of new arrivals and to train and equip them for their guard duty. While von Lutz could supply them with new soldiers, he had very few officers to spare and with the increased numbers Falkenberg had to delegate more duties to Ben. He was at the gate of the castle drilling new recruits, when von Lans's aide came across the courtyard.

"The Colonel wants to see you!"

"I'll be right there."

He dismissed his men, and followed the aide into the castle and upstairs to von Lans' office, the same room where he had handed over the Queen's box.

When he entered the room von Lans was at the window talking to Falkenberg, who stood next to him. Von Lans saw him enter, but held his hand up for him to wait, and continued talking to Falkenberg. Ben waited at the door. Finally the two officers stopped talking and von Lans turned, took a step into the room, and said. "Sergeant Fogel, come in!" The aide walked out and closed the door behind him.

Von Lans looked at Ben without saying anything, but then he smiled, and said. "Her Majesty wants me to express her appreciation for your work in finding the box that was so unfortunately lost on our journey."

Ben didn't know what to say, but managed to reply, "Thank you, Sir!"

"You did well, Sergeant, but there's more. As you've noticed, we've increased the size of the Guard, by bringing in more soldiers from Martinshof. We're changing our name to The Queen's Guard and Mr. Falkenberg has been promoted to Captain and will be in charge of the Guard under me. Two new Lieutenants are arriving in a couple of weeks, but we need one more."

He paused, looked directly at Ben, and continued, "You've done a good job. I've discussed this with Her Majesty, and she suggested that we should promote you. I've agreed and the Chancellor has approved that today, along with some other changes."

Von Lans took a paper from his desk and handed it to Ben. "Here is your letter of promotion to Lieutenant, signed by Her Majesty."

Ben looked puzzled. When von Lans mentioned the Queen's appreciation he hadn't known what was coming – a small present perhaps, but this was better.

"Thank you, Sir!" He took a deep breath and added, "Her Majesty is very kind, I'm most grateful to her."

Von Lans held out his hand, "Congratulations, Lieutenant, I'll pass on your thanks to Her Majesty." He shook Ben's hand, and continued, "Fogel, you'll carry on reporting to Captain Falkenberg together with the two new arrivals."

Falkenberg came forward, smiled, and shook Ben's hand, "Congratulations, Lieutenant. One of your first jobs will be to introduce the new arrivals to their work here. They're all young greenhorns who have just arrived from Sweden."

Von Lans looked at both of them, "Gentlemen, I think that's all for today. Tomorrow morning, let's have a full assembly, and I'll inform the Guard. It seems we will stay here until the spring, and then escort the Queen and the King back to Sweden."

Outside the door, Falkenberg turned to Ben and said, "Fogel, let's go find you a room in the officers' quarters and then have a schnapps to celebrate our promotions."

There wasn't enough space for all of them at the castle, but barracks had been built outside the walls of the castle. They had been mostly empty while the King and Queen were away, but now they were very useful. Three barracks formed three sides of a square, and on the fourth side there were stables for the horses. The courtyard in the middle was protected from the wind that blew in from the Baltic Sea, but during storms, the barracks shook in the wind, and damp, cold air seeped through the walls.

Ben didn't see much of von Lans, who left the day-to-day running of the Guard to his officers. The Queen had many demands, and von Lans became the conduit for executing her requests. A lot of this had to do with her late husband's appearances and whereabouts. She ordered new clothes and new riding boots with silver spurs for Gustavus, a new coffin made of tin, and even a new crown for the dead monarch. The new coffin was very heavy, and the morning it arrived, Falkenberg ordered the men to move it from the delivery wagon to the hall where Gustavus' body lay. Four of them couldn't budge it and they had to ask for more men. Finally they managed to get the coffin through the door, and onto two trestles in the hall. Ben turned to Falkenberg and said, "Captain, I think we'll need to get a new hearse. The old one may collapse under this weight, especially when we put the King in this coffin."

"You're right! I'll talk to Mr. Rubin."

Ernst Rubin had just arrived from Erfurt. He had been sent by Heidelman to manage the Queen's finances. Oxenstierna and Heidelman were concerned that Maria Eleonora would go on a spending spree, and Rubin's job would be quite delicate. He brought a letter of introduction from Oxenstierna to the Queen, which he tried to deliver personally on the day of his arrival. The Queen was not in a mood to see anyone, so Rubin sought out von Lans for his advice, and von Lans promised to deliver the letter and make sure Rubin could see the Queen as soon as possible. It would take a month before she would receive him.

Falkenberg found Rubin in his office and relayed the request for a sturdier wagon. The paymaster listened to him and replied, "The Queen has already asked for a better hearse, one that is more dignified and elegant, where you can remove the top for display of the royal coffin. She doesn't think the one we have is suitable for a King of such distinction."

He grimaced and continued, "The clothes and the coffin already cost a fortune, and this catafalque will cost even more."

He sighed, "Can you refurbish the old one?"

135

"I don't think that's possible. It's been traveling a long way and is in bad shape."

"Hm! Well, can you please bring the wagon maker here so we can talk to him. We'll try to hold the costs down."

Rubin's face lit up, "Perhaps we should put a collection box at the door and let the people pay to see him."

The Queen got her way. Gustavus Adolphus's embalmed body was spruced up with new clothing, and the tin coffin was decorated with his monogram, the Vasa lion coat-of-arms, crowns, and serpentine vines, all painted in gold. When the lid was open, the inside displayed three crowns embroidered with golden threads on the blue velvet background. Gustavus was made up and puffed up to look almost alive, just sleeping on his way home. The new hearse was magnificent, even Rubin had to admit that. The inside was like a fine room with polished wooden floors, pale yellow silk wall coverings adorned with Swedish crowns, and blue curtains around the windows. The outside was painted shiny black, and there was room for two coachmen on the front seat and two footmen standing at the back. Special mourning uniforms in black were made for the coachmen and the footmen. The hearse was to be drawn by six horses, and when Rubin saw the bill for the horses, he almost hit the ceiling. The Queen had insisted on perfectly matching black horses with two spares.

The Queen ordered the castle to be swathed in black together with the Swedish flag colors of yellow and blue. Curtains were changed, mourning crape put over the doors. Instead of flowers, tree branches were put in large vases and the black crape hung over them and tied around the vase with yellow and blue ribbons. All flags were at half staff, and every Guard member was ordered to wear a black armband. The household servants were already dressed in black, and the Queen herself never went out without a long black veil draped over her head and covering her face.

It took a lot of money, and almost all of von Lans' time. The Queen's chamberlain, Mr. von Pentz, arrived from Erfurt a couple of weeks after the cortege, and the two of them plus the paymaster, Mr. Rubin, were constantly trying to negotiate the Queen's demands. Not until the end of February did things quiet down, as the workers and artisans had finished most of the Queen's tasks. The coffin seamstresses had finished all the inside decorations, and in early March, Gustavus's body, dressed in his new clothes, was put on the soft mattress in the tin coffin. New oak trestles had been made to hold the weight of the King and the coffin. It was placed in the castle hall, where a cluster of flags was placed behind the coffin. There was a large yellow and blue Swedish flag at each end, and in the middle another, this one with three tails and a large GAII monogram at the center of the yellow cross. In between there were the flags of the house of Vasa, the duchies of Brandenburg and Sachsen-Weimar as well as several army standards.

While all the work was going on, the castle hall was very busy and noisy with people coming and going. Every once in a while the Queen would enter the room – she generally came unannounced, escorted by her ladies-in-waiting, but sometimes von Lans or Mr. Rubin would be with her. When she entered the hall, the people in the hall would hush one by one, and soon all you could hear were the footfalls of the Queen and her company as they walked up to the coffin. Often she would have instructions for von Lans or Mr. Rubin, but sometimes she would just come in and sit by the coffin for a little while, then leave. Those times she didn't seem to notice the other people in the hall, nor did she notice when most of them withdrew.

22.   Baltic Spring

Apart from allowing him to change his quarters, the promotion brought few changes in Ben's work. He and Falkenberg divided the Guard between them, and his days were filled with all the details of schedules, duty rosters, and training new recruits. His days were long, but whenever he could, he went to the castle kitchen to see Emilia. Mr. von Pentz was back in charge of the household, Mrs. Hahn was cooking, and Emilia worked as a maid. It was almost like being back in Erfurt. Emilia was always happy to see him, and they talked and laughed albeit the mood was subdued by the household being in mourning.

It was the end of March. They had moved Gustavus to his new coffin in the castle hall, all the arrangements were finished, and guards were posted day and night around the coffin. Ben had inspected the hall, and was on his way out of the hall into the courtyard when he was met by Korp. "Lieutenant, two new officers have arrived. I tried to find Captain Falkenberg, but he is in Wolgast with the Colonel."

"That's fine, I'll go and see them."

Two young men were waiting in the officer's lounge. It wasn't a grand room with a view over the sea, but a small, comfortable room facing the courtyard. It had been furnished with several armchairs and sofas, and there were bookcases along the wall opposite the windows. In the winter the sun never got over the castle wall across the courtyard to shine into the room, except occasionally by reflections from a window in the tower. On a table by the window, a steward was setting out glasses and bottles of wine, beer, aquavit, brandy, and other spirits.

Ben walked over to the two men, who got up. "Welcome to Wolgast!" he said, "Captain Falkenberg is away for the day, but I'm Lieutenant Ben Fogel."

The shorter of the two men spoke. "Erik af Portman," he said with a nasal voice that emanated from sinus cavities somewhere behind his eyes. He bowed his head slightly, and added, "Baron Erik af Portman," and his eyebrows applauded his sinuses.

The other man introduced himself, "Lieutenant Jan Walden." His voice was no match for af Portman's, but it was clear with a touch of dialect.

"Glad you're here, we need you. The Guard has doubled in size and the Captain and I have been working long hours to cope with the increased workload."

Walden asked, "What about the Colonel?"

"He spends most of his time negotiating with the Queen, who wants the absolute best – and most expensive – for the King. She comes up with new ideas every week, and the Colonel is in between her and the Chancellor. It's a very delicate job, and he leaves the day-to-day running of the Guard to Captain Falkenberg."

While he spoke, af Portman had gotten up and walked over to the window. Ben didn't quite know what it was, but there was something that bothered him about the man. Af Portman was looking out the window, his eyebrows slightly raised and there was a touch of a smirk on his face, when he smiled and said, "Look out there, there is one for me."

Ben came over to the window to see what he was looking at, there was Emilia. Reflected sunlight from a window lit up her face and hair as she crossed the courtyard on her way to the kitchen. Af Portman, oblivious of the darkness that came over Ben's face, smirked, "I bet it won't take me long to get between her legs. Heh – heh!"

His raw laugh reminded Ben of the crows on the dead horse at the roadside. Ben looked him and saw eyes with no warmth or laughter in them, only cold disdain, boredom, and arrogance. Ben, his anger rising, walked up to him, "Oh, no, you don't! She is too young. If you want whores, just cross the bridge to Wolgast. There are plenty of bars were you can find what you want."

Af Portman looked at Ben, as if he had just discovered him standing there, "Sorry, brother, I didn't realize you had an interest." He walked back to the sofa, sat down and continued, "I may follow up your advice about the bars in Wolgast."

It got very quiet in the room, but finally Walden broke the silence, "Well, Fogel, tell us what's it like here?" Ben, his anger subsiding, began to tell them about the Guard and the duties at the castle. Both men listened, but Walden asked most of the questions. Af Portman was polite but distant. After about an hour Ben said, "I must go back to the hall, but the steward will show you to your rooms, and bring your luggage. Captain Falkenberg will see you in the morning." He rose, said "I'll see you at dinner!" and left the room.

With Gustavus on lit-de-parade in all his splendor in the castle hall, von Lans expected things to be quiet for a while. He was wrong.

Many visitors started to arrive, some were invited, and some just dropped in, but they all came to pay their respects, or so they said. Nobility from the nearby duchies, big landowners, rich merchants, clergy, and sycophants in general – they all came to call. They paraded past the coffin, gawked at the Guard, inspected the flags, stretched out their hands to test the quality of the cloth and freshness of the flowers. Some were quiet and stood silently at the bier, others walked by, chatting with each other as if they were on a Sunday stroll. They brought little tokens and placed them at the foot of the bier – every night the Guard had to clear up the day's collection.

Officers from everywhere came to stand at attention, saluting their dead commander; many brought their regimental standards to be added to the collections of flags. It was seldom quiet around the dead monarch, and outside the castle courtyard sometimes resembled a busy market place. The visitors came by horse or by coach, and the traffic in and out of the yard was heavy. Falkenberg went to von Lans and proposed they should set up a holding area outside the castle walls near the stables and to hire more stable hands to help the visitors with water and feed for their horses. When von Lans brought the case to Rubin, he protested the extra expense, but von Lans took him for a stroll across the courtyard. When they came to the castle gate, Rubin's boots were soaked by the muck in the courtyard, and a coach coming through the gate made a wave that splashed more slush over the bottom of his trousers. Rubin quickly agreed to the expense, but muttered to himself, "We should charge an entrance fee."

The days grew longer, the sun rose higher and higher, and around spring equinox rays of sunshine came over the castle walls and began to warm up the courtyard during the middle of the day. Von Lans and Rubin were standing in the Queen's parlor; Maria Eleonora was sitting at her desk. She was dressed in her usual black, but without her veil. The

140

curtains behind here were drawn, but a small crack between the curtains let through a ray of sunshine that fell on a lute that was on the chair next to her. Von Lans knew that Maria Eleonora played the lute well. She used to play a lot in Erfurt, but she hadn't touched the lute since her husband died.

"Gentlemen, I would like to move the King to the church in Wolgast, where the citizens can pay their respect. I've written to the Bishop and he has agreed, and now I want you to arrange a procession from the castle to the church."

Von Lans nodded, "Very well, Your Highness."

"I want to have two kettledrums at the head of the procession, and I'll follow the hearse in my coach. The rest you can arrange as you see fit."

They discussed some of the minor details, and then the two men left the room. The Queen was still silently sitting at her desk, pensive and seemingly deep in thought.

Closing the door to the parlor behind him, Rubin turned to von Lans, "More expenses!"

"Yes, but this isn't so bad, and things will be a bit quieter here at the castle." He added, "But maybe you should consider charging that entrance fee you've been talking about."

Rubin's face lit up, "I know! We'll have a collection box at the church door, where the pious can pay tribute. We'll share the take with the church." Encouraged by his own brilliant idea, he sped off to write a letter to the Bishop.

Gustavus's visit to the Wolgast church went without a hitch. They had a problem finding trained kettledrum players but got help from the Duke of Pomerania who sent some of his own musicians. The streets and markets near the church were cleared of beggars and peddlers, and the cobblestones were swept before the procession started from Castle Island. In the church, Guard platoons took turns at the bier, and the citizens of Wolgast faithfully came by to view the pageant. Rubin was very happy; he told von Lans afterwards that the event paid for itself through the collections.

The King was safely back in the castle hall when Maria Eleonora called von Lans with new orders. Ben was in the officer's lounge with Walden when Falkenberg came into the room.

"I've just had word from the Colonel. Her Majesty wants to put on a banquet in the hall."

"A banquet?"

"Yes, but it will be a very solemn affair, a sort of a memorial State dinner with Gustavus as the silent host."

Falkenberg continued, "Mr. von Pentz will make the dinner arrangements, but we'll need Guards around the hall and around the castle."

Walden shook his head, "For being dead, the King is very busy."

Falkenberg didn't smile, "Another thing, a girl was found dead in the canal yesterday. It looked like she had been beaten badly before ending up in the water. Most likely she worked at one of the taverns in the harbor. Ask your men if they've seen or heard anything. I'll ask af Portman to do the same."

They all knew that it was unlikely they would find out anything, and Ben thought, "Another life disappears into the sea of dead – so many dead – what a waste." A shiver passed over him.

Over in his office, Von Lans was talking to Rubin, "This is a relatively small affair. The Queen is inviting a few people from Pomerania and Brandenburg. She wants the Chancellor to attend, but he's too busy in Heilbronn negotiating with the Germans."

Rubin frowned and replied, "But it's still a State dinner, and that means it'll be a lavish affair – and expensive." He added, "The King should be taken home, and given a proper funeral. Then we can stop worrying about the Queen's spending. What does the Chancellor think?"

Von Lans wrote regularly to Oxenstierna, who, with the King gone and Crown Princess Christina still a child, was the effective head of the government and represented Sweden in all of Germany. He replied, "He wants us to go back to Sweden as soon as possible, and I've just received word that ships will be sent to take the whole funeral party. We should be able to leave Wolgast in a couple of months."

"Good! Perhaps this dinner will mark the end of our stay in Pomerania. When will it be?"

"In the beginning of June."

The dinner was a quiet affair by royal standards, with only about a hundred guests. The guest of honor was Maria Eleonora's brother Prince Georg, Margrave of Brandenburg. The Duke of Pomerania, Bogislaw XIV was invited, but he was in poor health and sent his nephew Baron Ernst Bogislaw von Croy instead. Duke Wilhelm of Sachsen-Weimar and his wife were also invited but only Duchess Eleonore could come. Her husband had to stay back for the talks with Oxenstierna.

The preparations for the dinner kept everybody very busy. Ben hardly saw Emilia. He was busy organizing the guard for the occasion. Emilia was running around helping with setting up accommodations for those guests, and their servants, who would stay in the castle. Other guests would stay in Wolgast or nearby towns. Af Portman was sent with a group to Martinshof to find army tents for the coachmen, who wanted to be near their horses.

Ben's relationship with af Portman was a bit uneasy. They were very correct with each other, but tension hung in the air. Af Portman was the son of a high official in Stockholm, and he made no bones about the fact that he thought both Ben and Walden were well beneath him in the social hierarchy. He let it slip that servants were just a step above domestic animals, and once when he had had a bit too much to drink, he boasted about how he had "broken in the new maids" at his father's house. Ben was no prude. They all went to the fleshpots in Wolgast now and then, but he didn't like the way af Portman boasted about his conquests; there was a sinister quality to it. Ben suspected that the man had a special liking for humiliating any woman that came his way.

Walden was different, easygoing and with a knack for seeing the funny sides of people and things. He came from Sörmland, a province just south of Stockholm, where his father had a good-sized farm. Ben got along well with him, and on slow evenings when af Portman was duty officer, the two of them would go into Wolgast for a drink. Walden was very popular with the girls, and they had no problems in finding company. Sometimes they ended up in a couple of rooms upstairs from the bar, each in bed with a girl, and Ben would hear giggling and booming laughter from Walden's side of the wall.

Maria Eleonora had decided that Gustavus should be present at the dinner, and they had moved the bier with the coffin to the end of the hall so that the side faced the hall and all the dinner guests. Flags were put behind the coffin and along the wall, and there were fresh spring flowers on top of the coffin and in vases around it. Ben had been assigned the first watch and he placed two Guardsmen behind the coffin and two at either end. He and all the men had received brand-new uniforms from the camp store in Martinshof the day before. The men had pikes and the officers wore sabers that had been requisitioned for the occasion; the polished steel glistened in the evening light. In the corner to the left of the coffin, a timpanist had set up his kettledrums; he had put soft leather covers on the drum skins to mute them. Next to him a lute player was fingering his strings. Waiters were lined up along the left wall.

Mr. von Pentz stood in front of the waiters, dressed in his chamberlain uniform. He looked at his clock, and signaled for silence, and when the room was still, he nodded to Ben. On the stroke of six, two Guardsmen opened the door to the hall and stepped to the sides so the guests could enter. The Queen came first, on the arm of her brother. Behind them the guests formed a procession that slowly proceeded along the right side of the hall. The men wore uniforms with black armbands, and the women wore long black dresses. Scattered throughout the procession there were aides and servants, also in black, carrying wreaths and bouquets of flowers.

The timpanist struck the first muted note on the kettledrums and the lute followed with a long soft chord. With the slow haunting music in the background, the march proceeded along the side of the hall, turning at the bier. The Queen and her brother stopped by the side of the coffin and Prince George's aide brought a large wreath wrapped in ribbons with the Brandenburg colors, which the Prince placed on a stand in front of the coffin. He stood up, raised his hand to a slow salute, then took his sister's arm as they continued to their places at the head of the table, where waiters held their chairs ready.

On by one the guests filed past the dead King, placing their wreaths and flowers at the foot of the bier. There were officers, Swedish, Finnish, German, Scottish, and others in uniforms Ben had never seen. There were gentry from Brandenburg and Pomerania, the mayors of Wolgast and other towns with chains of office around their necks, landowners whose country origins were betrayed by their rough, reddened hands and stout wives, and clergy in white robes. Some guests stood out; one man had designed his own uniform with a black tri-corner hat with yellow edges, a long blue frock over a yellow vest, and shining black boots. Next to him was a woman, her face painted white, sharply contrasting with her black fur cape and the shimmering peacock feathers hanging from her dark hair. An old gentleman with long white hair and a hand that wouldn't stop shaking was on a rolling chair pushed by his valet.

Von Lans was last in the procession. He was accompanied by two Guardsmen carrying crosses made from green pine branches. Blue and yellow ribbons were tied around the crosses. Ben knew they came from Chancellor Oxenstierna and Field Marshal Horn. When von Lans had filed past the bier and paid his tributes to Gustavus, he sat down, and von Pentz directed the waiters to start serving. The timpanist faded the kettledrums leaving only the lutenist playing, the plaintive notes waning along their flight around the hall.

It began as a solemn affair, but as the night wore on and the guests relaxed from the food and the wine, the conversation picked up and the noise level increased. Speeches were given praising Gustavus, and when dessert had been served, Prince Georg waived von Pentz over and whispered something into his ear. Von Pentz nodded and walked over to the timpanist with a message. The musician picked up his mallets, and when Prince Georg, somewhat unsteady on his feet from the wine, rose from his chair, a long rising kettledrum roll rumbled through the hall. Conversations stopped, heads turned and the hall quieted down as everybody turned their attention to the prince.

He spoke eloquently about Gustavus, and praised Maria Eleonora for arranging the banquet. His initial manner was grave and earnest, but when he came to the end, he said, "I want to propose a toast, not only to our hostess, but to Gustavus whose demise is very untimely. We're still drinking his wine, and he's still with us, if not in spiritus, at least in corpus."

Everybody rose, the Prince turned to the coffin at the end of the hall and raised his glass, "Skål Gustavus! Thank you – farewell – and may your sea journey home be calm and swift."

The hall was dead silent while they drank their toast, raised their glasses again toward the coffin, and sat down. A moment went by, and then slowly the conversation started up again. Maria Eleonora patted her brother on the cheek, and whispered something to him. He smiled and put his hand over hers.

Ben joined Falkenberg outside in the courtyard; the last guests had just left the hall. His men were still posted at the coffin, but they would soon be relieved by Walden's platoon. In the hall the waiters and servants were clearing the tables, and Walden's men would move the coffin back to the center of the hall and rearrange the flags and all the tributes around it.

Inside the courtyard walls, they could only imagine the rosy sky in the northwest where the sun had dipped below the horizon. Above them the June sky was still light, but the walls of the courtyard were high and inside it was just twilight. Something moved in the shadows across the courtyard by the servant's entrance. Then Ben heard Emilia's voice.

"Let me go! Don't do uhmm….!"

He couldn't make out the last part, but it sounded as if she was choking. Ben ran across the yard, his saber clanging against the ground. He still couldn't see what was going on, but the shadows moved and dissolved into two, one of them disappearing into the darkness around the corner of the building. The other was sinking to the ground and when Ben came closer, he saw Emilia. She was sitting on the ground, coughing, her coat was pulled back, pinning her arms down, and the top of her dress was torn. He called out, "Emilia, are you hurt? What happened?"

She was shaking, and continued to cough while she was trying to regain her breath. Ben crouched down next to her and helped her get her coat back on to free her hands. He put his arms around her, and held her. Slowly she calmed down, the cough stopped and she began to breathe normally. Ben waited while she recovered, and then asked again, "What happened?"

"Somebody grabbed me. He pulled down my coat and put a hand over my mouth. I couldn't breathe."

"Do you know who it was?"

"No, I couldn't see him, but he smelled of drink and something else I've never smelt before – maybe some strange tobacco."

Falkenberg and two Guards had arrived at the scene, and now Falkenberg ordered, "Search the yard and the surroundings!" The two men unsheathed their sabers and left.

Around the corner the shadow moved, for a fleeting moment a ray of light, seen by none, fell on a figure with a contorted face, looking anxiously around. He moved and darkness swallowed him as he muttered, "I'll break that wench yet!"

The Guardsmen found no trace of any intruder, but he seemed to have vanished in thin air. Falkenberg had immediately ordered more Guardsmen to be posted in and around the castle, but as the guests and their entourage left, things slowed down and began to go back to normal. Emilia was not physically hurt, but she was still shaken by the experience. Ben went over to see her whenever he could. She was anxious and nervous, particularly about going out alone, but as the weeks went by her courage grew.

A week after the banquet, Maria Eleonora sent for von Lans; she was sitting at her desk by the window when he arrived. The servants had opened the window a crack, a mild summer breeze lifted the black mourning crape around the window and it fluttered gently. She returned his greeting with a nod, and said, "Colonel, you know that the Chancellor wants me to go back to Sweden. I've agreed, and I want you to make the arrangements."

Von Lans was well aware of not only Oxenstierna's wish for a speedy departure, but also that the Parliament in Stockholm was demanding the return of Gustavus for burial and closure. He replied, "Yes, Your Highness. We should have two naval ships arriving sometime in the next two weeks, and we could leave in the middle of July when the weather is good."

"I want the King to make a dignified departure."

Von Lans thought for a while before he replied, "The largest ship is Stora Nyckeln, a navy man-of-war. She'll have to anchor at the roadstead north of Wolgast. We'll bring the King in a procession from the castle to the departure wharf and from there by tender to Stora Nyckeln."

It was a hectic time for everybody, but in the middle of July the funeral procession that had rested in Wolgast for six months continued the final miles on Pomeranian soil. The royal hearse, the Queen's coach, the cavalry Guardsmen, followed by the Queen's household moved through Wolgast and through the gates in the town wall. They were preceded by a cavalry band of two timpanists with their kettledrums and a dozen trumpet players playing long flourish trumpets decorated with Swedish naval flags. Behind the cortege the people of Wolgast gathered. They wanted to see the end of the spectacle and followed the procession to the point of departure.

At the roadstead two ships were anchored, their bows into the light wind. The man-of-war Stora Nyckeln was closest to land and behind her Ben could see a smaller pinnace. He recognized it as the same ship he had seen going north when he first arrived in Pomerania; her name was Calmare Nyckel. Ben knew she would escort the man-of-war and bring extra freight for the Queen's household, servants, and a contingent of the Guard. The week before, Emilia had told him that she would come to Sweden with Mrs. Hahn. "I'm so glad," she said. "I want to get away from this horrible war." She and Mrs. Hahn would travel on the pinnace, and Ben was happy when von Lans assigned him and his men to the smaller ship.

A company of musketeers waited at the newly-built dock, but before the final salute was given, several speeches were held. A chair had been brought for Maria Eleonora, who was sitting next to the open hearse. The last speaker, the Bishop of Pomerania, concluded by turning directly to the Queen, "Farewell, Your Majesty, may God receive the Midnight Lion in glory, may He bless you and your daughter, and may He guide you on your journey."

The musketeers raised their weapons skywards and gave a salute. The coffin was transferred to a tender to be rowed out to Stora Nyckeln. Other tenders took the Queen and all the others that were going with her. Not until both the coffin and the Queen were safely aboard the man-of-war did the tenders return to embark the rest of the passengers and to load the freight. It took them several hours to finish. By the time everybody was aboard and everything loaded and secure it was getting dark, so they stayed at anchor.

At sunrise the seas were still calm, but around mid-morning a breeze started to blow. The two ships weighed anchor one after another. Stora Nyckeln led the way, and slowly the light southerly wind began pushing the two ships north toward the Baltic Sea. At the dock, people were clearing up from yesterday, and down by the water an old man and a woman were cutting reeds, tying them in bundles they could carry to the market. As the ships began to move, they saw a puff of smoke coming from Stora Nyckeln's portside followed by a loud "Boom!" from the cannon. Another puff came from Calmare Nyckel and the sound of her gun echoed the man-of-war's.

The weather was mostly good, the winds moderate and warm. Now and then the summer heat would bring a squall, but they never lasted long. Calmare Nyckel was a fast ship and she could easily have overtaken Stora Nyckeln, but her orders were to escort the royal ship and she stayed close behind it.

Ben and Emilia had very little to do, and they often sat on deck with the other passengers, talking and watching the sky and the sea. One evening as the sun sank below the horizon in the northwest they stayed up until a golden hue began to glow in the northeast. Around midnight the black sky was lit up by millions of stars. Suddenly one fell down toward earth – then another, and another. A shower of bright flashes fell into the sea ahead of them. Emilia called out, "Look, it must be a sign!"

"What kind of a sign?"

"Mrs. Hahn says that the King's death has angered God, and that he is giving us many signs of his wrath. She says that many cows have miscar-

148

ried, and houses have burned. Maybe this ship will go under." She moved closer to Ben and put her arms around his chest, "I'm frightened."

Ben, who to Emilia's great frustration, still thought of her as his little sister rather than a pretty young woman, put his arms around her and said, "Don't worry, I've seen stars falling before. Next time you see one, make a wish instead."

It took two weeks to reach their destination in Sweden, and in early August they landed in Nyköping, on the coast about seventy miles south of Stockholm. Standing at the railing as the Captain ordered the anchor to be lowered, Ben turned to Emilia, "I've only been away for a year, but it feels like a lifetime."

She replied, "I've never been this far away."

The ship's anchor grabbed hold, the chain tightened, and Calmare Nyckel swung gently around to face the dying wind. Tomorrow they would disembark and accompany Gustavus Adolphus on his return to Sweden. But that was tomorrow, and for now Ben was happy to be away from the war. His visit to Germany was over.

23.   The New World

I n July 1636, three years later, Axel Oxenstierna returned to Sweden. The war in Germany was in its eighteenth year and there was no sign of peace; the Swedes under Field Marshal Horn and Duke Bernhard had lost badly at Nördlingen two years ago to the Catholic imperial army under two Ferdinands, one the Archduke and the other his cousin the Cardinal-Infante. Over ten thousand Protestant soldiers had died. Horn had been captured and was still imprisoned in Bavaria. The Heilbronn treaty had been torn up, and Sachsen had entered into a treaty with the Catholic side. The war was not going well for the Swedes.

In October things looked up when word came from Germany about another big battle. It began as a shadow dance of armies roving around the countryside east of the river Elbe, a fleeting encounter near Werben, and finally a head-on confrontation at Wittstock. This time Sweden's General Johan Banér turned the tables and brought victory. The balance of power shifted once again, and Sweden was still a major power in Europe.

Gustavus Adolphus had finally been buried at the Knight's Church in Stockholm. The funeral was delayed because Maria Eleonora had insisted in keeping him with her for another year. Finally she let go, and a grand funeral cortege left Nyköping heading north. She hadn't yet given up the box with the heart, and after the funeral when the body had been finally placed in the marble sarcophagus, she insisted that she still be allowed to visit. Oxenstierna refused, and also asked that she should release the box. Eventually she had hesitatingly agreed, and the Midnight Lion was united with his Pomeranian heart. The lid of the sarcophagus was sealed.

Von Lans continued to work for Oxenstierna after the funeral. He'd been back and forth to Germany several times, but now that the Chancellor was back in Sweden, he spent most of his time in Stockholm.

The Queen's Guard had been assigned to the royal palace, but Falkenberg took care of the day-to-day duties of the Guard, leaving von Lans free to do the Chancellor's bidding.

In late October, a courier came to see him. He introduced himself as Lieutenant Arnem, and told von Lans that the Chancellor wanted to see him at his residence at Tidö. Wherever he was, Oxenstierna had regular courier service with Stockholm. Tidö was about sixty miles from Stockholm and a couple of small fast ketches sailed back and forth along Lake Mälaren with his mail. Von Lans asked Arnem, "When is the next mail boat?"

"Tomorrow morning, Sir. We can leave at six."

"I'll be there."

"Very well, Sir."

A strong northerly wind blew all through the night. The windows in von Lans' bedroom squeaked and moaned, and he didn't get much sleep. In the morning the wind was still blowing, and as he arrived at the stone wharf below the Knight's Church, the coachman had a hard time keeping the spooked horses still while von Lans stepped out of the coach. It was before dawn, but the mail boat was ready at the wharf, and he was greeted by Lieutenant Arnem, "Good morning Sir, we'll leave right away."

"But it's dark!"

"That's alright Sir, we have beacons to guide us, and it'll soon be light."

Von Lans looked out over the water. There were flickering lights here and there, but mostly it looked inky dark. He heard the waves splashing and the stays were humming in the wind. "Very well," he said and walked down the gangway. He handed his satchel to a sailor and followed Arnem, who led the way forward over the deck and down into a cabin. There was a lantern hanging from the ceiling above a table, and the light moved around the cabin as the ketch moved. On the port side there was a wooden stove and a counter, on the starboard side a closet, and on each side there was a long bench. There was a bulkhead with a door in the middle beyond the benches. Von Lans could see another smaller cabin with two bunks. The sailor put the satchel on the floor in the forward cabin and went back on deck. Arnem pointed to the cabin and said, "The forward cabin is for you, Sir. It may get a bit rough, from time to time, and you may be more comfortable in there."

"Thank you, Lieutenant, I think I may try to catch up on some sleep first. Then I'll join you on deck."

"Very good, Sir! We'll be under way soon." He walked past von Lans to the stairs, climbed up on deck, and closed the door behind him.

Von Lans slept for a few hours as the boat left the harbor, despite the boat's pitching and rolling. When he woke up it was light outside. The wind was still strong but the sky was clear and sunlight came in through the portholes. He got up, put on his coat and boots and climbed up on deck. He waved to the crew at the stern and, holding on to the railing and stays, he walked along the pitching deck up to the skylight over the forward cabin and sat down.

They had been crossing a large open bay, and were approaching a channel winding its way between several large islands. The wind subsided as they entered the channel, the pitching stopped, the force on the sails lessened, and the ketch leveled out. It got quieter as they sailed along the shores, and von Lans could let go of his handholds. The low October sun was shining along the water on the wooded shores, the light disappearing into bare branches, which the high wind had robbed of their last leaves. Now and then white stumps from beaver cuts at water's edge were lit up against the background of dark green fir trees. They passed small fields ringed by stone rows, and fields that had been cleared one stone at a time by generations of tenant farmers. There were small boats at the shore and nets hung out to dry; fishing was a way of adding food to the table or earning extra money at the market.

The cook came over with a steaming cup, "Here's some soup and bread, Sir."

"Thank you, sailor." Von Lans was hungry and the warm soup felt good in the chilly air.

The scene changed as the next islands rose with rock sides straight out of the water, and a stone quarry interrupted the natural shoreline. Von Lans could hear the sound of stone cutters chipping away in the quarry. A ship was being loaded with stones. They passed the quarry, and the channel opened up into a wide bay. He could see the whitecaps on the waves. The ketch heeled as the wind picked up, and their speed increased.

They made good headway, but when darkness came, they had to slow down and finally Arnem called a halt in a sheltered bay and ordered the anchor down. "It's just too dark," he said, "but we'll be there by midday

152

tomorrow." The cook prepared dinner, and an hour later von Lans was sound asleep.

Oxenstierna was very proud of Tidö. It was no palace, but with more than forty rooms, there was plenty of space to accommodate both family and the Chancellor's many visitors. A small coach drawn by one horse was waiting for them at the end of a long pier. Von Lans was on deck watching the landing maneuvers. All the sails but one were down and slowly they approached the end of a long pier. The last sail was let out to flap in the wind as the mail boat came to a halt, and two sailors jumped onto the dock, one from the bow and one from the stern. Each made a couple of half hitches around bollards on the pier.

Von Lans was ready to get off the boat. Arnem sent a man to get his luggage and said to him, "The coach is for you, Sir, I'll need to make sure everything is in order here before I bring the mailbags to the Chancellor."

"Thank you, Lieutenant, and thanks for the ride." Von Lans stepped ashore and went to the coach.

It was not far from the pier to the manor house, but it was uphill. Tidö was built on a rise to give its residents a good view over the lake. It was an old manor, but Oxenstierna had ordered a complete renovation. The work had started several years ago, and was still going on. There were scaffoldings and scores of workers both inside and outside. The front entrance was blocked, and the coach stopped at a side door where a valet met them. He opened the coach door and greeted von Lans. "Good morning, Baron! The Chancellor is expecting you. I'll take you directly. The footman will bring your luggage to your room."

He held the door to the manor open, and von Lans entered and waited while the valet went past him to lead the way. Von Lans followed him across wooden gangways through rooms where painters and masons were finishing walls and fireplaces. The valet said, "Please excuse the disorder, Sir, but soon we'll be in the finished part of the manor. The Chancellor is in his sitting room."

They walked through a corridor. The valet stopped and knocked on a door.

The Chancellor's voice answered, "Enter!"

The valet opened the door and announced, "Baron von Lans is here, Sir."

"Show him in!"

153

Von Lans stepped through the door; inside Oxenstierna was sitting at a table together with three other men. On the table were maps and papers, and each man had a tall glass of ale in front of him. Von Lans recognized one of the men, Admiral Clas Fleming, newly appointed Lord Mayor of Stockholm, but he didn't know the other two. Oxenstierna waved him to the table, "Von Lans, good to see you again." Von Lans walked over to the table and Oxenstierna continued, "I think you know the admiral, but I'd like to introduce you to Mr. Samuel Blommaert and Mr. Pieter Spierinck." All three men got up and shook hands with von Lans, and Oxenstierna added, "Sit down Baron." He called the valet over, "Please bring something for the Baron to drink." He looked at von Lans, "We make an excellent ale here at Tidö, and we're just trying our latest batch. Would you like some?"

"Yes, very much, thank you."

The valet brought another glass and a pitcher from a side table, poured a golden stream of ale into the glass, and put it in front of von Lans; the froth slowly rose to the rim of the glass. Oxenstierna nodded to the valet, "Thank you, that'll be all for now." The man left the room, as von Lans lifted the glass and took a swig.

"Aah – that's good!"

"I thought you'd like it."

Oxenstierna took a sip from his glass, put it down and pointed to the papers and the maps. "Baron, you may remember our first meeting, when we discussed the cost of waging war and the constant need for collecting taxes and tribute. Well, there is only so much you can take from the land, and in the long run we must have peace and commerce." He paused, got up and walked over to the window, looked out and continued, "It may take some time before we have peace, but we can still have commerce." He turned away from the window and looked directly at von Lans, "I brought you here because I want you to help us with a new project, an opportunity for Sweden to expand in the world, an opportunity to bring Sweden new income and more wealth."

He pointed to the wall and a portrait of Gustavus Adolphus, "The King was a great believer in the expansion of Swedish trade outside Europe, with Africa, Asia, and America, with some of the new colonies on these continents. For many reasons nothing has yet come of it, but now is the time to turn this idea into practical reality." His arm swept around the table, and he continued, "These gentlemen, I, and a few others

154

have formed a new company that will go to America, buy land from the natives, and establish a Swedish colony."

Von Lans had heard rumors about going to America. So far Sweden hadn't shown much interest in the New World. Most of the country's foreign trade was through others. Besides, the expansion in Europe and the participation in the war was a very large commitment. He had always thought that was the reason for why there had been so little interest in going elsewhere.

He said, "This is indeed a surprise to me." He stopped for a moment before he continued, "I must also confess that I know very little about America. Isn't it mostly wilderness, and aren't there large portions that are still unexplored?"

"Yes, but the colony will be on the eastern coast, which has been explored."

"I remember hearing about the Dutch building a new harbor city and calling it New Amsterdam."

"New Sweden will be south of New Amsterdam."

Oxenstierna's eyes lit up, "We'll have a new colony in a place where we may find gold and silver, grow sugar, spices, and tobacco, and harvest timber, all of it for trade. We'll bring merchandise from all our Swedish territories and use it for barter in New Sweden."

Blommaert broke in, "Baron, we'll start by bringing back fine furs and tobacco. Those we can sell with a good profit in Holland, Poland, and Germany, through my contacts."

"Is there land for sale, and how do you buy it?" asked von Lans.

Blommaert continued, "The man who will be in charge of starting New Sweden is Mr. Pieter Minuit. I know him well – like myself he comes from the Dutch West India Company. He bought the land that is now New Netherland from the natives, and built up the Company's trade with New Amsterdam. He knows how to do this."

Oxenstierna continued, "Baron, I have proposed to these gentlemen that you should be the government's representative for this project here in Sweden. You'd be working with Mr. Minuit and handle all the liaison between the government and the company – what do you think?"

Von Lans was trying to regain control over his reactions; this was totally new territory for him. "Colonizing America?" He hardly knew where America was. "Out west across the Atlantic somewhere."

"But," thought von Lans, "in for a penny, in for a pound." He said, "I'd be happy to do that."

"Very good! Here's what we want to do!"

24.   Emilia

I t had been three years since Emilia left Germany on Calmare Nyckel. She never hesitated about going. When Mrs. Hahn asked her if she wanted to stay with the Queen's household and go to Sweden, she decided right away to do so. The alternative was to go back to Erfurt and help her mother with the stand at the marketplace. She knew that her mother could barely make ends meet, and that Emilia would be a burden to her. She also wanted to get away from war-torn Germany and a conflict that never seemed to come to an end.

The first year in Nyköping was very hard. What had looked like a pleasant change in Wolgast became an exile existence in a small town among people that spoke nothing but Swedish. It was little comfort that all in the Queen's household felt more or less the same. Emilia cried many nights with the frustration of being in a new country. Maria Eleonora was too preoccupied with mourning her late husband to notice that her household was in turmoil.

When Gustavus Adolphus finally was moved to Stockholm and the funeral was over, the Queen decided to stay at the palace in Stockholm, and things slowly got better. With Maria Eleonora's agreement, von Lans brought in a tutor to teach the staff some Swedish. Stockholm also had a population of German and Dutch merchants with families and domestic staff. Emilia met some other girls who worked for these merchants, and she also gradually learned to speak Swedish. Now three years after her arrival, she was quite fluent even if her accent was still noticeable.

Another source of her frustration was Ben. He continued to treat her as a sister, and seemed oblivious to her hints that they should move on beyond their friendship. Since Ben was with the Queen's Guard, they saw each other often, and Ben continued to come to the kitchen, where he would sit by the table and talk while Emilia worked. When Maria Eleonora came to Stockholm, von Lans added additional men and officers, but he kept Ben, Walden and af Portman as Lieutenants of the Guard.

Although it was difficult in the close setting of the royal household, Emilia avoided af Portman. There was something about the man that bothered her – the way he looked at her. Mostly she saw arrogance, but now and then behind the conceit his eyes wandered up and down her body with raw lechery. She liked Jan Walden, he was open, friendly and laughed a lot. Ben and he had struck up a friendship, and often the three of them would get together. They would have a meal, take walks together, and in the summer they would bring a basket of food and have a picnic somewhere. Sometimes Walden would bring a girl with him. He was very popular but none of the girls had yet managed to get a grip on him for long.

It was August, tomorrow she would be nineteen, and they were planning a birthday party. First they would have dinner in the palace kitchen with all the others in the household staff. Mrs. Hahn had baked a large cake for dessert. After that Emilia, Ben, Jan and Kerstin, Walden's latest conquest, would hire a boat below the palace and row over to Lustholmen, where they knew there would be music and dancing. The island was a popular place for young people. The flat wharfs built by the navy, but not yet in use, were perfect for dancing. It usually began quietly but as the night wore on and the liquor bottles became emptier and emptier, the mood changed. Drunks would stumble into the woods and fall asleep, sometimes fights broke out, but mostly people were happy and enjoyed the evening away from the drudgery of hard work. It could get a bit unruly, but Emilia never felt threatened, since Ben was always there with her.

Lustholmen was a rocky island, much of it covered by woods, and there were several little nooks and crannies where lovers could sneak off to be by themselves. Emilia knew the place very well from other daytime visits, when they had been there on picnics. The August days were warm and clear and the heat of the day lingered long into the evenings. The light summer evenings were over, darkness fell early, but the moon would be full. Emilia thought, "Tomorrow night, Benjamin Hyeronimous, we'll go for a moonlight stroll."

For her birthday dinner she put on her best dress. One of the Queen's seamstresses had helped her to make it. It was made of linen dyed in Indigo blue. She had brought the cloth with her all the way from Erfurt, where her mother had gotten it at the Anger market. It was a plain dress with no ruffles; a bow in the back held the dress tight above her waist under a low curving neckline. Around her neck she had the amber necklace that Ben had bought for her in Prenzlau, and she wore a grey shawl over her shoulders.

She walked into the kitchen, where Ben had already arrived and was helping Mrs. Hahn put plates on the table. He said something, his back was turned to the door and Emilia couldn't hear what he said, but Mrs. Hahn broke out in a loud laugh. Emilia walked up to the table and said, "Hello!"

Ben turned around and replied, "Hello, birthday girl." He walked over to the counter by the window and picked up a bouquet of flowers, and handed them to Emilia. "Happy birthday!" He put his hands on her shoulder and leaned over to kiss her. Then something happened. He looked at her as if he saw her for the first time, hesitated a moment, smiled and pulled her closer and kissed her. It was only an instant, but the kiss lasted a little bit longer than his usually brotherly pecks, his hug was a little bit tighter than usual, and she pressed a little bit closer to him.

Ben released her gently and stretched out his arms. His hands were still on her shoulders, he looked into her eyes and said, "Emilia, you look beautiful." He let go, took her hand and led her over to the end of the table, pulled out the chair and said, "Tonight, you'll be our princess."

"Thank you, kind Sir."

The rest of the household staff arrived one by one, and Walden came with Kerstin holding on to his hand. Mrs. Hahn and one of the kitchen maids brought food and drink to the table, and they all sat down. When they had finished the first courses, the kitchen maids cleared the table and set out clean plates for dessert. Mrs. Hahn went into the cold storage room adjacent to the kitchen, and brought out her cake. She put it down in front of Emilia, put a candle in the middle, lit it, and said. "You should cut it, but first you must make a wish." She put a knife next to the cake. Emilia leaned over and blew at the candle; the flame brightened, bent over, and then went out.

"May I have some cake?"

The voice came from the door. They all turned and Mrs. Hahn replied, "Of course, child. Come here!"

The girl in the door was Christina, Gustavus and Maria Eleonora's ten-year-old daughter. As heir to the throne she had lived a very sheltered life. Her world was one of nannies and governesses and very few other children. Her mother was devoted to her, but Maria Eleonora's frequent depressions affected the child. After her father's death Christina became regent and Queen of Sweden, but until she would come of age, she was under parliamentary guardianship. In Gustavus's will he had appointed Oxenstierna to care for the girl in case of his death, and while he shared the guardian duties with four others, in practice Oxenstierna was her true guardian and the real ruler of the country.

Despite all the attention, Christina was a lonely child, and she would wander around the palace, often visiting the kitchen for a snack. Mrs. Hahn waved to the girl to come in, and Christina quickly ran up to the end of the table and took a seat next to Emilia. She looked at Emilia with a smile on her impish face.

"I want to have a big piece."

"So you shall." Emilia cut a piece of the cake and put it in front of her.

Christina had been taught manners by the best nannies, and she waited politely while all the others were served, but then she turned her attention to her piece of cake. She took a large piece and tried to put it in her mouth. It took some effort and a blob of whipped cream formed a white moustache. She laughed, wiped it off with the back of her hand. "Mama says I shouldn't do this," she said, and took another bite.

Soon she was finished. She got up, looked at Emilia and said, "Happy birthday – thank you!" and ran out the door.

Ben looked after her and said, "I wonder what will become of her?"

Mrs. Hahn replied, "I don't know, but I feel sorry for that child. First her father dies, and now her mother is not well." She sighed and added, "I heard yesterday that they may take her away from her mother."

Emilia asked, "But who will take care of her?"

"I don't know, maybe she will go back to her aunt, Countess Katarina. She took care of her while Queen Maria was in Germany."

The dinner was over, and Mrs. Hahn declined any help from Emilia. "It's your birthday." she said. "Go out, dance, and have fun with your friends." They thanked her, waved goodbye to the others and left.

160

They walked down toward the water, it was dusk and the shadow of the palace was falling on the bay between the city and Lustholmen. Down at the dock they found their rowboat. Walden looked at it, turned to Ben and said, "You're the sailor, you'd better get in first!"

"Alright!"

Ben stepped down from the dock into the rowboat. He gave Walden a line to hold and held up his hands. "Emilia, you're next. I'll catch you." He held her by the waist and helped her down into the boat. "Please sit in the back!" he said and she gingerly made her way aft. Next came Kerstin, but when she walked toward the rear, the boat shifted and she lost her balance. She reached for the railing, but missed and almost fell overboard. Ben grabbed her dress at the last moment. When she was safely seated, Walden sent down their baskets, and eased himself down into the bow where he sat down. Ben took the oars in the middle, Walden pushed off from the dock, and Ben began rowing toward Lustholmen across the bay.

The wind had died down and the evening sun came around from behind the palace. The three golden crowns on top of the palace tower glistened in the sun, a guard in the tower was getting ready to lower the flag, and the ripples behind the boat made long undulating reflections of the setting sun, lighting up the rocks and the trees on the opposite shore. A couple of young swans, their wings held high, made curlicues on the still water as they slowly swam around each other testing their newfound strength. It was quiet; the work at the old shipyard next to the palace was over for the day. Several ships were at anchor in the harbor, their anchor chains slack. A few fishing boats were on their way to bays further out, and other rowboats were heading for Lustholmen.

Emilia listened to the water rippling along the hull, and the squeaking of the oars as they grabbed hold and let go – grabbed hold and let go – grabbed hold and let go. In the middle of the bay, Ben stopped rowing and let the boat glide. It slowly came to a halt and drifted as they watched the sun sinking below the horizon. Walden, stretching out in the bow, said, "Ah, such pleasure! I wish you could hold on to moments like this."

Ben nodded, "The war seems so far away."

Emilia added, "I never want to go back."

Over at the old shipyard, in the shadows of boathouses and unfinished ships, another rowboat with only one oarsman onboard set out. It took a longer route to the other side of Lustholmen, where it landed by a grove of trees. The oarsman shoved the boat under some long branches and tied it to a tree where, in the growing darkness, you couldn't see it.

The music was already playing when they arrived, and they went directly to the dance floor next to the water on one of the docks. This evening there was a whole orchestra playing. It had two fiddlers, a lutenist, a hurdy-gurdy player, two dulcian players, and a drummer. They were playing a Polska, a Polish dance that had recently become popular in Stockholm. It was still early and the dance floor was not crowded. This was the time for the best dancers to have all the room they needed. The Polska was not fast, but it had a strong rhythm, and the dancers moved in perfect unison with the music. Jan grabbed Kerstin by the hand and went to the dance floor. Ben took Emilia's hand and they stood by the side watching the dancers. Emilia felt Ben's hand moving back and forth following the music.

The Polska was over, and the leader of the orchestra announced. "Now we'll play something new for you. It's an English dance called Longways." He paused, "That's a funny name. I think we'll just call it 'the English'."

He continued, "You'll be the first in Stockholm to try this. Here's how we'll do it. I want all the men in a line on one side and all the women in a line facing them."

They took their places and the leader showed them some simple steps and turns. They practiced a few times, and then he added the music. Ben and the others danced the English, the Polska and other dances. They danced four in a ring and two together until Emilia said, "Whew! I'm getting warm and tired. Can we pause?"

Ben took her hand and they walked off the floor. He said, "Do you want to take a little walk?"

"Yes, let's go up on top of the hill."

It had gotten dark, but the full moon cast its pale light over them and lit up the path. Ben led the way through a grove of trees up the hill to the highest point of the island. They sat down on a rock face that was still a little warm from the sun. Around them was an open area, and they could see the bay and the palace lit up by the moonlight. Beacons along the palace walls and at the top of the towers flickered in the night.

They sat close together. Ben had put his arm around Emilia's shoulders, and she curled up against him. He turned his face toward her and kissed her – slowly, slowly. Emilia put her hand behind his neck and pressed him against her. Elated, she thought, "This is what I have longed for – it's taken a long time, but here it is." Then she shivered.

Ben pulled back from the kiss and asked, "Are you cold?"

"Yes, a little bit. But I'm also very happy."

"So am I."

He put his hand on her arm, "You are cold. Where is your shawl?"

"Oh, I forgot it. It's in the boat."

"I'll go get it. It's not going to get any warmer."

Emilia sighed, "It probably would be a good idea. I can wait here."

"You're not afraid of sitting here alone?"

"No, it's a nice evening, and you'll be back soon."

"Alright then. I'll be quick."

He took off his jacket and put it over Emilia's shoulders. She pulled it tight around her and smiled at him. "Hurry back."

Ben disappeared back down the hill the way they had come. When she couldn't see him, Emilia got up; she needed to pee. She put down Ben's jacket on the ground, walked down the side of the rock, and went behind a tree at the edge of the woods, where she squatted down. When she was finished, she stood up and pulled down her dress, her back to the woods. Suddenly somebody grabbed her from behind, a hand over her mouth and another around her waist. A harsh voice said in her ear, "Hold still or I'll hurt you!"

Panic rose in her, the fear almost made her faint, adrenaline pumped out in her veins, and she tried to scream. At the back of her mind, a thought went past quickly, "I'm back in Wolgast. It's happening again." The man pulled her toward the woods. She tugged at his hand, and scratched it with her nails. Her dress got caught on a branch; she felt it tear.

"Stop it, you bitch!" The man pulled her head back, and she couldn't breathe. He continued to pull her away from the edge of the woods and in among the trees. She stumbled and fell. On her way down she grabbed at his sleeve and pulled at something cold and hard. Her head hit a rock, and then everything went black.

Ben ran down the hill to the boat where he grabbed Emilia's shawl and a bottle of water and started back up the hill. On the way he met Walden and Kerstin who were sitting on a blanket. He stopped, held up the shawl and said, "We're just out for walk, and Emilia was getting cold."

Walden replied with a grin, "Maybe you'll need a blanket? There is another one in the boat."

"Yes, that's a good idea." Ben turned around and went back to the boat to get the blanket. Then he started up the hill again, this time a little slower. He reached the top and looked over where they had been sitting. His jacket was on the ground, but nobody was there.

He called out, "I'm back."

No answer. He put down what he was carrying, picked up his jacket and put it on while he was looking around. No Emilia. He called her name again. No answer.

Where was she? A nagging feeling of worry began to spread in his mind. He thought, "She isn't in the open area, I can see that. She couldn't have gone very far, so she must be somewhere where she would get out of sight quickly." He walked over the woods and walked along the edge, calling her name. No answer.

He thought, "I'll need to go farther in, but where?" He came to the far end of the woods. He went in as far as he could see, and started walking parallel to the edge. Halfway along he saw something on the ground, it was a torn piece of Emilia's dress sleeve. He called her name again, and began walking deeper into the woods. It was so dark under the trees that he almost missed her. She was lying on the ground, her head next to a rock. When Ben knelt down beside her, he heard a noise deeper in the woods. Somebody was moving fast through the trees, but the noise faded as the person moved away from them down the hill toward the water. Ben let it go, he needed to help Emilia.

She was unconscious but breathing. She had a nasty wound on her head, and the rock next to her had blood on it. She must have fallen and hit her head. Ben didn't see any other wounds, but her dress was torn, and there were red marks around her mouth. She was on her side, her knees pulled up and her hands rested open on the ground. Ben took off his jacket again and put it over Emilia. He sat down and carefully lifted her head and put it in his lap. He held her and said, "Oh, what happened to you?"

Next to them Ben saw something glittering. It was the amber necklace, but there was also a golden button. He reached over and picked them up. He looked at his jacket sleeve; it had buttons just like the one he'd found. He sat there for a while, not sure what to do. Then Emilia screamed, and sat straight up. He grabbed her and held her, "It's alright,

I'm here." Her scream turned into a whimper, and she hid her face against his chest.

Down at water's edge, the shadowy man pulled out his boat from under the trees and slipped away.

25.   Revelation

Ben helped Emilia up to the top of the hill, where he held her while she sat down. He put his coat on and sat down next to her, wrapping a blanket around both of them. Emilia put her head against his shoulder and wept, while Ben sat quietly with his arm around her. The pale moonlight lit up the night. A thin layer of fog had formed over the water, making the buildings across the bay float like a ghost town in the air, the beacons on the palace blinking and fluttering like the eyes of spirits watching them. Emilia burrowed her face into the blanket against Ben's chest to ward off the world around her.

After a while she stopped crying and they sat silently. She put her head up and pulled the blanket around her shoulder; Ben dropped his arm to her waist and pulled her close. She looked away from him over the bay and spoke quietly, "I was so happy waiting for you to come back." Her voice trembled, "Someone grabbed me. I tried to scream but he had his hand over my mouth. He pulled me and then I fell." She paused for a moment to catch her breath. "I can't remember any more than that, but my head hurts."

Ben put his hand gently on the side of her head. "Is this where it hurts?"

"Yes, right here." She moved his hand a little.

Ben felt a wet patch and when he pulled his hand back and looked at it, there was blood on it. "It's bleeding, not much, but we better have somebody look at it. Can you get up and walk? I'll help you."

"Can we wait a little? I must tell you something – I think I know who it was."

Ben felt the heat of anger rising in him. "Who?" he asked.

Emilia was quite for a minute then she trembled. "I'm frightened," she said, "He may try again."

"Tell me – we'll make sure he can't."

"Remember the time in Wolgast?" Emilia replied.

"Yes, but that was years ago and in Pomerania, far from Stockholm."

"I think it was the same man."

"How can you tell?"

Emilia had stopped trembling. She looked at the bay where the fog was thickening into patches that floated on the water. She took a deep breath and replied, "Ever since Wolgast, I've had my suspicions that the man who attacked me was somebody I knew."

"Why didn't you tell me?"

"I wasn't really sure, and I suppose that deep down, I hoped I was mistaken."

"What made you think you knew him?"

"I don't really know for sure. He smelled of drink, but there was something else, a special tobacco maybe."

"Many men smell of tobacco."

"Yes, I know. That's what I thought at the time, so I dismissed it."

Emilia turned to Ben and looked him in the eyes. "You may think that I'm crazy, but I think it was the Lieutenant."

"Which lieutenant?"

She whispered, "Af Portman."

Ben thought to himself, "Oh, no!"

They both sat silently, Ben's mind filling with a growing rage. His eyes narrowed, and finally he said, his controlled voice like a rapier ready to slash, "I know the man is a bastard, but attacking women? How sure are you?"

Emilia replied, her voice a harsh whisper, "Whenever he's around, there is the same smell of tobacco, and he's always looks at me with those cold eyes that go up and down my body like the tongue of a giant snake."

She stopped to catch her breath and continued, "But now I'm sure. This man smelled of the same tobacco." She paused again, "And I recognized his voice."

"Damn the man!" Ben's voice had turned icy. "He's going to pay for this!"

Emilia felt a wave of fear going through her. She thought, "Ben mustn't get into trouble over this."

She said, "Be careful! His father is a very important man."

"I will. I'll talk to the Captain."

The fog patches were thinning out and slowly disappearing. They sat holding each other for a while, until Ben broke the silence, "We must get you to a doctor."

Emila held on to Ben as he helped her down the hill and back to the boat. Walden and Kerstin were on the dance floor, but came running over when they saw them. Walden called out, "What's happened? Is she hurt?"

Ben told them that Emilia had been attacked, but he left out the part about af Portman; he needed to think about this. They got back in the boat and Kerstin was sitting next to Emilia, who still had the blanket wrapped around her. Kerstin was holding her hand, and nobody said much. Ben rowed directly across the bay, and they landed below the palace. Walden jumped ashore and held the boat. He said to Ben, "Take her straight back! I'll take care of the boat." Ben and Kerstin supported Emilia up the hill to the servants' entrance into the palace.

It was late when they sat down in the kitchen. The night watchman had kept the fire in the stove going. Kerstin put water in a kettle, put it on the stove and said to Ben, "Go find the doctor! I'll help Emilia wash the wound on her head."

Ben went to get the surgeon who was on duty at the palace medical offices next to the guardhouse. The Queen's Physician in Ordinary had a small staff of army doctors, and one of them was always on duty. Ben knocked on his door and a sleepy voice answered, "Who is it?"

"It's Lieutenant Fogel, and I need your help."

"Just a moment! I'll be right with you."

The door opened and an elderly man stood in the doorway. "What's happened?"

He was Tor Nordman, an army surgeon who had served with Gustav Horn for many years. After being wounded himself and losing part of his leg, he had been sent back to Sweden. There was a rumor that Horn had pulled strings to get him the much sought-after job at the palace. He was a respected doctor, and Ben was happy to see that he was on duty.

Ben replied, "A girl has been attacked and she's hurt."

Nordman got his satchel and followed him to the kitchen. Along the way, Ben told him what had happened. Nordman listened to his story, and said, "This isn't the first case. During the last year I've been

168

called three times by the City Guard to look at other girls who have been similarly attacked. One was badly beaten."

"Have they found anybody responsible?"

"No, there are too few City Guards, their primary duty is to patrol and they're not really trained to investigate. They don't spend much time looking."

When they entered the kitchen, Emilia was sitting at the table. Kerstin had cut some of her hair around the wound, and was washing it with soap, while Walden was helping her hold back Emilia's long hair. Nordman took one look and said, "That's good, but we'll need something stronger." He brought out a bottle from his satchel and poured some aquavit on a clean cloth and applied it to Emilia's head wound.

She winced, "Ouch, that smarts!"

"Yes, but I think it cleans better."

He continued, "I'd better examine you." He looked around and added, "Everybody out!"

The others left the kitchen and went out into the hallway. A couple of candles lit up the passageway. Ben started walking up and down the passageway, Walden and Kerstin sat on a bench along the wall. When Ben passed them for the tenth time, Walden said. "Slow down, she's in good hands."

Ben stopped in front of them, "Yes, I know, but I'm so angry with myself for leaving her there. I thought she'd be perfectly safe for just a few minutes. He pounded the wall with the flat of his hand. "If I find the man who did this…!" His voice trailed off.

The door to the kitchen opened, and the doctor called them back. Emilia was resting on a wooden sofa along the kitchen wall. She had a pillow under her head and a blanket over her. Ben went over and sat next to her, and she took and held his hand. He looked at Nordman, "How is she?"

"Shaken, but apart from her head wound, fine."

The doctor added, "The cut is superficial, but her head has been hit. She may have a brain commotion and should rest. She blacked out from hitting the rock and can't remember anything after that." He looked at Emilia. "You're lucky Ben came as quickly as he did. I think the man got scared away."

Ben's eyes followed the doctor's and he squeezed Emilia's hand, "I'm so glad. How do you feel?"

"Tired."

"Well, it's late and I think we're all tired."

Kerstin offered to help Emilia to her room and settle her into her bed. Before they left Emilia gave Ben a hug and held her hand to his cheek. The doctor went back to his quarters, and Ben and Walden were left sitting at the kitchen table. It was very quiet, but Ben could still feel the effects of the evening's turmoil. He said, "I don't think I can sleep right away. Let's go have a beer, before we go to bed."

"Alright, but just one, I'm on duty tomorrow morning, and I need some sleep."

26.   Retribution

The tavern around the corner from the palace was filled with late-night drinkers, but they found a table in a corner and sat down with their tankards. The walls next to them and the steady drone of people moving and talking in the background gave Ben a sense of privacy, as if they were in a capsule floating on the murmur. Walden lifted his tankard, the beer swept down his gullet, and soon half the tankard was gone. He put it down, wiped foam from his lips, and said, "It's been a long evening. Now tell me what happened!"

Ben told him about the walk, how he'd gone to get Emilia's shawl and the blankets, and how he had found her when he came back. When he was finished he said, "I wasn't gone more than a quarter of an hour." He shook his head. "I shouldn't have left her alone! It's my fault!" His eyes filled with anguish, and he threw his head up and back so quickly that he hit the wall behind him. "Damn it!"

"Wait, slow down!" Walden reached over and put his hand on Ben's. "It's not your fault! Whoever did this is the one to blame."

He continued, "Does she have any idea of who it was?"

"Yes, but it's hard to believe….."

Ben was interrupted by a bang and a commotion at the front door. A man laughed raucously, and a woman shrilled, "Come home with me, sweetheart!"

The man laughed again. "Get off me! I need a drink!"

Ben froze in mid-sentence – that voice! He looked towards the door, shot up from the chair, knocking over his beer, and almost tripping over his own feet. Af Portman was standing there with a bedraggled woman hanging on to his arm. Ben felt a wave of anger welling up, and without really knowing what he was doing, he started toward the door. He bumped into several people along the way; they shouted at him, but he seemed not to notice. He ran right into af Portman and rammed him into the door; the woman fell and screamed. The door opened and af Portman stumbled and fell through the door into another group of people who were just about to enter the tavern.

The people scattered around them like falling skittle pins. Ben continued to push af Portman, who staggered backwards until the wall across the alley stopped him. Ben pinned him against the wall and shouted into his face. "You damned bastard, you should leave her alone!" Af Portman tried to raise his arms to ward off the attack, but Ben had a grip on his arms; neither of them could move.

Curious onlookers came out through the door, gathering around the two men. Walden had gotten up and followed Ben; he struggled through the crowd, and pushed himself in-between Ben and af Portman. "Are you crazy?" he shouted, "Stop it!"

Ben couldn't see anything but the hateful smirk mixed with fear on af Portman's face. In his head he heard the echo of Emilia's crying. He pushed harder to hold af Portman, but from somewhere a voice came through. "I said, stop it, you two." Ben let his grip go a little, and Walden pushed them farther apart, saying, "Break it up!" Other hands helped to pull the two men apart, and Ben backed off; af Portman was slumped against the wall, blood running down the side of his head.

Walden asked Ben, "What's going on?"

Ben pointed at af Portman. "He's the one who attacked Emilia!"

Af Portman touched the side of his head. He looked at the blood on his hand and said, "What are you talking about?"

"You were at Lustholmen tonight, and you attacked Emilia."

"You are deranged!"

"And it's not the first time," Ben continued.

"I haven't been to Lustholmen at all tonight."

"Let me see your hands!"

"Why?"

"Just hold out your hands! I want to see them."

Walden broke in, "Do as he says!"

Reluctantly af Portman held out his arms toward them with the palms of his hands upward. In the meantime Ben looked at his coat sleeves; a button was missing on the left one. He said, "Turn over your hands." Af Portman did as he was asked; on the right hand were two long red welts.

172

"Where did you get those?" Ben asked.

"A cat scratched me."

Ben reached into his pocket and took out the button that Emilia had given him; he held it next to af Portman's sleeve and said. "This must be yours, you're missing a button, and this matches the others."

Af Portman, who was regaining his composure, jeered. "You have exactly the same buttons, and so does he." He pointed at Walden.

"But we're not missing any!"

Walden took Ben's arm. "Let's go. This isn't helping." He pulled at his arm; Ben's anger froze him, and he didn't budge. He saw fear creeping back into af Portman's eyes. Walden pulled more insistently, and Ben turned and looked at him, nodded reluctantly, and allowed himself to be pulled away. As they walked up the alley away from the tavern, they heard another harsh derisive laugh, as af Portman swaggered back through the door into the tavern.

Ben tossed and turned in bed; his head was swimming with all the events from yesterday. He had bad dreams where Emilia's crying face was whirling around af Portman's sneer. His thoughts went round and round – what had happened? What should he do?

The next morning, Ben went to the palace kitchen, where Mrs. Hahn was busy at the stove. He asked, "Where's Emilia? Is she alright?"

Mrs. Hahn replied, "She had a bad night, but eventually she fell asleep. She is still sleeping."

"Tell her that I was here, and I'll be back later."

"I will, but how are you? I heard you were in a fight yesterday."

"News travels fast," Ben replied.

Mrs. Hahn shook her head, "Mind what you do, my boy. The lieutenant comes from a very influential family."

"I know. I'm trying to figure out how to handle it."

Ben walked down the hill to the water and continued along the docks. Across the bay at the old shipyard the morning work had begun, and he could hear the carpenters sawing and hammering. A couple of tenders were tied up at Lustholmen delivering material for the new shipyard. Along the docks next to him coastal ships were unloading and loading; goods were piled on the docks, some ready for loading, others awaiting delivery to the city. Horse-drawn delivery wagons were standing alongside. Further along, the fishermen from the many islands east of

Stockholm were selling their catches – many of them had spent several days sailing to the city.

Ben didn't notice much as he was deep in thought. He passed the southern end of the city, where the water from Lake Mälaren runs into the Baltic archipelago. He followed the lake shore back to the other side of the palace, walked up the hill and through the marketplace. When he came to the palace gate, he stopped and sat down on a bench. The late summer sunshine warmed his face, and he began to feel a measure of calmness settling over him. He had made a decision.

The guard at the gate came to attention and saluted when Ben walked through, Ben returned the salute and continued to the Guard's quarters. Captain Falkenberg was sitting at his desk when Ben knocked at his open door.

Falkenberg looked up, "Fogel, come in!"

As Ben entered the room, Falkenberg smiled and continued, "I hear you were in a scrape last night."

Ben closed the door behind him and replied, "Everybody seems to know about this, and it was only last night." He continued, "It was more than a scrape, and that's what I came to talk to you about."

"Sit down, this sounds serious."

Ben pulled out a chair and sat down opposite Falkenberg, "Here's what's happened," he began. Ben told Falkenberg all that had happened the night before at Lustholmen, how they brought her back to the palace, and that the doctor had seen her.

"How is she?" Falkenberg asked.

"Shaken, frightened, but not badly hurt. I think I came back just in time to scare him away."

"Did she recognize the man?"

"Yes, she did."

"Who is it?"

Ben took a deep breath – this was the point of no return.

"You are not going to like this. It's Lieutenant af Portman."

It was quiet in the room for minute before Falkenberg responded. "Oh, hell! Is she sure?"

"I asked her the same question, and, yes, she's sure." Ben went on to tell Falkenberg about the torn-off button, the scratches on af Portman's hand, and Emilia's suspicions that the same man had attacked her in Wolgast. He finished by saying, "She says she recognized his voice."

"He spoke to her?"

"Yes!"

Falkenberg asked, "What about the fight last night? What happened?"

"When he came into the tavern, I completely lost my temper. I confronted him, and if Walden hadn't been there, I don't know what would have happened."

"Was anybody hurt?"

"Af Portman hit his head on a stone wall."

Falkenberg sighed, "This is a mess. You're making very strong accusations, and either you're wrong, in which case you're in deep trouble, or you're right, in which case we have a very serious problem in the Guard. Either way, it's a mess."

He continued, "You know that af Portman's family is very powerful in the government. Are you sure you want to go on with this?"

Ben looked at him. "Captain, I've thought about this all night and all morning, but I keep coming back to one thing. Unless somebody does something, Emilia and maybe other girls will never be safe around here."

"Alright, write a report to me about this, and I'll take it to Colonel von Lans. In the meantime, stay away from af Portman as much as you can. I'll tell af Portman the same thing, but I'll leave it to the colonel to decide how to proceed with your accusations."

27.   Changes

A month went by and summer began to fade toward autumn. The leaves were turning, and soon they would fall; equinox arrived and the nights were rapidly getting longer and longer. Falkenberg was sitting in von Lans' office and they were talking about the attack on Emilia. Falkenberg said, "I've been talking to the head of the City Guard, Captain Andersson. He told me there've been several attacks in the last few years that have not been solved. Some of them are very similar to that on the palace maid."

"Does he have any suspects?"

"No, but they seem to have started after we returned from Pomerania."

"That could be coincidence."

"Yes, but there've been the two attacks on the girl, first in Wolgast and now this one in Sweden."

"Do you believe that af Portman is responsible?"

"I don't know; the button and the scratches on his hand are only indicia; the only concrete evidence is the girl's claim that she recognized his voice."

"Not much to go on."

Falkenberg replied. "I've talked to af Portman. He denies having been anywhere near Lustholmen that evening." He hesitated for a moment and then continued, "But there is something evasive about the man, and I think he's holding something back."

"It's a damned farrago!"

"I didn't know you were a farmer, Sir!"

Von Lans laughed, "My family has land, but my brother is the farmer." He added, "Now, what about Fogel?"

"Well, there've been no more fights with af Portman. I've ordered both of them to stay away from each other. I imagine the relationship is a bit strained, but they're both carrying out their duties as before." He went on, "I think Fogel is expecting that af Portman will be charged and held responsible for at least the last attack."

"Hmm!"

Von Lans reached into the drawer on his desk and pulled out some papers. "Look at this!" He handed them over to Falkenberg, who began to read. It was a two-page letter written on thick paper, embossed with a red and white crest with a picture of an arbalest and a tree. The handwriting was bold and large.

When Falkenberg was finished, he looked up at von Lans.

"This comes from af Portman's father?"

"Yes, Count Greger af Portman, member of Parliament, and a man of considerable influence."

Falkenberg looked at the letter. "He's very courteous, but behind his polite words the message is very clear. He wants to hear no more of charges against his son, and…" – Falkenberg read from the letter: "…he wants the slanderer disciplined."

"The veil on the threat is very thin." Von Lans continued, "Without much stronger evidence, we won't get anywhere. If Count af Portman goes to the attack, he'll not only destroy the girl, but also Lieutenant Fogel."

"And Fogel is clearly the better man."

"Doesn't matter! Lieutenant af Portman has his father to hide behind."

Falkenberg sighed, "We need to do something! I fear that otherwise discipline in the Queen's guard will suffer."

"Indeed! Let me think about it some more."

The boat trip back from Tidö took longer than did the trip to get there; the wind had turned to northeasterly and was often against them, particularly in the narrow east-to-west sounds, where it would turn to easterly. Lieutenant Arnem and his crew were good sailors, but they had to tack through many narrow sounds. It was getting colder, and several showers passed by, but whenever he could, von Lans sat on deck watching the islands drift by. He mumbled to himself. "From fighting a war in Germany, to guarding the Queen, and now to starting a Swedish colony in the New World – such strange times." He thought about the New

Sweden enterprise, making long notes about questions he had and things that he needed to do.

After the first meeting at Tidö, von Lans spent another day with Mr. Blommaert, who presented his plan for New Sweden. Admiral Fleming would join them from time to time, and in the evening they all had dinner with Oxenstierna. It didn't take long before the Chancellor asked, "Well, Baron, what do you think?"

Von Lans replied cautiously, "It sounds very interesting. Mr. Blommaert has given me an overall picture, but I'm sure I'll need to learn more about the details."

"I hope you'll take on the job."

"I will, Sir, but I need some time to get more familiar with the enterprise."

"Good! You should meet Mr. Minuit as soon as you can." Oxenstierna turned to Blommaert, "When is Minuit coming?"

"He'll be in Gothenburg in early December, unless the winter storms delay him," Blommaert replied.

"Can you be there then, Baron?" Oxenstierna asked.

"Yes Sir, but we must also consider the effect on the Queen's Guard. There are some problems that I need to sort out before I hand over to a new commander."

"Fine, do that." Oxenstierna turned to Fleming, "You have a new commander in mind for the Guard, don't you?"

"Yes, I do. He is Colonel Lennart Stureson, who's been serving under General Banér."

"To whom we are very grateful for the great victory at Wittstock."

"Yes, indeed."

Oxenstierna raised his glass. "Well then, gentlemen, we seem to be on our way. Here's to New Sweden! Skål!"

The three men raised their glasses and responded in chorus, "To New Sweden!"

It was evening when von Lans stepped ashore in Stockholm, and his carriage took him directly to his quarters. The next morning he walked onto the palace parade ground where the Guard had assembled for the morning formation, and Falkenberg was facing the troops, receiving the calls from each Lieutenant in turn. Von Lans stood off to the side. When the bells in the tower of the Great Cathedral next to the palace began to chime, Falkenberg called everybody to attention. The flags on the palace were hoisted slowly, reaching the top of the poles just when the major bell rang out the last stroke to mark the hour of eight.

Falkenberg gave out the orders for the day and dismissed the troops. He turned around and seeing von Lans, walked over to him. "Good morning, Colonel," he said.

"Morning, Captain. Walk with me! I've spent two days on a cramped mail boat, and I need to move my legs."

Von Lans led the way around the parade ground; most of the troops had left; only a couple of Guards were posted at the gate to the palace. Von Lans said, "I've been with the Chancellor, and heard that there've been some new developments." He paused for moment, "What I am about to tell you is in strictest confidence."

They passed the two guards at the gate and both men were silent until the guards were out of eavesdropping range. Falkenberg waited until von Lans continued, "Things are going well for our country, and we're going to start a colony in America. A company, called New Sweden, has been formed, and the Chancellor wants me to become his liaison with the enterprise."

"You'll be leaving the Guard?"

"I'm afraid so. But don't worry, the Guard's new commander is a good man. He's Colonel Stureson; he's coming directly from Pomerania where he fought under Banér at Wittstock. By the way, I think the victory at Wittstock has a lot to do with the Chancellor's optimism about the future."

Falkenberg thought for a while before he said, "I'll be really sorry to see you go, Sir. We've come a long way together."

"I know, but when Oxenstierna calls, it's very difficult to say no." Von Lans went on, "And I'm looking forward to my new assignment. Think of it – New Sweden! We already control a lot of Europe, and now we'll have a piece of the New World."

"Yes, I see what you mean, but this is different, isn't it? What do we know about America? Will anybody want to go there to live?"

"These are great challenges, but the company will be run by two Dutchmen who have done this sort of thing before."

They were back at the gate and their conversation stopped while they passed the guards again. When Falkenberg resumed, he said, "What about our two lieutenants? Can we resolve this before you leave?"

"Yes, I don't want to leave you with that boil festering. I have an idea." Von Lans continued, "Let's move both of them out of the Guard."

"Excellent, but where to, Sir?"

"I'll take Fogel as my assistant; he speaks fluent Dutch, and this way he'll be out of the gun sights of Count af Portman's."

"And Lieutenant af Portman?"

"He'll be posted back to Pomerania to one of Banér's companies. With the victory at Wittstock, his father will see this as a promotion. However, I have friends serving under Banér, and I'll let them know our concerns. I'll also explain this to Stureson, when he arrives – but that won't be for another month."

Von Lans shrugged his shoulders, "It's the best we can do – and who knows? – Maybe af Portman's bravado will make him a useful soldier in battle."

"Very good, Sir!"

The two men continued their walk, and von Lans told Falkenberg more about the new Sweden enterprise. Both of them knew that their futures were changing, but to what?

180

28. Departure

Ben was worried about Emilia; she went about her work as usual, but she was withdrawing into herself. When they were alone together she would sometimes cling to him, but she was tense and there was a rigidity in the way she held him. There seemed to be a shell slowly forming around her, a barrier growing up between them. Physically she was fine, and he just hoped that time would once again heal the injuries done to her spirit, and that she would become the Emilia he knew and had come to love.

Two months had gone by since the attack, and Ben came to the kitchen one evening. Mrs. Hahn was busy at the counter cutting vegetables, her knife moving up and down frenziedly. When her cutting board was full, she picked it up abruptly and scraped it over the soup pot so that little pieces flew all over the counter and the floor. Ben looked at her and asked, "Is something wrong?"

Mrs. Hahn banged the cutting board down onto the counter, "It's Emilia, she won't come out of her room," she said, her voice quavering.

Ben walked across the kitchen to Emilia's room and knocked on the door. "Emilia," he said to the closed door. There was no reply, and he opened the door again saying, "Emilia!" He stepped in to the dark room; on the bed Emilia was curled up; her eyes were closed, her hair in tangles, and her arms wrapped around her knees, which were pulled up against her chest. He sat down on the side of the bed, and put his hand on her arm.

"What's wrong?" he asked.

There was no reaction; he shook her arm, and she opened her eyes and looked at him. She started to cry, and when Ben put his arms around her, she let go of her knees and let him pull her close to him. She was shaking from the crying but he held her, and after a while she calmed down.

Ben asked, "What happened?"

"Nothing, it just comes over me. I have nightmares about him, sometimes even during the day." Her voice was just a whisper.

Ben didn't know what to answer; he just pulled her closer. Gradually he could feel that she relaxed, and finally she let go, he let go, and she sat up and said, "I'm fine now, I must get back to work." She got up and wiped the tears off her face and straightened her clothes. She took a brush from the table and brushed away the tangles in her hair. She turned to Ben. "I'm glad you're here!"

She bent over and kissed him lightly. "I'm fine now."

When they came back into the kitchen, Mrs. Hahn looked relieved, and when Emilia took the knife and started cutting vegetables, Mrs. Hahn sat down at the kitchen table with a loud sigh. Emilia put the soup pot on the stove, and began setting the table for supper. Other servants arrived and sat down, and talk filled the air. Mrs. Hahn got up and stirred the soup; it would be a simple supper of soup, bread, and cheese, and everything seemed to be back to normal.

When supper was finished, Ben got up, and said, "I'm working the night shift, I have to leave." Emilia followed him to the door, where he embraced her. He said, "Everything will be better soon." She smiled, but Ben looked at Emilia and thought, "Why is it that I don't quite believe her, when she says she's fine?"

A messenger came for Ben a few days later, "The Colonel wants to see you!"

When Ben came to von Lans' office, Falkenberg was already there. Von Lans greeted him, "Fogel, come in and sit down. Put your things over there!" He pointed to a chair standing against the wall.

Ben entered the office closing the door behind him. He was in full Guard uniform, and he took off his hat, sabre belt, coat and sat down next to Falkenberg. Von Lans waited until he was seated, then said, "I'll come straight to the point; I want to talk to you about your fight with af Portman; it's stirred up a real hornet's nest."

Ben squirmed in discomfort. "I'm sorry, Sir. I simply lost my temper."

"I know, and I can even sympathize with your feelings. But that doesn't help."

"No, Sir."

Von Lans paused a moment before he continued, "Captain Falkenberg has told me all about your allegations. We've turned the investigation of the attack on the girl over to the City Guards, but I have to tell you that I wouldn't get my hopes up."

Ben felt a rush of heat going through him, but he swallowed and nodded in assent.

Von Lans continued, "But there is still a problem here in the Queen's Guard, and the Captain and I have decided to make some changes."

Ben calmed down as he waited with a sense of dread for what was to follow; von Lans looked straight at him and didn't say anything. The room was dead silent, but finally von Lans said. "I'm going to offer you a way out, something that will give everybody time to forget this unfortunate incident."

Ben sensed a change coming over von Lans, who smiled and went on to say, "You'll leave the Guard, and become my assistant in a new enterprise."

"Yes, Sir!" Ben didn't dare to ask, "What enterprise?" but von Lans didn't keep him in suspense.

He continued, "We're going to America!"

Ben could hardly believe his ears, "America?"

"Yes! We're going to build a New Sweden across the Atlantic."

Von Lans went on to outline the venture and explain his own role. He finished by saying, "We'll use Gothenburg as our base, and as soon as Captain Falkenberg gets a replacement for you, which should be in a month or so, I want you to move there."

Ben, still reeling from the news, gasped, "I hardly know what to say, Sir."

"I understand. I felt the same way when Oxenstierna asked me to take on this task." Von Lans' eyes became very serious when he added, "I believe you're the right man for this job, but let me also emphasize that you really don't want to stay here in Stockholm. You have made some very influential enemies. Go to Gothenburg and America, and they will eventually forget you."

Ben thought about this and asked. "What will happen to Lieutenant af Portman?"

Falkenberg broke in, "He has been posted to our army in Pomerania; he left this morning."

Ben sat silently. Von Lans and Falkenberg stood up, walked over to the side and talked quietly to each other while they waited for Ben to let the order sink in. Many minutes went by before the two senior officers came back and sat down again.

Von Lans said, "Perhaps you can see the logic in this?"

"Yes, I can." Ben replied. "I also think I should be grateful to you."

"Only time will tell if we've done you a favor or not."

"What do I tell others?"

"Tell them only that you're being posted to Gothenburg."

The meeting was over; von Lans left it to Falkenberg and Ben to sort out the practical problems. When the two walked back to their own quarters, Ben said to Falkenberg, "Captain, please give me some time to talk to Emilia and explain this to her before I have to leave."

"Well, you'll be here until after Christmas – but don't wait until the last moment!"

It was getting close to winter solstice again, the days were short and when clouds shut out the weak winter sun, there was dusk all day. Emilia worked long hours and had only every other Sunday off, but when her day off arrived she went for a walk with Ben. They walked to the rapids north of the palace, where the lake water rushed down to add ever more fresh water to the archipelagic bays of the Baltic. They crossed the bridges between the islands that made up Stockholm. It was getting colder, there was a white mist forming around the rapids, and there were a few snowflakes drifting in the air. Emilia had wrapped a scarf around her head, and now she pulled it tighter to ward off the cold wind. When they came to the lake shore, the wind was whipping and the snow was flying sideways through the air.

"Let's find some shelter!" Ben said.

"Let's go to the church!"

"Yes – here!" He held his hand out.

Emilia took Ben's hand and they struggled against the wind and the falling snow up to a square and the Knight's Church. The front door was unlocked; they pulled it open and entered the church, shook the snow off their clothes, and Ben removed his hat. The church was empty; the snow-white daylight through the windows together with candles along the walls lit up the church, but there were deep shadows in the corners and behind the many columns. They walked down the side isle and came to Gustavus Adolphus' final resting place. The chapel was lit up by large candles casting light on the marble sarcophagus; through the windows behind they saw large flakes of snow flying by. Ben was reminded about another snowy winter night in Pomerania, but it all seemed such a long time ago.

They sat down in a pew across the aisle from the chapel. Emilia loosened her shawl, but kept it on. Ben put his hat on the pew, unbuttoned his coat, but pulled it tight. He said, "It's not much warmer in here, is it?"

"No, but at least we're out of the wind and snow."

There was an awkward moment of silence until both spoke at the same time. "I must tell you …." They stopped, looked at each other and smiled.

Emilia came back before Ben. "You first!"

Ben took her hand and said, "I have to go away."

"Where are you going?"

"The Colonel is sending me to Gothenburg."

Emilia looked at him. "Does this have anything to do with af Portman?"

"Yes, the Colonel thinks I'll be safer away from Stockholm for now." He added, "But don't worry about af Portman; he's being sent back to Pomerania. In fact, he's already left."

Emilia drew her breath in sharply and her eyes filled with tears. She heaved a sigh of relief. "Oh! I'm so glad to hear that."

The wind whistled through cracks in the windows and the candles flickered from the draft. Outside the snowflakes were thinning. Ben, still holding her hand, said, "I'll be working for von Lans directly on a new enterprise. I can't tell you more right now, but I may be away for some time."

Emilia pulled back her hand and wiped the tears from her eyes. "I've been trying to tell you something, and this makes it a little less difficult."

"Tell me!"

"Perhaps we were not meant to be together, but if we are, I need some time for myself to get over everything that happened at the end of a wonderful day, that awful evening at Lustholmen."

"So you don't mind if I go away for awhile?"

"Oh, I mind, I mind a lot! I don't want you to go, but you'll come back – won't you?"

"I will! I love you!" Ben put his arms around her and pulled her closer.

Emilia whispered into his ear, "I love you too, I always have! – Gothenburg is not that far away, and we can write to each other."

The snow had stopped falling; they left the church, coming out into a city covered by a blanket of white fluff. Hand in hand they half ran, half walked over the bridge and up the hill to the palace, the snow flying around their feet. They stopped, kissed, and ran again. Emilia picked up some snow, squeezed it into a ball and threw it at Ben, who caught it on the back of his head. Cold flakes melted down his collar on his neck; he bent over and scooped up a handful of snow that landed in Emilia's face. "Sorry!" he said while she wiped her face clean.

Emilia broke out laughing. "I'll get you!" she yelled and picked up more snow.

Ben slipped and fell, and when Emilia dumped the snow in his face, slipped herself and fell down on top of him in the snowdrift, he thought, "It's been a long time since she laughed like this."

That evening Emilia whispered to Ben, "Stay with me tonight!" It was five years since they first met in Erfurt; it felt like a lifetime and they thought they knew each other so well. But that night they discovered more about themselves and their love for each other – a love that had sneaked up on them over the years and made their tentative lovemaking the simplest and sweetest thing in the world.

Christmas was usually a very busy time at the palace, but this year Queen Maria Eleonora and Christina went to stay with Princess Katarina, the late King's sister. The Queen brought an entourage of maids and ladies-in-waiting with her, and life in the Stockholm palace quieted down. On Christmas Eve, Mrs. Hahn had prepared a goose, and Ben joined in the celebration. The next morning they all walked over to the Great Cathedral for an early service. It was dark outside, and churchgoers were carrying torches to light their way. More snow had fallen during the night, and the collection of torches placed in the snow drifts by the front of the church lit up the market place and the church façade. Vendors had set up little tables where bread, eggs, sausages, dried ham, and smoked fish from the lake were consumed together with warm ale to ward off the cold; churchgoers from near-by islands arrived by boat and walked up from the harbor.

At the stroke of seven, the church bells rang, the last stragglers entered, and the Christmas morning service began. They sang and prayed, and the Bishop of Stockholm preached about the joys of Christmas and about the coming return of the light. The church was packed; Emilia found a place in the last pew and Ben stood behind her with his hands on her shoulders.

The days went fast and soon they were into January of 1637. Ben's replacement had arrived and he was getting ready to leave. He had spent the last week with von Lans writing long notes with all his instructions for the next month. Pieter Minuit had been delayed by winter storms and wouldn't arrive in Gothenburg until March, but he had sent a list of requests and tasks, many of which von Lans asked Ben to take care of. Von Lans himself was staying in Stockholm; before he was to leave, he wanted to see Fleming and Oxenstierna as well as Pieter Spierinck Silfverkrona, another investor in New Sweden.

Ben and Emilia were lying in bed braided together in love, knowing this was their last night before he had to leave. A torch outside cast a dim light into the room; they could see each other's contours, but the world outside their cocoon was far away in the dark. Ben moved slowly and Emilia, holding her face against his, moaned with pleasure; he felt her breath against his cheek. They dozed off, woke up again, made love with less intensity this time, and finally they slept. Inevitably time went by and when Ben woke up, he knew he had to go. They both knew; neither of them said, "Don't go." But Ben felt Emilia's tears on his face when he finally left.

It had gotten colder, but the day was clear and a rosy sky heralded the sunrise. The coach was waiting at the palace gate, steam puffing from the nostrils of the four horses and from the heaps of pungent manure behind them. He put his satchels on the rack at the rear of the coach, and the coachman closed the cover. Ben turned and saluted the two Guardsmen at the gate. "Goodbye, boys!" he said.

The two guards came to attention and replied, "Goodbye, Lieutenant!"

Ben opened the door and stepped into the coach. The coachman climbed up on his seat; he released the brake lever, flipped the reins, smacked his lips, and urged the horses on. The coach started down the street to the city gate; Ben looked back through the rear window. The first rays of the morning sun were just hitting the palace towers, but he turned resolutely and looked ahead out the side window. His time in Stockholm was over.

29.   Home

The coach came to a halt. The last stop was in the Gothenburg harbor, not far from the Molen, his mother's inn. It had been a long trip, two hundred fifty miles of narrow bumpy roads, and they had also been delayed several days by snowstorms along the way. There were frequent changes of horses and coaches; sometimes they had to go by sled. Rumors of highwaymen in one of the large forests they had to cross caused further delays while they waited to join a convoy of several coaches under armed escorts. Luckily they were never caught out in the snow, but could stay in relative comfort at coach stations and inns along the road. Ben was the only passenger who would travel the whole way, but he was never alone in the coach. Many of his fellow passengers were seasoned travelers, and the snowbound days and evenings at the inns were filled with stories about snow delays, breakdowns, and mysterious riders appearing out of nowhere in the middle of the forest.

Leaving the midlands, they came to the Gotha River, and from there the road followed the river to its mouth at Gothenburg. It was getting warmer, and soon the ground was mottled by dark patches cutting holes in the shrinking fields of snow. Westerly winds carrying moisture from the North Sea added a rawness that crept inside the coach. The windows fogged up and they felt they were riding in a chilly gray box. By the time they arrived at the harbor, the ground was bare and there was a slight drizzle in the air.

Ben stepped out of the coach, his body stiff from days of traveling; he retrieved his two satchels from the trunk in the back, paid and thanked the coachmen.

"Ben!" It was a familiar voice. It sounded like his mother's. He looked around but didn't see any Anneke; he turned but didn't recognize anybody.

"Ben!"

A girl, who looked to be a few years younger than Emilia, was coming toward him. He looked again, and when the girl came closer, he said, "Alex?"

"Yes!"

She held out her arms – he was so surprised, realizing it had been so long since he left that his little sister had grown into a woman. He stood there dumbfounded with his arms pulled straight down by the two heavy satchels. Alex put her arms around him, locking his to his sides; tears were streaming down her cheeks. Ben felt tears coming to his eyes too as he stood there held tight by Alex. Finally he said, "Let me loose, or my arms will fall off." He put down his satchels and hugged his sister; he held her at arm's length and said, "Let me look at you!"

He brought out a handkerchief and wiped the tears from Alex's eyes, "How did you know I was coming today?" he asked.

"I didn't, but ever since we got your letter saying you were coming, I've been meeting every coach from Stockholm. Everybody is so excited!"

"How's mother?"

They had written letters back and forth, but mail took a long time and news was always sporadic. Ben picked up his satchels, and while they walked back to the Molen, Alex told him the latest.

"Mother is fine, a little older, but working just as hard as ever," Alex said, and continued, "You know that Oma died?"

Their grandmother had died while he was in Germany, and Ben replied, "Yes, I know, but it took a year for your letter to arrive; it caught up with me when I came to Stockholm." He added, "And how about Max?"

"He is working as an apprentice in the office of a trader, who somehow has managed to keep him from being drafted into the army."

"Are many men going to war?"

"Yes, but now they're hardly men, just young boys."

Alex squeezed his hand on the satchel. "It's a miracle you're back unharmed! So many don't come back at all, and most of those who do are crippled."

They arrived at the Molen; Alex opened the front door and they stepped into the inn. It took a moment for his eyes to adjust, but out of the darkness the shapes in the familiar room began to emerge. On the bar towards the rear of the room, there were glasses placed neatly in rows, a bowl of steaming hot soup in front of a customer, a basket of bread cut into slices, and two foaming mugs of ale ready to be served. On the wall behind the bar there were the familiar pictures from Holland with open fields under wide skies, boats on canals, windmills, and the village that his mother had told him was Volendam, where she first met his father. Alex called into the inn, "He's here!"

Anneke was at a table talking to a guest; she turned around, and when she saw Ben, she started crying uncontrollably. Ben put down his bags and, walked over and put his arms around her. He waited, and in a while she calmed down enough to say, "Oh, my boy!"

The man at the table stood up, and said, "Welcome home!" It was Harald Arneson, the old boatswain who had recruited Ben for his first sea voyage on Svala.

Ben said, "Harald! You don't look a day older."

"Now you're lying, but thanks anyway!"

Anneke, gradually composing herself, still held on to him, one arm around his waist. "I don't know where to begin," she said, "but have you eaten?"

Ben laughed, "Now I know I'm back home with my mother!"

The first week went by in a daze; there was so much to talk about. The Molen was open for business as usual, but Anneke had brought in extra help; in the evening, after when Max came home, they would all sit around the dinner table and talk. Ben told them about his time in Germany – the marches across scorched earth, meeting the King, the horrors of Lützen, the death of Gustavus, Wolgast, and his time in Stockholm.

Anneke talked about the death of his grandmother. "She was always hoping that you would come back before she died."

They told Ben about the hardship in Gothenburg when, one by one, young men disappeared to fight in the war in Germany, leaving women and old people to take over the men's work in the harbor and at sea. Many families starved and were reduced to begging; several women had died at sea when their small fishing boats foundered.

Max said, "It's getting a little bit better – it seems the army recruiters have eased off the pressure and they're taking less recruits." He went on, "And there are more ships coming in to the harbor. Without workers, we couldn't handle the docking, the loading and unloading."

Ben said, "What does your employer do?"

"He's a shipping agent, and his name is Gunder Olofsen."

"Norwegian?"

"His father was."

"What do you buy and sell?"

"Everything! Right now we ship lots of iron and copper to Holland. Yesterday we got a shipment of spices from Asia and tobacco from America."

"That's good!" Ben put a hand on his brother's arm. "You're lucky, Max, to be able to stay here. I wouldn't wish this war on anyone."

"I know. Most of the army shipments and troop transports go via Calmar, but now and then we get a shipload of returning soldiers. Many have lost an arm or a leg, some are blind, some can't walk."

"What can you do for them?"

"Not much. The army pays them to go home, but it's just a pittance. Those who can walk are on their own and for those who can't, we try to arrange transport, generally on the back of some wagon."

"Can you help everybody?"

"By hook or by crook most make it home. After that, it's up to them and their village." He added, "Whatever is left of it, with all the young men gone."

Max continued, "We can always tell when there has been a big battle because a few months later we'll get a ship full of wounded soldiers. Many are in bad shape, but they're still the lucky ones – the Captains always have lists for us of men buried at sea."

Ben asked, "What's it like right now?"

"It's been quiet for a while. The last troop transport carried soldiers who had been at the battle of Wittstock."

"That was a great victory for Sweden."

"Yes, and despite their injuries these soldiers were very proud of their deeds. They praised Field Marshal Banér for leading them to victory."

"You'd think they'd be angry."

"Well, some are, but most of them want to feel proud. Otherwise, their sacrifices would be worth nothing."

30.   Preparations

Von Lans had admonished Ben of the need for discretion about the New Sweden project; it was very important that the WIC, the Dutch West India Company, did not find out what the Swedes were up to. Minuit had been the WIC's Director of New Netherland at the mouth of the North River on the North American east coast. He traded with the local Indians, bought land from them, and established New Amsterdam as the center for the WIC. But this led to a dispute with his board. He was recalled to Holland and dismissed. Now, as the Director of the New Sweden Company, Minuit would compete head-to-head with his old employers in New Netherland.

In Europe, Sweden and The Dutch Republic were long-standing allies with strong relations in trade and diplomacy. They were fighting on the same side in the war against the Catholics, but even so the West India Company would not take kindly to competition in America. The WIC was not only a trading company; like most such ventures part of its charter was government-endorsed piracy. They had many large, well-armed ships, ostensibly to protect themselves against pirates and other unfriendly vessels. Nobody expected that the situation would come to blows, but the Swedish investors, from Oxenstierna and down, felt that it was only diplomatic and prudent to keep the New Sweden venture secret as long as possible.

Officially Ben was working for the government, buying goods and material to be shipped to the army. This was a convenient cover story, but everybody in the harbor knew that Ben was a Lieutenant in the army and that he'd been assigned to Gothenburg.

After the euphoria of the first week with his family wore off, it was time to get to work. Ben's first job was to find a warehouse, and he began by walking around the harbor. It was not a large harbor, only a few warehouses close to the water's edge. There was room for a few ships alongside the wharves and more ships waited at anchor. To get the ships in and out, poles had been put down along the channel, tenders would attach lines to the poles, and the ships would be hauled and turned as they were maneuvered into place in the dock or taken out. The wind and the tides would determine when a ship could finally weigh anchor and leave for the North Sea.

Behind the warehouses were more buildings that were used as offices by the shipping lines, agents, customs personnel, and anybody else that worked in the harbor. A few housed taverns and guest houses; the Molen was at the edge of the harbor away from the worst noise and clamor of people. The inn faced a small produce market, where local farmers and fishermen sold their wares. Gothenburg was a small town; its four thousand inhabitants lived mostly in houses huddled along narrow alleys on the hills behind the harbor area. It had two churches whose spires rose above the houses, and the market squares in front of the churches provided open areas for the stands of the farmers bringing their produce into town from the surrounding countryside.

Ben left the Molen and walked along the warehouses on the wharf until he came to the end. Behind the last warehouse there was small building with a sign over the door reading "Olofsen and Co. – Shipping Agents". Ben opened the door and walked inside. A young boy was standing next to a table wrapping small packages and putting them in a wooden box on the floor. On the other side of the room, Max was standing at a pulpit, writing in what looked like a ledger of some kind. When the door opened he looked up.

"Hello, brother! What brings you here?"

"Hello! I've been walking around the harbor, and now I hope you can help me." Ben looked at the boy, and continued, "Can we talk privately somewhere?"

"Certainly – in there!"

Max pointed the way and led Ben into a small backroom where there were bookcases along the wall, and in the middle a table with armchairs around it. Max closed the door and they both sat down. Max said, "Tell me!"

"I need to find a warehouse in the harbor; can you help me?"

"We can try. What do you need it for?"

"What I'll tell you must be kept secret. I don't want it spread out all over the harbor, particularly not to the WIC. Can you do that?"

"We trade with all the other shipping companies including the WIC, but Mr. Olofsen is very proud of his independence and doesn't talk about his dealings with others."

They heard a door open outside, and Max said, "I think that's him. Let me bring him in and you can judge for yourself."

Max went out of the room and soon came back followed by a tall blond man in his forties. He was dressed in a dark woolen suit over a white high-collared shirt; his golden beard was neatly trimmed, and his blue eyes looked straight at Ben. He smiled, shook Ben's hand and said, "Good day, Lieutenant Fogel, your brother had told me about you and your adventures."

Ben returned his firm handshake and replied, "Good day, Mr. Olofsen."

They sat down at the table and after a few polite phrases, the conversation quickly turned to business. Ben immediately took to the man. He soon felt very comfortable with Olofsen and with the idea of doing business with him. He asked Olofsen if he could help him find a warehouse and assist with buying the goods Ben would need. He explained, "My employers in the government want to ship some goods overseas. We will have two vessels coming after the end of the summer and I need to procure and have the shipments ready for them."

"We can help you with that, but you'll need to tell me more before we start."

"Well, for now I just need the warehouse, and someone who will honor my letter of credit. During the next month, my employers will come here, and then if we enter into a final contract I can tell you more." Ben had brought a valise, which he opened and took out a paper. "I've traveled for weeks with this sewn into the lining of my coat," he said as he handed the paper to Olofsen.

Olofsen read the text carefully and studied the signatures of the letter that was co-signed by Fleming and Oxenstierna. "With this you can buy the whole harbor if you wish," he said. He handed the paper back to Ben, and continued, "I think I have the right place for you; we have a warehouse next door. It has a small office and enough room for the goods, unless you're equipping a battleship."

Ben smiled, "No, not quite."

194

"Shall we go see it?" Olofsen said.

It was the end of March and winter was fighting its last battle against the advancing sun; the days were longer than the nights and the snow was melting. Ben was sitting outside the warehouse against the warm southerly wall; he'd opened up his coat and taken off his hat. He leaned against the wall with his eyes closed, feeling the warm sunshine on his face. Suddenly a wet blob of snow fell from the roof and landed in his lap; he looked up and saw snow overhanging the edge of the roof. It let go and more snow fell, some of it landing on his neck and running down inside his shirt. He leaped up with a surprised "Damn!" and stepped away from the wall, then brushed off the snow and pulled up his shirt to let the wet snow out. Somebody laughed; it was Max coming around the corner. He said, "You're sleeping on the job!"

"Well, I just closed my eyes for a moment." Ben tucked in his shirt.

Max handed him a letter. "This just came for you."

Ben took the letter, opened it and quickly read it. It was from von Lans; they corresponded regularly. It was all very military – Ben sent his reports and questions and von Lans replied with comments and instructions. Ben turned to Max, "The Colonel is coming here in a couple of days, and he's also expecting the director of the company from Holland."

"Very good!"

"Yes, but we'd better find them a place to stay."

"Mr. Olofsen has a guest house. I'll take care of it, but they may have to take their meals at the Molen."

"Mother will like that. The director is a Walloon, and he speaks Dutch."

Three days later von Lans stepped off the coach. It was late and he'd been traveling for several days. Ben met him and took him to the guest house, where he settled in for the night. The next morning he picked him up and brought him to the Molen for breakfast. Anneke was busy at the bar putting out plates of cheeses, boiled eggs, sausages, herring, butter, and several kinds of bread. Ben walked up to Anneke with von Lans and introduced him, "Mother, this is Colonel von Lans. Colonel, this is my mother, Anneke Magnusson."

Von Lans bowed slightly, "Delighted to meet you, Mrs. Magnusson."

Anneke nodded, "Welcome, Colonel, my son has told me so much about you."

"Glad to be here!" Von Lans looked at Ben, "You know, Fogel, I'd forgotten we'd changed your name."

Ben replied, "By now I'm so used to it that I think I'll keep it."

Von Lans laughed, "Very well!"

He looked at the bar where a small pot was being kept warm over a candle. He leaned over and smelled the steam coming from the spout, and said, "Is that coffee?"

"Yes," Anneke replied. "The ships bring in a lot of new things. Have you tried it? It's from Egypt."

"Yes, I have. An Ottoman merchant served it to me once."

"Well, I've set a table for you, so please help yourselves to the food and sit down. I'll bring you some coffee with your breakfast." Anneke pointed to an empty table at the end of the room.

Ben and von Lans filled their plates, sat down and began eating; Anneke brought them two tiny cups and poured some coffee for each of them. Von Lans tasted his and said, "That's very good, but it's strong."

Anneke replied, "Yes. Some of our guests dilute it with hot water, and some add milk."

"Milk! That sounds awful! I like it this way!"

The door to the Molen opened; it was Mogens, the boy from Olofsen's office. He came forward, took his hat off and handed Ben a note. It was short and Ben read it to von Lans. *A ship from Amsterdam is coming into the harbor. Will dock in an hour.* Ben added, "It's from my brother. I asked him to let me know when any Dutch ships are arriving."

Von Lans asked, "Might Minuit be on it?"

"Yes, he may. It's about the right time."

"Very well. Let's finish our breakfast and go meet the ship."

Ben turned to Mogens, who was waiting for a reply, "Tell Mr. Magnusson that we'll be there presently."

"Yes, Sir!" Mogens put his hat back on and ran out the door.

When Ben and von Lans came to the wharf, which was bustling with activity. A large square-rigger flying a Dutch flag was in the middle of the channel; it had drifted in from the North Sea on a light morning breeze. A forward staysail and the driver sail from the mizzen mast were still up, but the sailors had let them go and the sails were flapping in the wind. Four large tenders, rowboats with four oarsmen each, were pulling away from the ship towing thick lines that were payed out by the sailors aboard. At the edge of the wharf, the harbor master, dressed in full uniform, was

196

directing his crews. Men were getting ready to receive the first line coming from the bow of the ship.

The ship's three masts towered over the buildings. At the top of the aft and forward masts flew long red, white, and blue Dutch pennants, and at the top of the middle mast above the others flew a bleached yellow flag adorned by a large V overwritten by a smaller O and C. It was the flag of *Vereenigde Oostindische Compagnie*, the United East India Company.

Spectators were gathering at the wharf and Ben saw Olofsen and Max at the edge of the crowd. He led the way and von Lans followed him over to the two men. Ben greeted them and introduced them. Olofsen said, "Welcome to Gothenburg, Colonel! You came at the right time, it's not often we see a new VOC ship here."

Von Lans replied, "She's big, isn't she?"

"Yes, she barely fits in the harbor."

"What's she doing here?"

"I believe she's on a trial run, before she sails to East India."

They watched while the crews on land, in the tenders, and aboard worked to get the ship turned around and alongside the wharf at the VOC warehouse. Two tenders brought the ship's aft and forward lines ashore, where they were securely wrapped several turns around bollards and then held on the other sides of the bollards by crews of harbor workers. The two tenders rowed to join the third tender holding the other aft line, and the three of them began rowing away from the wharf. At first nothing happened; then slowly the stern began to move while the bow was held tightly in place by the forward line. The ship's captain ordered the driver sail to be tightened to help push the ship around. The aft crew on land payed out their line as the ship slowly rotated around the bollard to which the bow was attached.

The turn was orchestrated by the harbor master, who used a large megaphone. Aboard the ship a harbor pilot with another megaphone was standing next to the captain, and orders to the crews echoed off the rocky sides of the channel. When the ship's stern was straight out from the wharf, the fourth tender brought in the second bowline and the harbor crew changed the lines. The harbor aft crew got ready to let go. At this point the wind picked up, the driver sail stiffened, the bow lines slackened and the thousand-ton East Indiaman started to move forward toward the wharf. The tenders scurried to the rescue; one grabbed the released bow line and rowed upwind away from the wharf as the others gathered at the stern to hold her away from land, letting the stern drift downwind. The captain ordered, "Let go of the driver sheets!" The sail flew out and flapped in the wind.

The harbor master retained his superior calm, but his orders were rapid-fire and the ship's drift toward land stopped and she slowly, majestically turned around. Half an hour later she was safely alongside the wharf with her bow pointing out towards the North Sea.

Ben said, "Why didn't they just put down an anchor and let her swing around?"

Olofsen replied, "She's just a bit too large, and needs a very long anchor line."

A door in the side of the ship opened and crew members brought out a gangway. The first people out appeared to be passengers, followed by more crew carrying luggage that was put on the wharf. A middle-aged man with a graying beard looked around the wharf. "I think that's him," Ben said to von Lans.

They walked up to the man and Ben said, *"Bent u Mijnheer Minuit?"*
"Yes, I am he!"

"I'm Lieutenant Fogel." He took step backwards to let von Lans through. "And this is Colonel von Lans."

Von Lans held out his hand, "Welcome to Gothenburg, Mr. Minuit."

Minuit shook his hand. "Thank you."

"How was your trip?"

"It was very windy but we made good time," Minuit replied, and added, "We had an escort coming in over the Skagerrak."

"Oh?"

"A Danish man-of-war followed us from the North Sea until we started to drop sails outside Gothenburg."

"Well, things are still a bit touchy between us. Paying tolls at Elsinore to enter the Baltic is a thorn in our side, and the Danes don't like us bypassing the payments here in Gothenburg."

"Will it ever be resolved?"

Von Lans shrugged his shoulders. "I think so, but blood will flow first."

"But," he continued, "let's not think about that now! Let's get you settled in and then we have a much more exciting project to talk about."

Minuit didn't waste any time. He spent the afternoon with von Lans and Ben going through the minutiae of the New Sweden project. At the

198

day's end, he asked Ben to set up a meeting with Olofsen and Co. Ben went to see Olofsen and they agreed to meet the next day. Minuit and von Lans decided to dine in; Alex and Mogens brought them dinner. Ben was sitting with Harald at a rear table in the Molen when they came back. Alex came up to them and said, "He's a very charming man, your Colonel."

Ben looked at her as he thought of von Lans's conquests, and smiled at her, "Yes, but watch out. He's a real ladies' man."

At mid-morning they all gathered in Olofsen's meeting room. The preliminaries went quickly, and an agreement between New Sweden Co. and Olofsen and Co. was signed. Olofsen's eyes betrayed his curiosity about his new client, but he waited for Minuit to explain. Von Lans started. "Mr. Olofsen, as we've agreed, this is confidential, but the destination for our ships is America."

"America?"

"Yes, and I think Mr. Minuit would like to explain." Von Lans looked at Minuit.

"Thank you, Baron." Minuit smiled and looked at Olofsen. "I'm glad you sound so surprised. That means that we have been successful in keeping our mission secret. Let's keep it that way."

Olofsen replied, "Certainly! But you know that the WIC has spies everywhere."

"Indeed I do! I recruited many of them myself." Minuit leaned back in his chair. "But let me tell you about New Sweden! For six years I was the WIC Director of New Netherland. I bought land for the company from the Indians and built up a Dutch colony at the mouth of the North River."

"I've heard of it. We get shipments from New Netherland now and then."

"Very good! A little less than thirty years ago an English captain named Henry Hudson, working then for the VOC, explored the North American coast, and found a river he called North River. At the mouth of it there is excellent sheltered anchorage; that's where we put the capital on an island called Manhattan and called it New Amsterdam."

Minuit stopped, took out a silver case from his pocket, opened it and took out a cigar. "Do you mind?" he said.

"No, I think I may join you."

"Here, have one of mine!" Minuit sent the case around the table, and soon he, Olofsen, and von Lans were puffing away, as the smell of tobacco spread around the room.

Minuit continued, "The borders of New Netherland extend south to another river called the South River." He laughed, "We may have to do something about these names!" and went on. "The territory around the South River is virgin and there's sheltered anchorage. It's a perfect place for trading, for lumbering, for hunting, fishing, and farming." He took another puff on his cigar, "New Sweden will do what the WIC did with New Netherland. Our company has the backing of the Swedish government and it has both Swedish and Dutch investors. The WIC will not like it, but there is little they can do. By the time they find out, we'll already be in New Sweden."

"What about the Indians?" Olofsen asked.

"The Lenápe Indians, the biggest nation there, are very happy to trade with Europeans. We have so many things to offer; they have no metal tools and want our knives, adzes, spades, and hoes. They use animal skins for clothing, but think that our cloths are much easier to use. They welcome us, they have plenty of land and they'll sell it for our use in return for trade." Minuit paused and smiled, "And it's a beautiful land with large forests, meadows, rivers, and abundant wildlife."

"What would you bring back?"

"Mainly furs and tobacco."

"We can certainly sell some of that for you." Olofsen took a puff on his cigar and slowly blew the smoke out.

Minuit replied, "Very good! Now we need to get everything procured and ready for our first voyage. Two ships, Calmare Nyckel and Fogel Grip, will arrive here in September ready to be loaded."

"Then we'd better work fast to make sure everything will be ready!"

Minuit, von Lans, and Ben spent the next day going through what they would need for the voyage. Minuit knew very well what he wanted, and Ben spent long hours transcribing his scores of notes into procurement lists of supplies, weapons, and trading goods. Minuit was going on to Stockholm to meet with the principals, and he wanted von Lans to go with him. He said, "Colonel, you have been enlisting soldiers for Gustavus; you must know how we can find men to go to America with us."

Von Lans replied, "It may be difficult to find good freemen, but we can always go to the prisons and offer pardon to some of the light offenders."

"But we don't want murderers and thieves."

"Oh, no – these would be people with debts to the crown or those who don't want to be sent to the war in Germany."

Minuit turned to Ben, "Fogel, how are the procurement lists coming along?"

"I'm almost ready, Sir. I just need to make copies for you and the Colonel."

"Very good! As soon as you have them, we'll go see Olofsen one more time before I leave. You can deal with the details after that, but keep sending reports to the Colonel."

Two days later, Ben followed Minuit and von Lans to the morning coach. It was almost April, and spring was in the air; the snow was gone and they expected a fast trip to Stockholm; they had less than three hundred miles to travel, and it shouldn't take them more than a week.

31.   The First Voyage

Ahectic time commenced. Ben, with Max and Olofsen, got to work finding all the goods for the ships. Some of it was simple; general staples could be bought from ship's suppliers in the harbor. Others were more difficult, and Ben had to seek the help of von Lans in persuading the agent for the armorer to sell him the weapons he needed. A letter signed by Admiral Fleming finally convinced the agent that he would not get in trouble with the army, who normally bought everything he could deliver.

The warehouse started to fill up; in June there was a steady trickle of deliveries. Minuit had been through on his way back to Amsterdam and the next time he would arrive it would be for the final preparations and loading of the ships. Von Lans had accompanied Minuit to Gothenburg, but when Minuit departed von Lans returned to Stockholm. Before he left he gave Ben a list of names. "These men will go to New Sweden. Some of the men are soldiers, but some are minor felons who're getting amnesty in return. To make sure they don't run away, I've arranged a special transport with the soldiers as guards. They are bringing everything they need for the trip, but you need to find a place for them to set up camp."

Ben remembered the camp where he had first reported to become a soldier. "Can we use the army camp? It's practically empty now with so little recruiting going on."

"That'll be very good. Maybe we can get the army to feed them as well."

"I'll see what I can do."

"Very well!" Von Lans handed him a couple of letters. "Use these!"

Ben took the letters. One was a letter signed by Oxenstierna soliciting government agencies to provide general assistance to the New Sweden

Co., and the other, signed by Fleming and Minuit, authorized Lieutenant Benjamin Fogel to represent the company in Gothenburg.

"With those and the letter of credit you should be able to handle anything that comes up," said von Lans. "But you'll have to account for every rixdollar you spend." He smiled, "Remember Falkenberg tearing his hair out over all the paperwork? Well, now it's your turn. Think you're up to it?"

"I hope so!"

"Good – and don't forget the reports."

"No, Sir. I won't."

"Very good! I'll be back in September. Calmare Nyckel should arrive about then."

Von Lans left early on the next morning's coach; Ben saw him off and walked back to the warehouse. He sat down at his desk, a plain table in the corner office. It was six in the morning, and the early sun lit up the grey rocks across the channel. Work in the harbor started at sunrise, which in June meant about four o'clock. At seven the workers would stop for breakfast, but now the harbor was very busy with ships being loaded and unloaded, boxes, animals, and sacks swinging from cranes on turntables pulled around by horses. The pulleys and ropes creaked as the cranes turned and operators on the table cranked the handles to lift and lower their loads.

In front of Ben were several piles of papers – both Minuit and von Lans had left long lists of instructions. Ben shuffled through the papers absentmindedly; he wasn't sure where to begin. He leafed through a pile of letters that Mogens had left on his desk a few days ago. One caught his eye when he recognized Emilia's handwriting on the envelope. He had written her several letters since he left Stockholm. She had answered, but not as frequently as he had written. At first he didn't understand, but after a few letters, he realized that she had great difficulty writing. Illiteracy was common everywhere, and Ben knew many people who could neither read nor write; some had never gone to school and most had gone for only a few years.

Emilia's handwriting was sprawling, like that of child, her spelling imaginative to say the least, and her choice of words limited. It didn't bother him that she sprinkled her Dutch with Swedish and German, but when Ben read her letters, he felt like she was disguised inside a maze of distorting mirrors; only now and then could he catch a glimpse of the Emilia he knew. With time the mirrors were slowly becoming more distorting and opaque, and soon he wouldn't be able to either see or hear her.

She wrote about everyday things: *"I'm fine. Mrs. Hahn is fine. The Queen was back for a while, then left again. Jan Walden had been visiting and sends his regards. The weather is nice. I miss you."*

Ben always thought, "But how is she really?" He had asked and tried to draw her out, but so far he'd had no success.

He opened the letter in his hands and worked his way through it: *"I'm fine. Mrs. Hahn has a cough. The Queen's still away. Jan sends his regards. It rained last week."* Ben put the letter in his drawer; he wished he could talk to her.

At the end of September Calmare Nyckel arrived from Stockholm. She drifted into the harbor channel, dropped her anchor and slowly swung around into the wind. Lines were rowed ashore and she was pulled up alongside the wharf. Minuit, who had just arrived from Amsterdam, as well as Ben, Olofsen, and von Lans waited at the dockside. Von Lans said, "She's not quite the size of the East Indiaman, is she?"

"No, Sir, she's about a third that, but she sailed pretty well when we escorted the King back to Sweden," Ben replied.

"She looks a bit worn, doesn't she?"

"Yes, she's been at sea for some time."

The ship was secured at the wharf, a gangway was put out and the first to board were the Swedish custom officers. The rest followed them. They gathered in the officers' mess where Captain Hindricksen van der Water met them. They waited while the custom officers inspected the ship together with the second mate, Mr. Symonssen. When the inspection was finished and the papers signed and stamped, an inspection schnapps concluded the customs rituals. The customs officers left, Minuit poured another round of schnapps, and said, "Gentlemen, this will be our first journey to New Sweden. Let's drink to many more!" He raised his glass, "Skål!"

There was not much room to stand up, but they all raised their glasses. "Skål!"

The loading began the next day, and Ben and Max were frantically trying to keep track of all the batches of goods being moved around inside as well as in and out of the warehouse. Goods were shifted around and sorted according to Captain van der Water's instructions, and at the same time late deliveries arrived unannounced at the warehouse door. Ben scrambled to find room for goods and men to carry them, and he hired some of the émigrés to help them. From Minuit's instructions he had prepared detailed loading lists, but it was almost impossible to keep the shifting and changing batches in the order they were supposed to be loaded. The men spent long hours shifting loads from place to place

Fogel Grip arrived a week later, and tied up alongside Calmare Nyckel. She brought a full load from Stockholm, but there was no more room in the warehouse, and her unloading had to wait until they began loading Calmare Nyckel. It was chaotic, but slowly the trading goods and all the supplies, enough to take the new colonists through several winters in America, started to flow onboard and the holds filled up. Hard bread and candles were stacked next to bolts of bright cloth; salt fish and potatoes shared space with metal tools and vegetable seeds. They had axes, adzes, saws for cutting trees and shaping planks. Tents, mattress covers, and blankets were packed together with boxes of Bibles and hymnbooks. The trading goods included colored beads, strings, and extra rolls of cloth, which Minuit claimed the Indians cherished.

The last things to arrive were their weapons. Minuit intended to build a fort in New Sweden, and he had ordered several cannons in addition to a collection of swords, pikes, muskets, gunpowder, and ammunition. The armorer had promised delivery on time, but claimed that the army had ordered more than expected. Finally at the end of October, the last delivery arrived and was loaded on the ships.

At the army camp the men recruited to go to America were assembling. They were waiting to board the ship, but passengers would be the last aboard before departure. Finally it was time to get the passengers onboard, and Von Lans sent Ben to get the soldiers and the émigrés. Ben got a horse at the coach stable and rode out to the army camp. It was getting colder, and he found most of the men in their tents, some sleeping, some playing cards, and others just sitting around talking.

He went looking for Lieutenant Måns Kling, who was in charge of the New Sweden contingency of soldiers. He found him in one of the open areas next to the camps. Ben remembered it from his own first months in the army. Kling was standing at the edge of the field watching his soldiers practice shooting techniques. There were only about twenty men, not nearly enough for the classic Swedish square formation. Instead Kling had them in small groups of four each, two loading guns while the other two fired. He also made them move rapidly in between firings, taking cover behind knolls and in ditches.

Ben rode up next to him and said, "Good morning, Kling, the ships are loaded. It's time to get everybody onboard."

Kling called his men to a halt, "Take a rest!" He turned to Ben, "Hello, Fogel!"

Ben asked, "What are you doing – those aren't the exercises I remember!"

"This is such a small platoon, not even enough to make any battle-field formations. So, we're practicing to be fast and invisible – attack and run for new cover. I can't afford to lose any men, so they have to protect themselves, not just stand in the middle of a field firing and at the same time being perfect targets."

Ben got off his horse and tied the reins to a fencepost. "Very good!" He opened his saddlebag, brought out an envelope and said, "Here's the list of soldiers that are going. Are they ready?"

Kling took the list and looked at it, "Yes, they are, but where did you get some of these men?"

"Mostly from army brigs. They were serving sentences for things like getting into fights, insubordination, and desertion. By going on this mission they'll receive amnesty."

"Well, they seem to have accepted the conditions; going to America is better than being in jail."

"How about you, Kling?" Ben asked.

Kling's face broke into a smile, "I think it's great! It's the chance of a lifetime!" He paused for a moment and continued, "But I wonder what the women are like in America!"

Livestock from the holding pens behind the coach station were brought onboard and put in boxes, which had been built on deck. Horses neighed, cows mooed, pigs squealed, sheep bleated, hens cackled in their cages, roosters crowed, and dogs yapped. Fogel Grip's cat sat on the boom and watched the proceedings; one of the dogs stood at the foot of the mast and barked, but the cat, safe on its perch, ignored it. Finally the dog's owner came running over, kicked the dog, and it slunk off to a corner with a whine. Now soldiers and émigrés began to board; they were shown to their quarters in the forward hold. This was to be their home for several months to come – each had a hammock to sleep in and their worldly belongings were everywhere, hanging from hooks, stowed behind

206

nets on shelves along the sides of the ship, in the hammocks, and on the floor.

Minuit was standing on Calmare Nyckel's deck with von Lans and Ben when the last loads were brought onboard. Slowly things were calming down. Captain Hindricksen was at the bridge, and his sailors were making the ship ready for departure. If the wind allowed it, they would sail the next morning. Von Lans said, "Mr. Minuit, I've brought you a present – it comes from the Her Majesty." He handed over a soft leather case formed like a cross. "Please open it!" he said. Minuit took the case and untied the leather thong at the top; inside was a cross made of copper, which he carefully took out. In the middle of the cross was a single polished green stone, and at the foot the Vasa coat of arms had been painted under the golden letters CR. Von Lans said, "Christina Regina, our young Queen, wants you to bring this to the New World. She wants you to build a church and put her cross there."

Minuit made a slight bow and replied, "Please convey my thanks to Her Majesty, and tell her that it shall be done. When I come back I hope to be able to tell her myself." He replaced the cross into the case and tied it back together. A puff of wind caught the long blue and yellow pennant flying from the ships's top mast. Minuit's gaze went to the pennant before he continued, "This is it, gentlemen. The next time we meet I'll tell you all about New Sweden on the South River." He looked directly at Ben, "Fogel, when I come back, I'll try to talk Baron von Lans into letting you go with me to New Sweden."

It was early in November, 1637, and the two ships left the next morning. Ben and von Lans were at dockside watching them weigh anchor and slowly move toward the Kattegatt. They would never see Pieter Minuit again.

32.   Waiting

Letters came from Holland saying that the expedition was delayed. No sooner had Calmare Nyckel and Fogel Grip left Gothenburg than they were beset by a storm. This was not unexpected, as the North Sea was notorious for its rough weather in the fall. The ships were separated almost immediately, but before they left Gothenburg Minuit had given instructions that their first port of call would be Texel in Holland. He wanted to keep their mission secret from the WIC, and the island of Texel at the edge of the North Sea by Marsdiep, the shipping channel leading into the Zuiderzee and Amsterdam, was perfect – it was near enough to Amsterdam to be able to buy all the remaining goods they needed but far enough away from the center of WIC activity.

In early December Calmare Nyckel and Fogel Grip entered Marsdiep and were soon safely in the Texel harbor. The storm had battered the old ships. They leaked and needed repairs and it took another couple of weeks before they could finally leave Holland. In his last letter from Texel, Minuit reported that all repairs had been made, water and other supplies replenished, and both ships were in good shape.

The next batch of letters came four months later from Las Palmas on Gran Canaria, one of the Canary Islands. They were very general and all details were given in code – Minuit didn't trust any ship to convey messages without opening them. His reports were very optimistic; apart from more delays, this time due to calm weather, everything was going according to plan. The only change was that Minuit had decided to take the southern route, using the trade winds to get to the West Indies, and from there head north to America.

Von Lans was on his way to a meeting with Fleming and Blommaert, who was on one of his visits to Stockholm. The July sun warmed his back as he walked across the square by the Great Church. He ducked into an alley that wound its way toward the harbor on the Baltic side of town. He passed open doorways and he could see into backyards where workmen had set up their shops, and then a little square where children were playing amid the dirty streams of water and waste trickling down toward the harbor.

At the water's edge he entered a new building inside which the wealth of the merchants was displayed by impressive columns and tall ceilings, dark wooden furniture, and wall panels covered with imposing paintings showing faces of previous generations looking sternly down at the visitors. A few windows were open, letting the warm summer breeze come through as well as some of the harbor noise. A clerk led him through to a smaller study where Admiral Fleming, Baron Spierinck, and Patroon Blommeart were already assembled. Fleming met him at the door and held out his hand, "Welcome, Baron!"

They talked about Minuit's letters and, while the delays were a concern, they were not unexpected. Winds always shifted directions, there were storms, and ships could be becalmed for long periods. Delays cost money and should be avoided, and weather could blow a ship off course, or worse, cause it to disappear one way or another. Captains needed skill but they also needed luck. Fleming summed up, "Calmare Nyckel and Fogel Grip are in God's hands."

Spierinck said, "Yes, but while we wait for more news and their return, what can we do here?"

Fleming replied, "Let's get ready for the second voyage! This is just the start. We'll need to set up permanent trading offices here in Sweden."

He went on talking about how the furs and tobacco from America would make them richer. His enthusiasm was contagious and Spierinck looked as though he was anticipating his share of the profits with great pleasure. Blommaert was more cautious. "Gentlemen, we still have a long time to go. Let's at least wait until we hear from Minuit that he's arrived." He looked at von Lans, "Baron, I'd like to keep our office in Gothenburg and be ready for the return of the ships, but nothing grand."

Von Lans replied, "Very well. We can let Lieutenant Fogel stay there; he can work with the shipping agent, Olofsen, and learn what it means to be a trader. Olofsen owes us that, since he'll get our business."

Blommaert looked at Spierinck and Fleming, "What do you think?"

Fleming looked hesitant, he clearly would have liked a more active venture, but Spierinck nodded and said, "I agree, we need our man in Gothenburg. We already have plans for more voyages, but let's not spend any more money than we have to." He added, "Mr. Blommaert, as time goes by, can you use some of your old contacts in Amsterdam to find out what they know about our little venture in New Netherland? Our ships should have come and gone by now."

Blommaert nodded in agreement, "I'll see what I can do, but knowing Minuit, the WIC may still be in the dark."

Fleming said, "The darker the better! Mr. Blommaert, I trust you'll brief your Dutch investors and encourage them not to lose faith in New Sweden. Von Lans, why don't you come with me this afternoon to see the Chancellor. I know he's anxious to know what is happening to his plans to expand Sweden across the Atlantic." He paused, "Now, let's see what the cook has made for us." Fleming rose from the table and led the way to the dining room next door.

When the owners of New Sweden sat down to lunch, the Director, Mr. Pieter Minuit, was at his breakfast table aboard Calmare Nyckel, anchored at St. Christopher Island in the Leeward Islands during its return voyage. On the table in front of him was a crude drawing of a fort, but Minuit wasn't giving it much attention. He was writing a report for his employers. When he was finished he put it in an envelope, wrote the address on the outside, and finally put the letter in a box with all the other letters and reports he had written since they left Gran Canaria. He got up, put on his hat and coat, and walked out to where one of the ship's tenders was ready for him. Captain Hindricksen was on the bridge and Minuit walked up the stairs to join him. "Hindricksen, are you ready for our lunch on Het Vliegende Hert? I'm looking forward to seeing the Captain – he's an old friend of mine."

"I'm ready." Hindricksen turned to his first mate. "Mr. Symonssen, you've got the ship!"

"Ay, ay, Sir!" Symonssen pointed out toward the sea and a black cloud formation at the horizon, and continued, "There may be a squall coming our way!"

Hindricksen looked out at sea, and replied, "It doesn't look too bad, and it will probably pass us by. But maybe as a precaution you ought to batten things down. You never know!" He turned to Minuit, "Mr. Minuit, let's go see your friend." The two men walked to the side of the ship and stepped into the tender. Minuit waved to Symonssen and sat down while the sailors rowed them over to the Dutch ship.

Ben was very happy to stay in Gothenburg but the only thing that bothered him was that he couldn't see Emilia. They still wrote to each other, but less often than before, and Ben felt the increasing distance between them. At the same time he had a nagging feeling of guilt. Shouldn't he be more upset about not seeing her? He enjoyed his work with Olofsen, he helped out at the Molen, and he was not anxious to go away again.

It was still summer; Ben was at his desk when Max came storming in through the door. "Ben!" he cried out before he was through the door.

"Yes, what's happened?"

Max spoke between his gasps for air. "I've just heard from our agent in Calmar. A ship came in with several sick people aboard. Others had died on the way and been buried at sea. The plague has come to Sweden!"

Ben answered the only way you can when you need time to consider bad news. "Are you sure?"

"Yes, and they say it's spreading!"

No disease was as feared as the plague. Its origin and cause were unknown, and it seemed to appear out of nowhere. Its toll was high. Tens of thousands had died in the plague during outbreaks in Sweden, and the faithful were sure it was God's vengeance upon a faithless people.

Ben asked, "Has it gotten here?"

"Not that I know, but we're going to have to take precautions that will be very disruptive to the harbor."

"How so?"

"Every ship will be quarantined at anchor for forty days before anybody or anything can go ashore. The whole city will be closed and only visitors who have a health warrant will be allowed to enter."

"This will cause havoc to business, but it's better than having the plague. I've seen towns hit by the plague; people were dying like flies and whole villages would get wiped out." Ben continued, "Do we have any ships on their way?"

"I'm expecting another transport ship with wounded soldiers, any day. Now it'll have to be quarantined."

"That's the second troop ship in a month. There must have been another big battle."

"Yes, and we still have soldiers from the first who haven't been able to leave. We must get them out of the harbor in case we get quarantined ourselves."

"Yes, I know, they're all around me in the warehouse." Ben replied.

"Well, you know it was the only place we could put them."

"OK, let's see what we can do!"

They dropped everything else and concentrated on finding drivers, horses, and wagons. Ben went to the old army camp and cajoled them into lending them men and equipment. They bribed other agents into taking a soldier or two on their transports. A week later, the last wounded soldier had been carried out of the warehouse and gently placed in the back of a wagon heading northeast. Ben stood at the door of the warehouse surveying the disarray of mattresses and blankets spread around the floor, leftover clothes, bags of old food and other refuse the soldiers had left behind. Something glinted in a corner; he went over and picked up a button. It was marked with a Habsburg crest; some soldier had brought an enemy button as a trophy, only to forget it on the floor of the warehouse. Ben turned around and went to find somebody to help him clean the warehouse and make it ready for the next load of crippled soldiers.

The plague was spreading and the Governor of Gothenburg gave the order to quarantine all arriving ships. Luckily the town had been spared so far. Within a week four ships were anchored in the harbor with yellow quarantine flags flying from their spars. First in line was Valen, the troop ship Max was expecting, but the Governor wouldn't grant any exceptions to the quarantine for the wounded soldiers. Food and water were brought out to the ship in one of the harbor boats, but no person was allowed to board or get off. The fear of the Black Death was very strong, and armed soldiers patrolled the area in boats to guard against any attempts to escape.

The harbor came to a standstill. The ships already in it had been loaded and left, and no more would come to the wharf before the first forty days were over. The roads to the town were blocked, but there was hardly any traffic to speak of, as most of the commerce was done by ship. The mail was still being carried, and Ben wrote his reports to von Lans even though there wasn't much to tell. Von Lans wrote back, asking Ben to do as well as he could. He also told Ben that the plague had come to Stockholm, and there were many deaths. He concluded by saying he'd heard from Minuit and that they had arrived safely. They had bought land from the Indians, and they were busy building a fort and getting ready for the winter. New Sweden had been born.

They were four weeks into the quarantine, when some of the soldiers onboard Valen tried to escape it by swimming ashore. It was a foolish attempt, as the water was cold and they were not good swimmers. Both drowned and their bodies were found washed up on the shore by a fisherman. He took one look at their white faces and hollow black eyes and ran to the harbormaster's office.

"It's the Black Death! They're dead!" he bellowed as he barged into the office.

"Who?" the harbormaster asked, alarmed.

"There are two dead bodies on the shore! They came from the ship! The plague is here!"

The harbormaster brought a doctor with him and they went to see for themselves. The doctor concluded immediately that the two soldiers had simply drowned, and that there were no signs of the plague, but the damage was done and soon "everybody knew" that "there's plague onboard Valen". The rumor spread like wildfire, and doors were slammed shut, windows closed, and curtains drawn. Nobody dared to venture outside. Eventually the panic subsided as it became clear there was no outbreak, but for a while the harbor was dead silent, while everybody huddled inside.

Valen's quarantine was over, the harbormaster and the doctor had gone onboard and she was allowed to dock. Before the soldiers could disembark, Olofsen took Max and Ben with him and went aboard to see the conditions of the soldiers and make plans for their evacuations. Olofsen went to see the Captain while Ben and Max walked around the deck. They came to the forward deck, when Ben grabbed Max's arm. He pointed to a man sitting by the foot of the mast and said, "Look at that officer over there! I think I know him!" The man had a black bandage covering his eyes, and a red scar went across face. He was blind, his left arm was missing, and so was his right leg below the knee. A crutch was on the deck next to him; on his torn coat the faded stripes of a Lieutenant, marked him as an army officer.

Ben pulled Max back away from the forward deck and said, "I want you to do me a favor!"

"Yes?"

"Go up to the man, and ask him where he comes from and what's happened to him. I'll go along, but I won't say a word, and you mustn't let him know who I am."

"Who is he?"

"I'm not absolutely sure."

"Alright," Max replied, "but you must let me in on the mystery later."

"I will."

Max went first and they walked over to the man, and Max touched his shoulder. "Lieutenant!"

Startled, the blind man turned his face to him. "Who are you?"

"I'm Max Magnusson, and I work for Olofsen and Company. We're here to help you get home."

"Your voice sounds familiar. Have we met before?"

Max looked at Ben, whose jaws were clenched in a stony stare, and replied, "I don't think so." He continued, "What happened to you?"

The man's only hand began to shake uncontrollably; he searched for the crutch and clutched the handle. He said, "I was wounded during a battle in Thurgau. They left me for dead, but after the battle they found me." He held up his arm holding the crutch. "Then I almost died under the surgeon's knife." His voice turned to a whisper. "Now all I want is to go home!"

Ben felt a rush of heat flow up inside him. Gone was the arrogance and the drawn upper class elocution; the man's voice was weak and shaky. Ben turned around abruptly and walked away.

Max looked at his brother's disappearing back and said to the man, "Well, you're almost home. What's your name?"

"Lieutenant Erik af Portman!"

Max found Ben at the end of the wharf; he was sitting on a bench staring out over the water where three ships waited. The yellow flags on the quarantined ships hung limply under the spars, and along the railings they could see men standing and gazing longingly at the land they couldn't reach. Max sat down next to Ben. "What was that all about?" he asked.

Ben didn't answer right away, and Max waited. Finally Ben turned to him; he told him about Emilia, the attack, the fight, af Portman's disappearance, and his own enforced exit away from a vengeful family. Max listened without interruptions, and when Ben was finished Max waited a moment and then asked. "What do you intend to do now?"

214

"For so long I've wanted to get my hands on this man, but when I saw this wretched wreck from a war that never seems to end, all my will to bring him down blew right out of me. It was like the wind ripping a sail to shreds in a storm. There is nothing left, nobody to hate, no need for revenge, nothing!"

"I don't know if I understand," Max replied, "but I'm glad if you can leave it behind." He put his arm around Ben's shoulders, and continued, "I'll make sure af Portman gets sent home as soon as possible. You'll never need to see him again."

"Thanks Max!" Ben stood up, "Now I'm going home to write to Emilia. I want her to come here!"

The summer ended, fall came and the plague seemed to have burned itself out. Gothenburg had been largely spared, so the Governor lifted the quarantine rules, and life slowly returned to normal. Ben had written to Emilia several times, but he'd received no answer. It worried him, but the postal service had been erratic during the plague outbreak – that could explain it. It could take months before letters started to flow normally. One morning Mogens came in with a pile of letters; some had been on their way for a long time. Ben started looking through the pile and began opening them, and after a while he came to a letter from Stockholm. He turned it over and saw that it was from Jan Walden. He opened it and a small package fell out. He put the package aside and started reading the letter; Walden addressed him as fellow Swedish officers do.

"Dear Brother Fogel:

It is with great sorrow I write to you. I hope that you have been spared the wrath of the Black Death. It is the worst thing that has befallen our people in a long time. Our capital has been stricken hard, and I am particularly sad that God has decided to call our beloved friend Emilia back to him.

When the plague came to Stockholm, the royal family left to live in the country – as they should, God bless them. Emilia stayed behind, and shortly thereafter she came down with the fever. She was taken with other victims to a spital outside the town, but died there. She was not alone; hundreds of people were felled by the Reaper.

We tried to contact her at the spital, but it was not possible to go there. Mrs. Hahn, who is well, found a note and the necklace I am enclosing. They're for you.

215

I'll always remember Emilia, and I am so sorry for you.
Your old friend,
Walden."

Ben picked up the package and opened it, inside was the amber pendant he had bought for Emilia in Prenzlau together with a note; he recognized Emilia's sprawling handwriting. He read it.

"Give Ben the necklace and tell him I loved him."

Ben was stunned, and he sat motionless. His whole body felt like it was made of lead, and he couldn't move. He stared out the window at the sun shining on the ships in the harbor, the flags flying in the light breeze, and people going about their business as usual, but he didn't see them. His head was filled with the memories of Emilia and for a moment he saw her face clearly. She was laughing and her hands were playing with the amber pendant. Slowly a black shadow grew up behind her as she started to fade and blend into the shadow.

33.   The Second Voyage

Ben buried himself in his work – it was his only escape from the painful memories of Emilia. In the evenings he would sit with his family at the inn, quiet and morose, but gradually he told them more and more about Emilia and what had happened. At night he'd wake up with an intense feeling that she was right there, but slowly the opaque and distorted mirror would come between them. He tried to hold on to his memories, but as he worked harder and as time and seasons changed, they began to fade.

In December 1638 Calmare Nyckel finally arrived back from New Sweden. Storms, the need for repairs, controversies over permissions to trade, customs duties, and claims from the Dutch investors had delayed her in Amsterdam. No doubt, the interests of the WIC played a role in delaying any solutions, but finally Spierinck and Blommaert managed through negotiations and cajoling to get her released from Dutch custody, and to see her off on the final leg to Gothenburg. Her load of pelts was sold in Amsterdam, while the tobacco was going to Sweden.

Cold, strong northwesterly winds made it impossible for ships to leave Gothenburg. There was hardly any room for arriving ships, and Calmare Nyckel had to anchor at the edge of the harbor. The winds didn't let up for several days, and she had to ride out the storm at anchor. Von Lans, who had come from Stockholm to meet the ship, wanted to get aboard as soon as possible, and he, Ben, and Olofsen went out in one of the harbor sloops. The winds were gusty and the skipper hoisted only a small storm jib; water splashed over the side in their faces as they sped out toward the roadsted. The skipper was a good one. As the waiting ship slowly swung back and forth in the wind, he brought up the sloop in lee of the pinnace at the end of her swing, and let go of his own sail. They stopped as they came into the lee of the ship, and sailors aboard threw a line to the sloop's mate and soon they were moored alongside. Rope ladders were lowered down and they climbed up on deck.

"Do you want to wait?" Olofsen called down to the skipper.

"No, but we can be back in a couple of hours. Ask the captain to hoist a signal flag when you want to be picked up!"

"Very good!"

The skipper waited for the right moment before he ordered the mate to let the mooring line go and tighten the jib line. The tender swung out from the ship into the stormy waters and set a course back to the wharf.

Mr. Symonssen greeted them and they walked across the deck toward the officers' mess where they'd said goodbye over a year ago. The stays around the masts were vibrating in the wind; it was an orchestra of humming strings trying to find a harmonious song of bass and treble notes in the gusting winds. Symonssen closed the door to the mess behind them, and the windsong softened into a pianissimo, accompanied by the percussion of creaking wood as the ship moved.

Symonssen looked tired; it had been a rough journey from Amsterdam and he'd been on the bridge most of the time. The steward put steaming mugs in front of them, and Symonssen said, "This cider will warm you." He took a sip from his mug, and put it back on the table holding his big hands around the mug, savoring the heat. He said, "Where shall we start?"

Von Lans replied, "We've heard bits and pieces about the voyage, letters have arrived now and then, rumors are told and retold. First, tell us what happened to Minuit?"

Symonssen stroke his beard, hesitated a moment, and took another drink from his cider mug. Finally he spoke. "We were anchored in the Leeward Islands on our way home. It was a nice day, the wind a bit stiff maybe, but that's nothing unusual in the Islands. There were several ships anchored around us. One, Het Vliegende Hert, was from Rotterdam; Minuit knew the Captain and he and our Captain were invited over for a meal just to talk about old times." Symonssen looked at his mug and idly turned it around on the table. He continued, "Just as they left Calmare Nyckel, we saw a black cloud on the horizon, but we thought it was just a squall, not much to worry about. Minuit and Hindricksen were taken over to Hert in our skiff, and the boat crew returned. Minuit and Hindricksen would be coming back in one of Hert's boats."

"What about the squall?" asked Ben.

"Well, it took a couple of hours, but gradually the wind got worse and worse. Soon there was no way a small skiff would be safe in picking them up, but they were safe on Hert." Symonssen paused, "Or so we thought." His hands fiddled with the mug in front of him – by now the cider was cold, but he couldn't keep his hands still. He went on, "The winds got worse, and we realized that we had to move offshore to ride out the storm. I ordered all hands on deck, we put up a few storm sails, and pulled up the anchor. All around us the other ships were doing the same thing; one didn't quite make it in time and blew right up on land. Two others collided, and the crews had to cut tangled lines and spars clean before they got away from each other."

"But you managed to get away from land?" Olofsen said.

"Yes, but by now we realized that we had a hurricane passing by. Before it was over we had lost half a mast and several sails were ripped, but we made it through the storm. It took two days before the worst was over and we could return to St. Christopher Island. One by one other ships came back; some were unharmed but most were damaged." He took a deep breath before he continued. "But Het Vliegende Hert never came back."

It was very quiet in the room; Ben looked at Symonssen, whose face was grey with exhaustion. He asked, "What could you have done? You saved Calmare Nyckel."

"I know, but we should have seen it coming."

Olofsen said, "Mr. Symonssen, you did what you could, and you brought Calmare Nyckel back. We all know that a sea voyage is dangerous, and many men are lost at sea. When you set sail across the oceans you're in the hands of the Almighty God."

Von Lans asked, "What can you tell us about New Sweden?"

Symonssen pointed to a chest on the floor. "It's all there! Minuit wrote reports and letters. I left some in Holland with Baron Spierinck and the rest is for Admiral Fleming. I'm supposed to deliver it myself; no doubt the Admiral wants to ask me questions as well."

Von Lans replied, "Yes! You and I shall go to Stockholm and bring the documents to the Admiral. I can read them and we can talk on the way. We ought to leave in a couple of days."

"As soon as we've completed the unloading." Symonssen looked at Olofsen, "I assume you'll deal with the cargo sales?"

"Yes."

"What's it like? New Sweden I mean," Ben asked.

"Beautiful, but wild." Symonssen reached over to another table and got one of his charts. He spread it on the table, putting little bags of lead balls at each corner to hold it flat. He said, "Here is a chart of the American coast." He pointed at the upper right of the chart, and said. "First we have Nova Anglia, which the English claim." His calloused hand moved west, "See this long island that ends by the North River? That's in Nova Batavia, where the Dutch have a very strong position." His finger traced the coastline to the southwest. "Here is the South River. The Dutch claim the eastern side, but their settlements stop east of the river." He pointed further west. "This is Virginia – the English have settlements there, but coast is flat and swampy, and the air is unhealthy. Many settlers there die of fever diseases."

Symonssen pointed at the South River. "There is a better map along with Minuit's reports, but I can assure you that the river is deep. It's rocky but with careful navigation it was easy for our ships to enter, and there is good shelter during storms." His finger made a circle around the land northwest of the river mouth. "This is Nova Suecia!"

Von Lans asked, "Are there any natives along the river?"

"There are Indians living there, but there is room for everybody." Symonssen continued, "Minuit invited the chiefs of several tribes onboard. He gave them gifts and they agreed to sell us all the land on the west side of the mouth of the South River. We've established a harbor on Minquas Kill, a western tributary to the South River; it's an excellent harbor and it's away from New Netherland on the eastern side of the South River. During the year, Minuit bought pelts and tobacco, and paid with the goods we brought. The pelts were sold in Holland, but I have the tobacco for you."

"Are the men prepared for the winter?"

"Yes, I think so. A month before we left, we had finished Fort Christina; it was built where the Christina River – Minuit decided to change the name from Minquas Kill – flows into the South River, and it has a storehouse and a barrack for the men. It gives the colony both protection and shelter. They have all the weapons and ammunition, and in the bastions we left the cannons from Calmare Nyckel. There's plenty of game, large deer and big birds, and there're fish in the river, so they won't starve."

Von Lans said, "Very good, Captain. You and Mr. Olofsen need to get on with the paperwork. I'll take some of Minuit's reports back on land and start reading – Fogel can help me." He smiled, "But let's get together tonight at the Molen to celebrate your return." He turned to Ben, "Fogel, can you make the arrangements with your mother?"

"Yes Sir, I will."

Anneke and Alex worked at a leisurely pace at the inn. It was still early in the day and there were only a few customers at the bar. When Anneke heard Ben's request she said, "We'll set up a large table along the wall in the back, and I'll get a couple of extra girls to help."

Alex said, "I'll take care of it."

Anneke looked at her daughter. "I thought you were busy tonight?"

"I can do that another evening."

Ben, noticing that she avoided looking him in the eye, said, "This couldn't have anything with a certain older Colonel, who can be very charming with the ladies, could it?"

Alex's cheeks turned red, and she stammered, "No-no! He's not that old! I'd just like to…….. Oh, never mind!"

Anneke smiled, "Fine, you can do it. Get Olga to help you. She is still learning Swedish, but her Dutch is fine." She took off her apron and reached for her coat. "Now I'll go to the fish market and see if I can get something good from today's catch."

Von Lans sat at the head of the table, next to him were Symonssen and Olofsen, and Ben and Max completed the group. Anneke had been to the market. It was December and still stormy, but fishermen had put out their nets and pots in channels protected by the string of islands along the coast, and Anneke had friends among the fishmongers who would save the best for her.

Olga had brought tankards of ale to the dinner table, and von Lans proposed a toast. "Gentlemen, in our first toast I want us to remember Mr. Pieter Minuit and Captain Hindricksen, who by the will of God are no longer with us. Mr. Minuit worked very hard to get our venture started. I'm sorry he won't see it flourish, but we won't forget him. His name will always be linked to New Sweden." He stood up, raised his tankard and said, "To the first voyage – may there be many more. Skål!" They all stood up, raised their tankards and drank to New Sweden.

Alex and Olga brought the first course, a large steaming soup tureen full of mussels, clams, shrimps, and bits of lobster tails. Olga filled the first bowl, gave it to Alex who put it in front of von Lans. He picked up and unfolded the linen napkin, tucked the corner inside his collar, picked up the spoon and tasted the soup. "Excellent!" he said, "Did you make this?"

The room was warm, the soup was hot and Alex's cheeks were already pink, disguising any blushing. She replied, "Yes, but it's my mother's recipe."

"Well, make sure you take it with you when you marry. Your husband will love it!"

"Colonel, are you teasing me?"

Von Lans smiled warmly, "Maybe – but it is very good."

Alex served the rest of the guests, and between the good-natured slurps from soup spoons, a murmur of appreciation went around the table. Von Lans said, "This calls for wine." He got up and walked over to the bar. "Mrs. Magnusson, may I have a word?" Anneke looked at him and replied; Ben couldn't hear what they were saying, but he saw Anneke motion to von Lans to follow her into the back room where she kept her wine. After several minutes they both came back, Anneke carrying several bottles of wine that she gave to Olga to open. Alex brought glasses and poured each a glass of wine from Alsace.

The evening went on. After a main course of cod, turnips, and more wine, Alex served port from Portugal with cheese from Holland. Finally she brought them each a small apple tart on which she had poured a small sprinkle of plum brandy. Von Lans took a bite and rolled his eyes in appreciation. "Alex, please ask your mother to come over, and both of you sit down with us for a moment."

Max got two extra chairs and Anneke and Alex sat down at the end of the table. Von Lans, somewhat unsteady on his feet, rose and said, "Mrs. Magnusson, you are blessed. You serve a memorable meal, your son Fogel is serving the Queen and our new venture with distinction, your son Max under Mr. Olofsen's guidance is becoming an excellent ship's agent, and, I hope you don't mind my saying so," he paused and looked at Alex, "you have a beautiful and clever daughter." He raised his glass, "Madam, I salute you. Thank you for a splendid meal to celebrate the return of Calmare Nyckel from New Sweden."

There was brief silence while they drank their wine. Ben looked around the table and thought, "It feels good to be here among my family and friends. I only wish Emilia could have been here." Von Lans put his empty glass on the table, sat down, and said, "Now it's time for the second voyage to the New World!"

34. Changing Crews

The next morning Ben walked to the warehouse. Overnight another low pressure had swept in from the Atlantic and across the North Sea, bringing low clouds and rain with it. It was dark as night under the cloud-blurred skies, and the rain mixed with the mud and manure turned the streets into a smelly sludge. He stepped into the warehouse, took off his raincoat and hat, and tried to shake most of the water off before hanging them on the hooks by the door. He kept his jacket on. Mogens, the office boy, was in the office and had started a fire in the iron stove in the corner, but it was still cold in the warehouse. Ben called to Mogens through the open door, "God morning, Mogens, let's get something warm to drink."

"Yes, Mr. Fogel." Mogens scooped up some water from a water bucket on the floor, poured it into the kettle and put it on the stove. Today they would start unloading Calmare Nyckel, and Ben brought out his inventory books, making them ready for recording the arriving goods. Mogens brought a steaming mug; it was ale mixed with hot water. Ben was sitting at his desk warming his hands on the mug when the door opened and von Lans came in. The rain's intensity had increased and von Lans shook himself like a wet dog. His raincoat billowed out and the water sprayed all around. "It's miserable out there!" he said.

Ben got up and greeted him, "Good morning Colonel. Mogens will have something warm ready for you presently."

"Good!" Von Lans hung up his rain clothes and sat down opposite Ben. "When do we start unloading?" he said.

"She's still at anchor, but the harbor master has promised us a berth at the wharf sometime this morning."

"Very good! What does she carry?"

"Mostly tobacco; the pelts were sold in Amsterdam."

"Well, I hope we can make some money."

"I do too, Sir, but I'm concerned that there may not be much profit in the end. Customs duties in Holland, the crew payments, and repairs have drained a lot of our cash."

Mogens brought a mug to von Lans, who sipped at the hot drink. "That feels better!" he said, took another swallow, and continued. "Well, we can't stop now. I'm a military man, and if this venture is to be a success it's absolutely essential that we support the colony with good communications and a steady supply line in both directions between the mother country and the colony. Admiral Fleming is already planning another trip for Calmare Nyckel."

"Colonel, may I ask what Mr. Minuit reported?"

"Yes. I'll have to bring his report to Stockholm before I can give you any details, but he was very optimistic. He bought land from the Indians and made plans for building a fort at the South River. The colonists have built cottages and are settling in for the winter." He paused, "They're trading with the Indians, but they need more trade goods as well as supplies for next year."

The fire in the stove was warming up the office. Von Lans took off his gloves and jacket and put them on a chair before he continued. "The Chancellor is supporting more expeditions, but the deaths of Mr. Minuit and Captain Hindricksen were unexpected and the Board must find replacements." He drank from his cup, and said, "Fogel, I want you to go to New Sweden on the next voyage. I've proposed this to the Board and they concur. We need you there to support our new Commander. You speak Dutch and that is very useful, as the relations between New Sweden and New Netherland are likely to be problematic."

Ben didn't know what to answer; he understood that to say no to this request was not wise. He needed time to think, and just nodded while von Lans continued. "There is another problem. Count af Portman has made some suggestions at high levels of government that you should be sent to Germany to a regiment commanded by a friend of his. Have you heard about his son?"

"Yes, he was on one of the troop ships that came through here. He was badly injured."

"Did he see you?"

"No, he's blind, but I saw him. My brother arranged for his travel home."

"Well, it seems his father is very vengeful and he blames you. You'd be safer if you were away in New Sweden."

Ben didn't want to go away again; he'd just come home. But he knew that without von Lans' protection he was very vulnerable to the Count's threats. He didn't want to go back to the war, and he thought, "It can't be that bad, and there is no war in America."

He took a deep breath and replied, "Very well, Sir. When do you want me to leave?"

"You'll be on Calmare Nyckel's next voyage."

Von Lans continued, "You'll go as Lieutenant commanding the soldiers. Kling will be coming home on the return journey."

Ben had seen the soldiers that went on the first voyage and he remembered Kling's comment about the men. He asked, "Where do we get soldiers?"

"Admiral Fleming is making the arrangements." Von Lans looked directly at Ben. "This is confidential, but the Admiral has asked the Governor of Elfsborg County, Mr. Hindricksson, to find twenty-four able young men that want to go to New Sweden. They will be soldiers but should also have other skills that are useful to the new colony. We're building a new province, and we need men who are good at jobs like shoemaking, blacksmithing, carpentry, and masonry."

Elfsborg County included Gothenburg, where the Governor resided, and the surrounding countryside. Ben thought about how the villages had already been stripped of young men for the war, and said, "Colonel, most of the young men have already been conscripted. It may be difficult to find any more, especially good, skilled workers. The army has been through every village over and over again. There are only old people, women, and children left."

"I know, but I'm sure the Admiral and the Governor will come up with something."

Von Lans stood up. "I'm going back to Stockholm to help the Board find a new commander and a captain for Calmare Nyckel. You continue to take care of the unloading and the preparations for the next voyage, but I also want you to work with the Governor in finding our new settlers." He smiled, "I'd like to stay here and get to know your family. Your mother is a very capable lady, and your sister is a very sweet girl."

226

He paused and looked at Ben whose face stiffened, but von Lans laughed and added, "Don't worry! Miss Alex is too young for an old man like me."

Ben's face relaxed. Von Lans put on his coat and hat, went to the door and turned around. "Goodbye for now, Fogel! I'll be back in a couple of months." He stepped out into the rain and closed the door behind him.

Oxenstierna had summoned them to Tidö. In the three years since von Lans first had been there, the work on the manor had been finished, and Oxenstierna spent more and more time there. The valet brought him to the Chancellor's sitting room, where he knocked, opened the door and announced him, "Chancellor, Baron von Lans is here."

"Please bring him in!"

Von Lans entered the room and was greeted by Oxenstierna, Blommaert, Spierinck, and Fleming. He shook hands with each of them and after exchanging pleasantries, they sat down in armchairs placed in a ring around a low, wide marble table by the large French windows open to the garden. A warm June breeze came from the garden; von Lans could smell lilacs in bloom and a score of blackbirds were singing. Across the water he could hear a faint "Cuck-oo, cuck-oo!"

The Chancellor got down to business directly. "Gentlemen," he said, "Sweden is doing quite well in the war against the Catholic empires. Banér is moving toward Prague and we see no real threats there. Denmark is quiet; their Öresund duties are a sore point with us, but our trade routes from Gothenburg to the North Sea and the Atlantic are secure. It's a good time to expand our efforts in New Sweden." He looked at Fleming, "Admiral, let's start with our finances."

Fleming replied, "We've sold all the pelts and tobacco that Calmare Nyckel brought, and Fogel Grip will arrive with a second load soon. Unfortunately, there has been no profit so far; we've had unexpected expenses for the ships and crew because of repairs and delays. We've had to pay customs duties in Holland. The English in Virginia will not sell tobacco to us, so we had to pay higher prices elsewhere." He leaned back in his chair, puffed on his cigar, and continued, "Despite these setbacks, which I think are temporary and part of our learning process, I am confident about New Sweden's future. Minuit's reports are optimistic. The land is very fertile, and our people can grow their own food, the game is plentiful, the Indians are easy to deal with, and they want to trade with us."

He stopped for a moment, tapping his cigar so that the warm ash flowed through the air onto a plate on the table. "We will need additional funds to supply the next voyage – we knew this from the start – and the right thing now is to move on and send two more ships back. The colony needs more people as well as supplies and more trade goods."

Oxenstierna said, "Thank you! Admiral, I believe you also have some news about a new Director to succeed Minuit."

Fleming nodded, "Yes, I've interviewed Lieutenant Peter Hollender Ridder; his father is a Dutchman living in Finland and young Ridder has been in our navy for some time. If the Board approves his appointment, he is willing to go to New Sweden and take over as commander."

Blommaert added, "I know him, he's a good man."

Oxenstierna said, "I'd like to meet him."

Fleming replied, "I'll make sure he comes here to see you, Chancellor." He looked at von Lans, "Von Lans, can you take care of the arrangements?"

"Yes, Sir, I will. Where is he now?"

"He's in Amsterdam."

Spierinck broke in, "Gentlemen, I have a new captain for Calmare Nyckel. His name is Cornelis van Vliet, and he is also in Amsterdam right now." He looked at Oxenstierna, "Should I send him up to meet you and the Admiral as well, Sir?"

Oxenstierna looked at Fleming, who nodded in assent. "Very good!" Oxenstierna continued, "Well, that takes care of that." He looked at von Lans. "Baron, you seem to have your work cut out for you. Now, can you tell us about recruiting soldier-settlers?"

Von Lans replied, "It's not going as well as we have hoped. My man in Gothenburg has been working with Governor Hindricksson trying to find skilled young men that can go to New Sweden. He reports that it's very difficult to find any; over the years the army has emptied the villages of young men, who have been drafted for the war in Germany."

"Well, we certainly needed them for the war," Oxenstierna replied somewhat huffily, and went on, "I understand we're looking for only twenty-four men."

"I don't disagree, Sir, but the Governor is having a problem."

"What does he propose to do?"

"He now suggests that we – again – scour the villages for army fugitives and other delinquents."

"Very well! Tell him to go ahead, but to be circumspect about it and try not to press the people too hard; we don't want any upheavals! I'll sign the orders." Oxenstierna sighed, "I wish we could get some people to go voluntarily. It would be so much simpler."

Blommaert asked, "Perhaps we could make some concessions and offer the settlers some land to own and farm as free men, and allow them to trade freely. Let them work for themselves! They can trade between themselves, with the Indians, the Dutch, the French, the English; we supply the traders with goods to sell and we buy the pelts and other things from them."

Fleming laughed, "You're of course joking, Sir. If we were to let the people decide on their own what to grow, what to buy and sell, there would be chaos. The land in New Sweden belongs to the company, which in this case is the arm of the Crown. Only the Queen, who until she is of age is represented by her guardians, can make any land grants. Land is best kept in the hands of the nobility. We provide a service to the nation by employing many workers, some of whom may also be tenant farmers." He paused before continuing, "In the case of New Sweden, the ultimate landowner is the Company, but it also has the authority to act for the Crown. All Swedish laws and license regulations are in full force."

"But Sweden has a long history of free farmers – the Peasantry is after all the Fourth Estate?"

Fleming looked irritated, "Yes, yes! But don't forget that the First Estate is the Nobility."

Blommaert asked, "What about independent traders?"

"Most traders are independent, but they must be sanctioned by the Company and they buy from us and sell to us. Craftsmen and skilled workers will be employed by the Company or licensed to ply their profession. No country will allow free business establishments or free trading by individuals. It's unheard of, and New Sweden is no exception. Not only is it against the principles of good governance and common sense, but it would also cut heavily into our profits." Fleming leaned back and took another puff on his cigar.

Oxenstierna broke in, "It's an interesting notion to distribute the land among free men and leave it to them to best use the land. Others could set themselves up as smiths, carpenters, and masons, and yet others could become shopkeepers or start commercial ventures buying and selling what others make or grow or what we bring on our ships." He stopped and thought for a moment before he continued. "But how would they govern themselves? How would they know what is best for the nation and themselves?"

Blommaert replied, "They could vote among themselves."

"Oh, no! That would mean chaos! Only responsible citizens with a tradition of leadership, owners of land or other assets, and clergy sanctioned by the state can be allowed to lead. We can't have workers or tenant farmers voting. That would be irresponsible!"

Fleming laughed again and looked at Blommaert. "Soon you will say that women should also be allowed to vote!"

Blommaert shook his head in horror. "No, no, no! I was letting my mind wander, but women voting? If my mind wandered that far, it would be truly lost!"

Oxenstierna said, "Well, your ideas are very interesting, but I agree that the Crown must keep a strong guiding hand over New Sweden ... keeping in mind, of course, the commercial interests of the investors." He turned to his papers, shuffled them and brought out a couple of pages with elegantly written tables. He said, "We come to the more difficult matter of paying for the next voyage. These are the figures for expected expenditures for the second voyage." He handed the papers to Fleming, "Please pass these around!" and continued, "The Crown and the Swedish investors, including myself, are prepared to pay our share as a further investment. We believe in New Sweden and want it to be a success." He turned to Blommeart, "Mr. Blommaert, your Dutch group has expressed some hesitations, but I believe that this has been resolved?"

"Yes, Chancellor! There have been many questions about the prospects for the venture, and there has been considerable hostility from the West India Company. Many of my Dutch partners have been pressured by the WIC to get out. They are afraid that New Netherland may attack New Sweden and also that the English may want to get a share of the territory."

It was getting even warmer in the room, and Oxenstierna interrupted. "Gentlemen, let's be less formal!" He rang for the valet, stood up and took off his coat and opened up his shirt collar. The others followed suit, and when the valet arrived, Oxenstierna ordered, "Please get us some of our Tidö ale from the cooling cellar."

The valet bowed his head slightly and replied, "Yes, Mr. Chancellor, right away!" He left the room.

230

They sat down again and a breeze from the windows wafted through the room; outside the cuckoo had been replaced by a nightingale churring and singing in a copse. Oxenstierna looked at Blommaert, "Please continue!"

"These are the problems my partners and I have in Holland, but despite this, I'm happy to report that we will pay our share for the second voyage." He pointed to the papers. "Fleming and I have agreed on the numbers you see there."

The valet opened the door, and two maids accompanied him carrying pitchers of ale, mugs, and plates of bread and cheese. They put it on the table, and the valet turned to Oxenstierna and asked, "Will that be all, Sir?"

"Yes, for now. We'll have lunch outside on the terrace in an hour. I want to take these gentlemen on a walk through the garden."

"Very well, Sir!" The servants left.

Oxenstierna looked at Spierinck, "You've seen the figures and you agree, I take it?"

Spierinck nodded, "Yes!"

Oxenstierna turned to von Lans, "Baron, any comments?"

"Not really, Sir, except that the biggest risk is the ships. Both Calmare Nyckel and Fogel Grip are old and may need repairs."

Oxenstierna looked at Fleming, "Admiral, what do you think? Are the ships good enough?"

Fleming replied, "Von Lans is right, they're old, but it would be very expensive to get newer ships. I think they'll last for a few more voyages."

"Very well! Anything else?" Oxenstierna looked around the table; all the men shook their heads. He rose and said, "Let's take that walk!"

In August Fogel Grip arrived in Gothenburg, where she was unloaded. A few days later her anchor gave way in a storm, and from land Ben helplessly watched her founder on a reef. The Board decided not to replace her, but to send Calmare Nyckel alone on the second voyage.

It was dawn in the village of Stavbo, and Ben was on his horse waiting for Hindricksson's men to make their move. The were closing in on a cottage at the edge of the village, where, they had been told, a young man who had run away from the army was living with his wife. Jon Klasson had been drafted to go to Germany and serve with a regiment of musketeers in Banér's army. On the day he was to report for duty, he never showed up. The army had decided the pickings were getting poor in the

231

area, and they didn't want to expend much effort in pursuing a few fugitives. Klasson was one of several who had decided not to show up, and he and others were living openly at home.

When Governor Hindricksson received his orders to capture wayward soldiers to go to New Sweden, he didn't need to search hard. He simply went to the army, who provided him with a list of the recruits who had not reported for duty. Hindricksson's plan was to make several raids over a short period and, when he had enough settlers, stop. Ben's job was to accompany the raiding parties, and interview the captives. If they agreed to go to New Sweden, they would be sent to the old army camp outside Gothenburg; if not, they would be sent to the dungeons of Fort Elfsborg for some time to reconsider their situations.

Sergeant Persson from the Gothenburg City Guard headed the team that was moving in on Klasson's cottage. He waited until his constables were in place around the cottage, three at the front, three at the rear, and two on each side, covering any attempts by the fugitive to escape by the windows. Ben yawned – dawn came early in July – and none of them had gotten much sleep last night. The first dawn rays of the sun were beginning to light up the treetops at the edge of the woods across the field behind Klasson's cottage. It was quiet as the men slowly crept up to their positions. A thrush decided it was really time to get on with the day and began to sing; a rooster crowed in agreement, and more birds joined the chorus.

The men were in place, and Sergeant Persson walked up to the door and banged on it. "In the name of the Queen, open the door! It's the City Guard!" There was no immediate response; he waited a few moments before banging on the door again. "Klasson, open up!" They heard the door latch move, and the door opened slightly; one of the constables grabbed the door handle and pulled it open. A young woman dressed in a nightgown and a shawl around her shoulders stood in the doorway. She was barefoot and her hair was in disorder; she'd come straight from her bed. Her pale face showed fear and confusion. "What do you want?" she said.

Two constables went past her into the house, while Persson pulled her to the side. He said, "Don't be afraid! We're just here to get Jon Klasson. You must be his wife – what is your name?"

"Eva Eriksdotter, but what has my husband done?"

"He's a fugitive from the army, as I'm sure you know. Where is he?"

232

The woman stammered, "He's not here!"

"We'll see!"

There was a commotion inside followed by shouts from the back of the cottage. After a few minutes, the three men posted at the rear came around the side. Two of them held a young man who was limping between them; the third carried a pair of shoes and a coat. He said to Persson, "Sergeant, he tried to escape through the window, but he was in such a hurry he didn't have time to get dressed." The constable laughed, "He was very careful, he didn't see us and he dropped his clothes and shoes through the window before he came out himself."

Persson looked at Ben, who had joined them at the front door. "Lieutenant, do you want to talk to him here or at the camp?"

The young woman had moved up behind her husband. In his haste he had cut one foot and it was bleeding. She put her arms around him; two constables moved up and took her arms to pull her away, but Ben held up his arm to stop them. "Let's go inside. Eva Eriksdotter, you can attend to your husband's wound – it doesn't look very serious, but you should clean and bandage it. While you're doing that, I want to talk to both of you." He looked at Persson. "Sergeant, bring two of your guards and come in with us, but post the rest around the cottage." Ben looked straight at Klasson. "You're a fugitive from the army, and should go to jail for many years, but I may have a better alternative for you and your wife."

The small cottage had only one room; over in a corner was a narrow double bed with four posters and a canopy. The covers had been bunched up along the wall, the bottom sheet was wrinkled. The pillows had two dents from heads resting peacefully until fate hammered on their front door – the young couple had left the bed in a hurry. Everything else was neat and tidy; along the rear wall there was a counter with a basin and a pitcher of water next to it. The sun had risen a little higher by now and the morning rays shone through a small window on the side of the room. At the rear, a window was open where Klasson had tried to escape. In the middle of the room was a table with four chairs around it, and a fifth, partly finished, was standing in a corner.

Ben indicated to the guards to let the prisoner sit down at the table and for them to take positions at the door. He looked at Persson, "Let's sit down!" They pulled out two chairs and sat down opposite to Klasson.

Eva Eriksdotter went to the counter to get some soap and water; her husband was still pale but he looked resigned, and Ben was sure he was in no mood to put up a fight. Nobody said anything, everyone was waiting for Ben. He left the silence hanging in the air for a minute or two, then he looked at the fugitive man across the table and asked, "How old are you?"

Klasson wasn't sure what was to come, and he answered guardedly, "Nineteen!"

Ben looked at his wife, "And you?"

She looked up from her husband's foot that she was washing, "Eighteen!"

Bens' eyes turned back to Jon Klasson. "Why did you run away?"

The man didn't reply, he was looking at his wife dressing his feet.

Ben continued, "The army considers you a deserter and a fugitive. If you go to jail, your wife will have to fend for herself for many years. Unless she has her own family to help her, she will have to work very hard and suffer while you will be close to suffocation in jail." He paused to let the message sink in. Klasson's face fell and Ben repeated, "Why did you run away?"

Klasson looked at his wife, who nodded for him to answer, and he said, "My wife is with child, and I can't leave her." He reached out and took his wife's hand. "What will happen to her?"

Ben looked around the cottage and his eyes lit on the unfinished chair in the corner. "I see you make things. Are you a carpenter?"

Klasson was still cautious, but he answered quietly. "Yes!"

Ben continued, "I'm Lieutenant Fogel and I work for a Crown company that needs skilled young men and women to go to America and build a New Sweden. If what you say is true, I can offer you some reprieve for your desertion. You would go on a ship to America and work; you'll be a soldier but also a carpenter, and you'll be paid a soldier's wage. After two years you may stay or go home, but you will receive a full pardon for your desertion."

"But what about my wife?"

"She can go with you; we would like that."

The young couple looked at each other, confusion in their eyes. Klasson said, "How can we decide so fast?"

"The ship leaves in a month so you must decide now." Ben looked at Eva Eriksdotter, "We will take your husband with us; he can either go to jail or to America."

234

It got very quiet in the room; the young couple looked at each other. Eva Eriksdotter stood up and turned to Ben. "Lieutenant" – she hesitated – "where is America?"

Ben waited a moment before he answered, "You'll go south by ship past Holland and Spain, then across the ocean following the warm trade winds. The ship sails past tropical islands and then comes to America, where it follows the coast north to New Sweden. It's a beautiful country with good land, rivers, lakes, and forests."

Eva Eriksdotter asked, "Have you been there?"

"No, but the ship just got back and the Captain has told me this." Ben added, "But I'm going myself this time."

Jon Klasson and Eva Eriksdotter from Stavsbo decided to become settlers. So did Gunnar Gunnarsson, Peter Gunnarsson, and Anna Svensdotter from Ramberga, Sture Matsson, Anders Bengtsson, and Nils Eskilsson from Dalvik, Anders Larsson, Måns Andersson from Berga, Anders Bonde from Bro, and many more, some with wives and some without. Not all men were fugitives or in jail; several adventurous young men from Gothenburg signed up as free men.

A week later the ship was loaded, the crew was aboard, and the settlers were getting ready to board. Ben was sitting on the bench outside the warehouse. In his hands was Emilia's necklace. He held the amber pendant up against the sun and the light shone around the tiny moth that had been frozen inside millions of years ago. He thought, "Emilia, I might as well go to America now!" He put the necklace in his pocket, rose from the bench and went in to take care of the last-minute tasks before departure.

The captain gave the order and the deckhands started to sheet home the sails; they began to fill and the ship moved slowly upwind. The anchor line slackened. "Anchors aweigh!" the captain called from the poop deck. "Ay, ay, Sir, anchors aweigh!" the third mate called from the main deck, where the bosun echoed the command and sixteen men began to walk around the capstan forward of the main mast, severing their last connection with the homeland. The southeasterly wind filled her sails; Calmare Nyckel picked up speed and moved away from Gothenburg. In 1639 sailing ships did not travel fast. Her second voyage across the Atlantic to New Sweden was going to take at least four months.

The September weather was fair, and the sun lit up the rocks along the channel out to Skagerrak. Once there she would head west to the

North Sea, turn south through the English Channel, go past the Iberian Peninsula and along the African coast to the Canary Islands. Then she would let the trade winds blow her over to the Caribbean Islands. A couple of trading stops making deliveries, looking for return cargo, taking on water and provisions and she would set her sails for the final leg through the West Indies up along the North American coast to the mouth of the South River at what would much later be known as the Delaware Bay.

Ben stood at the railing looking at the rocky gray islands gliding by. On some of them he could see low weather-beaten houses, docks, and small fishing boats. Fishing was a way of life on the Swedish coast, but fisherman and their families lived hard lives. The villages on the islands didn't look very prosperous; tattered clothes hung out to dry fluttered in the wind, and most of the houses needed repair. Old ruins with fire-blackened wood covered by shrubs and weeds told of times of war when Danish soldiers had raided and burned down coastal settlements while the villagers fled inland.

They all had come to see him off, his mother Anneke and his brother and sister, Max and Alex. Anneke held him tight in her arms, crying, "I'll never see you again."

"I'll write," he said, "I can come back in two years, and this is better than being sent back to the war. In the meantime things will calm down with Count af Portman."

"You know I would have liked you to take over the Molen. I'm getting old."

"Max will be a fine innkeeper, and Alex can help," said Ben. "Remember the old sailor who used to tell us stories about traveling the oceans to the New World? Now I'll get to see some of these places. I'll write and tell you all about the Indians!"

The ship's tender was ready to take him aboard. He hugged all of them, and stepped into the tender. All the way out to the ship he waved shorewards. His family got smaller and smaller. Inside him everything was in turmoil, and to steady himself he kept repeating to himself.

"I'll be back in two years – I'll be back in two years."

The rocky islands were receding behind the ship. The breeze had picked up a bit, and Captain van Vliet had ordered more sails. Calmare Nyckel was doing about five knots. At that speed they could reach the English Channel in less than a week. The war that was to be known as the Thirty Years' War between Protestant and Catholic Europe was now in its 21st year; it would be prudent to take a longer but safer route and not go too close to Spanish Netherlands or France. Allowing for changes in winds and currents as well, the captain estimated that it would take at least two weeks.

Ben could feel the swells of the Skagerrak, and he was getting a bit queasy from the tossing of the ship. In the Atlantic a low pressure was forming, giving birth to a storm that would head toward the North Sea.

35.   Holland 1639

The pumps kept the water out, and Calmare Nyckel sailed through the Marsdiep and docked at Medemblik. Once the ship lay quietly at anchor the leakage subsided, but they couldn't go back out on the North Sea and the Atlantic without repairs. Captain van Vliet went ashore to find a shipyard that could help them repair the leakage, and after a few days they could move alongside a wharf at the yard he chose. Mr. Jongehans was directing the landing crew, and soon the ship was safely moored. Ben was standing on the side of the forward deck with Ridder, and both men were leaning their elbows on the railing, looking out over the shipyard. The afternoon sun warmed their backs. In front of them, several ships had been pulled up on slips, and shipyard workers were busy with their tools, replacing boards, scraping the hulls to get rid of barnacles and other varieties of Neptune's deposits. Some were tarring the hull of a ship. Flocks of seabirds were hovering next to the yard where the fishing boats landed, the raucous noise of gulls' screeches mixing with the sounds of hammers and saws and the shouts of the yard bosses.

Ridder said, *"Het oude land."*

Ben smiled, "Yes, but it doesn't look that old."

"No, but my father always talks about Holland that way."

"My mother sometimes does the same."

Things had quieted down, and a soft breeze came from the sea. Many of the settlers were on deck, some milled around, some were eating their meals, and one group was playing cards over in the lee of the forward deck. Ridder looked around. "Most of these people have never been away from their home villages. I wonder how they feel about leaving their old country?"

Ridder, thirty-one years old, nodded when Ben, six years his junior, replied. "Well, they're young. They'll adjust, like your mother and my mother did."

Mr. Jongehans joined them. "Gentlemen!"

"Good afternoon," they replied, and Ridder continued, "How are things progressing, Mr. Jongehans? Are we still leaking?"

"Yes, but it slowed down when we came into harbor, and my men can cope on their own." Jongehans continued, "But I'll need to get the passengers off the ship, and we may have to unload some of the cargo to reach the cracks in the hull."

Ridder looked at Ben and said, "We need to find some lodgings, but they must be very cheap."

Ben replied, "Well, maybe we can set up a camp somewhere. That's what I used for the soldiers in Gothenburg before we left. We have tents and other gear in the cargo."

"Excellent! Let's find a place to set it up!" Ridder looked at Ben, "I'll go see what I can find – why don't you talk to the harbormaster about finding a warehouse for our cargo?"

Ben turned to Jongehans, "Where is the Captain?"

Jongehans looked embarrassed. "Once we were safely moored, he went to his cabin."

"With a bottle?"

"I'm afraid so."

They all knew that Captain van Vliet liked his drink. In Gothenburg he had sometimes disappeared to his lodgings and not come out for days. Jongehans quickly added, "The Captain gave instructions for tomorrow. Carpenters from the yard will begin to work as soon as we have unloaded the ship."

A month later the carpenters were finished – or so they claimed; when Calmare Nyckel left Medemblik she began to leak again. Captain van Vliet ordered a return to Medemblik, and new carpenters from the shipyard went to work to seal more cracks. Again they left, but before they had passed Texel, the leaks were back. The Captain now gave the order to go to Amsterdam, where he hoped to get better work done.

For the third time, Ben and his troop of soldiers had set up a camp for the settlers, while the crew unloaded the ship. Spierinck had found them a field near the harbor in an open area. Autumn was over and winter was coming, and the settlers huddled around the campfires. On the day before Christmas they woke up to find snow on the ground and snow still falling. It was very quiet – these were holy days, and there would be no work in the harbor or at the yard until after Christmas. By the afternoon the snow had stopped falling; at midnight the churches in Amsterdam began tolling their bells and Pastor Torkillus called the settlers to service. He told the old familiar story about the travelers coming to the inn in Bethlehem, being turned away and having to seek shelter in a stable. He said, "We are also God's travelers – we seek shelter here while our vessel is being prepared for our voyage to the new land. It is a land where we will find fertile fields, woods full of game, and streams full of fish. Let us sing with the angels from the Gospel of Luke, and let us pray."

They sang:

"Glory to God in the highest,

and on earth peace,

and good will toward men."

And on the snow-covered white field next to the harbor of Amsterdam, the small flock of wayfarers prayed their Christmas prayers for the land and families they left behind and for the safety of their ship, but mostly they prayed for help with their fears of what lay ahead.

Calmare Nyckel was in a slip propped up by a timber cradle; two master carpenters were working on repairs to the hull. Ben stood at the side of the ship and watched as they replaced rusty old bolts and nails with new ones. One of the carpenters showed Ben a bolt that had rusted straight through, only the ends were left. "Look at this," he said, and handed them to Ben. "You wouldn't have made it across the Atlantic. Half of these are gone and the rest well on their way."

"How about the hull planks?"

"Mostly good, but we'll have to replace a few."

A group of men approached, their boots squelching in the mud along the water. It was Spierinck, New Sweden's Director, with van Vliet, Ridder, and Jongehans. Ben could hear Spierinck shouting. "Captain, this is a disgrace, this is the third time you're trying to get the ship repaired! This is costing us a fortune, not to mention the delay!" He was walking rapidly toward the ship; van Vliet tried to keep up, but slipped and fell on one knee in the mud. Jongehans held out his hand, the captain took it and pulled himself up. By this time Spierinck had reached Ben and the carpenter at the side of the ship. He said directly, "Explain to me what the problem is!"

240

Ben held up the rusty remnants of the bolt for Spierinck to see. "The carpenter was just showing me these. Most of the bolts must be replaced, we need some new boards, new caulking, and new nails practically everywhere."

Spierinck cursed, *"Verdammt!"*

Ben turned to the carpenter, "Show Mr. Spierinck around the ship's hull!"

They walked around the ship and the carpenter showed them how the bolts and nails had rusted and the boards separated, allowing seawater to seep into the hull. Ben thought to himself, "We're lucky we didn't go down!"

Spierinck asked several questions of the carpenter as they walked around the hull. He was agitated, and he was clearly looking for a quick way out of their dilemma. When they had finished the tour, he had calmed down some. He turned to the carpenter and said, "There is much more damage than I thought. We must get this repaired properly, but how long will it take?"

The carpenter thought for a while, and replied, "I can't say for sure, but at least a month."

Spierinck turned to van Vliet, "Captain, do you have anything to add to this?"

Van Vliet, his trousers muddy and wet, his face showing defeat, shook his head.

"Well, I didn't think so." Spierinck sighed, "I fear, gentlemen, that we have no easy way out of this." He turned to Ben, "Fogel, I want you to follow this closely. Keep Lieutenant Ridder informed, and report to me directly every week!" He said to the carpenter, "Thank you, Mijnheer Master Carpenter, please go ahead and make the repairs as quickly as you can." He turned to the others. "Come with me!"

He led the way to an empty area on a wharf; it was getting colder, and the wind from the North Sea had picked up again. The weak winter sun was low over Amsterdam's roof tops, shining through the smoke from thousands of fires burning to keep the damp cold out of the cottages and mansions along the city's streets and canals. Spierinck turned to van Vliet. "Captain, why in God's name didn't this get repaired in Medemblik the first time?"

Van Vliet wasn't going to give up without a fight. "The yard gave me their assurance that they had found the problem, repaired the damage, and that we were ready to leave."

"How could they? We've all seen the shape of the ship's hull. Did you inspect the hull yourself?"

"Well, yes...."

Spierinck interrupted him, "My people have been through the books, the logbook, and the accounting." He looked at the others, "Would you leave us, please, while I talk to the Captain!"

They walked along the riverside away from Spierinck and van Vliet until they came to a shed where they sat down on a bench. They could see Spierinck and van Vliet and hear the noise of argument. Both men's postures were aggressive, their hands waving angrily in the air. Ben said, "What's happening?"

Ridder replied, "Baron Spierinck has gone through the ship's manifest. It seems our captain has charged the company for much cargo that was never procured. That and the debacle about the repairs make very serious charges."

Jongehans added, "The men are about to revolt; several want to leave the ship here. They don't trust the captain, and some think the ship is cursed."

Somebody was shouting loudly in anger, "You're dismissed!"

All three looked toward the shouting. It was Spierinck and now he was waving them toward the shed, and calling, "Gentlemen, please come back here!"

Ridder, Jongehans and Ben joined Spierinck and van Vliet. The captain looked sullen and angry, while Spierinck looked oddly pleased as he addressed them. "Captain van Vliet has been relieved of his command of Calmare Nyckel. Mr. Jongehans will take over the command of the crew until further notice." He looked directly at van Vliet, "Sir, you must leave the ship immediately! Lieutenant Ridder and Lieutenant Fogel will accompany you to the ship, where you will hand over the Captain's keys, and immediately remove your personal belongings.

Van Vliet trying to retain some dignity, mumbled something to himself, but he was a defeated man, and none of them heard or cared what he said.

On February 7, 1640, Calmare Nyckel finally departed from Amsterdam. Newly repaired and considerably more seaworthy, she sailed through the Marsdiep on the outgoing tide. The northerly wind was strong and her sails were shortened. Captain Poewel Jansen was on the bridge; he'd joined them only a week before departure. As the waves of the North Sea began to build up and the ship's hull started to creak from the strain, Mr. Jongehans was down below checking for leaks. After a couple of hours he came up to the bridge and reported, "The repairs are holding!"

Captain Jansen replied, "Very good!" He ordered, "Helmsman, set course southwest directly toward the English Channel!

"Aye, aye, Sir! Course southwest!"

"Bosun, adjust the sails as we turn!"

"Aye, aye, Sir," The bosun echoed the order to the crew on deck, who scrambled to the sheets.

The captain added, "Bosun, when we're on course, I think we can add topsails. We don't want to waste any more time on our way to America!"

36.   Over the Horizon

Calmare Nyckel was at anchor in the bay of Las Palmas de Gran Canaria. The captain and the New Sweden factor, Mr. Joost van Langdonk, had gone ashore with a boat crew to get fresh water and other supplies for their Atlantic crossing. Captain Jansen had given strict orders that everybody should stay onboard; he wanted to leave as soon as they were finished. A mild breeze blew past the ship over the passengers that were lounging on deck enjoying the sunshine. Ben was sitting on deck when Ridder came over and sat down next to him. "It's good to be out of the storms," he said. As they left the English Channel to sail along the edge of the Bay of Biscay and past Portugal, they had run into several winter storms.

"Yes," Ben replied, "but the ship handled it pretty well."

From the water below the ship came a voice. "Ahoy! Calmare Nyckel, ahoy!"

They stood up and walked over to the railing. A tender from the harbor was approaching; four oarsmen rowed and the tender moved briskly toward them. It was the helmsman calling, "Calmare Nyckel, ahoy!" He ordered the oars up, and steered the tender alongside the ship to their ladder hanging over the side. One of the oarsmen put away his oar, picked up a line and tied the tender to a mooring line hanging down from the deck. Mr. Jongehans came down from the bridge, and stood by the top of the ladder looking at the tender. There were three passengers in the tender – a young man, a woman who looked even younger, and an older woman. The two young people resembled each other. Ben guessed they were in their twenties, they had that blond Nordic look, but their faces were tanned, and the hair of both had been bleached almost white by the sun. They were dressed in white clothes, which stood out

244

against the black of the boat and the grey clothes of the boatmen. The young woman wore a hat tied down by a thin white shawl, and the man had a round straw hat to protect him from the sun. The older woman was black, a deep, dark black, almost bluish color. Ben had never seen the likes of her. She was wearing a pale yellow dress, long and full, with meandering stripes of black woven into the yellow. On her head she had wrapped many turns of black cloth into a turban.

The man stood up and waved a paper that he held in his hand. "May we board? I have a pass here from Captain Jansen!" Jongehans gestured to one of his men to get the paper. The sailor climbed down the ladder. The young man handed him the letter and the sailor returned and gave the letter to Jongehans who opened the letter, read it, and handed it to Ridder. "What do you think?"

Ridder read the short letter out loud. *"Jongehans, I've granted Mr. Nystad and his family passage to New Sweden. They want to become settlers."* He added, "It's signed by the Captain." Ridder turned to Jongehans, "You'd better let them aboard, and we'll see what this is all about."

They sent down a bosun's chair for the women, while the young man climbed up the ladder. The oarsmen brought up the luggage, only three cases, and placed them on deck. The young man paid the boatmen, who returned to the tender and departed for land. The two women sat down on their cases; the young girl looked drawn and frightened. Jongehans looked at them and said, "I'm Mr. Jongehans, ship's officer. Who might you be?"

The young man replied, "My name is Esa Nystad, this is my sister Liisa, and our servant, Ellianah Moutakini. We've been stranded in Las Palmas, and we seek passage away from here."

Ridder asked, "Where are you from, and how did you end up in the Canaries?"

Ben looked at the young woman; she still looked very pale. The black woman put her hand gently over the young woman's shaking hands to calm her. Her brother looked at them before he replied. "We've been away from our home in Finland for two years. Our mother and father took us on a pilgrimage to Jerusalem. We were many pilgrims and we traveled by land, along the rivers of Europe, and by sea until we finally arrived in the Holy Land. The war made the travel very slow, and we often had to change plans. Our last sojourn was Jerusalem; after that we were going home. My father didn't want to return the same way, so instead he found us passage on a ship that sailed to the ports of North Africa and to Corsica, where we expected to find a passage on another ship going into the Atlantic and north around Iberia. All was going fine, but just before we arrived in Tunis, my father came down with a fever. The captain wouldn't let us stay aboard, and we were stranded in Tunis for many months."

It was getting hot on deck from the sun, but the breeze from the sea helped some. Nystad took out a kerchief, and wiped his brow; the black woman brought out a fan and started fanning herself and the girl. Ridder interrupted the story and said. "Mr. Jongehans, perhaps we can find some room out of the sun for these people. We can hear the rest of their story later." Jongehans nodded in assent, and said to one of the sailors, "See if you can find some bunks for them!" He turned to Esa Nystad, "I can only put you with the settlers."

They were interrupted by a high wail of pain from the foredeck – it was Eva Eriksdotter. Next to her, her husband stood up and called out. "She's going to have the baby!" Several women around them came over to Eva and tried to help her to her feet, but her legs buckled under her. Anna Svensdotter called for help, "We need to get her below to the women's quarters!" Ridder, Ben, and two sailors rushed over to help. They tried to pick up the mother-to-be, but she was getting very agitated and kept on wailing as the contractions became more intense. Over by the ladder, Esa Nystad said, "Mr. Jongehans, Ellianah has delivered many babies. Perhaps she can help!"

"Yes, whatever she can do. I don't think the others have much experience."

Nystad said something in Spanish to his servant, and Ellianah rose and swept across the deck; her long, loose dress flowing and rippling, winglike, in the air around her, before she kneeled next to Ridder, who was trying to lift Eva up from the deck." Nystad following behind his servant said, "Please let her have a look!" Ridder and the other men stepped back while the women formed a cordon around Eva. Ellianah said something to Nystad who translated, "She's having the baby now; we can't move her below." Anna Svensdotter came up to Ridder; "Lieutenant, can somebody put up something to shade her from the sun! I'll get some sheets for her to lie on and some hot water!"

Jongehans interjected, "My men will help you!" He turned to the sailors, "Rig up a sail for shade!" He added, "And can somebody find the surgeon!"

246

Peter Gunnarsson volunteered, "I'll help you with the sheets!"

Måns Andersson followed, "I'll get the water!" They all rushed off.

Eva was still crying out as the bouts of pain came, but soon she was at least comfortably shaded from the strong sun and lying on the softer bed as the other women turned their attention to the job at hand. Fredrik Uv, the barber-surgeon came running and kneeled down next to Ellianah. The rest of the men withdrew to the side, waiting for the outcome. It took several hours, but as the sun sank to the horizon behind Gran Canaria, the cry of a newborn baby rang out over the water. Call it serendipity or divine intervention, but at the same time the call for evensong went out over Las Palmas and the church bells began to chime. Uv, wiping his hands on a cloth, came over to Jon Klasson, "You have a little daughter!"

Klasson's voice trembled when he replied, "How is Eva?"

"She's tired, but otherwise fine. Go to her and see the baby."

Klasson hurried away while the barber-surgeon turned to Esa Nystad. "Thank you, and thank God Almighty! Your black woman must really be an angel in disguise. I've never delivered a baby before, and all of you were sent by the heavens just when we needed you."

The captain and the factor were still ashore, but tenders were bringing fresh water and supplies out to the ship. Two days later their supplies had been delivered, and in the evening Ben was on deck with Ridder, when a tender brought back Captain Jansen and the shore party. As Jansen stepped onto the ladder, they heard the tender helmsman say, "Steady, Captain, don't fall!" Two sailors at the ladder reached down to help the captain as he came on deck. He walked somewhat unsteadily toward his cabin. Ridder said to Ben, "I'm not so sure about the Company's luck in selecting ship's captains. They seem to like their drink."

They left Las Palmas early a few days later. The morning breeze filled the sails while the rising sun lit up first the top of the masts and then the sails. Captain Jansen ordered a northerly course to clear the islands before they turned west to let the trade winds carry them toward the horizon. Ahead of them was nothing but water and sky, but he knew that far over that line where the two met lay the new land. The volcanic peaks of the Canary Islands disappeared behind them in the east, and soon there was nothing but water all around them.

Calmare Nyckel moved slowly but steadily, mostly with all sails set, but sometimes the winds stiffened and the captain would send sailors aloft to reef the topsails. Under the ministrations of the other women,

Eva Eriksdotter recovered quickly. The baby was healthy, and during the morning service when the ship was moving steadily westwards in moderate winds, Pastor Torkillus dabbed water from the Atlantic Ocean on the child's head and baptized her Stina Eva Calmiana Jonsdotter.

The days went by slowly; the weather was pleasant and life aboard settled into a routine. The passengers spent most of the days on deck in the shade under awnings made from old sails. The swell of the ocean still caused some seasickness among them, but gradually everybody was getting used to the motion of the ship. The birth of little Stina had brought them together, and the women would gather around Eva Eriksdotter and, more often than not, the baby would be passed around from arm to arm. There were many more men than women, and the men would form small groups around the women like sentries protecting their flock. A community of settlers was forming, and they were getting to know each other. They talked about their lives, where they came from, the war, but most of all they conjectured about New Sweden. What would it be like? How would they live? Some had heard stories about red men killing and eating settlers. Others knew for sure that there were tigers and lions in the forests of America. It was all hearsay, of course, as very few of the settlers could read, and those who could were asked over and over again to read the scant descriptions they had of the new land. Ben and Ridder were always queried, and sailors who had been on the first voyage were endlessly interrogated about the slightest details from their visit.

Pastor Torkillus would hold services every day, a source of some annoyance to the Captain and other Dutch Calvinists, who didn't like Lutherans. Ridder tried to calm things down, but Torkillus's services were often disturbed by raucous calls from the crew's quarters. Ben, who didn't know much about Protestant factions, thought to himself, "First we fight the Catholics, now we fight each other. Is this the way of the world?"

Ridder was talking to Esa Nystad and his sister, when Ben joined them on deck. It was late afternoon, the sun was beginning to sink, and the air was cooling down from the midday heat. Liisa had taken her hat off and her blond hair was blowing in the breeze from the fan she was waving back and forth. Esa had a kerchief in his hand and now and then he would wipe the sweat off his brow. Ridder turned to Ben, "You must hear this!" He turned to Nystad, "Tell him your story!" The young man nodded.

"When my father came down with fever, we were taken in by Christians in Tunis. It was a very small group, which originally had come from Ethiopia. We were given rooms and board near their church. Luckily we still had some money, and we could pay for our lodgings. They never asked for anything, but the Church was very poor and we were glad to help, even if it wasn't much." He wiped his brow, and continued. "The congregation had been formed in Ethiopia about eighty years ago by Jesuit missionaries. Over time their faith became a mixture of Catholicism and ancient oriental Christianity. But then the Emperor declared that traditional Orthodox Ethiopian Christianity would be the single state religion, and he expelled the Jesuits. Some members of the congregation converted to the state religion, but others left."

He paused and Ben said reflectively, "More Christians fighting other Christians!"

"Yes, but the members of the Tunis congregation were very gentle people. Their faith was a mixture of Catholicism and the Tewahedo belief of the nature of man and God being one. They refused to change their ways and left Ethiopia. They suffered from drought and starvation; they were chased away by hostile villagers and raided by bandits. Some were killed, but they also met kindness, and they were helped by other nomads. After wandering around for two years from the Red Sea to the Sahara Desert, they found sanctuary in Tunis."

Ridder asked, "Isn't that where the Ottomans rule?"

"Yes, but they seem to accept the small group of refugee Christians, at least for now."

Nystad continued, "My mother nursed my father in his illness. There was a Muslim doctor living nearby. He would come by now and then, but there wasn't much he could do. He told us my father had typhoid fever. He got worse, and we were not allowed to even visit him. My mother was afraid that we would catch the fever. The families in the congregation had several slaves – it was part of their tradition and almost every family had slaves. Most of them came as children or were born to other family slaves, and most of them stayed with the same family for generations. They were part of the family but only as domestic servants, and they could be sold and bought anytime."

He went on, "When my father needed more care, two slave women were assigned to help my mother, and Ellianah was one of them. But then my mother became sick as well, the other woman also got typhoid, and the congregation decided to quarantine us." He paused, "And it got worse – first my father died, then the slave woman, and finally my mother. Their bodies were taken away as soon as they died, to be buried before sundown, and we were not even allowed to leave the house to see to it that they got decent burials."

Liisa had put her hands over her face and wept at the memories. Ellianah, sitting next to her, put her arm around her shoulder, trying to console her. Nystad continued, "Finally they agreed that the three of us had passed the normal fever quarantine time, but the congregation was still fearful, and they wouldn't let us stay any longer than necessary. Ellianah's family didn't want her back; they feared that she would carry the disease with her. They were going to sell her in the slave market, so we bought her ourselves. They put us on the first ship out, which turned out to be going to the Canaries. We had been waiting in Las Palmas since Christmas, and we were so happy when saw Calmare Nyckel with her Swedish flag coming into the harbor."

"But you know that we're going to America?" Ridder said.

Nystad glanced at his sister, and said, "We know, but with our mother and father gone, we don't have much to go home to. We're Protestants, and even though the Canarians don't seem to care much about our religion, there is always the Spanish influence; we don't feel safe here. And we're so tired of wars and all the ills of religious strife, and like the Tunis Christians, we're looking for a place where men of different religions can live in peace with each other." He smiled at his sister, "We'll take our chances in New Sweden."

The sun was just above the horizon, sinking slowly into the ocean, the wind had died down and the sound of the mainsail flapping spread over the deck as the ship rocked in the ocean swells. Nobody said anything, but then a loud, raucous laugh was heard from the bridge. It was followed by a drunken voice, *"Deze stomme Lutheraner!"*

37.   Arrival

Ben came up on deck at the break of dawn, just as the edge of the sun was rising over the eastern horizon. The wind had picked up overnight, and like an old person getting up in the morning, the ship was complaining. The hull was creaking, the stays were humming, and the ballooning sails were straining at the masts, all accompanied by the relentless splashing of waves along the sides. The waves had grown bigger since last night; now they came from behind. Calmare Nyckel would laboriously climb up the back of a wave, just to slide down the front while her stern tried to outrun her bow, causing a rolling, yawing motion as the helmsman corrected the course. At the bottom of the wave she dipped her bowsprit into the trough, and water would plume on both sides while the ship's bow slowly rose to attack the next wave.

Ben looked out over the sea; to the right of the sun a black cloud-bank had formed and under it curtains of rain were drawn back and forth across the water. He walked up to the bow, standing there as the ship pitched and rolled at the same time. Another splash and a sailor, all wet and dressed only in his breeches, climbed out of the net below the bowsprit. He nodded to Ben and said, "These waves do a good job of wiping my arse!"

Ben laughed – he remembered the cold seawater against his skin – and replied. "It's not as cold as in the North Sea, is it?"

"No, we're getting close to the West Indies." The sailor turned and disappeared below through a door. Ben sat down on the midship hatch cover. Since they were running before the wind they felt only a mild breeze blowing.

Other passengers began appearing on deck, though not as many as usual. Seasickness caused many to prefer lying down on their bunks, trying to shut out a world that wouldn't stop moving. Liisa Nystad sat down next to Ben. "Good morning!"

Ben returned the greeting, adding, "Where's your brother?"

"He's over there by the railing. He's not feeling so well." She pointed toward Esa who was standing on the lee side with several others. When Ben looked, Esa Nystad was bent over the railing. Liisa continued, "He says he's been throwing up on every ocean he's been on. He'll be fine in a couple of days."

"Well, it may get worse. Look over there!" Ben pointed at the cloudbank.

"Maybe it'll miss us!" It was Ridder, and he sat down next to Liisa.

Liisa turned from the cloudbank and looked in the other direction. "What's that?" Off in the haze on their starboard side something was moving across the waves. In the light of the rising sun it looked like a trident sticking out of the water, but it was far away, and when Calmare Nyckel sank down between waves the trident would disappear.

Ben replied, "It's another ship just over the horizon."

The distant trident appeared again, and Liisa shuddered, "It's a sea monster! Look!" She pointed, "It has speared something with its trident. It is wiggling from one of the prongs!" The trident sank below the waves.

Ridder said with a patient shrug, "I think that's just a pennant flying from a mast."

Liisa looked at him, and let out a sigh of relief. "Oh! I'm so glad!"

Ben replied, "I don't know if that's any better. These waters are full of predators – some are privateers and others are state-owned!"

On the bridge, Jongehans sent a man to get the Captain and ordered a lookout to the crow's-nest. The sailor climbed up the weaving mast, gingerly stepping into the basket at the top. He looked toward the ship on the horizon and called down. "It's a Spanish man-of-war!"

Captain Jansen came to the bridge, and he called to the lookout. "Is she getting closer?"

The lookout, holding on to the edge of the crow's-nest, strained to keep his balance as the mast rocked back and forth; it seemed as if the ship was trying to eject him like a stone out of a sling. He turned his face down toward the bridge and answered, "She's running almost parallel to us, slowly getting closer." He looked out again. "Wait! She's turning to port, and it looks as if she's trying to intercept us!"

"All hands on deck!" Captain Jansen's order was echoed by Jongehans to the bosun on deck, who ran to rouse the crew. All around them the deck became a hive of activity as the sailors came from their quarters and took up their places. "Make ready for a port turn!" Ben felt the minutes tick by – slowly, too slowly. The ship creaked, and the sailors finally were at their stations. Jansen called, "Helmsman, four points to port!"

"Aye, aye, Sir! Four points to port." The helmsman began his turn, while the sailors shifted the sheets to match the new direction. Nothing happened – then slowly the ship began to turn and to pick up speed.

Liisa looked at Ben. "What's happening?"

"We've been spotted by a Spanish man-of-war. Normally they wouldn't be interested in us, but you never know. We're still at war in Europe, and the Spanish captain may be looking for a trophy."

They could see the whole ship now – it had gotten closer, but with Calmare Nyckel's new direction the Spanish ship wasn't gaining on them very fast. "How can we get away?" Liisa asked. "It's a much bigger ship than ours!"

Ben pointed to the black cloudbank. "I think the Captain is looking for cover in the rain and mist under that cloudbank."

"That looks like a storm cloud!"

"Indeed it is! Out of the ashes into the fire! We'll soon see what this old ship is made of." Ben continued, "You and your brother had better go below."

Just then Captain Jansen's voice rang out, "All passengers should go below! Prepare for rough weather! No candles, and douse the fire in the galley!"

The squall hit them about an hour later. Ben was on his bunk, when all of a sudden Calmare Nyckel healed over and the noise of the wind outside rose to a crescendo. Boxes, pots, pans, bottles, bags, and clothes were thrown to the floor, where they piled up on the lee side. The seasick were sent into new paroxysms of agony, and more vomit mixed with the seawater sloshing on the floor. Two men fell out of their bunks, one, Sture Matsson, cried out when his arm broke. The ship righted itself, then fell over like a drunken man trying to take impossible side steps to counteract a world spinning around him. It got dark and the rain and waves pounded on the outside; somebody in the bunks was praying loudly.

Anders Larsson and Måns Andersson tried to lift Mattson back on a bunk. He screamed in agony when the floor under them fell away, and they tumbled toward the bunk. Finally they managed to get him on the bunk. Mattson was using his good hand to hold the broken arm, and the two others had to hold him so he wouldn't roll back onto the floor. The barber-surgeon, Fredrik Uv, made his way over to them. He had brought a broom handle, which he used as a splint to fix the man's arm.

Meanwhile the ship kept on rolling, and the noise outside was unabated. Ben stepped up the stairs to the deck door, opened it a crack, and looked out. A burst of salty water sprayed the crack and soaked him before adding to the slimy soup on the floor. He couldn't see much through the spray, but when Calmare Nyckel heeled over, the shape of a ship appeared off to the side behind them. A puff of smoke came from its side, but he couldn't hear the cannon shot in all the noise. Then the ghost ship was gone again. He closed the door, and came back down to his bunk.

"Did you see anything?" somebody asked.

"No!"

The commotion went on for what seemed like an eternity. There wasn't much they could do, and Ben closed his eyes. He didn't sleep, but the world receded some. When he came to, the noise had stopped and the ship's motion seemed to be almost back to normal. He stepped out of his bunk and made his way through the darkness to the stairs and up on deck. The squall was behind them and there was no sign of the man-of-war. Jongehans was on the bridge and Ben asked him. "Where is she?"

"We lost her!"

"Thank God!"

Ben looked around; two of the sails were ripped to shreds, one of the top spars was broken, and sailors were getting ready to make repairs. Ben asked, "How's the ship?"

"The hull is fine, and we're not shipping any water."

"Can you make the repairs underway?"

"Most likely, but the Captain has decided to make a stopover at St. Christopher Island. He wants to make some repairs, and we can get some fresh supplies. We'll be there in about a week."

"Fine!" The ship was still rolling, but much more gently. Ben added, "Will you allow the passengers up on deck again?"

"Yes! It'll probably do them good to get a draught of fresh air."

Ben went below again to tell the settlers and to see the damage from the storm. Down in the sleeping quarters, some of the settlers were

254

getting restless, and when Ben told them they could go up on deck several immediately headed for the stairs. The injured Mattson was in his bunk, moaning, his arm wrapped and held in place by several wooden splints. Anna Svensdotter was trying to clean and wipe the floor, and her husband was lying down trying to sleep away his seasickness. Eva Eriksdotter was sitting on a bunk propped up by sacks of straw that served as pillows; baby Stina was in her arms, her eyes closed contentedly while she nursed at her mother's breast. Ben asked, "How are you and the baby?"

Eva smiled, "We're fine. She slept through all the commotion, but now she is hungry."

"She's growing."

"Yes, and I think she likes being on the ship. She sleeps and eats, and in between she gets a lot of attention from everybody."

Ben nodded. During their long idle days on deck baby Stina often went from lap to lap; she seemed to provide comfort and assurance to the little cluster of humanity tossing in the wrinkles of an endless ocean that their lives had a future.

They had been at sea for two months since they left Amsterdam, but altogether they had been traveling for almost seven months. After their stop at St. Christopher Island, Calmare Nyckel set course northwards, away from the West Indian archipelago. The islands soon disappeared and once again there was nothing but water around them, and life was confined to the small ship. The northern half of the world began its annual tilt toward the sun and the advancing spring followed them on their northerly headway. The days became longer than the nights, and in early April the lookout sighted land. As the sun rose Ben heard him cry, "Land ho!"

Soon everybody was on deck trying to see; far ahead, off the port side, a low stripe of land glowing in the morning sun rose slightly over the horizon. Calmare Nyckel followed the land for several days until the captain determined they were far enough north. He waited overnight before ordering a course toward land, and in the afternoon they entered a large bay. From now on they would only sail during daylight, taking frequent soundings along the way; the bay would narrow toward the mouth of the South River, and there were many shallow and treacherous areas, sandbanks, rocks, and tidal flats along their way.

A couple of days later, Calmare Nyckel was at anchor at the western side of the bay. The wind had died down, it was just after high tide and the ship was facing into the water running out of the bay. It was a warm evening, the sun would be down in another hour, and most of the settlers were on deck escaping the foul closeness of their quarters. Ben, Ridder, van Langdonk and Esa Nystad were playing cards, using one of the hatches for a table. Liisa Nystad sat with her back to the forward mast; she had opened a roll of paper and was writing. Ben put a card on the pile between them, and turned to Esa Nystad, "Your sister spends a lot of time writing!"

"Yes, she's always done that. She keeps a diary of everything that happens and all the people she meets. We have a whole chronicle of our pilgrimage to Jerusalem."

"Where did she learn to write?"

"My father was a pastor, and he wanted me to follow in his footsteps. But both he and my mother thought that girls should also learn, so both of us had to have lessons. We read the Bible, of course, but we also had to learn arithmetic and geography."

Ridder, listening to Esa Nystad, said, "Perhaps your sister could be a teacher for us?"

"Are there any children in New Sweden?"

"No, and until now, no women either."

"So who will be her pupils?"

Ridder replied, "I'll decide when we get there, but I suspect that many of the settlers can't read or write." He looked down at his cards, and threw them on the table with disgust, "I pass!"

The sun was sinking over the horizon, and the water turned black as charcoal. A waning moon rose over the horizon creating a sparkling, glittering path across the bay; overhead the stars were adding myriads of little lights. But it was getting too dark to see the cards, and they sat quietly looking at the changing spectacle of darkness and incandescence. "We're looking at God, and he is looking at us," said Esa Nystad. "He sends the sun around the world, giving us strength and power to live, but lets us rest at night under the beauty of the heavens."

It was a time when great changes were taking place, but to these Europeans, at any rate, the belief in God and in God's hand in everything, was never in doubt. Earth was the center of the universe and the sun, the planets, the moon, and all the stars moved in some mysterious ways around the earth. Sailing across the oceans for many months, you were still on Earth, and the omnipresent God was there with you. But

Ben had a nagging doubt, and he asked, "But why, if God is looking at us, why doesn't he stop us from fighting? The war between Protestants and Catholics has been going on for over twenty years now. We can't even keep peace between Protestants; even the Dutch Calvinist crew members here on Calmare Nyckel hate the Swedish Lutherans."

Pastor Torkillus, standing behind Ben, broke in, "God moves in mysterious ways. Now he has brought us to these shores, where we'll build a church and deliver the heathens into his arms." He paused for a moment. "He has put the stars out there around the Earth to help us find our way."

Esa Nystad said, "On my pilgrimage, I heard a tale from Rome that a man named Galileo has been studying the heavens, and he was saying that the Earth and the planets revolve around the sun."

Everybody was quiet for some time until Ridder said, "That can't be! Is the Bible not right?"

"If the sun is the center of the universe, where would God be?" said Ben.

Torkillus replied, "God would still be everywhere. I always believe the Bible, but it isn't always easy to understand what is written and to reconcile it with what we see and experience." He put his hand on Ben's shoulder. "That is what these wars are all about. Different groups and cabals use the words of the Good Book to support their own call for power. I sometimes think the Devil had a hand in writing the Bible."

"Well, the Catholic Church reads it its own way. I also heard in my travels that the Pope has banned Galileo's book and the Inquisition has found him guilty of heresy," said Esa. "He barely escaped being hanged."

"I wonder what the natives of America believe about God and the universe?" mused Torkillus.

In the quiet that followed, they began to hear a noise. It was a humming sound that came from the direction of the shore; it grew louder. Ben said, "What's that?"

Ridder replied, "I think I know! Let's break out the smoke pots!"

Ben said, "When I wrote the manifest, I always wondered what they were for."

"Well, if I'm right, now you'll find out!" Ridder turned to a group of soldiers on the other side of the deck. "Larsson, get the smoke pots I told you about!

"Yes, Lieutenant!" Anders Larsson from Berga rose and went toward the door leading to their quarters.

The humming had turned into a high-pitched whine, and suddenly the whole deck was covered by a dark cloud of mosquitoes. The people on deck started swatting at them, but it seemed the bugs were everywhere, easily finding every bit of uncovered flesh. Some of the people pulled their shirts and coats over their heads, but the mosquitoes buzzed around their covers waiting for a chance to feed on fresh settler blood. Eva Klasson wrapped a sheet around Stina and fled for the inside; Ellianah pulled up her head cover and turned into a black tent. Anders Bengtsson from Dalvik got so agitated by the attackers that he ran across the deck swatting at them, his hands flying like wings in all directions. In his panic he hit the railing, stumbled and fell overboard; the mosquitoes followed him and a contingent guarded the place where he had disappeared under the surface of the water. Nils Eskilsson, also from Dalvik, came running, shouting, "He can't swim! He can't swim!" and jumped in after him, in the process drowning the contingent of mosquitoes. More men ran to the railing to see what was going on. Eskilsson's head came out of the water; he shouted, "I've got him!" His hand had a firm grip on Bengtsson's hair and he pulled his head out of the water, while he grabbed a rope that somebody had sent down.

Bengtsson was spitting and coughing; they pulled him out of the water and soon both men were back on deck. When they took off Bengtsson's shirt a large fish fell out. It wriggled across the deck, but Ben ran after it, picked it up and said, "Bengtsson, we'll cook this for you, but we'd better find an easier way to catch fish."

Larsson came back with the smoke pots; he put dry tinder and wood into them, lit the tinder and, when he had fires going, covered them with wet straw. Smoke from the pots began to drift across Calmare Nyckel, driving the worst of the mosquitoes away. From that night on, they had the same problem every evening, and learned to set up the smoke pots as soon as they anchored.

They worked their way cautiously up the river with the wind and the tides, and the settlers spent most days watching the land on the sides of the South River. The shorelines were green and they began to see more and larger trees. There were a few islands, and here and there tributary streams, which were draining into the South River. One day they spotted a canoe with two people in it, but they were two far away for them to see their first Indians clearly. The river was wide and the water clear, at their nightly anchorage they fished, and they often caught something they could add to their meager ship's rations. On April 17, 1640, a larger than usual tributary river appeared on the western side. Ben was on deck when he heard Anna Svensdotter crying out, "Look, a Swedish flag!" She pointed up the tributary, and far up the tributary, where it almost disappeared, a battered blue flag with a yellow cross was flying over the trees. Mr. Jongehans came down from the bridge and told them, "This is Minquas Kill, and up the river is Fort Christina – the end of our journey."

All the settlers gathered on the foredeck, while the southerly wind and the incoming tide drove them up Minquas Kill. As they came closer to the fort, Calmare Nyckel fired a blank shot from their cannon. From the fort came a white puff of smoke followed by a boom. They had arrived at New Sweden.

38.   The First Settlement

The captain had ordered all of the crew to their stations; sailors aloft were ready to change sails, anchor crews fore and aft stood ready to drop an anchor at a moment's notice, the ship's skiff was ready to be launched, and line crews waited for orders to pay out the berthing hawsers to the skiff or to cast pulling twine ashore. The captain and all the officers had put on their uniforms; Ridder was resplendent in his navy parade uniform, epaulettes shining in the sunlight, gloves in one hand, and the other resting on the handle of the sword hanging at his side. Ben had put on his Queen's Guard attire, and the two of them looked like a pair of grand capercaillie cocks from the depths of the Swedish forests with their tail feathers fanned, getting ready for a spring dance. It was a clear day, not too warm but pleasant; a light southerly breeze pushed Calmare Nyckel slowly up Minquas Kill. The shores of the kill were covered by trees and bushes; the leaves were a light spring green, and many of the smaller trees were covered with large four-petaled white and pink flowers.

The settlers gathered on deck to get a first glimpse of their new home – ahead of them a large flat rock came into view. "It's just like Minuit described it in his notes," said Jongehans, standing next to Ridder and Ben on the bridge.

Ben nodded, "A perfect wharf with deep water next to it."

There was a murmur of excitement from the settlers on deck. Ashore they could soon see people gathering on the rock and waving to the ship. They heard shouts, but it was still too far to tell what was being said. Closer and closer they moved, until the captain ordered, "Furl all sails, and secure the yardarms!"

From above came a bass chorus, "Aye, aye, Sir!"

Calmare Nyckel slowed almost to a halt with her bow about fifty yards from the rock, and the captain's voice rang out again. "Drop forward anchor!" A splash at the bow confirmed the order, and Calmare Nyckel swung slowly to face the oncoming river current.

The next order was, "Mr. Jongehans, please take care of our mooring to the rock!"

Jongehans came down from the bridge and oversaw the launching of the skiff. When the skiff was in the water, he followed the sailors down a ladder, where he took the helm while the sailors manned the oars. The line crews handed down the ends of the berthing hawsers, and soon the skiff was moving toward the rock face at the edge of the river while the sailors onboard payed out the lines. Willing hands ashore hauled up the ropes, and tied them around bollards bolted down into cracks in the rock. Sailors aboard began turning the windlass, others lowered pieces of timber along the side as fenders; slowly Calmare Nyckel moved to rest alongside the rock wharf she had left almost two years ago.

The excitement ashore wouldn't stop. The residents had waited a long time for the ship to arrive, and now they were beside themselves. Shouts of "Hooray!" and "Welcome back!" were mixed with laughter and hoots of joy. Ben was standing on the bridge looking at the people on the rock. It wasn't a large crowd as only two dozen men had arrived on the first journey. He recognized most of the men from the first journey, but there were also many new faces. Some looked Dutch or English, but some were different. "They must be the Indians," he thought. There were a few women; clearly some of the first settlers, all men, didn't want to live in celibacy. Lieutenant Måns Kling, also in full uniform, was at the front of the crowd, next to him was Hendrick Huygen, the factor, dressed in a black suit and with a round black cap on his head. On the other side stood a tall dark man, his hair in a braid on the back of his head, and his cheeks and chin marked by dark zigzag lines. His breeches and shirt were made of soft skins, as were his shoes. Around his neck hung a small leather pouch, and a large feather hung from his hair. Next to him stood a younger man dressed similarly, but he wore a woolen shirt that Ben recognized as part of the uniforms sent along on the first journey.

Four sailors came carrying a gangway; they laid it down and pushed it away from the deck until it rested on the rock. They tied and secured the end to the ship's railing, and when they were finished, Jongehans, who had stepped ashore from the skiff, inspected the gangway. Satisfied, he called to the bridge, "All ready and secured, Captain!"

"Thank you, Mr. Jongehans! Let the men stand down! I'll be right there!"

Captain Jansen turned to Ridder, "Well, Lieutenant, we're here, and you should be the first off the ship – welcome to your fiefdom!"

"Alright!" Ridder adjusted the brim of his hat and looked at Ben, "Fogel, come along! You know these people better than I do."

Ridder, with Ben right behind him, climbed down to the deck, walked over to the gangway and crossed the invisible border between the familiar and the unknown. As they stepped ashore the crowd cheered and gathered around them. Måns Kling, surrounded by the crowd, saluted them and held out his hand to Ben and greeted them. "Fogel, you're a sight for sore eyes!"

Ben shook his hand and replied. "It's been a very long journey. We'll tell you all about it later."

Kling looked at Calmare Nyckel. "Where is Minuit?"

"That's part of the story. I'm afraid I must report to you that Minuit is dead. He and the captain both died on their way home." Ben turned and held out his hand toward Ridder. "This is our new commander, Lieutenant Ridder."

Kling straightened up, put his hand to his hat in salute to Ridder and said, "Welcome, Lieutenant!" Ridder returned the salute, held out his hand, and he and Kling shook hands.

"Thank you! It's taken us a long time."

Kling turned to his aide and gave him a few orders, then turned back to Ridder. "Now I'd like to show you around, but first I want you to meet Chief Metatsimint and his brother Onoko, our Renapi Indian friends."

The tall, dark man next to Kling stepped forward, held out his hand, and spoke. When he was finished, the younger man said in broken Dutch. "My brother says that he hopes that our friend Kring will soon learn to say 'Lenápe'. He also wishes you welcome to the land of our people!"

Ridder laughed and shook Metatsimint's hand. "Thank you! Her Majesty, Queen Christina of Sweden sends honorable greetings to our good friends."

Onoko translated for his brother, who replied gravely, and waited for Onoko to translate, "We are very sorry to hear about our friend Minuit. Our people will be grieved."

262

"So will we, but his letters give us hope that your people and our people can continue living and working together in peace."

The Indian chief nodded, "Yes, we think we can do so."

Kling said, "Yes, this is terrible news about Minuit! I had no idea."

Ridder nodded, "Yes, but let's not spoil the joy of being here. We will remember him and honor him, but first we should let everybody savor this moment, when our long journey is finally over. Look at them!" He turned around; the new arrivals had begun to leave the ship. Some sat down and put their hands on the flat rock, caressing the land, some just walked around looking in awe at everything. The residents were equally excited, many grabbed the arrivals, shook their hands and started to talk to them, but some were choked by emotion.

Ridder continued, "Let's first give thanks for our safe arrival!" He looked at Kling, "We've brought a new pastor with us, and with your permission…." Kling nodded in assent, and Ridder turned to the ship and called, "Reverend Torkillus!"

"Yes, Lieutenant!" Torkillus answered from Calmare Nyckel where he was standing by the railing.

"Reverend, will you lead us in prayer, all new and old settlers, residents and visitors, giving thanks for our safe reunion with our countrymen? Ridder turned to Captain Jansen, "Captain, would you please allow Reverend Torkillus to stand on your bridge, where he can see the whole congregation?"

Jansen did not look happy; during the voyages there had been many derisive comments, usually under the influence of drink, by the Calvinist crew about the Lutheran faith, and Torkillus had often been the target. But Jansen nodded and said, *"Natuurlijk! Alstublieft, Mijnheer Torkillus!"* He pointed to the bridge.

On this, the seventeenth day of April, in the year 1640, from the bridge of Calmare Nyckel, the Reverend Reorus Torkillus held his first service to his New Sweden congregation, some still aboard, and the rest on the rocky threshold to the new land. Torkillus's voice was strong when he talked about the sea parting so Moses and his followers could reach the Promised Land. He said, "This is our Promised Land, and we have been delivered to it by the sea. We thank you, God, for your protection during our long and perilous journey." He prayed, and the voices of the residents, who hadn't seen a pastor in two years, joined those of the new arrivals; they sang and the chorus of prayers and hymns flew across the kill and into the woods, where they were absorbed like dew by the leaves and the flowers.

After the last "Amen" had drifted away, Kling turned to Ridder. "Tonight let's celebrate your safe arrival! We'll have a banquet and serve you a New Sweden meal!"

"Very good!" Ridder replied. "Tomorrow we can begin our new settler life."

The sparks from the bonfire rose and danced with the stars until they died. The fête of spring, an ancient Swedish custom, blended with the celebration of the arrival of the Calmare Nyckel and the new settlers. The settlers had been hunting a few days before the ship arrived, and now they had opened their storehouse and brought out several whole deer, which, skinned and gutted, were roasting over fire pits next to the bonfire. The unloading of the ship would start tomorrow, but Jongehans had managed to find a barrel of flour as well as some ale. They had baked bread and when the sun set over the trees in the west, the bread was ready, ale was poured into tankards, and the settlers brought out platters of smoked fish. "These have been caught in the South River," Kling said, as the fish was passed around.

"What is this?" asked Anna Svensdotter, pointing to a platter of yellow cobs held by Helge Gorun.

"It's maize. The Indians grow it, and we've started a small crop."

Anna took one of the cobs and asked, "How do you eat it?"

Gorun laughed. "Chew it straight off the cob. I hope you have all of your teeth!"

Anna grinned at him, "All but one!" Her laugh revealed a gap where the barber-surgeon had removed an infected tooth. She put the maize to her lips and gnawed at it. She managed to get a few kernels into her mouth and chewed. She grimaced, turned and spit. *"Tvi vale!"* She spit again, "Save that for the critters!" She reached for a tankard, "I need some ale!" she said and took a swig. "Can't you make something better out of that?"

Gorun laughed again, "I've been trying to make aquavit from the maize, but so far it hasn't worked too well."

Rolf Engvas, another of the first settlers, said, "Minnequa grinds the maize and makes flour, which she uses in baking bread." He put his arm around the Indian woman sitting next to him.

Gorun may not have been very successful in making maize aquavit, but he must have produced something, because there was a jug with the results of his efforts being passed around. When the jug came to Ben he poured a small amount from it into his empty tankard. It was a cloudy, thick, yellow potion that looked like a mixture of ale and milk. He tasted it; it was strong and had a sour taste. Ben shuddered and said, "I agree with you. This needs distilling."

"Yes, and I hope you have brought a still. I've used an open kettle with a cloth cover to collect the vapors."

"No wonder it tastes sour!"

From the other side of the fire music was heard; Anders Bengtsson from Dalvik had brought out his fiddle. He started slowly to get his hands warm and nimble, but soon a lively polska rang over the meadow with the ripples of his bow. Mattson picked up a wooden spoon with his healthy arm and added percussion with spoon and splint. Next Ellianah started ululating in the background. Jon Klasson got up and tried to pull up his wife with him. "Let's dance!" he said. Eva handed baby Stina to Anna, and got up to dance her first dance in the new land. Soon more people joined in. With the shortage of women, men danced with men, and others gathered around the dancers and clapped their hands to the music.

Bengtsson's hands were moving with abandon, and strands of bowstring and drops of sweat from his brow, backlit by the fire, were flying and colliding in the air. After two more polskas, he paused, and the dancers stopped, all of them breathing hard from the exertion. When the fiddler stopped, they heard voices coming from the side. Onoko and two other Indian men had formed a line and their firm bass voices had picked up Bengtsson's tune and kept it going. But it was not exactly the way Bengtsson had played it – Ben heard something in the chant that was alien, new to his ears. It was the rhythm, the notes, and the way the tones fell in between where he expected them. It was captivating, and for a minute all he could hear was the chanting and the crackle of the fire.

The chanting stopped, and the din of talking and laughing started up again. Kling went over to the fire pits, and asked Vidar Vidaris, his aide, and Jonas Persson, the cook, who were tending the roasting spit. "Is the roast ready?"

Vidaris replied, "Yes, Sir. We'll bring some to you!"

He began cutting pieces, putting them on plates while Persson added boiled ears of corn on the side. At one long table sat Lieutenants Kling and

Ridder, the old and the new commanders, Huygen and van Langdonk, the two factors, the Reverend Torkillus, Esa and Liisa Nystad, Gregorious van Dyck, one of Fleming's men, who had been on the ship. Ben and Chief Onoko shared a table. Ulf Ulfer, also a cook, lined up tankards on a table, filled them with ale, and put them in front of them, while Persson brought the plates of food.

When they all had been served, Kling stood up. "Gentlemen and lady, welcome once again to New Sweden. I'll soon be going home, but I hope I can return someday with a family. There is good fertile land here, fish in the rivers, and deep forests with plenty of wildlife. The Company trade with our Renapi friends and others is good, but we must bring more goods from Sweden. We need tools, but more than anything we need people, we need families. We also need reliable, secure shipping routes between the homeland and New Sweden, and we need steady support. If Sweden forgets its offspring, nothing will come of this."

He picked up his tankard before going on. "We've had our share of problems during these two years, but I'm an optimist. I'm going home to tell our owners that this new land has much to offer." He raised his tankard. "A toast to all of you who will carry on here and," he looked straight at Onoko, "to our Indian friends. God save the Queen and God bless New Sweden!"

They all stood up and a murmur of "Skål – Skål – Skål!" spread around the table.

The evening went on. A lot of ale was served, and Ben needed to relieve himself. He walked away from the light of the fires toward the river. It was another starry night, the waning moon casting a weak light, and by the water's edge torches had been lit around Calmare Nyckel and along the trail from the rock wharf. He heard sailors laughing – the Captain had a full night watch to guard the ship and its cargo. As the ale flowed out of him, a man came and stood next to him. It was Onoko, and the two of them stood there quietly in common pursuit of empty bladders. When they were finished, Onoko said, "You've come a long way across the water. Will you forget your home?"

"No, and someday I'll go back. I'm just a visitor!"

"Hmmh!" There was silence, then Onoko added. "I was born here and I'll die here; our people have always been part of the land."

"But you welcome visitors?"

266

"Yes, when they come in peace. You have things we want," he fingered his shirt, "and we have things you want."

"Well, tomorrow we'll start unloading our goods from Calmare Nyckel."

The Lenápe chief nodded, "Good!" he said, and walked off into the night.

Ben walked over and sat down on a rock nearby. He was looking at the silhouette of Calmare Nyckel against the moonlit water and at the shadows from the torches lighting up the rigging and dancing across the ship. Calmare Nyckel already looked smaller to him. He thought, "What a fragile line it is that ties us to our homeland!" He thought of sitting on a ship's deck many years ago with Emilia when they escorted Gustavus Adophus's body back to Sweden. He put his hand inside his collar and brought out the amber pendant, and held it up in the moonlight. "I still miss you, Emilia!" he thought.

Somebody came up behind him; it was Liisa, who was carrying his jacket. "I thought you might be getting cold," she said and handed him the jacket.

"Thank you!"

Liisa looked at the ship below. "It's so beautiful, with the lights, the moon, and the black sky." She looked at his hands holding the pendant, "That's pretty! What is it?"

"It's a moth caught in amber thousands of years ago."

"Somebody must have given it to you – somebody who cared."

Ben was quiet a moment; he took a deep breath before he answered, his voice unsteady. "I gave it to somebody I cared for. Then the Black Death took her away, and this is all I have."

Liisa didn't reply, she just put her hand on his shoulder. Finally she said, "It's all so mysterious. Some of us get to visit the earth for such a short time."

Ben felt her warm hand on his shoulder; suddenly he felt comforted. "The worst part is that I'm beginning to forget her face."

"Yes, I understand. I sometimes get the same feeling about my parents."

Ben turned and looked at her. "We must go on, mustn't we?"

"Yes, and this new land is a perfect place to begin anew!" As she took her hand away from his shoulder, it briefly brushed his cheek. "Let's go back and begin our new lives!"

39.   On Their Own

Kling was showing Ridder and Ben the settlement. They began inside the Fort Christina stockade. "As soon as Calmare Nyckel left two years ago, we began building," he said. "First the log cottages and then the stockade. There's an abundance of good lumber in the woods here. We can easily build as many cottages, cabins, barns, and storage houses as we need."

Ben looked around. The square yard was small and there were two log houses in the middle. What appeared to be two small storage sheds and a privy were built along one side of the stockade wall, and an army tent had been raised by the opposite wall. Several ladders led up to lookout platforms at the top of the stockade. Kling opened the door to one of the log houses, and they entered; inside were rows of bunk beds along the walls. In the middle was a long table flanked by benches, and at the opposite end of the house a brick fireplace. Everything was grey, there was no color anywhere, except in the middle of the table where there were two buckets filled with spring flowers. Ben recognized the pink and white flowers he had seen on the trees when they arrived. "What do you call these?" he asked.

"The Renapi call them 'Tuwchalakw'. The English call them 'Dogwood'."

Ridder looked around the house; the bunks were three beds high, and there were clothes, shoes, and other personal things everywhere. "It is very crowded," he said. "How can twenty people live here for two years and not be at each other's throats?"

"Well, it's not much different from army camps, and Swedes are also used to small cottages and being cooped up in them for long, dark winters. The winter is not as long here." Kling laughed, his laugh like a clucking

268

bird, "But believe me, we've had some real fights over trivial matters. That's why I've kept the tent up. It's a refuge when things get too bad."

Back in the yard, he pointed to the second log house. "Huygen and I stay there. Our office is there, and we have storage rooms as well."

He led the way through the stockade gate, to a clearing. "Here's where we have been logging, and now that we've cleared the land, we've been sowing a small field."

"What do you grow?" Ridder asked.

"We started with the seeds we brought, mostly barley, but then we've added maize. We bought seeds from the Indians, and they showed us how to plant it." He pointed over to the corner of the clearing. "Over there, we're trying to grow tobacco."

Next to the clearing were a couple of cone-shaped huts. "What are those, they look like Lapp cots?" Ben asked.

Kling replied, "Those are Renapi wigwams. They left them for us when we bought the land, and now they're used by some Indian women who have taken up with our men."

"Do the men live there?"

"Yes, and it helps relieve the crowding at the fort."

Ben said, "It reminds me of the soldiers who brought their families to the war in Germany. There were hundreds of women and children in those camps."

"So far there are only a couple of men who have found Indian girl-friends. One of the women is with child."

Ridder laughed, "Well, I'm sure Reverend Torkillus will look at this as a golden opportunity to convert the heathens and bring the sinners into the fold."

Kling replied, "We've been following the Church's commands, holding regular services every Sunday, but there hasn't been much time for missionary work."

"Don't worry! Torkillus has his instructions from the Bishop and the Crown to spread the word. We will build a church for our men and their families." He looked around, "But first we need more bunkhouses and cottages for the families. Let's get the new arrivals off the ship, set up our army tents and get to work."

Ridder was very enthusiastic, and as they walked back toward the Fort, he turned and said to Kling, who walked next to him, "You've done a good job, Kling, and my instructions are to move forward with building a new village with a fort and a church, plant fields, and expand the trade. The Chancellor wants New Sweden to grow, and one of my first tasks will be to purchase more land from the Indians."

"Very good!"

"But, as you said, the colony needs more people. You and Huygen will be going back on Calmare Nyckel to Sweden, and I want you to convey our enthusiasm, and persuade the Crown and the Company to send more settlers. Next spring I hope to stand here and welcome them to a prosperous New Sweden."

A month later, in the middle of May, 1640, Calmare Nyckel was getting ready to leave for Sweden. The days before the ship's departure were very busy. Ridder was finishing his report to the Company, adding more requests with details about supplies, people with skills the colony lacked, and trade goods. The ship had been unloaded, and the last goods to go back to Sweden were being put aboard. Van Langdonk and Huygen were writing long, detailed lists of everything coming and going. Now and then they requested Ben's help, and the day before departure, a messenger came for Ben. "Lieutenant, Mr. Huygen requests your assistance at your earliest convenience."

Ben was going through the personnel lists with Kling, and trying to find room for weapons, uniforms, and ammunition that had arrived on Calmare Nyckel. "I know we have twenty muskets, but so far we've only found nineteen," he said to Kling just as the messenger arrived. He sighed, "I'd better go see Huygen. I'll look for the missing musket when I get back." He rose and followed the messenger to the ship.

Huygen was standing at the dock next to a set of cages; the gobbling noise from the cages forced him to raise his voice and shout. "Lieutenant, what are these turkeys doing here among the tobacco and the pelts?"

"It's a special request from Chancellor Oxenstierna. He wants to raise turkeys at Tidö castle. He's very fond of roast turkey, you know!"

Huygen shook his head, "I hope they will survive the journey!"

Ben pointed to several bags next to the turkey cages. "Jesper Stolt, one of the soldiers returning home, will take care of the turkeys. He's bringing special feed compounded with the help of the Lenápe."

"Where am I going to put them?"

"Can't you use the stalls we made for the horses, and sheep?"

Huygen sighed, "I suppose so." He shook his head again, "What will they think of next?" Then his eyes lit up, "Perhaps I'll be lucky, and some will die. They do taste very good when they're roasted!"

Calmare Nyckel weighed anchor and drifted down Minquas Kill as the tide was going out the South River. The settlers had gathered on the rock wharf to see her off. Kling, Huygen, and van Dyck stood next to Captain Jansen on the bridge, and below them on deck a few soldiers were waving. These were men who had now served their time and whose visits to the new world were over. Ridder held his arm up as a signal to the fort; when the ship turned downstream, free of her tethers to the land and the river bottom, he lowered his arm. A loud "Boom!" from the cannon echoed across the river, "-ooom – ooom – oom" and a minute later a shot from Calmare Nyckel returned the farewell.

The ship disappeared behind a bend in the river. On land about four dozen souls watched their connection to the homeland being severed. Many of the young men looked grim, Eva Eriksdotter, holding baby Stina in her arms, was crying; her husband had his arm around her, and she hid her face against his shoulder.

Calmare Nyckel was gone, the crowd began to disperse, and Ben walked back to the fort with Ridder. They entered through the gate in the stockade. In the middle of the yard a man was sitting on the ground, his ankle shackled and chained to a pole driven into the ground. Ridder stopped in front of the man and looked silently at him. The man lowered his eyes, not looking at any of them. Ridder broke the silence. "Soldier Esko Munck, what am I going to do with you? You tried to stow away on Calmare Nyckel."

He looked at Munck who replied in a weak but defiant voice. "I just wanted to go home, Sir."

Ridder's stern gaze bored into his eyes, "Soldier, what you did is called desertion. We're not at war here, but if you had been serving in Germany right now, you would have been shot."

"Yes, Sir."

"Since Calmare Nyckel has left, there's no risk of you trying again. I'll let you free, but you're confined to the fort until we've arranged a tribunal to decide your case." Ridder turned to Ben, "Fogel, he's in your care! I'll be in the office." He walked off.

Ben waved to a group of soldiers at the gate. "Sergeant Rieser, over here!" A heavyset man separated from the group and came lumbering across the yard. He was breathing heavily when he arrived. "Lieutenant!" he said between gasps for air.

"Sergeant, you may release Munck. Let him work, but he's confined to the fort until further notice."

"Yes, Sir!" Sergeant Eskil Rieser, from Treryd in the forested highlands of Småland, brought out a key and unlocked the shackles around Munck's ankle, and said to the prisoner. "Go clean yourself up, and report back to me." Munck rubbed his chafed ankle, stood up and walked toward the bunkhouse.

Ben turned to Rieser, "Sergeant, one more thing," he said.

"Yes, Sir!"

"I think we may have a thief among us. Several things are missing from the load that we brought on Calmare Nyckel. Since most of the boxes and barrels were sealed when they came off the ship, I suspect that someone has helped themselves during the unloading and unpacking."

"What's missing, Sir?"

"Among other things a musket, bullets, and powder. I also think we are missing some food, and it looks as if somebody has tried to break into a box of the goods we've brought for trade with the Indians."

"I'll see what I can find out, Sir!" Rieser saluted Ben, turned and went back to the gate.

In the office Ben told Ridder about the theft. "This is much more serious than Munck's desertion," he said.

"I agree. Do everything you can to find out who's behind it all." Ridder continued, "I'm going to leave the settlement in your hands for a while. I'm going to visit the Lenápe chiefs and try to buy some more land from them. Van Langdonk is going with me."

"Very good, but..," Ben hesitated.

"Yes, go on!"

"I've been talking a lot to Chief Onoko, and I'm not so sure that the Lenápes look at these land agreements the same way we do."

"I know, but in the end it doesn't matter. I have strict orders coming directly from Oxenstierna to deal fairly and peacefully with the Indians. We'll do so with all the requisite pomp and circumstance, but in the end, without controlling the land, we have nothing. Also, if we don't get this land, the Dutch or the English will. So our view of any agreement must prevail."

"I agree, but can we avoid open conflict?"

272

"You've served in the Flaxen Guard in Germany, where I understand you had to collect tribute from the population?"

"Yes, I did."

"Well, then, you and I know that an agreement without battle is always the best for everybody, but the powerful have the last word in interpreting the law." Ridder added, "I don't think it will come to blows between the Lenápe and us. They seem to appreciate the goods we bring and the advantages of trading with us."

"What about the Dutch?" Ben said. "I understand they have been grumbling a lot about us being here. I wonder if they will try to scare us off?"

"I'm sure Governor Kieft in New Amsterdam is considering just that, but both he and I have instructions from our sovereigns not to bear arms against each other. I've also heard that Kieft has his own problems in the colony and with the WIC. That doesn't mean they may not try to rattle their swords. We can argue the legal points, but you'll need to keep your troops at the ready."

40.   **Letters From Home**

Ridder and van Langdonk successfully negotiated with the Lenápes for more land, and New Sweden expanded north along the western side of the South River past the tributary the Dutch called Schuyl's Kill, up to the falls of the South River. Ridder left most of the day-to-day duties to Ben, who was kept very busy overseeing the work in the fields, commanding the guards, and directing the building of new dwellings, barns, and storage houses. Logging crews were cutting trees, sawing them into logs, and, with the help of their few horses, pulling the logs to the building sites, where carpenters took over, shaping and cutting corner locks to fit as they stacked them to form walls. Land crews were clearing away the stumps and stones, expanding the fields where crops would be planted. It was hard work; most of the soldiers were illiterate and unschooled, and they knew little about carpentry or the cultivation of land, but luckily a few were quick learners, and after a few mishaps and false starts the work was going smoothly.

The leaves turned color and began to fall. Soon, thankfully, the people living in army tents could move to better housing – the men into a new bunkhouse and the families into the cottages. After the Sunday service at the end of October, Pastor Torkillus asked the congregation to walk with him around the settlement to bless the new dwellings. When they came to the end of the settlement, Jon Klasson invited them into his new cottage. Klasson had turned out to be a very good carpenter, and he had made sturdy furniture, plain but functional, for the cottage. The single room was small and low, reminding Ben of the cottage where they had caught Klasson – a double bed in the corner, a table with two benches alongside, a fireplace in the opposite corner. But something had been

274

added, a small wooden cradle stood next to the large bed. Stina, their first native-born New Swede would sleep well under her own roof.

In November, the Dutch ship Freedenburgh was sighted coming up Minquas Kill. The ship anchored in the middle of the river and a boat was sent ashore. Ben had been summoned by the guards, and he was waiting when the ship's boat landed. A portly man in a black suit asked permission to come ashore. Ben invited him onto the rock wharf, two guards helped him ashore, and when he was safely on the rock the man sighed loudly. "It's nice to be back on land again." He straightened his clothes and said. "You must be Lieutenant Fogel."

"Yes, I am. May I ask who you are, Sir?"

"Of course! I'm Joost van Boagert and I am here by permission from the Directors of New Sweden." Boagert reached into his valise, and brought out two envelopes. "I have a letter here from Mijnheer Spierinck to your Commander, Lieutenant Ridder. The other is for you from Colonel von Lans." He handed Ben the envelopes.

Ben read the address, *"Lieutenant B. Fogel, New Sweden, India"*, and he recognized the familiar handwriting of von Lans. He felt a wave of warmth rush through him. "This is a surprise! We're not as cut off from the world as it seems," he thought.

Bogaert continued, "I have more company reports and letters, and onboard we also have a bag of letters for the settlers."

Ben replied, "Welcome to New Sweden, Mr. Boagert. Please follow me, and we'll go see Lieutenant Ridder." He looked at the ship's boat and asked. "What about your men, Sir?"

"They can go back to the ship. We can signal them, or perhaps you can arrange to take me back later."

"Very well!"

That night Ben opened the envelope from von Lans, inside was a letter and another smaller envelope addressed, *"Lieutenant B. Fogel, private."* He began by reading the letter. It was a short briefing, its brevity typical of von Lans, on company activities in Sweden. At the end he asked Ben to write a report to go back with Mr. Boagert, and he ended the letter with his instructions.

"The Company is preparing two ships for the fourth expedition to New Sweden carrying about five dozen more settlers, including several families. Lieutenant Kling will be returning with his family, and he will take over the command of the garrison. At that time, you're free to return, but the Company

would like it very much if you were to stay as an agent. You will be paid your present salary, but you will also be allowed a commission on every trade. The Chancellor has approved that you will be given a land grant for your personal use, where you can build and farm as well. (The details are in the attached Letter of Appointment.) The Directors are certain that there is a good future ahead for New Sweden and that the trade with India will only grow."

Ben opened the second letter and began reading; after a while he understood why von Lans had decided to make it a private matter between the two of them.

"Dear Fogel,

There are several things that I want to convey to you alone, matters that I think should support you in deciding to accept the Company's offer and stay in New Sweden.

The New Sweden Company is about to go through many changes, of which you will become aware as time advances. While the profits of the Company for the first two years have not lived up to expectations, the Chancellor is still in very firm control and both he and Admiral Fleming support the Company. Our Dutch investors are under great pressure, originating from the Dutch West India Company, not to support New Sweden as it threatens the position of the WIC in New Netherland.

The long war in Europe, the support of our Army fighting the Papists, and the protection of Swedish interests there, make it difficult to get the Crown interested in the relatively small adventure of New Sweden. However, the Chancellor's influence may change that, making the New Sweden Company a matter of national concern. This will strengthen the Company, and if you accept the Company offer, you should be able to profit from this personally.

On another matter, your adversary, Count af Portman, still wants your head on the chopping-block. It would be wise for you to stay away from Sweden. A few more years and the matter may finally blow over.

Finally a personal note, one that starts with two tragedies, as first my older brother's wife died in childbirth, and then during the winter, my brother himself was struck down by the flux and perished. I am next in line, and I have taken leave of the army to take over the family land holdings. The Chancellor still wants me attend to Company affairs, and during these difficult months following my brother's death, I've had to spend much time in Gothenburg. I took most of my meals at the Molen, and over time your family has been a great comfort to me, especially your sister.

My warm feelings for your sister grew deeper, they appeared to be reciprocated, and now I've asked Alexandra to be my wife. I didn't think it could happen to me, but after all my dallying around I found myself totally enchanted by Alexandra, and wanting to spend my time only with her. I also can't think of anyone better for sharing my new responsibilities, both as a farmer and as parents for two young orphan nieces. Alexandra has agreed to marry me, and I'm happy to say that both your mother and brother have given us their blessing. I now hope that you will take this kindly and with approval.

Yours

Von Lans."

The Freedenburgh mailbag brought several more letters for Ben. He recognized Alexandra's careful penmanship, and opened her letter. She told him she was very happy.

"By the time you get this, Rupert and I will already be married. The deaths in his family struck him hard, but also brought out a more gentle side in him. Time is a good healer; Rupert is kind and takes his responsibilities to his brother's children very seriously. I want to share this with him even if it is a bit daunting to gain all at once a husband, two daughters, and a large household. Oh well, I'll just pretend I'm back at the Molen on a busy night trying to keep order among the cooks, the servers, and not to mention a few unruly customers."

Ben smiled to himself, "No need to worry about Alex," he thought. He opened and read a letter from Max, who reported that his work at Mr. Olofsen's agency went well. At the bottom of the letter there was a short note from Anneke. Her handwriting was hard to read, and Ben knew that she would have labored hard to write to him.

"My dear boy,

We're so happy for Alexandra – imagine that she'll become a Baroness! I am fine, but I miss you, and I hope God is treating you well. Come home soon!

Mother."

Ben sat quietly with all the letters strewn around him on the floor. For a little while the vast ocean had shrunk to a small lake, his family being just over on the other side. He thought of the aromas of food in the Molen, his mother's laugh, the noise in the Gothenburg harbor, the smell of fish being unloaded, the spring sun against his face, Max talking about a shipment of spices, Mogens stoking the stove in the office, and Alexandra standing next to the table looking at von Lans with a glow on her face.

There was a knock on his door.

"Enter!"

Liisa Nystad came in through the door. She looked at Ben and the letters on the floor and said with a voice filled with concern, "You don't look very happy. Have you had bad news?"

Ben shook his heads, "No. It's just that…." His voice trailed off.

"Yes, what?"

"It's good to hear from home. For a little while I felt as if they were very close." He picked up a letter and showed it to Liisa. "But look, this letter has been on its way for more than six months. In the meantime my sister has gotten married to my Colonel, he's left the army, and they are now living on his family farm. My mother says she's fine, but that was six months ago. If she were to die, I wouldn't know for another six months."

"I know, and that delay holds true for our soldiers as well." She held up a pack of letters. "I am going to read these for the men who can't read, and I already know that there are several with bad news. Naught can be done about it."

Ben looked at her for a moment before answering. "Well, you can't hide the bad news, but try to read it to them alone, and tell them that you will help them write a letter in time for the return of the Freedenburgh." He added, "Ask your brother or Reverend Torkillus to accompany you when you know it is very bad news."

"Well, luckily it's not all bad news."

Liisa pulled up a chair and sat down opposite him. She smiled, "Are you going to tell me your good news?"

Ben told her about his family, about von Lans and how he had served under him in Germany and now in the New Sweden Company. "I'm very happy for my sister. The Colonel is a good man, and if he's done with being a ladies' man, he'll make fine husband for her. He's older than she is, but I think that will be good for Alexandra. She's got a will of her own, and they're a good match."

Ben hesitated. "I don't know why I tell you this, but I feel very comfortable talking to you." He picked up the first letter from von Lans. "I'm being offered the opportunity to stay in New Sweden for several more years. There are great plans for the colony, and it's a very good offer. Besides, I can't go home because a man of great influence in Sweden wants my head for what he thinks I did to his son. Von Lans has been very helpful, and I really can't refuse."

"Don't you want to stay?"

"Yes, but why don't I feel good about it?"

"It's the curse of knowing there are other places. Like Eve in the Garden of Eden, once you have tasted other fruits, there's no going back."

Ben reached out for her hand. "How about you?" he said. "Do you want to go back?"

"Someday, perhaps. Now I'm all excited about what I can do here." She squeezed his hand. "I have to go see the soldiers. They are waiting for me to read their letters for them."

In November 1640, the Freedenburgh left New Sweden; it carried a load of over seven hundred beaver skins, thirty bear skins, miscellaneous other skins, and one small bale of tobacco. In Holland it would fetch enough money to pay for supplies needed by the colony. There was also a mailbag aboard which held Ben's letters to his family, his reports to von Lans, and a note telling his new brother-in-law that he was very happy for him and Alexandra. He also accepted the Company's offer for him to stay in New Sweden.

41.   A Troublesome Winter

Ben was at his desk when there was a knock on the door.
"Enter!"
Sergeant Rieser came through the door, together with a cold gust of wind. He closed the door, and walked over to stand in front of the desk. "Sit down, Sergeant!" Ben said. Rieser, wheezing a bit as always, pulled a chair over and sat down.

"Thank you, Sir!"

Ben looked at him, "How are you? You don't look well."

Rieser coughed – it was a rattling cough coming from deep inside him. Ben waited, and when Rieser finally stopped coughing, the sergeant replied. "It's just a chill, it'll go away."

Rieser took another wheezing breath and said, "I think I've found our thief!"

"Tell me!"

"Last Sunday when Pastor Torkillus asked us to walk with him, I took the opportunity to look around one of the new barns."

Ben nodded, "Go on!"

"Inside one of the stalls, I noticed a loose board in the barrier to the next stall. I opened it and there was the musket and everything else that was missing from what we unloaded."

"Do you know who had put it there?"

"Not at first, but I had my suspicions. With the barn finished, I expected that whoever it was would come back soon and move the cache somewhere else. Last night I took two of my best men, and we watched the barn. We were lucky. A few hours before sunrise, we caught the thief."

"Who is it?"

"Soldier Esko Munck."

"The deserter?"

"The same, but I don't think he was ever a deserter. I've had my suspicions about him for a long time, and he has been working on the barn. There was something wrong about his story of being a stowaway on Calmare Nyckel. He never struck me as the type who would want to go back home."

"But we caught him hiding in the ship."

"Yes, but I think he was there to steal, not to become a stowaway."

"You know that stealing can be a hanging offense?"

"Yes, Sir."

They sat silently for a while until Ben burst out, "Damn the man! The last thing we want to do is to hang one of our own. Lieutenant Ridder will hate this, but I don't see that he has much of a choice. What was Munck thinking of?"

"He says he wanted to go up north and become a trapper."

"Why couldn't he just wait? A few years of service here, and he could have gone wherever he wanted."

"I don't think he's the brightest of the lads. He's illiterate, and I doubt he thinks much about what may happen beyond tomorrow."

"You're probably right. Where is he now?"

"He's locked up in our new guardhouse, the first one to stay there."

"Very well. Keep him there. I'll report this to Lieutenant Ridder."

The military tribunal of Soldier Esko Munck was held on a day in late December when the nights were long and the cold of winter was upon them. Ridder was the judge, assisted by Ben and one of the few freemen in the colony, Esa Nystad. The case against Munck was presented by Sergeant Rieser. The tribunal listened, and after deliberation with his assessors Ridder ruled that Munck was guilty. His sentence would be:

"to have his back hide removed by the whip for the crimes of willfully stealing weapons and food stores worth in excess of twelve rixdollars, from the Company and Her Majesty's army; his crime being particularly wicked, stealing from the Colony's limited stores, thereby putting his fellow settlers and soldiers into unwarranted and serious jeopardy."

A note to the protocol from the tribunal read,

"At the request of the Reverend Torkillus, the lashing will be postponed until after the holy days of Christmas."

On Christmas morning a southerly wind brought warm air up from the south, and when the church bell woke them up before dawn, the settlers rose, dressed, and started walking toward the church. They were building a new wooden church on the rise above Fort Christina, but while the building was going on, Torkillus had commandeered several of the army tents and converted them into a field church. Outside they had built a wooden bell tower, and at the top hung a bell that had been brought from Sweden. Inside the tent Torkillus had set up a makeshift altar under the Queen's cross. There were only a few seats for the women and children, so the rest had to stand until the carpenters could build more benches.

It was dark, and the settlers carried torches to find their way to the church and the Christmas service. Before they entered the church, they planted the torches outside in a circle around the front. When everybody had gathered, Torkillus walked up to the altar; the congregation hushed and silence spread over the church. In the distance from outside the thin walls a clinking noise started up. It swelled to a clanging at the door and continued into the church. They all turned around and escorted by two guards, Munck came in with his shackles and chains clanging as he shuffled down the aisle. The guards took him to an empty chair at the side of the altar, where he sat down and averted his face from the congregation.

Reverend Torkillus gave his Christmas sermon with its message of goodwill to all men. He made no reference to Munck until the very end, when he said. "We pray for the soul of our brother who lost his path, and we pray that he, after receiving just punishment and paying his dues to his fellow settlers, with God's help, shall find his way back." The service was over and the congregation left the church, some stealing a furtive look at the condemned man. When the church was almost empty, the guards helped Munck to his feet and escorted the prisoner back to the guardhouse.

The morning was cold; the clear night had robbed the land of what little warmth the winter sun had reluctantly given it the day before. All the soldiers had been ordered to assemble in the courtyard to witness Munck's punishment. Ben stood next to Ridder at the front of the troops. A small crowd of settlers and Indians stood off to the side, while Rieser and two guards, Gunnar Gunnarsson and Måns Andersson, waited at the door of the guardhouse. When Ridder signaled to Rieser, a murmur of anticipation went through the crowd. Rieser opened the guardhouse door, and the two guards brought out Munck. His chains clanged as he approached the whipping post, his bare back shivering in the cold. His hands were released from the shackles only to be tied to rings bolted into the whipping post. Andersson checked the knots, and, satisfied that the prisoner couldn't escape, he stepped back. Gunnarsson stepped forward to stand behind the prisoner; he put down one of the slim wooden rods he'd been carrying, and held the second one in his hand. They were ready.

Liisa Nystad was alone outside the fort in the cottage she shared with her brother. When he asked her if she would come to the whipping, she replied. "I couldn't bear it. I know he is guilty, but it is such a cruel punishment, especially for a man who doesn't really understand what he's done." Liisa, at Ridder's request, had become a teacher – her first class was a group of soldiers whom she was trying to teach how to read. Ridder wanted them at least to be able to read their letters from home. Munck was in the group. He was a very slow learner, and she understood how hard things were for him.

A drum roll came from the fort, followed by sharp slaps. There were a few loud cheers and laughs, but they faded quickly, and soon all she could hear was the sound of the lashes. Then came the screams; Liisa tried to shut them out by covering her ears, but they became louder despite the pressure of her hands, coming to a crescendo until – suddenly – there was silence.

Munck hung unconscious from the whipping post, his back covered by deep red welts; the skin was sliced open and hanging like red rags between the gashes. Ridder walked up to the prisoner, then turned to Rieser and ordered, "That's enough! Cut him down and return him to the guardhouse, and ask the barber-surgeon to look in on him!"

"Yes, Sir!"

That was the end of the whipping of Esko Munck. The crowd slowly broke up, the soldiers were dismissed, and they returned to their duties. When Esa and Ellianah came back, Liisa was sitting at the table, her eyes red from crying. In the courtyard Ben walked over to Chief Onoko, who stood by the whipping post; on the ground lay the two used rods now drying a into a brownish red hue. Ben asked, "Do your people punish thieves like we do?"

Onoko reached down and picked up one of the rods, he looked at Ben for a moment before answering, "Yes, we do." He hit the whipping post with the rod leaving a red mark of Munck's blood on the wood. "But I think your chief Ridder was wise to stop the flogging before the man died; it is better to have the man hoeing the ground than being buried under it."

Winter on the South River was not nearly as harsh as in Sweden. The days were longer and generally warmer, but now and then a snowstorm would come through, and with the wind blowing hard, large snowdrifts would form. It never lasted long and the settlers were seldom forced to take cover. The logging went on all winter, hunters went out, and the river never froze long enough to prevent ships from anchoring. Dutch, English, French traders came by, and the settlers sometimes traveled to New Netherland, Virginia, and New England. The Lenápes, who lived all around them, visited frequently, bartering pelts, grain, and tobacco for wampum, cloths, and tools. The Swedes also traded with the Minquas from the Susquehanna Valley, a nation of aggressive hunters and sworn enemies of the Lenápe. The Minquas thought nothing of raiding Lenápe villages, and the name Minquas Kill was given to the river, because the attackers would often come by water.

The interaction of European settlers and the Indians brought not only the exchange of goods, but also an invisible invasion of a different kind. It was the end of February, 1641. Ben was at the rock wharf overseeing the unloading of pelts; two trappers had arrived that morning in two canoes loaded with beaver skins. Van Langdonk had just concluded the purchase and trade of supplies, and two soldiers, Anders Larsson and Måns Andersson from Berga, were loading the pelts on a wheelbarrow to be brought to the storeroom in the fort. Larsson stood up and stretched his back, looking out over the river. "Look!" he said, and pointed down the kill. "There's another boat coming."

A small boat with a torn brown sail came around the bend downriver in Minquas Kill. The tide was on its way in, and a light breeze pushed the boat slowly up the river. They watched as it approached the rock wharf, and when it got closer they could see one man at the tiller, and two others lying on the deck before the mast. The boat came closer, and the helmsman called. *"Ahoy, op land! Kunnen jullie mij helpen?"*

Ben called, "What is your problem?"

"I have two dead Indians aboard, and I am feeling very poorly myself."

"Who are you, and where do you hail from?"

"My name is Martin Holter from Eckersdorp in New Netherland."

The boat came closer, but Holter was too weak to get the sail. He managed to steer the boat toward the lower end of the wharf, and turn it at the last moment. The side scraped along the side of the rock; he untied the sheet and the sail flapped in the wind. Larson reached down and picked up a bow line and tied it to a bollard. The boat came to a halt and settled along the wharf, but Holter stayed slumped on the aft thwart clutching the tiller. "I can't stand up," he said.

Ben looked at the men in the boat. The two Indians in the bow were lying on their backs on a stack of pelts; they seemed very comfortable wrapped in blankets against the cold, but they looked at him with the blank eyes of the dead. Their faces were covered by sores, blisters that had festered and disfigured their skin before the sickness claimed their lives. Holter had no visible blisters, but his white face and shivering body bespoke a racking fever. Ben asked Holter, "What happened to the Indians?"

"They come from a village near us, and we have often trapped and hunted together. This time, after we had left they told me that many in their village were sick and several had died." He stopped to catch his breath. "They wanted to get away, but it must have been too late; both of them came down with the fever several days ago, and they both died yesterday."

"How about you?"

Holter couldn't stop shivering. Clutching the tiller with one hand, he reached out with the other for a blanket next to him and tried to pull it over himself. His teeth chattered as he replied. "I got ill as well, but I have no blisters anywhere, just the fever, and aches all over."

Ben turned to Andersson. "Go find the barber-surgeon. I want him to see this before I let the man ashore."

"Yes, Sir!"

The soldier went to find Uv, and Ben said to Larsson. "Stay and guard the boat. Don't let Holter come ashore and don't let anyone near the boat!"

He turned back to Holter, whose shivering seemed to have subsided. "Do you have water?" he asked.

"Yes, I have some here."

"Good. We'll wait for our doctor, and then we can decide what to do."

The arrival of a strange boat had attracted villagers and visitors to the rock wharf, and Onoko and a couple of Lenápe traders were standing at the edge of the rock looking into the boat. Ben walked over to him and asked, "Chief, can you tell me who these Indians are?"

Onoko turned to the Lenápes and spoke to them in their own language. The men nodded and replied, and there was an exchange of words accompanied by heads shaking and nodding. Ben waited until Onoko turned to him and spoke in Dutch. "These men are Lenápe people from a village on the other side of the Lenápewhittuck, the big river you call the South."

"Do you know them?"

He looked at one of the Lenápe traders, "My friend Tatamy has met them along the river earlier. He doesn't know them well, but he has spoken to them."

Andersson had found Fredrik Uv, the barber-surgeon, and they arrived out of breath from running all the way from the fort. While Uv caught his breath, Ben told him about the boat and its passengers, and asked. "I want you to look at them and tell me what you think they have. I don't want the boat to bring any perilous contagion to New Sweden."

Uv, wearing a coat, hat, and gloves against the cold, wrapped a large kerchief around his head to cover his mouth and nose and stepped down into the boat. He looked at the two Indians in the bow, and using a stick, he lifted the blankets to look at their necks and chests. There were more blisters as well as red pockmarks on their bodies. He walked over to Holter in the stern, removed his cover, and asked him to pull up his shirt; Holter's pale, white skin was free from blemishes. Uv put the blanket back over him, rose, stepped back to the side of the boat, and climbed back up on the wharf. Ben followed him off to the side, away from the ears of the crowd. Uv said, "Lieutenant, it may be masels, but I think it's the pox!"

"Are you sure?"

"Yes, I have heard there have been several outbreaks among the Indians."

"What can we do?"

"Not much, it'll have to run its course."

"How about our own people?"

"It seems we're not as vulnerable as the Indians. Holter has no pockmarks or blemishes. Let him stay, but we must keep him quarantined, and especially away from the Lenápes, until he is well." Uv hesitated.

"Yes, go on!"

286

"These diseases are caused by miasma, poisonous air, and with the dead bodies in the boat, the air and everything in the boat is permeated with miasma. Holter can come ashore, but we can't let anything else from the boat come ashore. We must burn his clothes and belongings, and he must wash himself with lye soap. You should burn the whole boat."

Ben sighed, "Thank you, Uv. I must speak to the Chief about this."

Onoko walked with Ben up on a knoll at the side of the river. They sat down on a log looking at the water, the low February sun warming them a little bit. Onoko listened to Ben who said, "This illness is caused by miasma, evil spirits in the air, which are very dangerous to your people. You should take them away for a while until we're sure the spirits are gone, and there is no more illness."

Onoko replied, "I have heard about many villages where our people get sick and die. The air surrounding the white man has brought new illnesses to our land."

"Yes, so it seems, but it can no longer be undone. There are many mysterious illnesses in this world. I've seen whole villages in Europe being wiped out by the Black Death."

"We must bury our dead people."

Ben sat quietly; he had been thinking about how to bury the two Indians in the boat. He said, "Chief, it would be very dangerous for your people if we take anything from the boat. In my country we sometimes bury our people at sea. Our ancestors would place the dead in a ship filled with everything they would need for the long journey. They would take the ship out to sea and set it afire to light their path and free the souls to find their way to the kingdom of the dead."

Onoko looked at him. He nodded but didn't say anything.

Ben continued, "I want to send the two Lenápes to the Kingdom of the dead the same way. We'll let the man Holter come ashore, but he will not be allowed to bring anything from the boat. Then we'll take the boat out with the tide and burn it at sea. I promise it will be a solemn ceremony befitting the Lenápe people."

Holter was too weak to protest; with Uv's help he slowly managed to take all his clothes off. They had to hold him to keep him from falling; his teeth were shattering in the cold, but they saw no blemishes anywhere on his pale body as he entered New Sweden naked as a newborn baby. A tub had been fetched and filled with hot water. He washed himself, wincing as the harsh lye soap scoured his skin, then Larsson put a new blanket over him and they led him to the wheelbarrow, where the exhausted man laid down. Uv said to Ben, "There is an empty wigwam outside the fort where I can put him." He signaled to Larsson and Andersson, who grabbed the handles of the wheelbarrow and began pushing the sick man toward his new abode.

To thwart any temptation to steal the pelts from the infected boat, Ben posted guards at the landing site. Next morning he assembled a crew for the settlement's own boat; one of the men was Anders Bengtson who brought his fiddle. He had asked Reverend Torkillus to come along, but the pastor of the Lutheran Church had refused. "Lieutenant, what you're proposing is heresy. I can't condone a pagan ceremony."

Ben talked to Ridder, who shared his concern about the contagion. Ridder suggested that he bring Esa Nystad. "After all the man had been training to be a missionary."

Nystad agreed directly. "I don't want that boat and its contents anywhere near the village."

They collected firewood and filled Holter's boat, covering the two bodies and everything else in it. The boat became a huge funeral pyre. When Ben was satisfied they launched the settlement's own boat and, catching the outgoing tide, they sailed down Minqua's Kill and the South River towing Holter's boat on a long line behind them. As they entered the South River, three canoes joined the procession. Onoko had brought some of his people to the funeral, and the Lenápe men in the canoes had colored their faces with black ashes and hung large feathers from their hair.

The next evening, in the middle of the South River, with the tide going out and hardly any wind, they lit the pyre. Esa Nystad read a prayer for the dead, Bengtson took up his fiddle and played a slow, lamenting funeral hymn from Berga, his home, and like Vikings once had done, the two Lenápes left the living on a blazing ship drifting toward the sea. A full winter moon rose in the east, and Ben watched the Lenápe canoes turn into shadows in the silvery path of moonlight on the water. Holter's boat was far away, the pyre still glowing orange, when Ben ordered his crew to weigh anchor. It was calm, and in the pale moonlight they rowed back up the river to find a place to camp until daybreak.

288

42.   The Missionary's Daughter

The settlers were subjects of Sweden, and they had brought with them not only language, law, customs, and religion from the homeland but also the way their society was run and rules about who had power and who did not. This way the order of their new world was never questioned. It was comfortable, the social hierarchy was familiar, privileges were afforded according to rank, and everybody instinctively knew his place among his fellow settlers. In their small village, mixing across unseen but firm social borders was frowned upon.

Their Commander, Lieutenant Peter Hollender Ridder, was at the center of their society, and orbiting around him were the military officers, the Company officers, the Clergy, plus a few otherwise meritorious members – including Liisa, the missionary's daughter, and her brother, the missionary's son, now himself a missionary – who had been anointed by the center cluster. Farther out, the next ring held the freemen. They claimed the status that farmers held in the homeland, but they still had to make their small landholdings productive before they could exert any significant influence. In the outermost ring were the conscripted soldiers; many of them were also farming, but they didn't have any landholdings and were poor tenants of the Company.

In the small ring around the Commander they were all literate, generally skilled and well informed, while in the outermost orbit most had little or no schooling, and they could neither read nor write. One of the first things Ridder did was to set up a school for the men who needed it. He asked Liisa to become the teacher, and he told her. "These young men are so ignorant, but they're all we have, so whatever you can do will be good for them and us."

He asked Ben to help her in selecting the men who should attend Liisa's school. "Tell them," he said, "that I want them to be able to read their own letters from home."

When Anna Svensdotter and Eva Eriksdotter heard about the school, they came to Liisa and asked if they could join. Liisa talked to Ben about it, "I can't have women in the same classroom as men!"

"Why don't you teach them separately?"

When the other women heard of this, they also wanted to join, and soon Liisa was teaching two groups, one with some of the men, and one with all the women. She started with simple reading, and writing, but Reverend Torkillus pointed out to Ridder that the homeland laws about the teachings of the Church and the practice of the true Lutheran faith applied in New Sweden as well. The pupils absolutely must get a proper dose of religion, and they should learn Luther's Small Catechism. Since they couldn't read or write yet, it would have to be done by rote, but this was as it had always been done. The Reverend Torkillus and Esa Nystad, the missionary, took turns in the catechism classroom.

Liisa enjoyed being part of the inner circle of the settlement. She was the only woman with that status, and attracted a lot of attention. She learned to play cards, and added her contagious laughter to van Langdonk's bass blasts and Ridder's melodious howls. The men were courteous to her, even as there were occasional glimpses of longing passing over their eyes. There were only a few women among the settlers. Not many of the soldiers and only some of the freemen had dared to bring their families along. The war in Europe demanded more Swedish soldiers all the time, and there was nothing unusual about young men going off alone without wives or girlfriends to serve in the army. Besides, when you're a young soldier away from home, part of the adventure is to find women wher-ever you are. But New Sweden wasn't Germany, and there was a definite shortage of women. So when Madam Isabel's small whore boat flotilla came from upriver and made one of its irregular visits to the Minquas Kill settlement, men of all social standings could be seen hurrying down to the wharf.

When the first boat of the flotilla was seen coming around the river bend, a tremor went through the settlement. First came boats with tents and furnishings, and a crew of strong young men who would set up several crib tents around a large pavilion where drinks of an unspecified nature going by fanciful names such as India Gin, Baby Killer, Fire in the

Hole, or River Ale would flow freely. The word of their arrival spread like lightning around the bunkhouses, and the men from the settlement were drawn in anticipation to the harbor like moths to a candle, or as Liisa said to Ben, "Like lambs to slaughter." When the tents were in place, Madame Isabel Theodora Achterspeel arrived together with her girls. They would make their entry at dusk, when the dim light was merciful to aging faces and sagging flesh, and drinks had already put foggy filters in front of the young men's eyes. All they saw was beauty, and all they felt was desire – if they weren't sick from too much drink. The men would line up at the crib tents, and each was given just a few minutes of bliss before the girl called, "Next!"

Presiding over it all was Madam Isabel, born and raised in Amsterdam. She had learned her trade at the brothels in the alleys by the Amstel river, where sailors from the whole world would come and go in a steady stream. When she was twenty, she followed one sailor to New Amsterdam, where he promptly proceeded to get himself killed in a knife fight. She went back to her old trade, and discovered that she also had an entrepreneurial talent for getting others to do the work for her. She was adventurous, and decided there were opportunities along the rivers where many settlements suffered from a great shortage of women.

She knew how to ingratiate herself with the leaders of the settlements. She paid "taxes" where she had to, and she was known to make other special arrangements for the men at the top. Her young men kept order among the guests, not allowing any serious fights. When the sun began to light up the eastern sky, Madam Isabel and her girls left before the magic and the merciful cover of the night wore off. Her young men would pack up the tents and be gone as well by the end of the day. That day half the male population in the settlement walked around in a daze from sleep deprivation and the effects of too many India Gins.

Ridder tolerated Madam Isabel's establishment, as long as things were under control. Ben remembered the many traveling inns, brothels, hawkers, and con-men that followed the armies around Germany. By comparison, Madame Isabel's establishment seemed pretty harmless. Reverend Torkillus was of a totally different opinion; to him they were like the sinners and evildoers of Babylon leading their seduced victims on a road to perdition. At first he tried to stop Madam Isabel. He would come to the pavilion with a small group from his congregation, and they would try to dissuade the men from entering. The men were not very receptive to his arguments against sin and the devil drink. They were, on the contrary, delighted to get drunk and to sin in all manner of ways, and the Pastor who had such power during the day was invisible to them at night when their noses had picked up the strong scent of hands-on debauchery. The Reverend Torkillus soon gave up his nightly sermons, and saved his talk of hell and damnation for the Sunday services.

Another spring arrived. The dogwoods were in bloom again, the weather was mild, and Madam Isabel had just left. Liisa knew that on the day after Madam Isabel's departure many of Liisa's pupils would not be very attentive. Torkillus, smarting over yet another defeat in his battle against sin, had offered to spend the day teaching the Catechism to the men while Esa taught the women. Liisa looked forward to the day off, and after breakfast she walked down to the river. They had built a wash house where the settlers could wash their laundry in a tub filled with hot soapy water, and then rinse it in the river. There was also a bathhouse, where every Saturday, in the Finnish and Swedish traditions, they would fire up the sauna, and take turns washing and sweating the week's dirt off their bodies. Below the bathhouse and the wash house there was a wooden dock attached to rocks at the edge of the water and extending out over the river. It was held in place by poles and at the end a ladder led down into the water. Many bathers – even in the winter – would finish their sauna baths by immersing themselves in the cold river. Others would simply pour a bucket of water over themselves.

Liisa sat on a bench by the bathhouse enjoying the warmth of the spring sun. Her servant Ellianah was down on the dock rinsing clothes, holding them in the moving water, picking them up, spreading them out on the dock and beating them with a paddle. Two mockingbirds were having a singing contest from the tops of trees not too far away. It reminded Liisa of her home in Finland, where the village women would go down to the lake to do their wash. In the spring they would be serenaded by blackbirds. She was just getting up to help Ellianah when Ben and Onoko came walking toward the bathhouse.

Ben and Liisa saw a lot of each other, as it was a small village and they were both part of Ridder's circle. They liked each other, got along well, and inevitably they were drawn to each other. Love is contingent upon many practical matters, mainly proximity and availability. At Fort Christina the possibilities were limited, these two were always near each other, and the outcome was inevitable – even if neither one had yet come to this epiphany.

The two men greeted her, and Ben said, "The schoolteacher is taking the day off, while her pupils are confined to the classroom?" He smiled.

Liisa returned his smile, "The men are doing penance with the Reverend for having gone to Madame Isabel's."

Onoko went down to the water, where he sat down watching Ellianah beat the clothes; her bare black arms glistened in the sunlight reflecting off the water. She was old enough to be his mother, but before Ellianah arrived at the settlement, Onoko had never seen a person with such black skin, and he was fascinated by her. Ellianah didn't mind, but they had no language in common, and their conversation was limited to a few words, gestures and nodding or shaking their heads. Ellianah looked at Onoko and held out a shirt and a paddle toward him. He laughed and shook his head. This was work only for women. She raised her eyebrows, shook her head, shrugged and went back to manhandling the wash.

Ben and Liisa sat down on the bench. Ben said, "I've decided to stay."

Liisa nodded, waiting for him to continue.

"I've talked to Ridder. He had a similar offer to stay, but he wants to get back to Finland."

"Who will become the next Commander?"

"I don't know. Ridder wants to leave in a couple of years, and the Company will appoint another commander."

"What will you do?"

"I'll find that piece of land that the Company wants to grant me, and I'll become a trader."

"Where do you want to go?"

"I'll stay in New Sweden, but I want to go to the new land the Company has bought along the South River. There is some up north and some across the river on the eastern side. I don't want to go too far from Fort Christina; this is the center for Company trading and the harbor for our shipping."

They sat silently until Ben continued, "Ridder wants me to go and look at the new Company land, and he suggested that I could look for a suitable parcel for myself at the same time. He's been authorized by Admiral Fleming to make the land grant. Onoko will go with me as interpreter."

Liisa looked at him, her face lit up by excitement. "This is wonderful! I wish I could go with you!"

Ben's face relaxed in a smile; he took a deep breath before he went on, "I wish you could, but it won't be an easy trip." He continued, "We'll leave in a couple of weeks."

"Well, the minute you come back, I want to hear all about it."

"I promise!" Ben looked straight into her eyes, and before he knew it, the words came tumbling out by themselves. "When I come back, and if I have found some land, will you go with me when it's time for me to leave?"

Now it was Liisa's turn to change color. "Lieutenant Benjamin Fogel, what are you saying?"

"Come with me! I don't want to do this without you!"

"Do you want me to be your mistress?"

"No, I think I'm asking you to marry me!"

Liisa put her hands on his cheeks, pulled his face slowly toward hers and kissed him. She let go and looked at him. "Do you really want to marry a missionary's daughter?"

"If you can marry an innkeeper's son, I'll gladly marry a missionary's daughter."

Liisa stood up, threw her hands into the air, and spun around so that her hair flew out around her like a sunflower. She laughed and said, "Yes, I'll marry the innkeeper's son." She stopped moving, dropped her arms, and looked at him with a more somber expression on her face. "I'll have to talk to my brother."

"Do you think he'll object?"

"No, but I don't want to abandon him. He wants to be a missionary, but I think he's counting on me to help him."

"But you must live your own life."

"Yes, but Esa and I have never talked about that."

"Do you want me to talk to him? We get along fine."

"No, let me do it first. Let's keep this a secret until I've talked to him."

Ben looked toward the wooden dock, where Ellianah, with Onoko as a spectator, was beating her wash. "Yes, that's fine, but I don't think we'll be able to keep this a secret for very long. This village is too small for such secrets."

"I'll talk to him soon."

294

"Wonderful!" Ben stood up, took her hands, brought them up to his face, and kissed them. He said, "I surprised myself, but the thought of leaving you all of a sudden seemed unbearable." He put his arms around her and they embraced each other.

"Lieutenant!" It was Bengtsson's voice; he was coming toward them from the direction of the rock wharf.

They quickly disentangled themselves, and Liisa sat down again, Ben pulled at his coat and straightened it. "Yes!" he replied.

"There is a small boat coming up the river. It has a Dutch flag."

"I'll join you right away!" Ben held out his hand toward Liisa who touched it briefly. He followed Bengtsson toward the wharf.

There were only four people in the boat, a helmsman, two oarsmen and one passenger, a woman. She was wearing a long dress under a grey cloak, and on her head she had a straw hat shading her face from the sun. When the boat approached the wharf the helmsman called to the shore. "We have a passenger who wants to disembark at Fort Christina."

Ben replied, "Where do you hail from?"

"Fort Nassau! Our ship is anchored downstream in the South River."

It was not unusual to see Dutch ships on the South River. Fort Nassau, on the east side farther up the river, was a trading post used by the WIC. It was not very successful as a trading post, but since the Swedes had arrived, Fort Nassau had become very important to the Dutch as a sign of their rightful presence on the South River.

Ben replied, "Very well. Is your passenger well?"

The woman looked up at him from her seat, and before the helmsman could reply, she interrupted him. "I most certainly am!" Her thick Scottish brogue gave away her origin.

Ben bowed slightly, "Sorry, Madam, but with the pox epidemic, we can't be too careful. But I'll accept your word." He turned to the helmsman, "You may let the lady disembark!"

Their visitor was a small, dark-haired woman in her mid-twenties. The sailors helped her ashore, and one passed her a valise made of soft leather. "Goodbye, Madam!" he said. "Godspeed!"

"Thank you and God bless you!" The woman waved.

The boat left, drifting down Minquas Kill, and the woman turned to Ben. "Good day Sir, I am Caitrin Edina MacHarold."

Ben bowed, "I'm Lieutenant Fogel. May I ask what brings you to New Sweden?"

She put down her valise on the dock. "I'm a missionary from Edinburgh. Are you familiar with our city, Lieutenant?"

Ben thought of his one and only visit to Scotland aboard Svala, on a mission to pick up Scottish mercenaries for Gustavus Adolphus's army. It seemed such a long time ago. He replied, "I am."

"Then you may know of our deep devotion to the Protestant faith."

Ben's experiences in Edinburgh were limited to drinking at several inns in the harbor. None of them would qualify as having anything to do with any faith other than that of more robust corporal pleasures, but he nodded.

"I've been sent out to preach the true faith to the people of the new world. I want especially to spread God's word to the heathens."

Ben's first impression of Caitrin MacHarold was that of a very determined woman. She had a pretty, lively face, and spoke pleasantly, her hands accompanying her replies with animated gestures. He said, "I'll see if we can find you somewhere to stay while you're here. We have our own missionary pastor, and perhaps he and his sister can provide you with temporary accommodation." He thought to himself, "I hope Esa will see eye-to-eye with her when it comes to who has the true faith!"

He picked up her valise. "Let's go find Liisa Nystad, and ask her!"

Esa Nystad and Caitrin MacHarold were like two matching pieces of the same puzzle, two people on similar missions to save souls for God, and the force of their convictions brought them together. It was love at first sight, and once they'd met, there was no way to break the bond. At first, Esa was upset because he had to move into bachelor's quarters to give room for their boarder, but after a few days his objections were silenced. He came to the cottage for meals, and he and Caitrin would soon engage in long talks about missionary work and being a missionary in a foreign land.

A couple of weeks after Caitrin's arrival, Ben stopped by to see Liisa. Caitrin was washing dishes at the table, and Esa was drying them. When Ben entered the door he heard Esa say, "I want to build a church of my own, where I can bring the gospel to the Indians." He turned to Ben and waved the towel, but quickly turned back to listen to Caitrin.

"That's exactly what I have been looking for! A new church in the New World!" She glanced toward the door. "Hello, Lieutenant!" she said and her eyes went back toward Esa.

Ben walked up to Liisa. So far she had not wanted to show him any affection in company, but now she reached up and gave him a kiss. He kissed her back, but asked in a puzzled voice. "It's no longer a secret?"

"No. I've talked to him. But look at them. It's difficult to get a word in edgewise with these two, though I think he heard me, and he said 'Fine!'" She came closer and whispered, "Let's try this again!" This time he put his arms around her, and they lingered in a longer kiss.

They didn't notice that it got very quiet behind them. "Hrmph!" A discreet cough broke the spell, and when they let go of each other, Esa and Caitrin were looking at them. Esa looked sternly at Ben and said. "Lieutenant Fogel! I sincerely hope you will take good care of my sister!" His face broke into a broad smile, he held out his hand and the two men shook hands.

Caitrin said, "I'm so happy for you two!" She walked over to Liisa and gave her a hug. "I want to stay for the wedding!"

"Yes, do!" Esa said. "I want to talk more with you about building a new church."

That night Liisa and Ben met for a walk around the settlement. Ben had brought a blanket, and Liisa a basket that she had packed with cold pieces of heath hen, corn on the cob, bread, and a drink made from cranberries. They found a secluded place at the edge of a clearing at Minquas Kill, where they put out their blanket and watched the sun set while they ate their New Sweden fare. As dusk fell, a thin slice of a moon rose. In a quiet, natural way they slowly undressed each other and lay naked in the warm night. Fireflies twinkled over clearing, and the weak moon cast a pale light over the river. When Ben entered her, Liisa cried out in a moment of pain, but that was soon forgotten, and the newly engaged couple stayed embraced and made love, clinging to each other on the earth of the new land.

43.   River Travel

The sick Dutchman, Holter, slowly got better, his fever went down, and he never developed any rash or blisters. Uv kept him quarantined for an extra couple of weeks, just to be sure that his disease wouldn't spread. Toward the end of the quarantine, when the March sun began to warm up the land and the last snow was gone, Uv would let him sit in a chair outside the wigwam, and the settlers could talk to him as long as they kept a respectful distance. The man didn't speak any Swedish, and most of the settlers didn't speak any Dutch, so the exchanges were generally brief and accompanied by a lot of hand-waving.

Ridder asked Ben to find out more about the man, and Ben went to see Holter, as he sat in the sunshine. He was still in quarantine, and Uv had put a chair about twenty feet away, just far enough so that Ben had to raise his voice for Holter to hear. Holter, on the other hand, was still weak and didn't have the strength to shout. Ben's questions rang out across the field and echoed against the wall of the fort, while Holter's replies often were whisked away by the wind before they reached Ben's ears. Nevertheless, during the course of their undulating conversation, Ben found out that Holter was a trapper who worked together with several Indians nations along the South River. He had heard that the Swedes would pay more than the Dutch, and was on his way to sell his pelts in New Sweden when he and the two Indians caught the fever. He said, "You should know that the WIC and Governor Kieft are very unhappy with the competition from you. They don't like anybody to undermine their trade with the Indians."

"Do you think he'll attack our settlement?"

298

"No! His orders are not to seek a confrontation with New Sweden, but at the same time he should resist any further encroachment on the South River."

Ben reported his conversations to Ridder, whose comment was, "Well, two can play that game."

"Well, it may actually be three! Holter told me he had heard that the English are on the move."

"Ah, the English! What can they do?"

"I know they're not as powerful as the Dutch, but the tobacco-farming in Virginia seems to attract more settlers. We've also seen the pelt trade with the Indians along the South River go down recently. Some English traders have been offering better prices than we have."

They were sitting in Ridder's office; he got up from his chair and walked over to the window. It was midday, the sun was warming up the building, and water from last night's rain was dripping down from the edge of the roof. Ridder looked out the window at the soldiers who were posted at the gate to the fort. He tapped his fingers on the windowsill, turned around and said, "We can't have them trading in our territory, without our permission, and outside our control. The Company can't afford to give away trading privileges. We need to stamp this out!"

Ben replied, "I agree! Holter also says that he has met some English traders who told him the English are planning an expedition to bring settlers to the South River – which they call the Delaware."

Ridder was pacing back and forth across the room. "I don't mind settlers, as long as they're allegiant to the Swedish Crown. We do need more people." He continued, "The Utrecht settlers at Upland seem to be doing fine. Do you think we can get the English to accept being settlers in New Sweden?"

"It depends. If the Governor in New England is testing our resolution, he'll send people who won't."

Ridder stopped pacing and looked at Ben. "Take some men and an interpreter, and make a tour of our new land. If you see any illegal settlers, make sure they know they're under the laws of the Swedish Crown, and that the territory they're in is owned by the New Sweden Company, who has procured it legally from the previous Indian owners. If they want to stay and they qualify, they can either lease or buy land from us." He added, "Oh, and the land won't be expensive, but they must have that lease or deed from us."

"Very well, but how would they qualify?"

"Loyalty to the Crown is obligatory. As for the rest, it's a matter of what they can do. We need more of everything – farms to grow food crops and raise cattle, tobacco plantations, fishermen, millers, bakers, carpenters, blacksmiths, hunters, and trappers." Ridder's voice filled with optimism, "It may take a little time, but New Sweden will grow and provide the investors with a very handsome return."

The spring flood had swelled the South River and currents were very strong. The level finally came down and the water flow slowed, but it was mid-May before the expedition could get underway. Onoko was their Lenápe interpreter, but Ben also brought Rolf Engvas, the early settler who had learned a few words of Lenápe from his Indian wife, Minnequa. Sture Mattson, Nils Eskilsson, and Jonas Persson, the cook, completed the party. They loaded up the ship's boat that had been brought from Sweden. It was a sloop large enough to hold them and their supplies. They would sail wherever possible, but the boat also had oars. The plan was to camp along the river, though if necessary they could sleep onboard. Onoko told them there were long stretches of marshland, especially downriver on the eastern side, where landing could be very difficult.

Ben was at the helm, everything was loaded, and the soldiers were aboard. Onoko was in his canoe in the middle of Minquas Kill. When they reached the South River he would tie it to the boat and climb aboard. A southeasterly breeze was blowing, it was slack tide, and by the time they reached the mouth of Minquas Kill the tide would be coming in, a perfect time to go up the South River. Ben ordered, "Set the jib!" Eskilsson hauled up the jib sail and secured the halyard. The jib flapped in the wind. Ben continued, "Cast off!" Mattson pulled the mooring lines aboard, Eskilsson hauled in the lee jib sheet, and the sloop began turning and moving down Minquas Kill.

A group of settlers had come to see them off, Liisa, Esa, and Caitrin among them. Ben waved and Liisa waved back and shouted, "Come back soon!"

The sloop sailed slowly up the river, pushed by the tide and the wind. The river flow from the land up north and the slow swing of the six-foot tides created a constantly changing seascape of open water, channels, mud banks, shoals, and underwater rocks. It went from as far up the river as they had explored and all the way down and across the wide bay that ended in the Atlantic Ocean. The Indians who fished the river were used to this; they knew where the dangers lay in the shifting waters, and in their canoes they could pass through most shallow areas. The sloop drew more water and had to travel in deeper channels. Sometimes they would take a dead-end channel, and when the tide was low, put down an anchor and wait for the water to come back. The South River at Minquas Kill was wide, but in the main channel, particularly when the tide was running out, it took a strong wind for the sloop to move upstream.

Ben's plan was to follow the western side and come back along the eastern shore. Slowly they made headway up the river. At night they made camp on the shore, either on land along the river or on offshore islands. They tried to find camps at high tide when they could bring the sloop near the shore; there were often small coves where eddies had made pools of deep water. Then there were the nights when they couldn't find any landing spots, or when they couldn't reach land before the tide ran out. During the early part of their expedition, they sometimes had to sleep in the boat, but they quickly learned to start early and find camp well before dark. Onoko's canoe came in handy; he would go ahead and investigate the shores and when they couldn't reach land, he would ferry them ashore. Ben and Onoko also went up some of the tributaries to explore.

They came to Schuyl's Kill, and landed at the mouth of the tributary. They were sitting around the campfire one evening as the sun was about to set, when five Indians approached the camp. One man was older than the others; he was carrying a spear, while three of the younger men carried bows, and the fifth, who looked like he wasn't much more than twelve years old, carried a large quiver full of arrows. Onoko got up and greeted the older man, who returned the greeting and spoke at length to him. Onoko listened and nodded, and when the man was finished Onoko turned to Ben. "This is Mexkalaniyat, he is a friend of my father, and he was present when Minuit first came here and asked for land."

Ben got up and held out his hand. Mexkalaniyat took it and shook Ben's hand vigorously. He said something to Onoko, who translated: "He wants you to bring his greetings to your young queen, but he wants to know why you don't have a king instead?"

"Tell him we had a great warrior king, but he died in battle, and he left no sons."

When Onoko translated, Mexkalaniyat shook his head gravely.

Onoko said, "Mexkalaniyat says he understands, but he hopes that your queen has some older chiefs to help her."

Ben thought of Chancellor Oxenstierna and replied, "She does! Our most powerful chief is at her side, guiding her." He continued, "He is also the chief of our people here, and he wants us to be good friends with the Lenápes." He waited for Onoko to finish translating and then added, "And he likes to eat roast turkey!"

Mexkalaniyat laughed heartily. Onoko said, "He says your chief should come for a visit, and we shall prepare a feast for him!"

"Thank you! I will tell him that."

Ben invited the Lenápes to join them at the campfire, offering to share bread and ale with them. They spoke, but the conversation, accompanied as it was by gestures, signs, and heads nodding and shaking, was slow and deliberate as Onoko translated. Ben asked about hunting and trapping, and if Mexkalaniyat's people could bring pelts to Fort Christina for trade. Mexkalaniyat replied that they would gladly do so, but he also told them that both the Dutch and the English wanted the same thing, and that perhaps they would give the Lenápes better offers than the Swedes. Ben replied that they should always trust the Swedes to give them good trades, and that the others were trespassing on the good relations between the Lenápes and the Swedes.

Ben went to their supply packages and brought over a clay pipe and a piece of cloth. He gave the pipe to Mexkalaniyat. "This is for you." He handed over the cloth. "Your wife can make comfortable clothes from this cloth." Ben added, "We can bring more of this and other things you may need."

Mexkalaniyat felt the cloth and passed it to the other men, who also fingered the cloth and talked among themselves.

Engvas whispered to Ben, "I think he likes it!"

When the ale was finished, Mexkalaniyat brought out a pouch, which he opened, took out a pinch of tobacco, and filled his new pipe. He leaned toward the fire, lit a small twig and held it over the pipe, while he puffed on it to light the tobacco. Satisfied that the pipe was properly lit, he held it out toward Ben, and spoke. Onoko said, "He wants you to try his tobacco. He says they can bring tobacco leaves for trade."

"Excellent!" Ben said and reached for the pipe.

The Swedes and the Lenápes sat by the fire. The pipe went around from hand to hand, and each man solemnly took a puff and passed it on. Ben thought of von Lans' stories about cigar-smoking during meetings with the New Sweden board. "They'll like this!" he thought.

The Indians left, but the next morning they came back and showed them the fading Swedish flag at Schuyl's Kill. It had been put there by Minuit to mark the northern end of his purchase. Ben asked Mattson to get a new flag to replace the old one. Mattson went to the boat to get the flag while they waited. Mexkalaniyat asked, "Where are you going now?"

"Up this side of the river to Sankikan and then back down to Naraticon Kill and our land on the other side, all the way to Varkens Kill."

The Lenápe Chief stroked his chin with his hand and nodded while he listened to Ben and Onoko's words. He said, "There are evil spirits across the river. Many of our people have been taken ill and many have left the land of the living. Be careful!"

Mattson was finished with the flag. The men boarded their boat, and as it moved away from shore, Ben held up his hand in a farewell to Mexkalaniyat, who returned the gesture gravely.

They moved on up the South river. The land along the western shore slowly began to rise. The river narrowed, and there were less marshlands. The trees were in their late spring green, and in the morning they were often awakened by birdsong rippling from the shore. The river was still wide, but slowly getting narrower, and the current picked up. Most often when they camped along the river, they would have Indian visitors. Ben had brought some hatchets, pipes, knives, and scissors as well as wampum along, and he would sometimes trade for a beaver or fox pelt. The room in the sloop was limited, but he wanted to make it known that the Swedish settlement was a marketplace where the Indians could come with their wares. He had also showed them their own pots, pans, knives, axes, and other things they had onboard. "These are some of the things we have for trading with you!" he said.

They turned around at Sankikan, the South River falls that marked the northern end of Ridder's land purchase. The eastern shore was claimed by New Netherland, and they didn't make any landfall on the eastern side until they came to Naraticon Kill halfway between Sankikan and Schuyl's Kill. Earlier that year, Ridder and van Langdonk had bought land on the eastern shore, from Naraticon Kill south down to Varkens Kill below Fort Christina. They arrived at the mouth of the tributary late in the afternoon, and had to find a landing place and a campsite quickly before darkness and the outgoing tide made it impossible to land. Ben spotted a small beach on the south side of Naraticon Kill. When they came closer they saw a pole with the Swedish flag marking the end of the eastern shore land. In the fading light he made out two raccoons sitting next to the pole, gazing curiously out at the approaching oddity.

The marshy land was low, but the Naraticon Kill had cut a deep channel through the marsh. They didn't want the sloop to be stranded in the marshes at the edge of the wide South River, where strong winds often blew without warning, and they continued up the Kill. Onoko went ahead in his canoe to search for a better campsite. The wind had died down and the men put out the oars and followed him. In a little while he came back. He swung around and maneuvered the canoe next to them.

"There's a good site for landing up ahead," he said. He shook his head, "But something is wrong!"

"Why do you say that?" Ben asked.

"It's too quiet. No people!"

Engvas said, "Lieutenant, remember Mexkalaniyat's warning about evil spirits taking people away!"

Ben did, but the sun was getting low, and they needed to find a place before it got dark. Ben replied, "Yes, but I think we'll be quite safe for the night. Tomorrow we'll look around." They continued up Naraticon Kill, and Onoko led them to a place where tree-covered ground rose up from the river. Next to the shore there was a deep-water pool where they could anchor.

It was morning, but overnight a thick fog had crept up from the South River. It was white all around them, dead quiet and a bit chilly. They had to wait for the fog to lift, and they gathered around the campfire. Eskilsson was putting firewood on the fire, and the frying pan was filled with slices of pork ready to cook. Persson, their cook, had been up a small stream to collect water and he was pouring it into a kettle hanging on a wooden tripod over the fire. He put five eggs in the water, took out a loaf of bread and cut slices for everyone, and said. "These are our last eggs, so savor them!" They had supplies for at least a month. The settlers were used to eating venison, heath hen, turkey, as well as rabbit and squirrel. Ben and his men augmented their diet by fishing, hunting and trapping.

The smoke from the fire mixed with the fog, a trail of white that wreathed around the trees on the hillside. The trees drifted in and out of the whiteout, and sometimes they floated in the white air. There was movement in the fog, a creature appeared next to an oak, then disappeared as the fog thickened. Mattson cried out, "Somebody is out there!" They all peered into the fog, and Ben reached for his sword. Mattson pointed, "There!" For a brief moment an opening appeared in the fog, and they saw a figure moving away from them; his legs were hidden by the fog and he seemed to float away. It looked like a man in a long cloak, his long white hair waving behind him. Then the hole in the fog closed and the creature was gone.

Ben looked at Onoko and asked. "What was that?"

Onoko's face was pale. "It was a ghost, a visitor from the dead. Perhaps your boat didn't reach its destination, and the two dead men are still looking for the kingdom of the dead."

Ben shook his head. "I am sure the boat is gone from the world of the living. I think it was just a Lenápe man who was curious about us."

Onoko got up, "We must leave this place! There is death here!"

"As soon as the fog lifts."

Two hours later, the morning sun had burned through the fog, and they packed up their gear and put it in the boat. Just as they left the shore, something made Ben look back. In a clearing on the hillock he saw a man standing still. He was wrapped in a blanket, and his white hair shone in the sun.

They moved slowly up the river as it meandered among patches of tall reeds and low land covered by small trees and brush that grew all the way down to the water's edge. A green carpet of creepers and vines drooped over the brush into the water as the incoming tide lifted the river. They entered a wider area; at the far end poles rose from the water. As they came closer they could see that the poles were part of several fish weirs built to catch the fish going up and down the river. Ben said, "It reminds me of home. Where I come from we also fish."

Onoko replied, "Naraticon people along the river are good fishermen." He looked around and pointed up the river. "Up there is a village." The expression on his face changed and he looked worried. "But where are they? There is no smoke, and I see no people."

The tide had filled the river and it was about to change direction. The river current grew stronger, and the wind was turning easterly against them. Ben was at the tiller and he ordered the sail struck. "It's not far, but we'll need to row!" he said. "Eskilsson, you and Mattson take the oars!"

The two men put out their oars and began rowing. Soon they arrived at a small landing at the edge of a clearing that continued up on a hillock rising several feet above the high water. Two canoes had been pulled up on land, and on the flat top of the hillock there were several wigwams.

On the beach there was a pile of baskets, a stack of poles that looked like those that were used to build the weirs, balls of twine that also must have been used for fishing; farther up, next to a tree at the edge of the clearing, there was a wooden rack holding paddles.

The tiny village looked abandoned; there were no sign of life anywhere. Ben ordered the anchor out, and the sloop came to rest in deep water at the edge of the river. They all looked at the village, but nothing moved. Ben looked at Onoko, "What do you think? Is it a trap?"

"No, these people are very peaceful, and they know me. I fear something is very wrong."

Ben thought for a moment. "Let's go ashore and look, but only you and I will go! The rest of you stay here. Load a couple of muskets and keep them ready, just in case."

Onoko stepped into his canoe and brought it alongside the sloop to let Ben board; it was a tricky maneuver keeping the narrow canoe from tipping over, but soon they could push off. They landed at the beach, stepped out of the canoe and pulled it up on land. Ben strapped the scabbard holding his sword around his waist, while Onoko carried a small tomahawk in his hand. They walked up towards the wigwams. There were several fireplaces outside but no fires. There was a large wooden rack on which pelts had been hung out to dry; flies were circling around the skins. Onoko pointed at a couple of wooden figures that lay on the ground. "These are children's dolls."

The doors to the wigwams were open. Ben approached one and looked through the door. "Nobody is here," he said. "It seems to have been empty for a while."

They looked into the rest of the wigwams, but they were all empty. Onoko was getting fidgety and looked more and more agitated. "Where did they all go?" he said. He picked up one of the dolls. "This is new. No child would leave it behind." He held up the figure for Ben to see. The crude face was painted white, the eyes had black rings around them, and red tears were drawn on the white cheeks. "This is an image of great sadness."

They walked past the wigwams away from the river, where there was a trail that led toward the woodlands beyond the clearing. The trail was open, but the dusty surface showed no traces of footsteps. The trail went along a small field planted with a crop of maize. The growing stalks reached up to Ben's midriff. At the end of the field, they came to a burial ground; Onoko spotted it first and he stopped. "Look!" he said. "This is where the villagers are!" Over half of the graves were new, the mounds of dirt rising like a pod of black whales out of the ground.

Ben looked at the mounds and said, "This must be almost the whole village! It's as though the Black Death has been here." He looked back, but Onoko had already turned around and started back. Ben entered the burial ground and walked in among the graves; he wanted to see if there were any clues to what had happened. The burial ground didn't offer any explanations, and he soon turned back to the village. Onoko was waiting at the landing. He looked distraught, and he said, "We must leave! This is a bad place full of spirits." They climbed into the canoe, but as they pushed off, a large eagle appeared low in the sky from behind the wigwams. The majestic bird made a circle around them, its wings slowly pumping the air. It flew one more circle around the village, then rose high over the river and disappeared on the other side. Calmness came over Onoko's face, and he said. "This was the last spirit to leave. Now this village will be at peace."

Ben wanted to continue up the river, but the currents were getting too strong for rowing the sloop. He decided to make a short excursion with Onoko, who was still reluctant to go on, but agreed when Ben promised they would be back before dark. Before they left, they went ashore one more time to get one of the Naraticon canoes for the men in the sloop. Ben asked them to go ashore and collect some maize from the field. He had also seen a flock of heath hens at the edge of the clearing, and a little hunting diversion would do his men good.

Ben and Onoko made good progress up the river despite the currents. The rise of the river was slow, and Onoko knew how to take advantage of the calmer water along the edges. Bushes, trees, flowers, and reeds passed in review as they moved upstream. Now and then they would come to an area where the river would go around a small hill. They saw birds, the occasional deer, a beaver den, and fish in the water, but no people. They passed more villages with no signs of human life. After the last village, they came into an area of marshland along both sides of the river. They couldn't see how far from the river the marshes went because the reeds were too tall for them to see over, but the current slowed down, so they must be in a wider part of the river.

They followed the main channel around a bend, and Ben, in the front of the canoe, was the first to see two bodies caught in the reeds.

He signaled to Onoko to slow down and pointed at the bodies. They approached carefully; it was two men dressed only in breeches, they were tangled up in the reeds behind an obstacle of floating branches, one floating on his back and the other on his stomach. The bodies were bloated by being in the water, but Ben could see clearly that both were covered by pockmarks and sores. He said, "I think it's the pox, the same malady that killed the two Lenápes in the boat."

"A white man's disease!"

"Yes, but your people are much more vulnerable than we are."

Onoko shook his head, and started paddling backwards away from the bodies. "Let's leave this place of death."

Ben nodded, "Yes!"

They turned the canoe downstream, this time going out into the mainstream. The Naraticon Kill went through flat country, and the natural flow was not very fast, but the trip downstream was still faster than it had been upstream. They arrived by the sloop just before dusk. Engvas, Eskilsson, Mattson, and Persson were waiting at the landing. They had started a fire, fresh maize was in the kettle to be cooked, and two plucked heath hens waited to be roasted. Ben was concerned that Onoko would object to staying near the village where so many had died, but Onoko told him, "The eagle is guarding the peace of this village."

In the morning they left Naraticon Kill and continued their travel south along the eastern shore of the South River. Their sails were set for a long tack, and the warm sou'wester coming across the water pushed them down the fetch. They were making good headway and the men relaxed while the wind did the work for them. The eastern shore drifted by, but all they could see were endless flat marshes where reeds grew out of the water and little channels meandered among the reeds. Now and then an occasional knoll rose slightly above the reeds. As yet another channel disappeared in among the reeds Engvas, who was at the tiller, remarked, "Not very attractive country, is it?"

Ben nodded, "No." He turned to Onoko. "Do many Lenápes live here?"

Onoko had made himself comfortable against the windward side of the leaning sloop. He had put out a deer skin to sit on, and he had put on a straw hat that was tipping forward over the top of his face to shield against the sun. He looked like he was dozing off, but now he lifted the brim of his hat and replied, "Our people live here. Some of these channels

308

lead to dry land behind the reeds." He pointed toward the land, "Look, there are some of them fishing!" Two canoes were at the mouth of a small channel. In the rear of each, a man was maneuvering the hollowed-out logs using his paddle. What looked like the ends of a net was strung between the forward ends of the canoes, and two women were pulling at the net while the men held the canoes in place. In the middle of one canoe, a child – Ben couldn't see if it was a boy or a girl – was sitting, splashing its hands in the water.

Ben ordered the sheets to be let out; the sails lost their wind and the sloop came to a halt. Ben raised his hand in a greeting, "Good morning!"

Onoko echoed, *"Woapanacheen!"*

The man nearest to them replied, *"Woapanacheen!"*

Onoko continued talking to the fishermen. They replied and Onoko translated, "They are a family of Siconese Lenápes, and they live on the eastern shore."

"What do they fish for?"

"They catch shad fish, and they also get shellfish."

"Ask them if they have seen any white men along the shore?"

A brief exchange in Lenápe followed, and Onoko said. "They say that a group of white people arrived at Varkens Kill."

"How many are they?"

"They don't know, but a large ship came with men, women, and a few children."

"Do they know what nationality they are?"

This took a lot of talking between Onoko and the Siconese fishermen; clearly they had great difficulty in telling one white man from another. Finally Onoko said, "I think they are English."

"Very well, Lieutenant Ridder told me about them. We'd better go and have a look. But before we go, ask them if they have any fish to trade."

They exchanged a few colorful beads for a basket of crabs, after which Ben held up his hand in a farewell and said to the Indians, "Thank you!" The Siconese men returned the gesture, and Ben ordered the sheets pulled in. The sails filled again and they continued their journey down the South River.

They passed Finns Point, where the river turned southeast, and by late afternoon they entered the mouth of Varkens Kill. It was too late to explore the Kill, so they anchored by a small island and went ashore to set up camp for the night. After having been cooped up in the sloop for the better part of the day, it felt good when Ben stretched his legs. The high June sun had been beaming down on them all day, and it was a great relief to see it set in the west across the river. It was warm, and soon crickets and tree frogs started their nightly concert. For dinner Persson cooked the crabs and served them with a mixture of maize and wild onions that he had found at the Naraticon village. They sat around the fire talking until one by one they dropped off to sleep. Ben stretched out on his blanket looking up at the myriad of stars against the dark sky. The Big Dipper slowly moved, pointing its scoop at the North Star, a beacon showing the way home across the oceans. His last thought before falling asleep was, "Or maybe my home is here now?"

Next morning they became soldiers again when it was time to visit the English settlement. The sloop moved up Varkens Kill and they soon arrived at a wooden wharf next to a group of small cabins and tents. The Swedish flag flew from the boat's aft pole, the men had put on their army coats and hats, Ben had strapped his sword to his belt, and two muskets were placed prominently within easy reach. Even Onoko had dressed for the occasion with two large eagle feathers decorating the tail of his long hair, and a knife at his belt. Eskilsson and Mattson were at the oars, and Engvas manned the tiller, while Ben took up his place at the bow. They approached the wharf held by poles that had been pounded into the muddy bottom, and on Ben's order the oarsmen lifted their oars straight up. The sloop came to a halt alongside the wharf. Persson jumped ashore and tied the mooring lines to the poles that held the wharf in place. When he was finished he stood at attention at the bow of the sloop, looked at Ben, and said, "Lieutenant, all secured!"

"Thank you, Persson!" Ben stepped out of the boat and onto the wharf.

A small group of people had been gathered on the shore. Behind them there were two log cabins and a couple of tents surrounded by piles of boxes, barrels, and general debris that the settlers had brought. It reminded Ben of their first days at Fort Christina when the Calmare Nyckel had been unloaded and they didn't quite know where to put it all. Men were working on the cabins, others were clearing land at the edge of the settlement, but now they put down their tools and came down to the shore. One man walked out on the wharf and greeted Ben. "I'm Captain Nathaniel Turner of the Delaware Company. Ben put his hand to his hat in a salute, "Lieutenant Ben Fogel from Fort Christina."

310

The situation was tense; the Swedes considered the English to be trespassers upon land they had bought from the Lenápes, but when Ridder visited Varkens Kill a few months earlier, he was told that the English had also bought the land. Neither the Swedes nor the Dutch recognized the English purchase, but then again, the Dutch thought of the Swedes as trespassers as well. Add to this that the Indians didn't look at the purchases as actually giving up their own usage of the land, and that different Indian chiefs would claim the right to barter the same land, confrontations between all these groups were inevitable.

But not now! Ben was very much aware that he didn't have the manpower to challenge the English at Varkens Kill. That would have to wait, but he wanted to show the flag and assure the settlers that the Swedes were not giving up their claim to the land on the eastern shore. He said, "We come in peace, Captain Turner, to see how your people are adjusting to their new lives in New Sweden."

Turner smiled, recognizing the opening gambit. "With respect, Lieutenant, we feel we have purchased this land from the rightful previous owners, making it a part of New England."

"Well, as you know we claim this land to be part of New Sweden by prior rights. We're happy to see settlers arriving, as long as they recognize Her Majesty, Queen Christina as their sovereign."

Turner looked at the sloop, where Onoko and the four soldiers were following the exchange. He replied, "I don't think you have come to settle this issue here and now."

Now it was Ben's turn to smile. "No, I think we shall wait for our masters and governors to resolve this."

"Very well!" The positions had been made clear, and Turner now became the gregarious host. "Let me show you around!"

44.   Changes

It had taken them the better part of a month to travel around the edge of the South River. Ben had kept a diary during the journey, and when he got back to Fort Christina in the middle of June, he wrote a report for Ridder. The two of them plus van Langdonk were sitting in Ridder's office, and Ridder was asking questions about the journey. He was concerned about the incursion of the English. "Lamberton and Turner's expedition is the thin end of the wedge," he said. "The English want to take over the whole area, and they have started another settlement at Schuyl's Kill." He shook his head, "And if you think the Dutch are bad in their treatment of the Indians, wait until you see the English! They'll walk all over the Lenápes."

Ben replied, "The settlement at Varkens Kill doesn't present much of a threat, though. It's a miserable area, and since most of the pelts come from up the river, it's not a good place for trading with the Indians." He continued, "Varkens Kill may be good for fishing, but the marshes are damp, full of insects, and probably infested with miasma. There were several of the English who looked like they suffer from the ague."

"Very well, we should concentrate on their settlement at Schuyl's Kill. Perhaps we can get some help from the Dutch. I'll send a letter to Governor Kieft."

Ridder put down the report. "Have you found any land for yourself?"

"Yes, I'd like it to be at Schuyl's Kill. It's a good place for trading, with access to both rivers, good land for farming, hunting, and forestry." Ben smiled, "And it's beautiful up there along the river."

"Very good! Van Langdonk, can you draw up the papers for me to sign?"

Van Langdonk nodded, "Yes, but I'll need a description and a map."

Ben replied, "I'll take care of that right away."

Ridder said, "Good! I can only wish you good luck. I'm a bit envious of you."

"Well, why don't you stay as well?"

"I can't do that. I have family and other responsibilities at home." He looked at van Langdonk. "What about you?"

"No, I will be happy going home. This feels too much like a place of exile." He looked at Ben. "You'll need a family to help you out."

Ben grinned. "You know that Liisa and I are engaged?"

"Yes, Reverend Torkillus has already read the banns. Congratulations!"

"When is the wedding?" Ridder asked.

"On Midsummer Day."

"Wonderful! Let's make it an occasion for the whole village to celebrate together."

From time immemorial, Swedes have celebrated summer solstice and the magic of long light days when the sun dipped below the horizon only for a couple of hours, if at all. Darkness, where death and disease ruled, was banished, and the people would celebrate light and eternal life together with the gods, be they Freja, the ancient goddess of fertility, or Martin Luther's Almighty. It was a feast of love and procreation, and an occasion for rituals and supernatural revelations. But in New Sweden the sun moved differently. At noon it was high in the sky, and at sunset it would fall straight down below the horizon, sinking into darkness and languishing there until belatedly it would rise on the other side of the world. Even in June the nights were not very short, they were dark and there were different beings and spirits to reckon with, but to the Swedes it was still midsummer and an occasion to celebrate.

Pastor Torkillus had opened up the sides of the church to let the warm summer breeze blow through the shade under the tent roof and to make room for more people along the sides. During the spring they had added rows of roughly-made pews on each side of the center aisle, and there were benches for the latecomers along the sides. It was also the place for several Lenápes, some chiefs, some friendly traders, some who had been converted to Christianity by the unflagging efforts of Esa Nystad and Caitrin McHarold, and some who were there out of sheer curiosity. The altar was decorated with wildflowers from the meadows and the woods around them; blue and yellow Swedish flags stood on each side. Colorful turkey feathers had been added to the yellow tassels hanging from the tops of the flagpoles. Over the altar hung their new cross. Jon Klasson had made it from the wood of a black walnut tree, and he had polished it to a dark brown color; in the middle he had put Queen Christina's cross.

The congregation rose from their seats and the murmur of talk quieted down as Torkillus entered the church followed by Esa Nystad, both dressed in white robes and holding bibles in their hands. They strode up to the altar, bowed to the cross, and turned to face the congregation, Torkillus at the altar and Nystad at his side. The church was quiet when the bell outside started ringing.

When the last clang of the bell drifted away, Bengtsson, outside the church, started to play his fiddle, a bridal march that he had learned from his father. Bengtsson led the wedding procession into the church, behind him came Ridder in full regalia, and next to Ridder, Chief Metatsimint dressed in Lenápe clothing, two eagle feathers tied to his hair, carrying a staff decorated with many-hued bird feathers in his hand. Behind them came four more soldiers – Sergeant Rieser, Classon, Mattson, and Eskilsson – in shiny new uniforms, their boots and leathers polished, and their wide-brimmed hats decorated with flowers around the edges. The last to enter the church were Liisa and Ben, he in his Flaxen Guard dress uniform, and she in a long white dress. On her head she wore a wreath of flowers, and she had a bouquet of more wildflowers in her hands.

The procession walked slowly down the aisle. When he reached the end, Bengtsson went off to the side, while Ridder and Metsamint took their places in the first pew. The soldiers took up their places on each side of the church, while Liisa and Ben stopped in front of Pastor Torkillus. Bengtsson continued playing, softer and softer until the last note of the bridal march ended in a hushed whisper. Torkillus gestured to the congregation to sit down and spoke. "Dearly beloved......"

It may have been darker than in Sweden, it may have been warmer, and it may have been in a place where the animals, the plants, the trees, and the native people were different, but the midsummer wedding and the village celebration in New Sweden were still the same as at home. The music was all familiar melodies, the dancers took traditional steps, they sang songs they had learned as children, and sometimes they forgot they were thousands of miles from home. When darkness fell, and the glow of the fires began to fade, Ben and Liisa, their faces glowing, walked around among the many men and few women to thank them for celebrating with them. Midsummer in Sweden is a time for dreaming about your future,

314

and after seeing Liisa as a bride holding the arm of the man she loved, many a guest went off to sleep and dreamt of the lover they would meet some time soon.

After the wedding, Ben and Liisa had moved into a new cottage that had just been finished. With the chronic shortage of housing in the settlement, Liisa and her brother had to give up their cottage when Liisa moved out. Esa stayed at the bachelor's quarters, but Caitrin moved in with Ben and Liisa. Their new cottage had an extra room just large enough for their bed to fit. Caitrin's bed was behind a curtain in a corner of the main room. With Esa coming around almost every day, Ben felt as though he had gone directly from being a bachelor on his own to having a family of four. He didn't mind; from his youth he was used to the commotion always surrounding him at the Molen.

Caitrin and Esa seemed more and more inseparable, and it didn't surprise either Ben or Liisa when one evening at supper Esa held Catrin's hand on the table and announced, "We are also getting married!"

"Wonderful!" Liisa's eyes filled with tears, and she got up to embrace Caitrin while Ben shook Esa's hand.

Their wedding was held after the autumn harvest was safely in the barn, and the whole village turned out once again, happy to have another cause for celebration. It was a warm Sunday in late September, when the deep green of the surrounding woods contrasted with the yellow stubble of the fields. It was the time of Harvest Home, and the celebrations went on for three days.

In November they sighted two ships coming up Minquas Kill; this journey from Gothenburg had taken Calmare Nyckel and Charitas four months. The new settlers were in poor shape, disease was rampant, several had already died at sea, and more died a short time after arrival. Nonetheless the size of the colony almost tripled, and several men came with families. During the year, the settlers had built several new cottages and another bunkhouse; but with the new arrivals there was still a shortage of beds, and many of the newcomers had to move into tents. It was crowded, but there was still more room than the newcomers had had onboard the ships, where they had been cooped up during the long sea voyage. Ridder was optimistic, "This is only temporary." he said to Ben, as they were standing at the wharf watching the unloading of goods. "Several of the newcomers are skilled craftsmen. It will hasten the building of more cottages, barns, storehouses, and everything else we need." He continued, "Look at this!" and handed the list of new settlers to Ben.

Ben looked over the names and the comments made by the New Sweden recruiters. "It seems we have our usual crop of minor felons, debtors, blasphemers, poachers, forest burners, and deserters." He flipped through the page. "But there are several free men and several wives that are coming with their husbands." He read out loud, "Olof Stille, farmer and mill builder, with his wife, and two children."

"We'll get him to build a mill right away."

"Måns Svensson, tailor, with his wife, two daughters, and a son." Ben continued, "Pastor Kristoffer, on recommendation by Admiral Karl Karlsson Gyllenhielm."

"Gustavus Adolphus's half brother?"

"The very same!"

"So now we'll have three pastors!"

"Well, I think Nystad wants to build a church of his own soon."

Ridder thought for a moment, "Fogel, now that Kling is back, you can spend all your time on expanding the company affairs. With your new land on Schuyl's Kill, you could start a new Swedish settlement. Take Nystad along, and he can build his new church there."

"I'll need to bring more people!"

"Yes, and you'll get them. We have to start more settlements, and yours could be one of the first ones."

"Well, I have thought about that."

"Good. With you up there we can keep the English under control. Right now they're ruining our trade with the Indians."

"Have you heard from Governor Kieft?"

"Yes! He wants to meet with me."

When the time came for Calmare Nyckel and Charitas to leave, their loads of New Sweden goods were small. Because the ships arrived later than expected, the Swedes had run low on trade goods, and they were not able to buy as much from the Indians as they would have liked. The effect on trade of the English presence was also worse than expected. The Indians had been offered better prices by the English, and therefore they had less to sell to the Swedes. The English were also blocking tobacco sales by their farmers directly to the Swedes. The Dutch suffered as well, their trade on the North River and their more frequent sailings helped, but they were getting ready to pounce on monopoly trespassers.

It was May 1642, and it had been a terrible winter. It began with one settler sniffling and getting a fever, and it spread around the settlement. Several people developed lung fever, coughing and hacking. Two children, one woman, and one man died. When spring came the worst was over, and only a couple of people remained sick. All of this, though, had slowed down their work. The healthy had to work harder, but they were behind on building cottages and getting ready for the planting season as well as in their trade with the Indians.

Ben and Kling were called to Ridder's office, where he invited them to sit down. "Feel this!" he said and put a beaver skin in front of them. It was soft and dry, perfect for the fur trade in Sweden.

"Very nice!" Ben replied.

"Yes, but we can't get any more of these."

"Why not?"

"Because the English on Schuyl's Kill bought them all!" He looked straight at them; the expression on his face and the resigned look in his eyes betrayed his feelings of uncertainty. "It's time to go see them!"

Ben asked, "What do the Dutch say?"

"Governor Kieft is ready to move against the English."

Kling asked, "Aren't we jumping from the frying pan into the fire? How do we know the Dutch won't take over?"

"Kieft and I have sent letters back and forth, and then I met with him halfway between here and New Amsterdam in a little village called Zomerdorp on the Lenápe trail. We've agreed that he will send some twenty of his troops and we will send as many as we can spare – which won't be many since we also must be able to defend Fort Christina – and assist in the mission."

Ridder's fingers played unconsciously with the beaver pelt, stroking the soft fur. "Here's what I want us to do! Fogel, you take five men and go with Captain Jan Jansen – his ship will arrive from New Amsterdam soon – up to the settlement and talk sternly with the English."

Ben knew that stern talk meant that unless the settlers surrendered, their village would be burned to the ground and people arrested or killed.

Ridder turned to Kling, "You and I will stay here, but we must be prepared for the possibility of an attack." He looked at Ben, "That's why you can only have five soldiers."

"I understand!"

Ridder stood up and walked over to a side table where he picked up a bottle and three glasses and brought them to the table. "Let's talk about the detail, but first I want you to try my aquavit made from maize. I think we may have solved the problems with the distillation!"

Liisa was nestled up against Ben in bed, she was resting her head on his arm, she her hand idly twisting the hair on his chest. "I love you!" she whispered.

"And I you!"

He reached out for an envelope on the table next to the bed, and pulled out some papers. It was the deed for the land that he had been granted. He held up a map so that Liisa could see it. "Look at this!" he said. The map showed Schuyl's Kill going north from the South River. He pointed to lines that were drawn on the west side of Schuyl's Kill, not too far from where it entered the South River. "This is where we're going! It's a perfect place for a trading post right along the river. The land rises away from the river, and there are woods, meadows, and streams and it's flat enough for us to clear land for fields."

"But you're not a farmer!"

"No, but Ridder will let me take some settlers to help us build and clear the land. He wants more people to settle there, and some of them can become tenant farmers for us. Later they may want to get their own land."

"Will the company give away land just like that?"

"Not just like that! First they will have to show that they are good people, willing and able to work, and then they will have to pay for the land. It may not be much, but it'll come out of their income. This way we can winnow out the good people, who can help to build the colony."

"You're beginning to sound like a country squire already!"

"Well, I expect that we'll have to work hard, both of us."

"What about the trading?"

"That's the most important thing for me. Look!" He pointed at the map. "We're right on the water and next to both rivers. It's a perfect place to build another trading post with its own harbor!"

"Is it far?"

"No, you can easily sail from Schuyl's Kill to Fort Christina in half a day if the wind is right."

Liisa turned on her side to face Ben. "Who will go with us? I know Esa and Caitrin want to build their new church."

318

"They're coming and they'll bring Ellianah. As for the rest, Ridder has promised to let me have at least five men. One or two should be married, so that we'll have a few more women."

"When are we going?"

"Soon, there is some work to finish first." He told her about the English settlement on Schuyl's Kill. "Ridder wants me to go there together with the Dutch and drive out the English unless they recognize Swedish sovereignty."

Liisa's lifted her eyebrows, creating little furrows across her brow, and a look of worry came over her face. "I had hoped that we'd left all this strife behind us," she said.

"Well, it seems that we are born to strife." He put his hand gently against her breast. "But not always."

Liisa moved closer. "Promise me you'll be careful!"

"I promise, and I expect this mission won't be very dangerous." He continued, "After it's finished we can start thinking about moving."

"I can't wait!" Liisa's face relaxed. She went on, "I'm glad Ellianah is coming. I'll need her!"

Ben turned to face her looking at her with an expression of puzzlement. He remembered Ellianah helping with the birth of Stina onboard Calmare Nyckel. He put his hand on her cheek, and said, "Are you with child?"

Liisa caressed his chest, her hand slowly moving down his stomach and finally disappearing under the cover. "No, not yet, but I want to make sure that it happens soon."

45.   New Sweden Grows

Leaving one of his large sloops, the Real, anchored at the mouth of Minquas Kill, Captain Jansen took the other, St. Martin, up the Kill to Fort Christina. Jansen was coming to pick up Ben and his men, and this group would join the Dutch soldiers in their action against the English settlement at Schuyl's Kill. Ridder and Ben were waiting on land while the Dutch moored the sloop at the wharf. Jansen was a man in his forties, short, his thick hair gray at the temples, with a full beard also streaked with gray. It was a hot day, and he was wearing a white shirt with long sleeves to protect his arms, and on his head a wide-brimmed white hat to shade his face and neck from the glaring sun. His hands and face were already a dark brown, deeply tanned from many days at sea under a tropical sun.

St. Martin was almost as long as Calmare Nyckel, but the sloop was lower and had only one mast. The skipper steered her alongside the wharf, and berthing hawsers were cast ashore and secured. After they had made fast at the wharf, Jansen stepped up on land where he was greeted by Ridder. "Welcome, Captain Jansen!" They saluted each other and shook hands, but both men were reserved. While they would join forces against the English, the Dutch and the Swedes had only temporarily set aside their own differences. Ridder introduced Ben. "This is Lieutenant Fogel, he and his men will go with you."

Jansen saluted Ben. "Lieutenant, it shouldn't be a difficult mission, but you never know."

Ben replied, "I've been to the settlements at both Varkens Kill and Schuyl's Kill. The people may have arms, but they're no match for a platoon of soldiers."

Jansen nodded, and asked, "Have you ever done this before?"

An image of the Flaxen guard collecting tribute in German villages flew through Ben's mind. "Yes, but I'll tell you about that when we're underway."

Ridder said, "Captain, I've set up a table in the shade over there, and I have taken the liberty of arranging breakfast for us." He pointed to the bath house, where they had put up a large piece of sailcloth as an awning over a table. He went on, "We can look at our maps and discuss any final details of the mission at the same time."

Jansen replied, "Very well. Can my men wait here?"

"Yes, my aide will see to that they are taken care of." He waved to Vidaris, who was arranging the table by the bath house. "Vidaris, over here!" His aide quickly walked along the wharf to join them, and Ridder said to him. "Make sure our visitors get something to eat and drink, while Captain Jansen, Fogel and I have our breakfast."

It was early morning three days later, and the St. Martin and the Real were approaching the English settlement on the shore near the mouth of Schuyl's Kill. The English had selected a place where large ships could get in close to shore for loading and unloading, but this also made them vulnerable to attacks from the water. The two sloops were not huge, but on the narrow river they stood tall, and when the first sunlight struck the top of the main masts, and slowly began to light the stage of the new day, they made a statement of power. Jansen was aboard the St. Martin under a Dutch flag, and Ben was aboard the Real, flying a Swedish flag for the occasion.

When the sloops were outside the settlement, Jansen ordered the anchor to be lowered and the St. Martin swung to point her bow upstream. The sails were secured and the soldiers lined up with muskets in hand along the side facing land. The Real positioned itself closer to the shore upstream from the St. Martin, and the soldiers onboard lined up the same way. The crews uncovered two cannons, one on each foredeck, and pointed them toward the shore. Ben looked at the settlement, where people were gathering at the shore, but he saw no soldiers, and nobody appeared to be armed. For the next hour, they made no move toward the village; Jansen wanted the impression of the armed sloops to sink in and to create fear and a sense of inevitability in the settlement. More people gathered, and they counted at least fifty people, men, women, children, plus a few Indians.

They had agreed beforehand that Ben would go ashore first, and when Jansen gave the signal, he boarded the small ship's boat with four soldiers, and two oarsmen rowed them ashore. As they struck the shore the people on land backed off; Ben and his five soldiers jumped ashore, muskets in hand. Ben walked up toward the crowd and asked, "Who speaks for you?"

There was some shuffling among the people until a man came forward. "I do!" He was a young man in his mid-thirties.

Ben looked at him, "I'm Lieutenant Fogel from Fort Christina. May I ask who you are, Sir?"

"John Smith, from New England."

"Where are Mr. Lamberton and Captain Turner?"

The man looked uneasy, but replied, "They have left. They took their ship and left several days ago."

Ben looked around. The settlement was only a few cabins and a couple of storehouses. The settlers had obviously begun clearing land, but hadn't gotten very far. There were a few small boats at the shore which he assumed were for fishing, since there were nets hanging on poles to dry. The people looked healthy and well-fed, but the expressions in their eyes were sullen and revealed a wariness of strangers. He asked, "Did Lamberton and Turner abandon you?"

A look of embarrassment went over Smith's face. "I'm not sure, but before they left they warned us that you might appear."

"Well, here we are." Ben smiled, and continued, "Since you were warned, I'm sure you know you're on land belonging to New Sweden."

"They didn't tell us that, and when we left from New England, they claimed that this land belonged to the English Crown, who'd bought it from the Indians."

Ben sighed, "Well, they're wrong." His eyes went around the settlement again, stopping at a pile of discarded pieces of skins that looked like they had been trimmed off pelts of beaver, fox, and other furred animals. He pointed at the pile and said, "It looks as if you have been trading with the Indians?"

Smith hesitated before he replied, "Yes, anybody can do that."

"No, all the trade privileges here belong to New Sweden."

Smith didn't answer. Ben went on, following the plan they had agreed on at the breakfast at Fort Christina a few days earlier. "We welcome new settlers to New Sweden, but there are two conditions. First, you have to swear loyalty to the Swedish Crown, and abide by our laws. Second, unless you get permission to do otherwise, you must trade only with the New Sweden Company."

Smith said, "This we cannot do, for we would go against the expressed orders of our governor."

"Well, I will give you a moment to discuss this among yourselves. In the meantime I will ask my Dutch collaborator to come ashore. I'll need an answer by the time he gets here." Ben turned and walked down to the shore where he signaled to Jansen that it was time for him to arrive. The settlers withdrew from the shore, and the noise of their agitated voices grew. The Real's ship's boat was in the water and Ben could see soldiers boarding and the boat starting toward the shore. It took four trips to get them all ashore. Jansen himself waited until the last trip.

It was a slow but deliberate process, and Ben could see how the settlers looked increasingly alarmed as more and more soldiers came ashore. While this was going on Ben, escorted by his men, took a quick walk around the settlement, opening a few storehouses and checking for possible ambushes. They found very little evidence of any presence of soldiers, except an abandoned, empty cabin. Lamberton and Turner had apparently left the settlers to fend for themselves. They walked back to the shore and the others.

Smith was arguing with Jansen, their voices loud, angry, and agitated. When Ben walked up to them they stopped and looked at him. Ben said, "Mr. Smith, your storehouses have piles of fresh pelts that you must have bought recently. I also found barrels of imported goods that you must use as barter with the Indians. This is against Swedish laws, but I've given you a way to make amends. Have you decided what your answer is going to be?"

Smith's face was red from shouting, and looked very distraught. But his voice didn't quaver when he answered, "We don't have any money, and if you've been to our storehouses, you've seen all the goods we have. It's not much." He paused for a moment, and went on. "We are all English patriots, and want to remain loyal to our King. The answer is 'No'."

Jansen looked at Ben, and said, "That's that. Let's get on with it!"

Ben nodded in agreement, and Jansen turned to his men and gave the orders. The population of the English settlement on Schuyl's Kill was rounded up and put under guard. The soldiers cleared out the storehouses and brought the few valuable goods aboard the ships. It took them two days, and on the third day the settlers were allowed back one by one to pack small bags of their personal belongings, after which they were brought to the shore. Animals were let out to run free, and when everybody had been counted, Jansen's men went around and deliberately put the torch to the buildings. The settlers were transported to the ships, and when only ashes remained of the settlement, the Real and the St. Martin sailed down Schuyl's Kill and on into the South River. Ben and his men got off at Fort Christina, and Ben stood with his men on the wharf watching the St. Martin disappear around the bend of the river. The two ships were going back to Manhattan in New Netherland, where the English settlers would be incarcerated. He thought of his time in Germany, where whole cities would be burned to the ground for refusing to pay tribute. "I hope sometime we can do better here," he thought.

While the Dutch and the Swedes joined forces against the English at Schuyl's Kill, the owners of the New Sweden Company met in Stockholm. Oxenstierna, still the most powerful man in Sweden, hosted the meeting at the chancellery. The company had gone through many changes, but the Chancellor remained a champion of the venture. Political pressure in Holland from the West India Company had forced the Dutch investors to remove themselves, and Oxenstierna had orchestrated their replacement by the Swedish Crown. He had also brought other members of his family into the company. Both Fleming and Spierinck remained, but for all practical purposes the New Sweden Company was now a Crown matter.

Von Lans and Spierinck were the first to arrive, and they were shown to the Chancellor's meeting room. It was a warm summer evening, and the sun lit up the room from across the lake. Through the wide open windows they could hear the noise of the city – people shouting, animals neighing and cackling, boats splashing, and wagon wheels clattering over the cobble stones. A steward had arranged a buffet of food and drinks on a side table. Before he withdrew he pointed to the lavish display of cold fish, smoked meat of various kinds, patés and sausages. the platters of ribs, lamb, and pork joints kept warm over candles, the pitchers of ale, water, and cider, the bread and cheeses and the cakes and pies for dessert, and said, "The Chancellor has sent word that he may be a bit late, but he wanted you to help yourselves to what his house has to offer."

Von Lans had been traveling all day and he was hungry, he filled his plate, poured a glass of cider, and sat down at the table. Spierinck looked at the buffet and decided to try the slices of fowl. He came to the table, put the plate down and said, "This must be the Indian turkey meat that Oxenstierna raves about." He sat down, cut a piece and put it in his mouth. "This is very good! Here, try some!" He handed a piece to von Lans, who tasted it.

"Excellent!"

The two men started to eat and the room was quiet, the only sound was the city noise coming in through the windows. Finally Spierinck broke the silence. "Well, Baron, what do you think of the new order in the company?"

Von Lans thought for a moment before he replied. "With the benefit of hindsight, I think it was inevitable. The power of the WIC in government circles made it almost impossible for our Dutch investors to stay, and when the profits Minuit promised didn't materialize, that was the end of their participation." He took a drink from his glass and went on, "How about you? As you're from Holland…?"

"Not every Dutchman likes the WIC. They've become too powerful and arrogant. Besides, by now I'm more Swedish than Dutch, and I still believe in New Sweden."

"So do I, but the results so far are not encouraging. We'll need more people, more trade, and more ships."

"This will cost a pretty penny. The trade profits aren't enough. Who's going to pay?"

Von Lans replied, "Well, I must say that I admire the Chancellor's strategy. Bringing in the Crown is the only way to keep the venture from collapsing, especially with the Dutch investors bailing out. The Crown is the only one who has the staying power and the money to support New Sweden during the time, the very long time, that it'll take to get the venture going."

Spierinck smiled, "Not to mention getting the Crown to assume most of the financial risk. The founders should consider themselves lucky they haven't had to suffer any serious losses. It's been very helpful to have high representatives for the Crown who are also private investors."

"Well, it's the way of the world, isn't it? Certain privileges come with the responsibility of ruling."

The door opened and Fleming entered the room followed by two men. Von Lans and Spierinck got up to greet them, Fleming shook hands with both of them, then stepped back to let the two men come forward for an introduction. "Gentlemen, I want you to meet our new treasurer, Mr. Johan Beier and Lieutenant Colonel Johan Björnsson who has been helping us recruiting more settlers." He turned to address the two newcomers, "Baron von Lans works for the Chancellor, and you know Admiral Fleming already, I believe."

Everybody shook hands and von Lans looked at the two men. Beier was of average size and build, but next to Björnsson he looked like a dwarf. Björnsson was the biggest man von Lans had ever met. He must have weighed over three hundred pounds, and he was a head taller than any of them. He shook hands with Spierinck, then turned to von Lans and held out his hand. Von Lans was not a short person, but next to Björnsson he felt small; he took the man's hand and was not surprised to feel the strong grip of a large hand that enveloped his own.

The three newcomers went to the buffet, filled their plates, and joined von Lans and Spierinck at the table. Beier sat down next to von Lans and Spierinck with Björnsson and Fleming across the table. Von Lans turned to Beier, "Mr. Beier, I understand you are our new Postmaster General?"

Beier, who was born in Germany, spoke Swedish with a heavy accent. "Yes, the Chancellor has asked me to succeed Frau Wechel. She and her husband have done a wonderful job setting up the postal service, but now with her husband gone, she wishes to retire."

Von Lans had been with Oxenstierna back in 1636 when the Chancellor asked Anders Wechel to start a Swedish postal service. A year later Wechel had died and his wife took over the job. Von Lans replied, "Does the Post Office handle mail to New Sweden?"

"In a small way. We have an agent in Gothenburg who delivers mail to ships, but we have nobody to distribute the mail in New Sweden. That's up to the company."

"But could we establish a branch of the Post Office in New Sweden?"

"Yes, in principle that's fine," Beier replied, "but it may be a bit early with so few settlements."

Von Lans nodded in agreement, "Yes, I know." He went on, "But you see, one of the most important matters of concern for New Sweden is to have strong links with the homeland. We have ships for supplies and trade goods, but we also need to have the best mail service. If we could rely on the mail, I could receive regular letters with reports of trades and advance notices of shipments. This would give us a head start over our competitors in selling and we could get better prices."

Beier nodded, "Baron, you're absolutely right, but I'm afraid it will take some time before we can offer you safe, regular service to New Sweden."

The door opened again and the steward held it open for Oxenstierna. The others stood up while the Chancellor walked around the table greeting everybody. He seemed in a good mood, and took his time exchanging a few words with everybody. When he came to von Lans, he said, "Good morning, Baron. I have some good news about your old commander!"

"Good morning, Chancellor! What news, may I ask?"

"Horn has been released by the Catholics. We exchanged him for no less than three imperial generals."

Field Marshal Gustav Horn, who was also Oxenstierna's son-in-law, had been captured at Nördlingen in one of worst defeats for the Protestants. He had been held prisoner since then, and von Lans replied, "That is indeed good news, but it's been eight long years. Is he well?"

"As well can be expected. You must come and see him."

"I will!"

"Good!" Oxenstierna continued, "And how is your new family?"

"Very well, thank you. We have a new baby boy."

"I'm glad to hear that. What's his name?"

"Pieter."

"Pray that he will grow up healthy and well."

A pensive shadow passed over Oxenstiernas face. Von Lans knew that most of his many children had not survived infancy, and of those who did, two had died young. They sat down and Oxenstierna quickly took charge of the meeting. The first important topic of discussion was the company finances; Calmare Nyckel's latest load had been a disappointment, and there was no profit to report. Ridder had requested more supplies as well as more settlers, and it would be necessary to spend more of the investors' money. Oxenstierna, with the support of Fleming, was nevertheless still optimistic.

"Look at the Dutch!" he said. "Look at how they are profiting from their trading companies in both East and West India. The future of Sweden is in more trade, and I am convinced that we can do the same thing! So let's move ahead and build New Sweden into a profitable venture!"

They decided to send two more ships with more settlers, which brought them to the topic of settlers. Oxenstierna turned to Björnsson. "You have been recruiting settlers for us. How is it going?"

Björnsson replied, "We have a few volunteers, but generally it is still very difficult to find people who are willing to go. They think it's too far, too dangerous, and that they'll never come back. So we've resorted to the usual way of offering amnesty to minor law-breakers in return for a few years in New Sweden. This way we've now recruited enough people for the next shipment."

Fleming said, "It seems from Ridder's reports that despite their histories, some of the settlers adjust quite well."

"Yes, not all of them, but some find it a real opportunity for improving their own lives. Some stay beyond their conscription times."

"But we still need more people?"

"Absolutely, it's the only way that the colony will grow large enough to become profitable, and it's the only way we can stand up to any threats from other nations."

"Very well!"

Oxenstierna looked around the table and said, "That's settled. Let's turn to the topic of finding a replacement for Lieutenant Ridder, whose term is at an end. As you know Lieutenant Colonel Björnsson has agreed to become the Governor of New Sweden."

Björnsson quickly asked, "Should I leave, while you discuss this?"

"No, we've already discussed it among ourselves, and I think we're all in agreement."

The men around the table nodded in assent, and Johan Björnsson became the first Governor of Sweden's newest province. He was given an annual salary of twelve hundred rixdollars, a land grant, and trading privileges. He was also knighted and changed his name to Printz, which had been that of his maternal grandfather.

That was the end of the meeting, but Oxenstierna had one more thing to tell them. "Gentlemen, as you know, Queen Christina comes of age in two years. She is still young, but it won't be long before her interests start influencing the direction of the country. In the greater scheme of things, New Sweden is a small venture, and the Queen will be facing so many other more important matters. I'm convinced we can make New Sweden a prosperous adventure, but we must show real success during the next few years." He looked directly at Björnsson, "Governor, the board will give you our strong support, but you'll be the man on the spot. Good luck to you!"

46.   The New Settlement

In New Sweden the August heat was almost suffocating. The humid air was still. The birds, too hot to sing, were hiding in the shade of the woods, but the loud, high-pitched sizzle of cicadas and tree frogs sliced through the humid air like a swarm of knives. Rolf Engvas and his wife were sitting in the shade of a tree outside their wigwam. Next to them in a cradle their little boy, Ragnar Nutimus, almost two years old, slept peacefully. Minnequa was Esa Nystad's first convert to Christianity, and before the child was born, she and Rolf had been married by Nystad. The child was the first in the colony to be baptized in their church; he was named Ragnar after Rolf's father and the name Nutimus had been given to him by the Lenápe elders. Minnequa had learned a smattering of Swedish and she was listening to her husband speaking a mixture of Swedish and Lenápe. "Lieutenant Fogel has asked if we want to go with him up the river to Schuyl's Kill. I've served my time, and I'm now a freeman; I can do what I want. If I want to go back, the company will give us passage to Sweden, but if we go with Fogel, we could soon have some land of our own."

"What could you do in Sweden?"

"Become a tenant farmer and work for some big landowner."

Minnequa shook her head. "No, I think it's best we stay. We can live on land where the Lenápe have lived for all time. This is good land, look at it!"

The settlers had cleared land and planted corn, squash, rye, barley, tobacco, and several small vegetable patches. The crops had grown tall during spring and summer. Soon it would be time to harvest, and it would be their biggest yield yet. They had also built more cottages, storage houses and barns. Stille had constructed a mill, which would be ready by the time of the harvest, the church was almost finished, and the wharf had been extended and improved. Fort Christina was beginning to look like a real village.

Schuyl's Kill was about twenty-five miles up the river, and Ben had been back and forth several times since the expedition against the English. He had surveyed the land and made a map of a new settlement that would start with his land grant. The easiest way to get there from Fort Christina was by boat, and Ridder had let him have one of the boats. They had also found a way by land. It was a Lenápe road that for centuries had wound its way over hills, through woods and shrub lands, and around marsh-lands along the South River. The road was narrow, more like a trail, but good enough for men and animals, and this way they would bring horses and cattle to the new settlement. Ridder had also let him have a few extra men, but some of them would return to Fort Christina after they had built cabins and shelters for the winter. In addition to Engvas and his family, Mattson and Eskilsson wanted to come. They were still under obligation to serve the company, but Ridder decided that they could do that working for Ben at the new settlement. Esa Nystad would be their pastor and his wife Caitrin would assist him. Liisa, of course brought Ellianah, and Ridder also let him have Persson, the cook. "You'll need him, and we will soon get more people on the next ship." Two brothers, Kiell and Torvard Augustsson from Vasa, who also had two more years to serve the company, were already at Schuyl's Kill clearing for the site along the river where their first buildings would soon go up.

Liisa came outside but stayed in the shade of the cottage. She was heavy with child and had only one more month to go. She felt fine, Dr. Uv thought she was fine, Ellianah thought she was fine, but the heat and humidity of the summer was hard on her. Ben and Ridder were sitting at a table with a piece of vellum made from deerskin in front of them. On it Ben had drawn a map showing the South River from Varkens Kill up to the falls at Sankikan. He and Ridder had worked many days to draw the South River, the tributaries large and small, hills, and all the villages and settlements. Ben had just added the Lenápe trail from Fort Christina to Schuyl's Kill. It was a rough map of New Sweden with a lot of blank areas, but it showed the progress they had made, the new settlements at Varkens Kill, Upland, Finland, and now the next settlement on Schuyl's Kill. There were also many dots showing Indian villages.

Liisa sat down at the table. "How are things going?" she asked.

Ben replied, "Very well! I think we may leave after the baby is born, and you have recovered."

Ridder said, "We need a name for the settlement."

"Yes, Liisa and I have tried many new names, but for a long time we couldn't agree on any suggestions." He went on, "But, last night, in the middle of the night she woke me up and said she had the perfect name." He looked at Liisa, "Tell him!"

Ridder looked inquiringly at Liisa, who replied, "I think we should call it New Calmar!"

"After the town on the Baltic?"

"Yes, but mainly because of the ship. Calmare Nyckel, the Key from Calmar, opened the door to West India, to America. We should remember that."

Ridder sat quietly for a minute thinking, and then said, "I like that! New Calmar it is!" He turned to Ben, "Put the name on the map!"

Liisa went into labor early one morning, and after a struggle with Ellianah on one side and Dr. Uv on the other, their first child was born. Ben had been pacing back and forth outside the cottage, listening to Liisa's cries of pain, "I don't want to do this. Stop it! I want you to stop it!" He couldn't bear listening and walked down to the wharf, and around the fort, just to be drawn back. He had to know what was going on; it seemed to take an eternity, but about noon, Liisa's cries stopped and he heard a baby's cry instead.

Soon Uv came out and said, "It's a little boy. He took his sweet time, but he and his mother are fine. Come in and see for yourself."

Ben had been sitting down, and when he got up he noticed that his legs were a little shaky, but it soon went away, and he walked in through the door of the cottage. There in bed was Liisa. Ellianah had washed her face and combed her hair. It was very hot inside and Liisa had no clothes on, only a sheet pulled up to her midriff. In her arms was the baby, nursing at her breast. He was at first sight a scrawny little thing, all red and wrinkly. Liisa looked tired but happy, gone was all the pain. Ben thought she looked radiant and that her eyes were sparkling despite her tiredness. He sat down next to her, leaned over and kissed her brow. Liisa looked at him then at the baby, and said, "Isn't he beautiful?"

"Yes, he is!"

The boy was named Magnus – after Ben's father – Seppo – after Liisa's father – Benjaminsson Fogel. He grew fast, and his mother recovered quickly from his birth.

Ben had to make another journey to New Calmar to oversee the work. Onoko came with him and together they went to see Mexkalaniyat and his Lenápe tribe, whose village was closest to New Calmar. Mexkalaniyat received them with great gravity. They smoked his tobacco, examined his pelts, bartered them for tools, wampum, and corn liquor, and they talked about future trading between the Lenápe and New Calmar. The building work was going well, one cottage was ready and being used by the workers. In a month two more would be ready; one was for Ben and his family. A fourth one was going up. It would serve as a house for Esa and Caitrin, but also as their church. Ben returned to Fort Christina and told Liisa, "I think we can leave in early October. Are you and Magnus ready to travel?"

"Yes, I'm sure." The boy was in his cradle sleeping. "Look at him," she said. "He's eating like a little pig and he's growing fast." She stood up and whirled around. "Look at me! I'm eating like a pig myself to keep him supplied, and I'm getting thinner!"

"You look fine!" Ben pulled her down in his lap. "If you're sure, I'll tell Ridder we'll be leaving soon."

Liisa bent down and kissed him. When she sat up again she looked concerned. "What about the school? Who'll be teaching there, when I'm gone?"

"Well, Reverend Torkillus and your brother have kept it going while you've been away. I think Torkillus will manage until the next ship arrives. We're expecting many new settlers, and there must be somebody who can help Torkillus."

In November of 1643, Ben Fogel – the innkeeper's son, sailor, soldier, traveler, settler, trader, and soon-to-be farmer in New Calmar on the South River at Schuyl's Kill – left Fort Christina with his wife, and child, accompanied by a group of settlers from Sweden, Finland, and North Africa. One group had already left by land when Ben and Liisa stood on the wharf ready to board the boat. Ridder, normally very reserved, reached out and put his arms around Liisa and hugged her. His eyes had tears in them when he let go and turned to shake Ben's hand. His voice quavered when he said, "Godspeed to both of you. I hope to see you before I leave for good."

Ben replied, "We're not going that far. Let us know when the next ship arrives, and we'll come back to see you off."

It wasn't far, but it was the end of their known world, and they had little or no idea of what was laying in wait for them. They boarded the boat, and the men on land let go of the mooring line. Mattson pulled in the line and tightened the main sheet. The westerly wind filled the sail, sending the boat off down Minquas Kill. Ben looked back at Fort Christina. As they went around the bend in the river, the fort disappeared, but the Swedish flag could still be seen over the treetops. Slowly, though, the flag got smaller and soon it disappeared. They reached the mouth of Minquas Kill and turned north on the South River; the next day they would be in New Calmar, the end of their journey.

Epilogue

The autumn went by, then Christmas, and it became another year. In the middle of February the ships Fama and Swan came up Minquas Kill, almost four months after they had left Gothenburg. Fama had lost her main mast and Swan had some damage on deck. It had all happened in a winter storm at the mouth of the South River. When the ships appeared, coming around the bend in Minquas Kill, the word of their arrival spread with lightning speed around the village, and everybody went down to the wharf to meet them. The first to step ashore was a man dressed in the uniform of a Lieutenant Colonel. He was tall and the great bulk of his body seemed to strain the seams of the uniform. Anna Svensdotter whispered to her husband, "He must weigh four hundred pounds!"

Onoko echoed her sentiment, "Big belly!"

Ridder walked up to the officer, saluted and said, "Welcome to New Sweden! I am Lieutenant Ridder."

The officer replied, his voice booming, "Lieutenant Ridder, I'm very glad to finally be here. I'm Johan Printz, your successor as Governor."

And yet another era was beginning.

Breinigsville, PA USA
29 March 2010
235149BV00002B/2/P

9 789197 494113